To Diane

THE HOUSE ON 4TH STREET

a novel in stories

~ ~ ~ ~

CONNIE WESALA

Connie Wesala

– 2017 –

This is a work of fiction. Names, places, characters, events and incidents are the products of the imagination of the author or are used fictitiously. Historical persons and information have been changed for the sake of the novel's story-line. Any resemblance to actual events, locales, or persons, living or dead, is entirely coincidental.

Library of Congress Catalogue-in-Publication Data. 2015
ISBN-13: 978-1508989165
ISBN-10: 1508989168

Cover photograph and design: Michael W. Wesala

"And now these three remain: faith, hope and love. But the greatest of these is love."
— 1 Corinthians 13:13 Holy Bible, New International Version

"Where there is great love, there are always miracles."
— Willa Cather

Inside the house on 4th Street is an attic. In the attic is an old steamer trunk. In the trunk are pieces of the past including journals and diaries from the 1800s through the 1970s. Within these diaries are stories of love. From those stories we learn that love often requires forgiveness, a willingness to change, acceptance that we must put our own needs last, and sometimes even the courage to let go or leave.

Chapter 1
June 2009
Oklahoma

This was the last place on earth Karen wanted to be. Her
starched white cotton shirt clung to her back. Though barely
June, the humidity had aligned with the temperature, and at 10:00
a.m. she was already sticky with perspiration. Fanning herself
with her left hand, she felt a slight breeze graze her cheek, and
with it, a vague sensation—almost a memory—washed over her
like a tissue-thin curtain.

Karen's adoptive mother had died just three months ago this
week; outliving her adoptive father by ten years. Her inheritance
consisted of the family home in Colorado and this 1922
Craftsman in Oklahoma. She was determined to sell both over
her summer break. She didn't want them hanging over her head
when her teaching schedule began in September. Karen had lived
here as a child thirty-four years ago, though she had to dig deep
for any memories.

She pushed her hair behind her ears and rummaged through
her purse for the large shamrock keychain she'd found in her
mother's dresser drawer a week after the funeral. This would be
her last visit, if the realtor was any good.

She had to admit—the house had a definite charm. The one-
story bungalow was a soft butter-yellow with white trim built on
traditional red-brick cove. Curved flower beds lined the front of
the house; their color just budding out. At the far end of the

front porch, a white swing swayed on metal chains, and a basket of red geraniums hung beside it. The ninety-year-old oaks in the front median created a canopy of shade, and a couple of squirrels scampered along their broad branches.

The set of keys seemed to emerge of their own accord, and she gave a deep sigh as she fumbled with the lock and stepped inside. She'd neglected to inspect the attic during yesterday's visit. As the front door creaked open, the quiet of the empty house enveloped her. Karen stood in the silence, felt the void creep into her, and wept.

She pulled a Kleenex from her bag to wipe the tears from her cheeks and entered the living room. During the night, small bits of childhood had flooded her dreams. With the morning sunlight streaming through the window, she could almost see a Christmas tree in the corner next to the fireplace. She saw herself as a four-year-old sitting beneath its branches, gazing up at the bright colored bulbs, waiting for Santa. Maybe she was just remembering an old photo.

She shook off the memory and turned right, through the dining room. In the short hallway between the two bedrooms, she opened a door, flipped the light switch, and carefully climbed the steep staircase. Karen held tightly to the handrail. The steps were so narrow; she struggled to keep her footing. At the top of the stairs, she was pleased to find a finished room with an A-frame ceiling and paneled walls. She walked to the center and looked up at a framed skylight. *Hope that thing doesn't leak.* The appraiser would arrive within the hour, and she didn't need any surprises. As she continued the length of the room, Karen spotted another door. It seemed an odd location, so close to the front of the house. Something felt familiar, though she had no clear recollection of seeing it before today.

The rusty old hinges complained as she turned the knob and entered a small room tucked inside the front dormer. It couldn't be more than eight-foot square. A wood clothes-rod was mounted on each side of the raftered ceiling. A few metal coat hangers hung at disjointed angles from one of them. Cardboard boxes and a rolled-up oriental rug nearly filled the room. She walked to the front, turned the brass latch and pulled open a small window. A slight breeze relieved the dank smell of the worn-out carpet. She'd keep it open until after the inspection. As she turned to leave, she caught sight of something in the far left corner where the floor met the steeply sloped roof line. She bent down and pulled an old trunk by its worn leather handle into the center of the room. The decorative brass draw bolts held the lid in place, but the locking mechanism was secured by wire. She began to untwist the thick strands.

She knelt on the floor, feeling like Alice in Wonderland when she grew too big for the room. She cautiously lifted the heavy lid, watching for spiders, or worse. A torn faded newspaper clipping fluttered to her feet. She took one item after another from the box and placed each carefully on the floor. Letters, birth certificates, legal documents. She glanced at dates. 1974 – '63 – '45 – '23 – 1890. It was packed with baby blankets, rattles, a yellowed lace wedding veil—packed full of the past.

Amid its contents, Karen spotted hand-written journals. She picked up one thick leather-bound missive. The spine was worn but holding together, the ink faded in places, making it somewhat difficult to read. She slid her finger gingerly along the pages and opened it carefully. The handwriting was precise and straight as if there were invisible printed lines on the page. She began to read:

Millicent Granger died from Typhoid yesterday. I sat with her to the end. Today I will help prepare the body for the viewing. I will miss her companionship. I counted her as a good friend. Karen flipped to earlier pages and read another excerpt.

Charles tells me that rail employees are not allowed to participate in the land run because of the unfair advantage of living here. How will we ever be able to build a house if we have no land? Some days I consider returning home to Papa and settling in Abilene.

As she turned another page, the doorbell rang. She leaped to her feet and headed toward the stairs. At the last moment, Karen couldn't resist one backward glance at the trunk. There was just too much history here to leave unexplored. And she had to know the name of the woman who had written these heartfelt entries.

Downstairs, she greeted the realtor, and they waited together for the inspector to arrive. The woman's engraved name tag read: Vickey Smith, Prosper Realty. Karen guessed her to be around forty, close to her own age. She was tall and thin with a blonde chin-length bob and she wore a tailored navy pantsuit and low heels. Her kind smile put Karen at ease immediately.

"You have a lovely home," she said. "I've always liked this area of Edmond."

Karen smiled. "It was perfect for my parents when we lived here. They were professors at the college, as you probably know." Karen glanced around the empty room. Except for a few scuff marks in the living area, the original wood floors gleamed.

"I was sorry to hear about your mother's death," Vickey said.

Karen nodded. "Thanks," she whispered. Her throat knotted each time she thought of her mom's last days. The chemo had made her mother so ill, she couldn't eat and she'd dwindled from a size ten to a size six in less than nine months. Karen had never felt so helpless. Several times recently she'd forgotten her mother was gone and had reached for the phone to call her; until a sudden sharp pain told her to hang up.

"Did you know my parents?" she asked.

"Our office leased the property for them all these years, though I never had the chance to meet them personally." Vickey said. "You live in Denver now?"

"Yes, my husband, Gary, is an architect and I teach high school history. It is a lovely old house," she said. "Do you—"

The appraiser interrupted them as he walked through the open front door with an out stretched hand. Within an hour, he had completed his paperwork, and Karen had signed the listing agreement.

"How long are you going to be in town?" Vickey said.

"I flew in yesterday and unless you need me, I'd planned to catch a flight back to Denver day after tomorrow."

"That's fine," Vickey said. "We can do it all by e mail."

Karen followed her and stepped outside.

"Well, it's immaculate and in a prime location. I have no doubt we'll get a quick sale, as long as you're okay with our listing price." Vickey stepped from the large front porch down the two concrete steps to the sidewalk. "You leaving the porch swing?"

She nodded. "Oh ...Vickey," she said, "I almost forgot. I found something in the attic that I'd like to check out—an old trunk. Is it okay if I come by again tomorrow?"

"Absolutely, you still have the keys until we close escrow." She waved good-bye as she hopped into the Suburban parked in the ribbon driveway.

Karen closed the front door and stood alone in the home her parents had purchased over forty years ago. The emptiness echoed through the vacant rooms.

The following day, she pulled into the drive, grabbed her purse and McDonald's coffee, and approached the house. She let herself in and walked slowly through each room. She took time to visualize her parents living here—young and in love. The living room was long and narrow with a white-stucco brick fireplace at one end. Its room-length mantel sat atop bookshelves with glass-paned doors and crystal knobs. She wandered into the front sun-lit bedroom and looked out to the drive and the row of crepe myrtle just beyond. Down the short hall, the full bath, though small, had been renovated, and a few steps beyond, looking onto the back yard, was a second bedroom painted a soft mint green.

This must have been my childhood bedroom. She stepped through the doorway and examined the miniature closet to her left. She felt herself slip below another layer of history: a basement of unknown ghosts.

She had always known that she was adopted at birth. Her parents had never kept secrets from her. The two things they insisted she know were her biological mom had died in childbirth and how lucky they felt to have her. She'd always assumed her birth mother had been a very young woman whose boyfriend had probably skipped, though no one had ever said that. This assumption had made for an easy explanation as to why her biological father had never tried to find her.

Her reverie was broken when the carillon from the nearby Methodist Church chimed the quarter hour. She wondered if her mother had stood in this very room listening to the same familiar hymn. She could forgive God for her father's aneurysm ten years ago, but as difficult as that had been to accept, her mother's death after a two-year battle with cancer felt like a personal attack. Sadness knotted in her chest at the reminder that she was an orphan.

Unless ... If her birth father were still alive, she might, in fact, not be an orphan at all. She hadn't really considered that possibility. She'd always assumed he was out there somewhere, of course, but she rarely thought much about it. Sure, in high school, she'd asked the usual questions that every adopted teen asks. Had her mother been pretty? Were her blue eyes from her dad? Would she be tall like a model? She'd been content with the few facts her parents had provided. But ever since her mother's funeral, she'd felt this huge void and found herself wondering more about her biological parents.

Shaking off the past, she remembered today's mission and headed up to the attic. Once again she knelt on the floor and opened the trunk lid. As she lifted the items on top, something landed at her knee. She picked up a Purple Heart medal from World War II and ran her thumb across the plastic center. By noon, she had assessed most of the trunk's contents and headed back to her motel room. Being back here had left her emotionally drained and exhausted. And yet the house seemed to be calling to her, and she felt the need to stay a few more days. There was no reason to race back. She had packed extra stuff in case something with the listing had gone awry.

That evening, she counted as their Colorado phone rang and rang, and she waited impatiently for Gary to pick up. "Is he ever home?" she asked herself.

Suddenly his breathless voice came on the line. "Karen? Sorry ... I couldn't find the damned phone."

Karen had seen that movie a million times: Gary running from room to room chasing the sound, usually finding it just as the caller hung up.

"If you'd ever keep it in the charging cradle, you wouldn't have to search," she said.

"What's up?" he asked, not biting on the invitation for an argument.

She spent some time describing her recent find and finished by adding, "I'm staying on for just a few more days, Gary; I really want to research some of this."

"Ever the history teacher." There was a smile in his voice.

"It's more than *that* this time. This is where my parents lived; where I was born." Her words took on a sharpness she hadn't intended. Gary always understood and supported her; why did she act like this? "I just feel like there's something here—some answers about my adoption, my father ... I don't know."

"I wasn't criticizing, Karen—just making an observation and a teasing one at that."

"I know," she said. "I'll call with my flight details when I make them." Before she hung up, Karen, uncharacteristically, told Gary she was sorry for her tone.

She phoned Vickey Smith next to tell her she was staying a while longer.

The next afternoon she drove to the title company to obtain

the abstract papers for 311 E. 4th Street. For the next two days, she perused the sixty pages of documents and read each transaction, dating back to April 5, 1922 when the land was originally sold. That entry made her curious. The property lines were clearly demarcated, but she noted that a portion of land had been transferred from the adjoining lot prior to construction.

On Friday, she pushed against the heavy front door of a native red sandstone building four blocks from the house and stepped into the dimly lit foyer. She used both hands to close it against the strong wind that had nearly blown her across the parking lot. The Edmond Historical Society and Museum had been converted from an armory built in 1936 by the W.P.A. Its depression style modern architecture matched buildings at the college and looked just as it must have looked in the '30's.

The short, round, gray-haired woman who peeked around the corner at the end of the long hallway reminded her of one of the little grey squirrels she had seen scampering in the yard. She smiled at Karen and motioned for her to join her.

"Windy afternoon, isn't it dear?" the older woman said.

She introduced herself as Hazel Wycoff, and Karen followed her into a chilly, cavernous room. It was lined with floor-to-ceiling bookcases. In the center stood several long mahogany tables stacked high with tattered and faded books. One wall held rows of hinged wood dowel rods for larger items, like city and street maps, and over-sized papers too large to be folded. Several large silver-handled magnifying glasses sat on a shelf close by.

"May I help you find something specific," Hazel Wycoff asked. Her smile warmed the room.

Karen told Hazel about the house she'd inherited from her mother and the trunk she'd found in the attic. "As a history teacher, I'm always curious about the past," she said, "and I was hoping you could help me do some research."

"Of course," Hazel said. She walked towards one of the bookcases that bowed under the weight of the heavy volumes.

"The information on the abstract states that a Davis Lee built the house," Karen said.

"That's possible," Hazel said, "but H.W. Clegern owned over forty acres south of the university, between Boulevard and Rankin. In 1903, he divided a portion just north of Capital View into housing lots." She smiled before continuing. "Very astute of him, because when statehood arrived four years later, Edmond grew overnight, making him a very wealthy man."

Karen could see that Hazel was a fellow fact-finder. She smiled and listened closely as the older woman shared her knowledge of Edmond's past. The woman seemed to be enjoying her captive audience.

Hazel continued. "Many entrepreneurs back then. A lot of them from Europe, actually. They came when the railroad was built from 'Oak' City out to Guthrie, even before the Run. Lands, I'm boring you silly. I'll leave you to it, dear."

Karen watched the older woman shuffle off; then opened one of the massive books.

A few hours later, she stopped at the house—her house, she reminded herself—before heading to the nearby motel. She walked back to the kitchen and found a plastic cup for some water. New white glass-front cabinets and butcher block countertops brightened the room. As she filled the cup from the sink faucet, she looked out the lace-trimmed curtains at the side yard. The home next door was nearing a falling-down state, although the remainder of the neighborhood seemed well maintained.

She'd intended a two-day in-an-out visit, just long enough to see the property, get it on the market with a competent realtor and get the thing sold as quickly as possible. Yet here she was, days later, hanging around, looking for answers to questions she hadn't quite defined. The house had triggered feelings deeper than she had expected. Her high school history classes would fill her time in the fall, but for now there was nothing calling her back to Colorado—nothing but her mother's belongings and getting the family home ready to sell. *I'm not ready*, she thought, *not for that.*

Gary wouldn't miss her. Between work and weekend golf, he was seldom around. She wondered if most twenty-year marriages were like that. You got busy with your own lives, your own careers, and then? But it irked her every time he headed out to the country club. She couldn't remember the last time they'd even gone out to dinner, except for business. And then she felt like a third wheel; the guys talking about the latest coup over another prestigious firm; the wives talking about children in college, children in sports, children in theater productions. Karen nodded politely, occasionally mentioning a student's sudden turnaround in grades, or her plans for summer break. She watched their eyes glaze over. No, she may as well stay on. Perhaps he might even miss her if she stayed.

The following morning was Saturday, and Karen decided to spend some time combing the neighborhood. She parked on the street and slowly rambled past homes that had seen nearly a hundred years of history. It amazed her to think about the families—the generations—this place had seen. So many families had passed through the very home her parents had lived in. *What were their stories?* She wondered.

She nodded hello to a young woman pruning roses in the side yard of the two-story Victorian on the corner; then continued down the four blocks to the campus. She'd heard dozens of stories from her parents, but the memories were opaque as cobwebs after all these years. College professors in the '70's— anti-war demonstrations—her own adoption. She strolled along the university gardens and sat on a bench beneath the canopies of tall oaks and the few elm trees that had survived the blight.

The bell in Old North Tower chimed on the half-hour, and she could imagine her parents racing across campus to their respective classrooms. She wondered if they had been happy here—as happy as they were later in life? Or did they, too, go through rough patches of endless days of marriage? She and Gary had separated a few times over the years, but never more than a week. And they'd always managed to reconcile. She wondered if it was just simple inertia. Each day they headed off in different directions, and, if she was honest, she stayed as busy as Gary with meetings, teaching, grading and tutoring. She shook off that line of thinking and headed back to the house. She owed Gary a phone call. They could hardly work things out if she continued to postpone her return.

Vickey Smith met Karen at the house the following Monday with an offer. They went over the contract, worked through the numbers, and Karen surprised herself by turning it down.

"We can counter," Vickey said.

Karen nodded. "I just hate to take the very first offer, you know?" She knew that pissed off realtors. What was the adage? A bird in the hand. She was certain Vickey would say "you may not get another," but she was polite enough to smile as Karen signed off on the counter-offer with a flourish.

"Do you have a little time?" Karen asked.

"Of course," Vickey said.

"Can you tell me a little more about the house itself? I mean the little things. The reason it's historic—the reason I'm asking an arm and a leg," she joked.

Vickey put aside her briefcase. "Have you ever noticed this?" She pointed to the opening between the living and dining rooms. The plaster wall arched between two brick-topped columns. "It's called 'carpenter style.' The trim carpenters decided what might look nice, and designed their own thing. Probably different in every house in the neighborhood."

Karen's hand grazed the niche in the dining room wall. It was the first clear memory she'd had since arriving—her mother untangling the long black phone cord and her three-year-old self standing on the wooden heat vent in the floor a couple feet away.

"Every house had a telephone niche, even in the '20's," Vickey said.

"The plaster cove ceilings and wide crown moldings are typical Craftsman too. And your leaded windows are all original. Looks like maybe a pane or two have been replaced over the years, but not many."

Just beyond the kitchen was a narrow laundry room and beside it a tiny half bath.

Vickey pushed open a large set of folding doors to show Karen the back room. It was large and open and lined with windows on all three sides, making it bright and cheery. For some reason Karen saw sheer white curtains on each. She envisioned an antique desk and reading chair.

"It was possibly an addition," Vickey said, "however the windows are the same as the rest of the house: double-hung casements from that era. Some of the sash cords have broken and the windows won't stay up. Buyers may request a fix."

They walked back through the laundry room, out to the rear deck, and down three steps toward the detached single-car garage. Two pecan trees in the neighboring yard hung over the fence, covering much of the deck. Pecans lay everywhere from last fall's yield, and Karen picked up a few as she walked her realtor to the front driveway.

"They're still good if you want to take a bunch; plenty to make a pie if you have the stamina to crack them all," Vickey said.

Karen answered the realtor's warm smile with a wave good-bye. "Thanks for everything," she called as Vickey got into her car to leave.

She walked through the house one last time. She envisioned her mother moving from the stove to the kitchen sink, talking to her father as she prepared a meal. She wasn't certain why, but she just had a feeling that his office had been in that large back room, and that they'd conversed easily in the open warm banter they'd always shared. Oh, how she envied them.

Two days later, she loaded the rental car and headed to the airport. On her way out of town, she stopped at the Fourth Street house and watched as the shipping company carefully crated the trunk and all of its contents except one thick leather-bound diary. She was already intrigued at Lily's life as a pioneer woman in the late 1800's. An hour later, Karen settled into her window seat for the short flight to Denver. From her carry-on bag she pulled out the old journal then switched on the over head lamp as the plane headed west toward home.

Chapter 2
March, 1887

Lily cried out sharply as the right side of her body slammed against the curved ash slats of the prairie schooner bonnet. She watched the other five women as they jostled for space along the hard wood benches that lined the interior. The wagon leaned to the right, and the wood wheels finally found traction. Lily closed her eyes tightly, pretending to be anywhere but here. If they bounced over one more rutted riverbed, she'd get out and walk the rest of the way.

The taut canvas covers rattled with the incessant March winds. Each morning the women and children squeezed into the cramped schooners; the men rode horseback. Lily peered through the front opening. Eight riders protected each wagon; two on each side and two in front and rear. Three Indian braves, hired by the Atchison, Topeka and Santa Fe Railway, rode well behind to protect against marauders intent on robbing them.

The train ride from New Mexico to Kansas had seemed endless at the time, but it was nothing compared to the wagon trail Lily and her husband, Charles, were now enduring. The ten-day journey from Arkansas City to the unassigned lands of Oklahoma was becoming a dusty blur, and now her two-year-old son, Davis, refused to ride in the wagon. He insisted on sitting with his father astride the Spanish-bred Andalusian.

On the third day, Lily fell into a slight stupor as the wagon swayed slowly along the unmarked trail that led south across the barren red land. She became more nauseous each day and was often unable to eat. She didn't have a mirror and was glad of it. Sanitation was nonexistent. The smell of sweat was new to Lily;

her rancid odor unfamiliar, and she begged to wash in the few streams they found along the way. She could smell herself even now, and she curled her body further into the rear corner of the wagon until she heard the order – Pull Up! The other wives climbed down quickly. She was the last to emerge and welcomed the hand that reached up to assist her. "Thank you," she said. Her step was wobbly, but she managed to find her balance. It seemed to Lily that the other women were faring much better.

As he did every evening, Charles, the foreman of his rail crew, positioned the twenty prairie wagons into two large circles. In the center of each, the men built a large fire pit of wood and cow chips. Lily looked about her as she and the other women prepared their one hot meal of the day. She was sick of beans and smoked ham. She checked on the soda biscuits and cornbread that baked in cast iron skillets over the fire.

Lily had shipped their belongings ahead, and made do with the few pieces of clothing and toiletries essential for what seemed like an endless trip across miles of Indian land. She had one skillet and one pan to boil water and heat the provisions the Santa Fe Rail, her husband's employer, provided them. Each dawn, the women stoked the embers and boiled water from the nearby springs for coffee and gruel.

As the women cooked together, Lily approached the youngest. "Here, Becky Jo; let me help with the baby." Lily took the tiny girl into her arms and rocked her as she tended the pan of porridge bubbling over the fire. After dinner, she approached Annie who had a son about the same age as Davis and one on the way.

"Here, give me that," she said, as she offered to finish mending a toddler's flannel shirt. "I can watch Billy too." Sensing Annie's hesitation, she insisted. "Go on," she said, "go walk with your husband. You haven't seen him all day."

Annie smiled gratefully. "You are too kind, Lily."

Billy ran to Davis and gave him a toddler hug. Lily laughed. "Here you go," she said as she opened a burlap bag of maple wood building blocks and put them on the ground for the boys. "Sit here and be good."

As she meticulously brought the needle up and down in tiny stitches along Billy's shirt sleeve, Lily looked down at her own tattered dress, the hem slowly releasing itself and dragging along the ground. Less then three years ago Lily had walked the streets of Abilene in shantung silk and cashmere dress coats, and the finest leather boots buttoned from thigh to ankle, ordered from Italy.

She was the only child of Captain John Davis, a man who had used his Confederate Army skills to become an assayer for the railroad. The Atchison, Topeka and Santa Fe Rail was the largest company in the southern U.S. with extensive holdings in Texas. Her father was highly successful in business, and provided Lily, whose mother had died when she was just fifteen, the best money could buy—their large home in Abilene, a nursing degree from University of Texas in Austin, a year in Europe and a job as his assistant once she returned.

Her stitches slowed as Lily's mind returned to Abilene and all she'd left behind. It hadn't seemed a sacrifice, for she had fallen in love with Charles the night they'd met. And she smiled at the memory of that evening—a formal dinner dance given by the rail company in 1884. She could still feel the quickening of her breath when Charles turned those broad muscular shoulders in her direction, tipped his hat and grinned at her across the room. A moment later, Lily felt her right foot tapping nervously as Charles shook hands with her father; then asked her to dance. His steel blue eyes exuded confidence bordering on braggadocio, much like her father. Lily lowered her eyes and cautiously placed her white-gloved hand into his.

Even now, through the unabating dust of the plains, Lily could see the ivory brocade walls of the ballroom that night, the pink satin gown tracing her décolletage, and the light from the crystal chandeliers that lit them with a golden glow. It took only two months for Charles to win her hand in marriage. She remembered the day he'd asked her father for her hand. He had promised to make her happy and give her the best life could offer. She had put aside her nursing degree, her independence and even her concerns that their polarity of politics mattered.

They had married in April. The wedding was simple and elegant and attended mostly by company men and their wives. She knew the travel Charles' position required, just as her father did. She leaned heavily on the Captain's arm as he walked her down the aisle, and she fought back tears of both joy and loss.

As a foreman for the Santa Fe Rail, Charles oversaw crews of a hundred or more men at each location to which he was assigned. When they married, he was posted in New Mexico, and within a week they moved into a two-bedroom cottage outside Albuquerque. Lily had been happy there, and in mid-May she told Charles she was pregnant and wrote her father to tell him the good news. Their son, Davis, whom they named for the Captain, was born the following February.

Two years later, Charles came home with a telegram. His crew of a hundred and twenty-five men was to complete a well digging operation that was taking too long and costing the ATSF too much money. It was urgent that the water well along the North Canadian River be completed quickly so the tracks could be laid. They were heading into unassigned lands. Lily chose to face the move with a sense of excitement and adventure. She realized how naïve she'd been, but she had never questioned her own abilities and strengths … until now.

Lily pulled the needle through one last time, knotted the end and clipped the thread with her teeth. "Davis, Billy," she said as she rose. "A cup of milk, and let's get ready for bed." The small boys washed the red dirt stains from their hands in the pail of water Lily provided, then sat on the wooden wagon bench drinking the milk, still cold from the pottery crock.

Each night, in the purple-streaked dusk, Lily watched as small scouting parties of umber faces approached along the horizon. When the guides rode out to greet these visitors, she watched them exchange supplies, food or trinkets.

She was beginning to realize what Charles' station would mean for the tribes of the Indian Territory. The Santa Fe was simply one piece of the maze of tracks now crisscrossing the country. Charles' crew would finish the well for the watering and coaling station in Oklahoma that would complete the puzzle. *But at what cost?* She wondered.

One evening, after she tucked Davis under a heavy mound of wool blankets, Lily turned to Charles, her eyes gleaming with questions. "Do you ever wonder if our work here will be the ruin of all this?" she asked.

Charles looked up from the camp fire he was tending. She saw his look of exasperation. Lily knew he was once again resenting what he called her liberal ways. His response didn't surprise her, though she wished it had.

"Progress always comes with a cost, Lily; you know that."

She kept her thoughts to herself. They were tinged with a tight ridge of anger these days, but she was too tired to argue.

Lily was experiencing something she'd never felt before. Loneliness—most definitely—but also a deep separateness from the others. She had felt so positive when they left Abilene; foolish she thought now. The women on the trail were kind, respectful of their husbands, and pleasant to Lily, but few could read and most were unable to sign their names. She ran out of conversation and patience soon after leaving Arkansas City. During the day she smiled, but after dark the desire for home opened its mouth and devoured her.

It was in those dark hours that she recalled a conversation with Charles early in their courtship. It had been their second evening out together and almost their last. It was a cold Texas evening in late February, but Lily had insisted they didn't need the carriage. As they strolled from her stately home the few blocks to the theater, she gave him a cursory glance from head to toe and wondered what her attraction had been that first evening. He looked gangly in his pressed black wool suit, his tie askew and in need of a haircut. He reminded her of the silhouette of a large crane, one foot in the water and the other curled under a wing. "So you find the Republican party too liberal for your liking?" Lily had asked.

"I simply find myself in favor of a more realistic and traditional style of government is all, Miss Davis," he said. "I don't find the Republican ideals to be of much use in this time of American growth and expansion."

"Why do you say that, Mr. Lee?" She watched his face closely.

"Well, we've freed the blacks. I wonder what is next."

"What do you fear will be next?" she asked, pointedly. Lily was startled at his reply.

"There's talk in Washington about change on the reservations as well. What have the native tribes done for us except slaughter us in the most vicious warlike ways?"

She knew her wide-set green eyes were flashing with anger. "Mr. Lee," Lily said," I wonder … what would you perhaps do if someone tried to take over your lovely home in Bowie that you've so fondly told me about?"

Charles threw back his head in laughter. "Miss Davis, your point is well made."

Lily suspected that most of the women Charles courted were vapid and quiet, most likely deferring immediately to his male opinions. She had no intention of playing those silly games.

"Tell me later how you like the play we're seeing this evening," he said. "I'm sure we will enjoy some lively banter over its content."

"Mr. Lee, I hope you aren't baiting me," Lily replied, "just because I have my own views and opinions about what we are doing to the Indians. Taking their land; as if we had eminent domain over every mile of this country."

"Not at all," Charles said and smiled down at her. "I find it quite entertaining to spar with a woman of your intelligence and charm."

Lily leaned backward and met his gaze. She returned his smile. "Well, don't let the A.T. and S.F. hear that."

Later on, as they walked back home, Lily found herself unusually quiet. The play had been amateurish at best and there was no need for discussion as he'd suggested earlier. As they reached her father's front porch, Lily turned and met Charles' eyes. "Mr. Lee, you'll have to forgive me for my strong views. My mother taught me at an early age that helping others was more important than the wealth my father was accumulating. And, though my father wore Confederate gray, he would have gladly worn blue."

"I respect your views, Miss Davis," he said. "I'd like to hear more of them, in fact."

And, so, Lily thought, as she lay her head on a rolled up blanket inside a cold, damp wagon, here we are. Charles would provide a pile driver he had operated in New Mexico, and he and his crew would work ten-hour days for the next year and a half, if it came to that, in order to complete the drilling of the well that would fuel the steam engines. Summit Station would connect Arkansas City, Kansas with Gainesville, Texas.

The Kansas Rail and the A.T.S.F. were in a race to reach the midpoint on the Canadian River. The tracks approached them from either direction like a snake looking for its next meal. They stood in the center and waited for the snake to swallow them.

On the ninth day of their journey, Charles returned to camp excited and anxious. The crew had come upon the Canadian River that afternoon, wide and flowing swiftly from the earlier spring rains.

They followed the river for another full day, and at dusk that evening, the first wagons halted over an outcropping, and they saw the make-shift settlement below. Lily could hear the whoops and hollers of the men on horseback as they returned to the schooners.

Charles rode to the wagon fourth in line, pulled Lily side-saddle behind him and placed their son into her arms. The three of them rode the grey rapidly over the slight hills that surrounded the make-shift town and down into the valley below. Lily hugged Davis tightly, and tears burned to be released. Unassigned had a new definition as she surveyed their future home.

A tall conical structure, thirty feet in diameter, had been built over the limestone rim of the well: the well Charles was to complete on schedule. Beside it stood a little red pump house which would eventually pump water from the well to the water tank and fuel the steam engines of the ATSF, but for now would be their home. It was nothing but a sixteen-foot square shack thrown together with wood siding and a shingled roof. Light showed through half-inch cracks between the boards and around the shabbily framed door and front window. At the rear a tall tin smoke-stack emitted a dark gray flume of coal smoke. Lily stepped gingerly up the uneven step to the porch and steeled herself before opening the door.

The boiler and pump for the well sat in the far corner of the one large room Charles and Lily would now call home. Lily shook her head in disgust at the ugly structure that took a third of the room, but she knew it would provide them with winter warmth. She thought longingly of her home in Abilene where her father still resided and of Charles' home in Bowie. Lily suddenly yearned to feel the softness of freshly laundered linens and to eat meals prepared and served by their hired cooks, though now that seemed lavish and wasteful.

"Charles Lee," Lily whispered, "you will pay for this the rest of your life." Then she set about moving the few pieces of make-shift furniture the rail had supplied and found linens to cover the wall-hung bunk beds. Lily had no time for tears.

*

In less than a week, life for the crew settled into a routine. The men worked from sunup to sundown digging the well which, when complete, would measure thirty feet in diameter and a hundred and twenty-eight feet deep. The women tended babies, fires for cooking, laundry and warmth, and gardens to feed them. It was not an easy life but the wives were used to uprooting and living in tents for months at a time. Most had married young and had children before the age of seventeen. It was a life Lily had never experienced.

If it was Charles' role to take care of his men, it fell to Lily to look after their wives and to make certain they had the necessities for life on the plains. She was the wife of the foreman and she took her responsibilities seriously. She kept a small leather journal with her, noting items and food rations that Charles would request of the ATSF. On the first Friday of each month she read the list of needed provisions while he telegraphed the company. Cornmeal. Coffee. White cotton batting. Thread. Salt.

Twice a week, Lily walked the muddy path that took her east from the well site to the enclave of tents that housed the other families. The canvas dwellings were just one step above the schooners that had transported them, and Lily came to appreciate the pump house the company provided. On those days she visited each woman and inquired about their needs, taking note of each item they required. And as a nurse, she tended to their illnesses and injuries.

It was on one of her morning visit days that Lily let go of Davis' hand and allowed him to meander just a ways ahead of her, keeping him clearly in sight. They were just steps from the pump house when he began to duck and bob among the cedars and the few weeping willows that lined the creek. Lily scolded. "Davis, come back closer to mama … now."

Davis grinned mischievously; then ran off to his left and out of her line of vision momentarily. She spotted his green jacket and shook her head. "You are going to get a licking, young man," she called. He began to tease her by running back and forth across the rutted path; just far enough into the dense briars to scare her before racing back to her skirts; then off again.

"Mama, look," he called from the left side of the path. He ran a few steps further into the wooded brush, and Lily called for his return. She couldn't see him but she could hear his small voice as if talking to someone. "Davis …" Lily wasn't sure which way his voice was echoing. "Davis," she shouted. She was running now, heart pounding.

It took only a few seconds to reach him, but she was breathless when she did. *Thank God.*

"Look, mama," Davis said again.

Following his outstretched arm, Lily walked to where he was pointing.

A young Indian boy lay on the ground sobbing; his right arm twisted at an unnatural angle beneath him. He looked to be eight or nine years old, and he gazed up at her with wide anxious eyes. A small roan pony stood a short ways off, waiting patiently. As Lily approached, he shuffled to a sitting position; his face scrunched tightly in pain; his knobby thin shoulder blade forced backward.

Lily spoke softly, though she knew her words would have no meaning. "May I look at your arm?" she said. Apparently her tone conveyed her desire to help, for the boy wiped away tears and scooted toward her. Davis hung behind her skirt now, his eagerness replaced with a look of concern.

"Oh, my," Lily said. It didn't appear to be broken; most likely pulled from its socket. It would require additional pain in order to help him. She wasn't sure she should treat him, but they were miles from the nearest reservation; in fact she questioned what he was doing so far from home. But she couldn't just leave him here.

"Davis, come here," Lily said. She took the blue bandana from around his neck and began to roll it into a sling. "Hmm." How to tell the boy this was going to hurt badly?

She knelt on the ground and held the scarf in front of her, carefully showing the boy her intent. She wrapped it around her own shoulder and pulled. Lily let out a sharp cry when she pulled it toward her chest to show the boy what she was going to do.

The boy shook his head wildly—No.

Davis spoke for the boy. "No, mama, no."

Lily laid a hand on Davis' head to reassure him; then reached forward and gently touched the boy's cheek. She whispered, "It will only hurt for a moment. I promise."

Before he could move away, Lily brought the folded cloth over and around his shoulder and pulled. The boy screamed in pain for a moment; then a look of relief flowed across his small tear-stained face.

She clasped his hands in hers and looked closely into his eyes. "I'm so sorry I hurt you," Lily said. His lips turned upward into a smile.

"Here, we'll leave this on for awhile so you can get back to your village," Lily said. She gently bent his elbow and tucked his arm toward his chest; then tied the sling around his shoulder forming a cradle for the injured arm.

"There," she said as she lifted herself from the ground. "Come, Davis," she said. She didn't have to ask twice. He was right on her heels. Lily bent down and helped the boy to his feet. Brushing his backside to remove leaves and dirt, she walked him to the pony and easily lifted him up and onto its back. Lily handed him the rope reins and waved him off. But she stood for some time watching the boy grow smaller and smaller. Just as he turned into a small dot on the horizon, she saw a dozen other dots moving slowly east toward the reservation. After a few minutes, she took Davis by the hand and turned toward home. She was too tired to walk to the tents today. She would go tomorrow.

A week later, Lily watched out the front window in amazement. "Davis," she called, "get under the kitchen sink and close those curtains around you, hear me?" As the dust began to settle, four riders came into focus. "My, lands!" Lily gasped as the men rode into the yard and up to the house.

Lily had seen photographs of lavishly adorned Indians in magazines but having them outside her front door was another thing. Her heart beat a bit faster and she considered what to do. She reached for the rifle which stood just inside and to the left of the doorframe. Lifting it by one hand, she held it pointed downward at her side, ready to take aim if she had to. One of the first things Charles had taught her was to use a gun, and her tin can average was fairly decent for a petite citified woman. Opening the door a crack, she called out, "How may I help you?"

One of the burnished copper men wore a full feather headdress and sat astride his pinto with his right hand raised. The other three were dressed in similar leather chaps and moccasins and wore headbands with a single feather. Sitting bareback behind one of the men was the little boy she'd tended in the woods.

Lily opened the door a little wider and nodded her head at the leader, and when she did he lowered his hand and nodded back. She stood quietly in the open door as he dismounted and opened one of the saddlebags that hung on each side of the tall horse. Lily clasped the rifle tighter but kept it lowered, just grazing her skirt but in full sight of the Indian chieftain. From the bag he pulled a buffalo-hide parfleche, placed it on the step to the porch and began to untie the rawhide straps. In it Lily could see slabs of meat, carefully portioned and salted.

The chief spoke slowly in his native language using his hands and eyes to convey his intention of the gift. Lily smiled and leaned the rifle against the door frame, then carefully walked toward him as she spoke in English, "My husband and I thank you."

He lowered his head, turned and mounted his horse, and the party headed slowly east back toward the Kickapoo reservation.

When Charles arrived for dinner, Lily met him on the small wood porch. "Charles, you won't believe what happened today. Come see. We have meat. I cooked antelope for dinner."

The quizzical look on Charles' face suddenly changed to recognition when he saw the envelope-shaped buffalo hide lying in the corner of the room.

His face screwed up into an anger Lily had never before witnessed. "Tell me you did not open the door to those murderous Indians, Lillian Lee," he yelled.

She stood in silence; then swished her long skirt around her as she walked away.

"Lily, don't walk away from me."

She felt his hand pull at her arm as she continued to the kitchen area Charles had partitioned from their sleeping quarters with a bolt of fabric.

"Damn it, Lily," Charles said, but he didn't follow her. His voice trailed into an angry hiss.

At the stove, her red face mirrored the heat from the large cast iron skillet where she had seared the piece of venison and simmered it with onion and carrots all afternoon.

That night, dinner at the small square table was quiet enough to hear each fork chink against the chipped china plates Lily had so lovingly packed in the wood crates shipped from New Mexico.

"Davis," Lily spoke formally to her son, "please pass your father the bread before it gets cold."

Charles gave a sigh of resolve. "Lily," he said as he pushed his plate to the side, "I'm sorry for my tone. But need I really warn you of the danger you put yourself and our son in today?"

"They were quite respectful and, not in the least, dangerous," she said.

"They are not to be trusted, Lily. Were they Kickapoo or Iowa?"

"I have no idea, Charles, does it matter? According to you, they are all heathens and murderers."

Charles removed himself from the table and walked to the front porch. Lily could see him through the window as he sat down in a rickety straight-back chair, leaned against the side of the house, and watched the sunset. She heated water on the wood stove to wash the dishes and helped Davis into the one pair of clean pajamas she could find. Her back ached from bending over the washboard; she put the task off as long as long as possible. But tomorrow she'd drag the heavy oak tub to the backyard.

As much as Lily had hated the wagon train, she now longed for companionship. She envied the bonds the other wives had formed in the close-knit city of tents. Her weekly visits made her even more aware of her isolation. She spoke to Charles several times about her feelings, trying hard not to sound complaining.

"For God's sake, Lily," he said one evening following dinner, when she'd brought it up again. The candles flickered in the lanterns that lit their one small room. "You never complained in New Mexico about being lonely."

Lily sat opposite him on a hard bench she'd cushioned the other day. "We were newlyweds, Charles. And I was pregnant and gave birth to Davis soon after."

"Still," he said, "you knew it wouldn't be Abilene when you married me. Surely you knew that."

Tears slid down Lily's cheeks and onto the table.

"Oh, Lily, I'm sorry if I've hurt you. Come on now. Is it really that bad?"

"There is no one to talk to within miles, Charles, except Jones at the general store when I walk into town or Mr. Franks at the postal office. A woman needs companionship."

Charles tried to interrupt, but she cut him off.

"No, don't say I should be busy enough with Davis or that I have plenty to do. That isn't the issue. You have your crew all day long. I hear how rowdy your men are and the banter between you. Don't you think a woman needs that as well?"

"We live in town, Lily. Do you really want to move into the tents? You'd be even more unhappy. Have your father send you more books. You love to read."

And that was the end of the conversation. Still … she longed to walk in Abilene again: to glance at fashions in the store windows; to visit the museums followed by an evening at the theater. She missed her days at the hospital where she felt fulfilled and the intellectual debates with her father. It did no good to look back. She had known Charles was a company man when they married, and she knew that he would go where the rail sent him from now on … and next time it could be even worse.

At least the plains were beautiful in their own way. The endless red landscape seemed to float before her for miles. The large sky was broken only by occasional billowing clouds that rose upward into soft charcoal pillars, bringing winds and rain. She'd simply have to make the best of it. For surely, by this time next year the station would be operating, and they could build a real house of their own, or move to a larger city if Charles obtained a higher position with ATSF. It will be fine, she assured herself. She sighed and let the loneliness wash over her.

It was several weeks before her visitors returned. This time Lily raced to the makeshift pantry to retrieve the flour and sugar she had managed to put aside. She was standing on the porch as they dropped from their horses, one step below her. No rifle in her hand this time. She understood their intent and welcomed it.

Handing the chief her two small sacks, he smiled and grunted, then surprised her by clearly saying, "Thank you, Missus."

Lily could not hide her pleasure and reached her hand toward him. She realized immediately he had no idea she was indicating a handshake. Her hand dropped quickly and she tucked her head and lowered her gaze. "You are welcome," she answered.

"We bring wild turkey. You like?" The man to his immediate right handed down a heavy cloth bag which the chief presented to Lily. He gave a quick bow and jumped onto the pinto. They were gone before she could find the words to thank him.

This time Lily made sure to salt the meat again and hide it in an upper cupboard. She would tell Charles she had shot the thing herself when she served it on Friday.

*

By summer Lily had created a home out of the one room shack. She sewed curtains for each of the three windows made from fabric she had bartered for her canned beets and snap peas at the one general store in town. Magazines and newspapers were hard to come by, but every few weeks *The Arkansas Register* arrived. Jones, the store owner, had grown quite fond of Lily and always saved her a copy. Lily looked forward to seeing the large rotund man on days when she walked into town. His fleshy red face always held a warm smile when she walked in.

Sometimes she took a small basket of baked goods when she went. He teased that only his mama in Germany could bake biscuits as light as Lily's. She thanked him for the newspaper and handed him a nickel. She sat at night after reading to Davis and cut out pictures that she nailed to each wall. Flower arrangements, formal city events, museums and even art work adorned the room.

Some nights she sat and gazed at them in the glow of candlelight and pretended to be standing inside the Abilene art museum just blocks from her father's home.

At two and a half, young Davis was growing quickly. It was all she could do to keep him in clothes. He played at her feet as she pushed the treadle on the sewing machine her father had sent her from Texas, letting out hems and sewing new overalls. Lily bent over the grooved washboard each week trying to purge Charles' shirts of the embedded red clay, her hands shriveled from hours in the hot water which she boiled on the old wood stove.

It was a hot, sticky afternoon in August when Lily spotted the small cloud of dust kicked up by two riders: one Indian man and the young boy she had helped in the spring. She stood at the horsehair clothesline that stretched from the back of the house to a wooden pole that Charles' foreman had cemented into place in the yard. She wiped her hands on her apron, untied it and walked into the house to check on Davis as he napped.

The horses were lathered from the hard ride. The riders dismounted and walked quickly to her door. "Come," the man said when she met him on the porch.

"Come?" she asked. She shook her head. "I don't understand."

The man hung his head for a moment; then repeated, "Come." This time he pointed east toward the reservation, and Lily realized what he was trying to say. But why come for her? The natives seldom asked for outside assistance. The boy walked directly to Lily and pulled aside his leather shirt, showing her his shoulder. He smiled broadly, and Lily slowly understood. He had apparently told his elders about the woman with "good medicine."

Lily was reluctant. Davis was sound asleep, and she wasn't certain she could be of any help. Charles will be furious, she thought. She considered running the short distance to the site to tell him, but she knew how he would respond. She penciled a quick note to him, reached beneath the bed and slid out her leather satchel; then lifted the sleeping child into her arms. The tall, thin man led the way to his horse and she handed Davis to him. Lily hesitated. She hoped she was making the right decision.

The Indian helped her onto the back of his horse side-saddle and pulled himself and Davis up with the saddle horn and reins. The boy rode bareback on his pony and kicked its sides to keep up with the older man. It was barely fifteen miles to the nearest Kickapoo colony, but the trip took nearly an hour. It was an hour Lily filled with self doubt.

The reservation covered over a hundred thousand acres and bordered the North Canadian River. Small separate villages divided the land. The smoke of tanning animal hide and the strange odors of food stored in tree-bark containers slowly settled around Lily, mixing with the permanent smell of dirt encrusted in her nostrils. Rows of horses stood idle, lifting an occasional hoof, trembling to shake off the black flies that settled on their backs and in their manes.

The Mustang they were riding slowed, and Lily watched closely as they sauntered through a tall tightly-bound cedar-pole fence. She took in the foreign surroundings of wickiups and grass-thatch lean-to's. The giant cone-shaped shelters were fifteen to thirty feet in diameter and resembled balls of bark scattered along the ground. Short bursts of smoke from the inside fire pits floated up and through a round opening in the center of each hut.

She took Davis and slung him over one shoulder, then followed the man toward one of the largest wickiups at the far end of the circular enclave. The man she recognized as chief and who had visited her home several times stood outside. He nodded his permission and lifted the deer hide opening for her.

Davis, now wide awake, hugged his mother's neck for a moment before she placed him on the smooth ground outside the entrance. An old woman spoke to him in a hushed voice and presented a small wooden toy to draw his attention, and Lily cautiously entered.

A buffalo skin had been hung at the rear of the dwelling to give privacy to the girl who cried out in pain. Just behind it stood two young women, as young as the girl herself. A middle-aged woman approached Lily and took her hands. Her eyes pleaded. *Her daughter*, Lily thought. She assessed the situation quickly. The girl was no more than fifteen and much too small for this birth. She seemed dazed from the pain, *or more likely*, thought Lily, *an herb tea the wet nurse had given her.* As she reached into her leather bag, her hand stopped midway and she hesitated.

Her eyes met those of the elderly woman now peeking around the edge of the doorway.

Lily swabbed the girl's abdomen and inner thighs with Mercurochrome, then wet a rag with a solution from a brown bottle and placed it between the girl's mouth and nose. The girl immediately sank into a deep sleep, and Lily opened her legs and felt for the baby's head. It was in the head-down position but it was facing the mother's front instead of her back. Posterior presentation she remembered from nursing school, and she prayed that the cord was not around its neck. Lily glanced at the mother and nodded. The girl lay still as death, unable to help push the child from her womb, but as Lily pressed on her abdomen, the contractions of her labor continued.

The room was silent, but Lily felt eyes in the dimness around her. The death of this girl could mean her own. The responsibility fell like a cloak around her tense shoulders. The girl's contractions became dangerously slow. Lily began to hum softly and moved her palms in gentle circles along the stretched skin of the girl's tight abdomen. She spoke softly. "Come, little one, come."

She felt one sharp contraction that bumped hard against her hands. A moment later, she saw the dark, wet hair of the crowning and waited briefly as the head emerged. She prayed for the next contraction that would tilt the shoulders and let the baby slide into the world, but it didn't come. She would have to turn the child herself and hope it wasn't too large for this young girl's body. Holding the head in one hand, she slipped two fingers into the canal and turned gently. Within seconds, the baby slid into her hands, and she thanked God. Lily patted the tiny brown infant until it let out a raspy cry; then placed her into her grandmother's waiting arms.

With relief, Lily stooped down to retrieve the after-birth. Instead, an enormous surge of blood erupted from the frail girl. Lily gasped, and with widened eyes, begged silently for assistance from the two young women standing behind her. They raced to Lily's side. She nodded with her forehead to the rolls of cotton inside the open black leather bag at her feet. Four hands fed her the gauze as quickly as they could unroll it, and within a moment, Lily managed to staunch the flow and pack the area. There was no guarantee the girl would live, but she had done all she could do.

As she stood, Lily's shoulders crumpled from the fear and exhaustion she now allowed herself to feel, and the girl's mother embraced her. Both women wept in the silent hut. Lily washed with lye soap in the basin of water the women provided and wished she could lie down to rest. The ride back would be long.

When Lily pushed through the opening and reached for Davis' hand, the men nearby raised spears and bows and released a flood of strange noises and words that frightened the child and caused him to cry.

It was just after dusk when her rider reined in the horse and stopped just shy of the house. He jumped from the Mustang and helped Lily and Davis dismount. At that moment, Charles slammed through the front door, rifle aimed at the man, finger on the trigger and half cocked.

Lily's clothes were red with the blood of the young woman, and she knew he thought they'd been harmed. "Charles, it's all right!" she yelled at her husband. "We're fine. We're home."

Charles interrupted her, "Get in the house, woman."

"I'll do no such thing, Charles Lee; you will listen to me."

Charles' face flushed full red, his mouth tightened in anger.

"Davis, get in the house," he said sternly. "Lily," he yelled in her direction again. "Where the hell have you been?"

It took less than a minute to list the afternoon events, and Lily watched each gradual movement of Charles lowering the rifle inch by inch until he leaned it against the house. She saw his anger slowly dissipate into relief. He turned to the still, ghost-like native, put forth his hand, and motioned for him to bring his horse to the watering trough at the side of the house. Lily watched Charles' back and barely heard his next reply. "This is not over, Lillian Lee."

"You are something," Charles said to Lily later that evening. She had bathed herself and Davis who was now slumbering quietly in one of the bunks.

Charles rose from his corner chair. "You will never go against my wishes again. Do you hear me, Lily? Do you have any idea the danger you placed yourself in … and my son? These are Indians, Lily. Savages."

"Please don't be angry, Charles," she said. "The girl would have died …."

Before she could add more, Charles shook his head in resignation. She watched as his eyes crinkled with a slight hint of humor, and he led her to the bed.

A few days later, Lily left Davis with Annie Grover, her closest neighbor and the wife of Charles's crew leader. She told Annie she was delivering medical supplies to a few families north of town and that she would return in a few hours.

Then Lily saddled her mare for the long ride to the reservation to check on the young girl and her infant. As she rode into the wide circle just inside the reservation walls, the chief again welcomed her. He led her to the farthest wickiup where she found the young mother sitting near the fire-pit suckling the tiny baby. She knew the girl had been too drugged to recognize her.

She approached cautiously and raised a hand in welcome. Just then the girl's mother stepped into view, and when she saw Lily, she walked to her with outstretched arms. The girl, named Tahnee, listened attentively and beamed up at Lily when she realized this was the woman who had saved her life and that of her daughter's. She placed the baby into Lily's arms, and Lily exchanged the child for the gift she had brought with her. Tied in a clean patterned flour sack was a hand-knitted pink blanket. Tahnee rubbed it against her face; then wrapped her daughter carefully in its softness and bowed. Hand signs took the place of language, but the three clearly understood each other, and for an hour, Lily enjoyed the warmth and comfort of being within the large family of tribal women.

On the ride home, she pushed the mare hard. She had to get back before suppertime or face the wrath of Charles. It had been one of the best days she'd had since leaving Texas and she didn't want it to end. Washington was already pushing to force the tribes to conform to the white man's ways, and during the afternoon a thought had taken hold. On her next visit she might speak with the chief about teaching English to the younger women so they could function in the new world that was destined to overpower them. Perhaps in trade, she could learn from the tribe's medicine man about the native herbs and flowers they used medicinally out here on the plains.

A week later she once again lied to her good friend so Davis could stay behind, and she wasn't sure if that was better than the lie of omission she was making to Charles. Once she was welcomed onto the reservation, she sought out Tahnee and asked for her help. It took the better part of the afternoon to learn the words of the Kickapoo by using hand gestures and mime: speak – English – book – teach. It was harder to express her offer as the gift she intended it to be. Emotions were difficult words in another language. She knew the Chief spoke some English; he had spoken to her many times in her own words, but she wanted to try to use his language if she could. Tahnee asked her husband to speak with the Chief on behalf of Lily to get her an audience. And by late afternoon, she sat with him outside on a blanket in front of the cooking fire where his wife made a warm tea. He nodded often throughout the conversation and he smiled at her poor grammar and lack of Kickapoo words.

"Your people are our enemies," he said. "White men want land—our land. But you are wise. The future is coming and the railroad will bring it quickly. Many of our young people would welcome your English words. You have my blessing."

Lily couldn't believe how late the day had gotten. She would need a very large lie for her lateness. But somehow that was becoming easier for her. This was something she felt compelled to do. All she really had to give was her education and it brought purpose into her life again.

That night she wrote her father and asked for his assistance, and within a week the package arrived. Lily placed the box out in the horse stall where Charles would not see it.

She couldn't continue to lie to Annie, so for the next several months, weather permitting, Lily filled her saddle bags with the Beginning Readers her father had sent from Abilene, and after lunch with Charles each Thursday, she settled Davis onto the saddle in front of her, and they rode east. Every week, as Lily rounded the last bend along the river, a smile spread wide on her face and long dampened feelings of purpose and excitement, and yes, even happiness, filled her. The secret ate at her, but nothing would stop her now.

September rolled into October and then to November. Her lessons with the medicine man continued until snow covered the plants they needed. As she taught the young women, she began to learn their native language. It was difficult on her tongue, but she welcomed the chance to respect their heritage.

A week before Thanksgiving, Lily woke with anticipation of her visit to Tahnee and her other students, but as she rose from the thick down bed covers, she glanced outside. An early snow had blanketed the red plains and the slight warmth of the sun was turning it into a sheet of ice. Her heart sank for a moment, but she pulled herself upright, reached for her heavy chenille robe and ankle high slippers and walked across the room to stoke the boiler. She started a fire in the cook stove and poured water into a kettle to boil for coffee. Charles woke soon after and he hollered to Lily that he and Davis were going to relieve themselves. She chuckled. Davis hated using the chamber pot and preferred to suffer an ice cold out-house.

A few moments later she heard the door slam and Charles cursing. Lily raced into the living quarters. "What on earth?" Her question was met with large glaring eyes and a dead silence.

Davis was at her side and behind her skirts before she could say another word. She waited, expecting Charles to wreak some punishment upon their son for whatever he had managed to do between the facilities and the porch.

Charles pulled his hands through his hair and stomped into the kitchen, and Lily followed. She poured coffee into his favorite tin mug and then her own. When he sat down at the kitchen table, Lily decided it best to remain silent and wait. She joined him at the table. It was several minutes before Charles cleared his throat and spoke.

"Davis tells me the snow is going to keep you both from going to see his Indians."

Lily's last sip of coffee sputtered from her lips, and her eyes grew wide. She glanced across the room at Davis who sat on the floor by his bed, playing with a small wooden train.

"Charles ... I can explain."

"So now you are taking our son to 'his Indians' for visits? Exposing him to their heathen ways? Lily, even after all this time, I am shocked at *this*."

She tried to interrupt, but he raised his hand to silence her.

"Never again! Do you hear me, Lillian?" He was yelling in

rage, and Lily could hear Davis crying as he crawled under the blankets on his bed and began to sob.

Charles stood quickly, reached for his heavy leather jacket and cap and walked from the house. She could see him going toward the station through the side window, and she went to comfort her son. She knew she should have told. Poor Davis—feeling the wrath of his father for something she had done. Lily sat on his bed and took him in her arms and rocked him and soothed him and told him it was all her fault.

It was a week before a word was spoken in the Lee home. Charles worked extra-long shifts, and Lily helped the other women with chores and canning and preparing for the upcoming holidays. Thanksgiving was tense but civil, and the turkey Charles had killed for the feast was unusually tender.

The following Thursday she woke early and dressed for the ride to the reservation.

"Davis will be staying with Annie while I teach at the reservation today, Charles," she said. His look confirmed that he thought she was mad.

"If these people are to become Americans as you want, they will need to speak English and be able to read and write. Isn't that what you want? That they become civilized?"

Charles hung his head for a moment. "I do not condone this, Lily so don't think I do. But you are hell-bent to do this. As long as you don't take my son ...then go."

That night they talked about the well and the weather and how many eggs the hens had laid, and a calm settled between them once again.

On Christmas morning, Davis woke Lily and Charles early. Beneath the blackjack Christmas tree Charles had dragged in the week before, sat a toy drum and a simple wood rocking horse. The three-year-old screeched with delight and hugged them both. After lunch they stood on the short unstained wood porch and posed for the traveling photographer passing through town. Lily smiled broadly, barely able to contain the news of her pregnancy. She prepared a dinner of roast beef, potatoes that had cost her dearly, and string beans from the garden Charles had planted for her last summer. As she served the cherry cobbler, still warm from the oven, Lily could hold it no longer and burst forth with what she hoped would be good news.

His wide grin said all she needed to know, but she grasped his hand anyway. "So you're fine with your errant wife giving your son a brother or sister?" Charles shook his head and gave a loud laugh. "I ask just one thing, Lily. No more visits on horseback; do you understand?

This time Lily agreed without hesitation. The early snows could mean a hard winter and it would be difficult to ride.

*

One cold morning in February, eleven months after their arrival, Lily read the headlines of the newspaper, threw it on the table, and let out a howl that frightened Davis and panicked Charles.

"Is it the baby, Lily? Should I get Doc Taylor?"

Lily glared at Charles for a moment before speaking. "Well, you and your rail people have gotten your way again, haven't you?" she said.

Charles sat back down, a look of resignation crossing his face. He picked up the paper and read aloud, "President Cleveland, on this day, February 8, 1887, has signed the Dawes' Act." Charles shook his head and looked at Lily who stood stiffly behind him, arms crossed.

"Do you know what this means, Charles?" she asked. "Have you read about this bill?"

"Of course, Lily, and I understand you've become friends with the Kickapoo, but they will be fine."

"What?" she yelled, "fine?"

Charles read from the article. "The head of each Indian family will be granted 160 acres. Other adults will receive 80.

Children under 18 – 40 acres. "

Lily glowered. "Go ahead … read the rest, Charles."

He laid the newspaper face down on the table and left the room.

Lily glared after him and glanced back down at the newsprint. She knew what this meant: that the natives could no longer hold communal property; the reservations they'd been forced onto would be dissolved; and they would be forced into farming and required to adopt the habits of "civilized life".

An hour later, Lily saddled up the new mare Charles had given her last year for her birthday. Her three-month belly pushed slightly against her gray flannel dress, and she pulled the wool blanket closer around her against the cold February wind. Tears streamed down her cheeks, and she hoped they'd freeze and divert the other pain she was feeling—the loss of the Indian friends she knew was coming. It would most likely be her last visit to the Kickapoo who had welcomed her into a strange, foreign land.

As Lily reined in her horse at the entrance of the reservation, she sat silently and waited. She hadn't been here since the early snows of December. She now wished for more time. Her approach had been visible for several miles, and a small welcoming committee greeted her. One of the men helped her from her saddle, and Lily turned to find the chief standing a few feet in front of her, silent and stoic. He nodded for her to enter his hut, and she followed. Tea was already steeping atop the fire, and one of his wives presented her with a pottery mug. In less than a year, the ways of the tribe had shifted. The chief now wore wide-legged cloth britches and a flowing cotton shirt with his moccasins, and ribbons were carefully woven into two thick black braids of shoulder-length hair.

"Atto. Hello," she spoke in Kickapoo and the chief smiled and motioned for her to sit. His simple English was clear and pure. "We will miss you," he said, and he sat down to join her as the silent woman filled their cups.

"Inenie. Thank you, sir." She took a sip from her cup. "I am so sorry," she said; then repeated the words in Kickapoo. He nodded.

Lily watched as his face slowly closed into repose of acceptance.

"When?" she asked, in his language.

"Soon," he answered, in her own.

"Taanahi. Where are you …?" She swept her hand wide along the horizon.

"Some here; some away." His eyes clouded, and Lily saw the distance in his eyes before she felt it. Was she even welcome here, she wondered? She was as white as the men who had signed the documents taking their land. Tears choked in her throat, and Lily could think of nothing more to say. She finished her tea quickly and stood, stretching to her full height. The chief lifted himself from the ground as well and stood before her.

Without speaking a word, he walked her to the tethered mare. Lily reached out her hand toward the chief, and he took it in his own. Instead of a hand-shake, he unexpectedly lifted her hand to his lips and placed a gentle kiss on her knuckles. "We will speak again," he said, and he motioned to a young man who formed a step with his hand and lifted her onto her saddle.

Just as she was leaving, Tahnee and several of the students she'd been teaching rounded the corner between the huts to her left. In Tahnee's arms were the dozen reading primers Lily had used for her lessons. She shook her head and refused to take them. Her throat choked closed, and she was incapable of saying good-bye, so Lily waved silently as she turned the mare toward home.

The next five months moved slowly, as hours ticked into days and days into weeks of labor for both the men and the wives. Chilling March winds and rainy April days finally turned into blue skies so the children could scatter among the wild flowers where they bloomed among the sage and brush of Oklahoma. Everyone was looking forward to the completion of the well and the bonus they hoped the ATSF might dole out if they met the deadline.

Lily startled awake at the sound of bellowing male voices. The Thursday afternoon in early July, 1888 had been relatively quiet, and she had lain down with Davis in the hot airless room to take a nap. The sounds of construction had become a constant background noise after all these months. She instantly heard Charles' voice above the cries of the other men.

She knew immediately that something had gone terribly wrong. "Stay here," she cautioned Davis as he opened his eyes. She hoped her look of threat would keep him inside. The closer she got to the site, the more convinced she became that Charles had been hurt. What would she do? How could this happen?

Then she saw him … barking out orders; the men digging out rock with their bare hands, with shovels, with anything that could possibly help reach the man buried beneath the crushing limestone.

Lily stood silently and prayed. For thirty minutes the men refused to give up. She watched knowing that they also knew it was impossible to reach him in time. The women from the outlying tents raced toward the building site and stopped alongside Lily. Whose husband had given his life for the railroad this time?

It would be another half-hour before Charles would walk to the women who stood tearless and frightened, small children in their arms, babies at their breasts, toddlers grasping their dirty skirts. He reached for Annie Grover and took her into his arms, and the other women bellowed with cries of relief and anguish. The remaining men arrived within seconds, finding their wives and crying together as they returned to their tents.

Charles would not go to bed that night. He sat with a bottle of whiskey while Lily listened to the details yet again. In order to prevent the well from collapsing, it had to be lined with a two-foot-thick wall of rock. They were near completion when the accident occurred. The men had carried one hundred and nine loads of rock from a nearby rail car to the gaping mouth of the well over the past six months. Today, on the hundred and tenth load, the heavy metal chute that slowly fed the limestone to the men below groaned with the weight and gave way. A ton of rock released too quickly for Jim Grover to react, and he was buried in a stone grave. How could one of his men die in the final load?

Lily knew that Charles considered his crew his brothers. They were family; had worked together for many years in New Mexico. He prided himself on keeping them safe. Robert Billings had contracted dysentery in January, a horrible illness that swept through the camps of men laying track. But losing a man to illness was one thing. Lily knew that in Charles' mind, accidents did not happen on Charles Lee's crew.

She grieved with Charles and with Annie, but she couldn't help but remember that Jim Grover marked the second man to die since they arrived fifteen months ago. The women had not fared as well. Within that first year, Lily attended to five wives and helped bury three of them. Two graves held both the birthing mother and the still-born child she had given her life for.

Millicent Granger, wife of Charles' foreman, had contracted typhoid, putting the entire group in quarantine for more than a month. Lily had wrapped one of Davis' grey-white diapers around her mouth and nose and brought broth and sat with the woman wiping her face with cool water to ease the fever. On a Friday afternoon, as Lily turned to open the one lone window to give the woman some fresh air, she heard the all too familiar death rattle. She turned sharply and raced to the bedside as the woman gave over her spirit. Lily wept silently, closed Millicent's eyes, and walked to the work site to tell her husband.

*

On July 15, 1888, the first train whistle blew into the new

watering and coaling station. Lily stood beside Charles like they were royalty. She looked around at the crowd that had gathered. The entire town of two hundred residents, mostly rail crew, stood in the dirt streets waving flags and banners made of anything they could find.

As the steam shooshed and the engine pulled to a stop at the makeshift wooden platform, the engineer jumped from the train and shook hands with them both. Edmund Burdick, a Santa Fe traveling freight manager, greeted the rail crew on behalf of the ATSF.

Lily watched as Charles proudly introduced each and every man on his team. A few moments later, her voice joined the rest of the crowd who cheered as the first load of coal slid down the chute and dropped into the engine's coal car parked below; water flowed into the fire tube boiler and the steam pushed gray through the territory's blue skies.

She stood with her hands clasped together; supporting her huge eight month belly. Davis clung to his father's left leg. The photographer who snapped them on the station deck caught them looking into each other's eyes with pride.

A few weeks later Elizabeth was born, and by September, Charles, Lily and the children were among the few inhabitants left in town. With the project complete, Charles' crew returned to Texas where they would be reassigned by ATSF to other rail projects. The company sent Charles two new employees to man the station and the recently completed telegraph office. Lily stood on the porch every morning and surveyed the emptiness around her. Hundreds of ranchers had moved into the Territory with their families, but they were spread miles apart. Lily could go for weeks without seeing another woman.

Two trains a day came through the coaling station—one passenger and one freight. And Lily, not a woman to remain idle, discovered a new passion. One day she noticed the rail men taking a break for food and water. Most had nothing more than an apple or a piece of cornbread. She felt sorry for them. The next day she made lunch baskets and gave them out to the men as the engine was refueled. As she walked back home, she hit upon an idea.

Within a week, the men spread word of Lily's cooking skills, and she seized the opportunity. Her days filled with cooking and selling. A month later she stood in her kitchen and tossed the cold coins in her hand. She was making nearly two dollars a day from the hungry train crews.

She could see Charles shaking his head as he watched her each day from his office inside the new brick station. One evening he approached her regarding the matter. "Lily, you don't understand the ways of men. I urge you to be more cautious in your dealings with them. I don't want you or the children harmed."

"Oh, Charles, please. These men are simply hungry and tired from working the train for days on end. They are no more a danger than any worker in this town."

"Woman," he responded. "They *are* different; they ride the rails; they are vagabonds and unknown to us. They drink and carouse with women of the night and test their wills in fistfights at every saloon around. I will not have you go against my wishes on this."

Lily stood quietly, contemplating her husband's words. "I will be cautious in my dealings, Charles, but the money I make is providing us with much needed provisions. The Santa Fe Rail certainly doesn't care if we ever own a home or not. I know we'll never return to Abilene, Charles, but I would at least like a house with walls and doors. Is that asking too much?"

She hesitated and watched his face cool from anger to near-acceptance. She lightened her tone. "I'm at the station no more than an hour each day, and I'm well within your sight, God knows, at all times … and I will continue with my sales, with your kind permission."

Charles was left without words; then muttered, "You have my permission."

*

The fall and winter passed quickly. With Davis and the new baby and her thriving business, Lily was so tired by evening that she often fell asleep shortly after dinner.

At breakfast one morning in early 1889, she read an announcement in the local gazette and turned to Charles. "We will finally be able to build a real house," she cried out.

Charles looked up at her excited face and listened as she read.

President Benjamin Harrison had just signed a proclamation setting the stage for a great land rush into the Unassigned Lands in the heart of the Territory. It would begin at high noon on April 22, 1889 and offer a hundred and sixty acres per family to agrarian homesteaders.

She hesitated for a moment. Her mixed feelings surprised her. She missed the bustle of Abilene; this would bring much needed growth to the town, as well as land for her and Charles. And yet … the quiet solitude around the station would now be swept forever from the frontier.

"Good news," Charles exclaimed. "Great news for us, really. More people mean more jobs and more need for the trains. And who knows? In another year, if things go well maybe the Santa Fe will …" Lily didn't hear the rest. She was already visualizing their piece of land.

Throughout the day, as she did her daily chores, Lily could not stop thinking. She could see the new house in her mind—a real house with wood floors she could keep clean, a separate room for herself and Charles and a kitchen with cupboards instead of gingham fabric over broken down wood shelves. Her life would be easier; she might even have time to read or join the new Women's Society.

In the chicken coop as she stooped for the eggs, Lily glanced at her course hands, lined from the labors of washing laundry, drawing water from the cistern, tending the garden and snapping chickens' necks for the evening meal.

Her creamy complexion had thickened and burned in the heat and wind of Oklahoma summers, and the incessant humidity made even the slightest attempt at beauty futile. Her once lustrous, braided auburn hair had turned a dull brown. She was tired and worn from running dawn to dusk. She was no longer the lovely cameo she had once worn about her alabaster neck. The luxurious gowns and petticoats she'd foolishly shipped from Abilene had been torn into strips for wiping, bathing, and monthly woman days.

One morning she'd said, "Here!" and made Charles take their one mirror from the room. "I can't stand to look at what I've become."

Every few weeks she waited anxiously at the post office for a package. As much as she longed for her youthful figure and her beauty, what she missed most was the use of her bright and curious mind.

"Afternoon, Mr. Franks," she said.

He smiled broadly. "Yep, came this morning." He went to the rear and came back with a small box. "Sure is heavy for its size," he said.

Lily smiled.

"From Abilene, says here."

She waited for him to finish his jesting. "Ok, Mr. Franks." She took the package from his hands and walked outside. She couldn't wait to get home to open the box of books her father sent monthly. The children fell asleep early giving her a few hours to read by the oil lamps she had purchased at the general store. She wanted so badly to claim their 160 acres and build a lovely brick home, or even a frame cottage with several rooms and indoor plumbing.

That night, she crept into the kitchen after Charles fell asleep.

She stood on tip-toe in front of the kitchen pantry and reached to the highest shelf. The tin coffee can fell into her hands, and she sat in the light of a candle and counted. She'd saved every penny from her lunch business, and they added up to the price of her precious piece of land. She would save more to build the house as quickly as she could.

Two days later, Charles shared the news with Lily that the rail employees were not eligible to participate in the run. Living in town would give them an unfair advantage.

"I'll be assisting the surveyors and handing out deeds to those who make the run," he told her.

"What?" Lily nearly screamed when she heard the news. "That cannot be, Charles. I have waited long enough for a home. I've sacrificed for too long. You promised my father to give me everything life could offer. Do you not remember that promise? I swear I will return to Abilene with the children, if you do not take me seriously, Charles Lee." She regretted her words immediately.

"There is absolutely no legal way for us to participate, Lily. Here, read it for yourself." He slammed the company letter onto the writing desk and stalked from the room.

Lily watched through the window as he stood on the front porch, board-stiff with his head hung low. She felt a slight remorse for the harshness of her words. It was unfair to attack his ability to provide. She knew Charles wanted to build a home for them, wanted to keep his promise to her father. And he had cared for them, had protected them.

If she hadn't been so angry at the ATSF, she might have reached out to him. She could feel his spirit darkening with shame, but she couldn't fix it. She wanted that land; it was unfair. She wanted Charles to fight this, and she also knew he wouldn't take a stand against the company.

The morning of the run reeked of tension—windy, and cold. All morning, Lily kept busy cooking hams, baking bread and making coffee in preparation for the great rush of new town citizens. At noon she watched from her kitchen window. Dust billowed along the horizon, and she imagined herself on her roan flying across the barren land to stake her claim. She had put up with this one-room shack for two years already; how much longer could she be patient?

By nightfall, the Lees were joined by roughly a hundred and fifty newcomers, mostly men. Tarps were thrown up like patches of tall sagebrush for miles. Lily offered food to the tired, dirty people who hadn't eaten for some time. The days of great buffalo herds, bronze-skinned warriors on horseback, dusty cattle drovers and blue-coated cavalrymen were gone forever. As much as she'd longed for her own piece of earth—her own home—she couldn't help but think of the Kickapoo who had been stripped from their own land; who had paid such a high cost.

The next morning, a special edition of The Gazette was delivered. The pictures told the story. Those who had sneaked over the line during the night took off in wagons or on horseback rushing to the land they had picked out during their long wait in the woods. Their ribboned stakes held high, they rode to the sites and stabbed them into the hard red ground of the Oklahoma territory, then rode to the station office to stake their claim and pay their owed money. Oh, how Lily wished she could be that woman on the inside page—Annie "something"—standing on the platform of the train as it roared toward the station; jumping to stake her claim, and jumping back onto the last car as it kept heading west. Eddy B. Townsend, a local rancher, stood proud and tall as he staked the first claim of the day. There were questions of his ethics.

There was a photo of Charles as he greeted the new land owners and took their cash. In the background, surveyors handed out deeds to each property. In another, he was shown breaking up a fight between men claiming the same property.

She laughed when she saw it. Charles, of all people, caught in the melee.

Within months, Lily barely recognized the city growing around her. Tents quickly gave way to wood frame stores, and houses grew along Broad Street and Second Street. Banks were built, barbershops, the Hotel DeHoss and numerous restaurants. By fall a school was opened and a teacher hired for the many pioneer children. Davis and Lucy were among the first students. The newly named town of Edmond was being birthed.

Lily wondered where her friend Tahnee was now. She hadn't visited the reservation in some time. It made her sad to see the small farms and cattle ranches that now dotted the once cohesive tribal lands. The division of the reservation into allotments had led to corruption on both sides—within the tribe and by the white men overseeing those transactions. What she had feared years ago on the long wagon train ride into Oklahoma had come to pass.

A year later, Lily stood in her makeshift kitchen, her anger reaching a depth she'd never felt. That morning she had stood her ground with Charles.

"Lily," he had raged, "you don't know what you're talking about."

"Oh, and you do?" she answered. "Forget it—you've always hated the Indians."

"And you've always protected them, which I have never understood," he said.

The old arguments had taken on a new dimension. What had once been disagreement had escalated over time, and Charles felt like a stranger. The man she had married had thrived on the excitement and change that the Santa Fe had provided him. He'd been eager to take on the wilderness and the growth of the rail. Now he seemed to be stuck while younger men moved on.

Each morning he dallied over breakfast, often staring out the window for an hour or more before he walked across the road to the desk that seemed to consume him. His bouts of blackness had worsened over the past winter, and Lily often smelled liquor on his breath and wondered where he threw the bottles.

One morning she nudged Charles with her elbow as she stood to clear the dishes. "You don't look well, Charles. Is everything ok?"

He sat silent, reading the newspaper, refusing to either look at her or answer.

"Charles," she said again.

This time he looked up and held the front page in front of her. "Here you go," he said. "This is the government's answer to gaining our much needed land."

Lily grabbed for the paper and began to read. "I don't understand this Curtis Act, Charles; what does it mean?"

"What it means is that the Indian governments have been dissolved. Your Kickapoo were given a lot of acres, Lily. It isn't like they were thrown off their land."

Lily suspected what Charles had failed to mention: that the rest of the Indian land could now be sold—to non-native settlers, the railroad, and corporations.

"No," she hissed, "they most certainly *were*. The Dawes Act divided their land, but this will dismantle their government. They will be assimilated into white society soon. Now you understand why I was hell-bent on teaching the women our language."

"Lily, you are ..."

"Don't talk to me Charles Lee. You and your damned railroad started all this grasping for land." She stormed from the room before Charles could say another word.

She cried that night for the first time in a long time. She went to the chicken coop and wept for an hour or more. She longed for Abilene. She longed for her father. She wrote him a letter asking him to send for her; then tore it up the next day.

Lily gave birth to her third child, Willard, that fall.

*

Because of his position with the railroad, Charles was included in Edmond's circle of community leaders. Lily was surprised when he was invited to lunch with these well-educated men. They were lawyers, physicians, and businessmen as well as ranchers and cattlemen, and they hailed from nearly every state in the U.S. as well as England and Europe.

"We still live in a tiny two-room pump-house, Charles. Why ever would we think we could socialize with these people?" The morning he mentioned a late breakfast with Milton Reynolds, known to the community as Kicking Bird, she laughed. "You're dining with the founder of the newspaper? Next it will be Anton Classen."

Charles grumbled. "Money isn't everything, Lily; nor is a house. As far as they care, I run the rail around here."

Shortly after Anton Classen built his new home north of town, he and his wife, Mildred held a garden house-warming party. Classen was a young lawyer from Michigan and making money hand over fist in the newly formed city. Lily gasped when Charles insisted they attend.

"And what would you have me wear, Charles? A frumpy housewife's cotton muslin, no petticoats, not even a pair of fashionable shoes?"

"Lily, you are being unreasonable. These people are my colleagues. You will go and be gracious to these newcomers. They are our future." But as he turned to get ready for bed, he stopped. Reaching back for her hand, he pulled her behind the curtain that served as their bedroom. Once away from the children, Charles nuzzled her neck, but she pulled away, unshed tears gleaming in her eyes.

"Here," he said handing her a long white envelope. He watched as her questioning eyes opened in surprise. The envelope held eight dollars in silver coins. "Take the train into

Oklahoma City and spend the day," he said. "I'll ask Becky Miller to watch the children."

"Oh, Charles," she whimpered, "I was so mean."

Charles took her in his arms. "You are never mean, Lillian Lee. You are kind and patient and you put up with too much from me. I don't deserve you, you know?"

"That is most likely very true, Mr. Lee," she laughed, already thinking how she'd have her hair done in an up-do, get a proper manicure, and purchase a soft floral party dress with pearl buttons down the back. No one would say Mrs. Charles Lee was anything but fashionable and well-educated. She lay in bed for hours worrying and planning. That night in her dreams, Lily danced with a young Charles, her pink satin gown tracing her décolletage, and the light from the crystal chandeliers throwing a golden glow on the ivory brocade-covered ballroom.

On the evening of the party, their hostess greeted her guests on the spacious, covered front-porch. The home was painted with whitewash and though not fancy, it held many pieces of imported furniture and paintings brought from their home in Michigan. Though just six small rooms, the home was still a showcase, and at the sight of the new kitchen, the women swooned.

The latest appliances filled the room, and electricity operated everything. Lily thought how wonderful not to have to stoke the fire inside the old black stove to bake biscuits. And to be able to go to the bathroom right inside the house without chasing rats out of the outhouse in the middle of the night. She could barely breathe with the jealousy rising like bile in her throat. These thoughts were consuming her more often these days; so often she'd considered returning to Abilene with the children. She was hanging on by one short thread—her love for Charles, who looked so handsome tonight in his best pin-stripe suit.

"You look stunning, my dear," Mrs. Classen said, as she touched the ruffled bodice of Lily's long-sleeved emerald silk dress. "It makes your pale skin look almost porcelain."

Lily blushed and returned the compliment, suddenly remembering how it felt to be in the company of fashionable, wealthy and well educated people. "Thank you," she said, "Not as nice as my gowns in Abilene I'm afraid." Porcelain, indeed, she thought, much used pottery might be more apt.

The party proceeded to the back yard gardens, lush with peonies and roses and honeysuckle. They must have cost a fortune, Lily mused. Charles held her elbow as he introduced her to the city leaders. She felt self-conscious at how little they had in comparison. They settled into an evening like those they'd known in the not too distant past, and Lily was determined to have a home in which to entertain by the following year. Charles was paid a decent salary by the railroad though he had become something of a figurehead. But land had become a commodity that only the rich could afford. She simply had to get the land on which to build.

She watched Charles closely as he moved among the newly self-appointed movers and shakers of Edmond. His confidence amazed her. They'd been shut off from society for so long. She wasn't sure she still had it within her. Standing at the fringe of the party, she couldn't help but wonder if she was even the same woman she'd been three years ago. She had helped birth Indian babies and bury white women. The well-groomed, fashionably dressed crowd faded into a recent recollection.

Six weeks ago, just before the crews returned to Texas, Lily had been approached by one of the neighborhood children. The little boy led her to one of the make-shift homes a mile south of the tracks. As they approached the tent, Lily saw nothing amiss, and her face questioned the child. He pointed beyond the structure, and Lily told him to stay. As she rounded the tent Lily took in a sight that shook her to the depths of sorrow. She recognized the body of Kathleen Taylor, eighteen years at most, broken neck hanging limp from a large oak in the yard. She'd found a way to escape the abusive marriage she'd suffered for years.

Lily shook the image from her mind. Which woman defined her now? The young naïve girl raised with privilege and wealth or the hardened prairie wife and mother she'd become? Was it possible to return to an old life she had all but forgotten?

She strolled along the outskirts of the group, bending occasionally at the long linen-covered serving tables filled with fois gras and pastries. She wondered about these women. Had they, too, suffered the hardships of life while their husbands bartered for position in the newly developed territory? She knew little of these women, and she wondered about their secret lives outside this gathering.

Toward the end of the party, Lily joined Charles and a small group of men who had been conversing for some time. Charles nodded when she indicated it was time to leave, and she stood beside him and listened patiently. When she overheard Anton Classen speaking with a Mr. Howard about propositioning the government for the new Normal School, she took a step forward and spoke clearly. "What a wonderful idea, and Edmond would be the perfect city. I would love to be on the committee to approach the governor."

She felt Charles nudge her elbow as he pulled her closer. "Forgive my wife," he said. "She's much too busy to take on such a responsibility."

Lily pulled away slightly, not daring to glance at her husband. She felt faces turn. She didn't care. "Nonsense, Charles," she spoke her words carefully. "Gentlemen, I am a college educated woman from Abilene, and I would be most pleased if you would allow me to join you in this important venture."

Anton Classen smiled and took Lily's right hand, lifting it to his lips. "Mrs. Lee," he said, "We would be honored to have you join our small group. I will contact you this week."

A moment later, Charles took her arm and led her from the

gathering, politely thanking his host and hostess and nodding good-bye to the other men as they departed.

Without a horse and buggy, the Lees walked the dozen blocks to their rail station home. The return was quiet and tense.

The following morning, Lily woke to a strange yet vaguely familiar feeling. She felt refreshed and full of an energy she thought forever lost. It was almost like waking up back home in Texas. She hopped out of bed, spread her arms wide before the open window, and looked forward to the day. She took a mid-morning phone call from Classen, and, in the kitchen, she marked the Carter's Seed Company calendar with her first Normal School committee meeting.

Six months later they celebrated their success with a small gathering at the Hotel DeHoss. J.W. Howard and his committee, including Lily, had convinced the government to place the Normal School on a hill to the north of Edmond. Classen backed up his promise and donated the land. J.W. raised his glass of champagne as the committee and their spouses sat in the dining room beaming with pride. He toasted each member by name, and when Lily stood, she held her head high and accepted the recognition with pride. The only person missing the evening's dinner was Charles Lee. She had left him at home halfway through a bottle of scotch.

In 1891 the Normal School opened. Lily was there to welcome the first students, mostly women. She knew that J.W. and Classen had high hopes that the school would grow and make Edmond a center of wealth and education. She was satisfied that because of her involvement, other women were being educated to become teachers.

*

Lily approached Charles over breakfast in the summer of '93. "Charles," she said, "I've been asked by J. W. to teach at the Normal School. I have my degree and I want to put it to good use again."

Charles stared blankly at her as if she were an apparition. "Our children need you, Lily. Teach *them*," he said.

"The children are in school, Charles, as well you know. Why would you stand in the way of this? Why would you deny me something I need so badly?"

"I cannot deny you anything, Lily. You've made that very clear these past ten years. You are headstrong and will do as you wish."

"I have done nothing without your approval, Charles. I have been a loving and respectful wife. I have put up with our lack of wealth in this town and held my head high. I will do this, Charles, with or without your approval this time."

"As if I didn't know that, Lily," Charles growled, slamming the door behind him as he exited the house.

That night Charles stayed out late, and the next morning he left before she rose to wake the children for school. She had grown used to his dark moods, but his recent wanderings worried her. She wondered if she was pushing too hard, but the thought was a fleeting one. Besides a house of their own, she wanted nothing more than to be the woman she had left behind in Abilene. And so later that morning, she stood in front of the committee and accepted a teaching position at the school.

A few months later, Lily walked to the rail office to speak with Charles about gossip she had overheard at the university. He sat gazing out the back window of his office and didn't see her approach until she cleared her throat.

"Charles." She spoke softly to avoid startling him.

"Oh … Lily … What brings you here this time of day?"

"We need to talk, Charles. I'm hearing all kinds of rumors about how you spend your days. I don't want to believe any of them."

Charles frowned and spun his chair to face her. "Gossip, huh? This town is always good for gossip, isn't it?"

"Then tell me what is going on, Charles, so I can at least deny them." Charles sat quietly for a moment; reflective, she thought. "Well?"

He cupped his hands over his eyes as though he couldn't look at her, cleared his throat and began. "I spoke with Burton last month—head guy of ATSF these days, you will remember. I asked for a promotion and was denied." He finally looked up at her.

"Oh, Charles ..."

"It's pretty obvious I'm stuck in this role of rail master, whatever the hell that is. Lily, I'm sick of having nothing to do. Sure, it gives us a fair income, but I'm weary, Lily, weary."

She didn't know how to respond. She was shocked that after all these years the ATSF would place younger men ahead of a man of his experience. She remembered him as a young man who had dreamed of growing with the Santa Fe.

"We'll manage, Charles," she said. "I know you are unhappy, but we are settled now, and the children are growing older. They will be off on their own sooner than you can blink an eye."

She knew her words meant nothing; his eyes had glazed over the minute she spoke.

"Lily, Lily," he said, "always the optimist. I wish it were as easy as that."

There were nights when Charles came home long after she'd fallen asleep. He smelled sour and smoky as he fell onto his side of the narrow bed, nearly ripping it from the wall. Lily woke cranky from troubled sleep and irritated at what she now considered his adolescent behaviors. Several times she confronted him in the haze of pre-dawn.

"Charles," she said, "Are you trying to get fired? Everyone in town is talking about your drinking."

"They can all go to hell," he answered. "Besides, the Santa Fe would never fire me. Who else would sit here with nothing to do day after day?"

"Make something to do, then, for heaven's sake, Charles! Or ask for a transfer back to Texas."

"Your attachment to Texas and your old life is growing old, Lillian. If you want to go back to Abilene, then go."

It was at those moments Lily questioned her loyalty to Charles. After all, he'd dragged them here; wasn't it his duty to make this work? She knew it was a harsh thought, but nothing else seemed to work. Davis was now old enough to question his father's nightly absences and she was growing weary of creating excuses.

Meanwhile Lily's presence in the community grew. She joined the Women's Aid Society and the new Methodist church, and when she wasn't teaching or with the children, she was doing volunteer events and fundraisers for the college. There were days when she left the house early in the morning and went back out after dinner.

During one late-night argument, she made a pot of coffee and made Charles sit with her at the kitchen table. He refused to speak for some time, but she waited him out.

He finally met her eyes. "I'm not needed, Lily—not at work, not at home. You do it all—work, raise the kids, feed the poor. What use am I to your life?"

Lily was shocked. "Oh, Charles, that is not true. The children need you; I need you."

"No Lily—*need* is not even close." He hung his head and walked out.

She sat silently contemplating Charles' words. Had she stopped needing him? She felt a slight pang of remorse and sadness.

She grew more concerned as weeks passed, but each time she approached him, he pulled further away. All she could do was keep their home quiet and stable for their three children. As Charles withdrew, so did Lily, until their home felt estranged and empty.

For the next few years Lily watched silently as Charles grew more distant and more depressed. They no longer fought for it got them nowhere. Lily focused on teaching, her community involvement and the children.

One sunny afternoon as she walked down the steps leading to the grassy lawns below Old North Tower where she taught, she saw Charles approaching from the south, a letter in hand.

"I'm sorry, Lily," he said as he handed her the letter. "They had no time to reach you before he passed."

Lily fell into Charles' arms and sobbed. She had seen her father twice in the ten years they'd been in Oklahoma. Both visits to Texas had been alone without children or husband. This time they would accompany her to her father's final resting place.

*

In the summer of 1897, Lily was introduced to a new resident of the city. Harry Clegern and his wife had recently arrived from Scotland and had purchased a large amount of land to the east of the Normal School and not far from the Classen holdings. His intention was to build a large farm among the groves and to sell off a parcel or two to make payment for the remainder.

J.W. Howard introduced them at lunch, and Lily could barely breathe with excitement. She had saved for years for this day.

"Mr. Clegern, I am interested in a parcel if we can afford it."

He smiled. "For such a lovely lady, I'm sure we can make it work, Mrs. Lee."

J.W. bellowed with laughter. "Harry," he said. "This woman will take advantage of you if you let her. Beware!"

Lily gave her most infectious smile; just short of flirtation. She wasn't going to let this opportunity slip away.

"We just need a small lot close to campus to build a home," she said. "And I do have cash," she added, hoping that would make a difference in the deal.

A half hour later, Lily was beside herself with excitement as she literally ran along the red brick side-walks to the rail station.

"Charles," she cried out breathlessly as she swung open the heavy wood door. "Charles, where are you?"

Charles appeared in his office door way and moved to her quickly. "Lily, what's the matter? Is it one of the children?"

"Oh, Charles, I found our land." She stopped and took a deep breath before she could continue. "We're going to build our home. I've met the owner of the land just today."

"Whoa, Lillian," he said sternly. "This is man's business. Who did you say you met?"

She walked into Charles' office, sat down and spread her hands out on his desk. "I will not be spoken to in this manner, Charles Lee," she said.

Charles sighed. "Go ahead," he said, and he sat down behind the desk and waited.

Lily told him about Harry Clegern's purchase of the large acreage northeast of them. "He's selling off a small portion just across from the normal school. I have the money, Charles," Lily said in a softer tone. "I've saved nearly everything I've made these past few years. Let me do this for us, Charles. The children need a home. Please say yes." She watched as her husband rose quickly from his chair and stood before her, glaring.

His face reddened, and his raised fist startled Lily. She knew Charles would never strike her, but the fact that he was angry enough to consider it, made her lean back.

"Charles," she cried out, "Charles, I'm sorry."

His fist hit the top of the desk like a hammer, and Lily startled. Then, as she watched silent with fear, the skin on his face sagged downward; his body seemed to deflate.

"Damn it," he said as he wiped the sweat from his brow. "When will you stop, Lily? When will you let me be a husband?"

Charles straightened his broad shoulders, adding height to his frame, and his chin pushed upward as he walked toward the door of the office. He turned. "I'll meet with the man tomorrow morning in your stead."

She nodded as he left the room and closed the door behind him. Lily sat in silence, contemplating his every word. It had never been her intent to shame him, to make him feel less than a man. She had wanted to be herself, and it was true, she'd gotten her way in everything since leaving Abilene. She had wanted for nothing.

She lowered her head into her hands and wept. She had put her needs first for many years; had wanted to be strong in her own right; wanted Charles to respect her opinions; wanted others to appreciate her talents and abilities. But she hadn't meant to do it at the expense of the man she loved. And she did love Charles. Had loved him from the moment she saw him across the ballroom so long ago. She had wanted a home since the day she saw the silly red pump- house they still lived in. Now all she wanted was her husband's happiness. There had to be a way to make things right.

Lily didn't wait up, but she was aware of him in bed some time during the night; could smell the bitterness of alcohol upon him. She prayed for God to present an answer before she awoke.

The next morning she watched as Charles prepared to meet with Clegern at ten. He put on his best wool suit, crisp white shirt and tie, and wing tips. He apologized for last night's outburst while they ate breakfast.

"No, you were right, Charles," she said. "I am sometimes too hard-headed."

She left at nine, while Charles sat with his coffee and newspaper. "Faculty meeting," she said, and she left without giving him her ritual peck on the cheek. She took a detour through the kitchen and scooted out the back door.

Lily walked with her coffee cans into the Edmond Bank and Trust. Along with her personal savings of bills and coins, she deposited a check from her father's estate that had arrived only days prior. The account she opened was in the name of Charles Lee.

She left the bank with a smile on her face, and just past the general store, she saw Charles walking toward her. The sun glanced off the brim of his black hat, and she smiled at the image he presented. How proud she'd been when he'd courted her and walked her along the streets of Abilene for all to see. He wanted only her happiness, even back then. Her stubbornness and need for personal success had somehow gotten in the way of that very happiness. It wasn't his fault as much as hers.

She waited until he reached her halfway down the block.

"Headed to Clegern's office," he said.

She smiled and handed him the cashier's check she pulled from her purse.

It read: To the Order of Harry W. Clegern—from the account of Mr. Charles R. Lee.

His mouth opened, but words wouldn't come. He finally managed, "But Lily ..."

They could only afford a small piece of land, but it was enough for the two-story brick home that Lily had imagined for so many years.

"It's our money, Charles. Go cut us a deal." She winked. "Oh, and here," she said as she handed Charles a large bundle of rolled-up papers.

His eyebrows arched in surprise. "What ..."

"They're drawings of the house." She laughed. "I'll meet you at home," she said, "after you finish your men's business."

That evening, Lily sat with Charles and walked him step by step through her drawings: the downstairs sitting room, formal dining room and his study; then up the narrow stairway to the four bedrooms above. And it was within five blocks of the Normal School which was expanding nicely under the tutelage of the new principal.

"Charles," she said in a quiet voice. Her eyes moved slowly up to his. "I have asked J.W. to give me just one class next fall."

Charles tried to interrupt, but she continued. "No, I want to;

I want to be a wife and mother in our new home and I won't give up teaching forever, just fewer classes. I want to do this for us, my dearest husband."

"I guess I didn't fulfill that promise to your father, did I?" he said.

"Charles, you gave me love and respect and three beautiful children. What more could I have possibly wanted?" She bent close and whispered in his ear. "I love you." He smiled and took her face in his hands, then bent to kiss her.

"What is this off to the side?" Charles asked a few moments later. He pointed to a sketched-in building at the back of the house.

"That, my dear Charles, is called an automobile garage."

"We have no need for an auto, Lily."

"If we're going to drive to Oklahoma City we will, my dear," she said. Her eyes sparkled.

Charles chuckled loudly, and Lily saw the slightest glimmer of wetness in his eyes. "Anything to make you happy, Lily— anything to make you happy.

Chapter 3
Back in Colorado

Gary was waiting at the luggage carousels when Karen arrived at Denver International. She could see him below as she descended the escalator. He was a perfect two inches taller than her 5'5" height. His olive complexion, brown hair and dark chocolate eyes were a distinct opposite, yet a perfect complement, to her blond-haired paleness. She surprised herself by putting her arms around his neck in a tight hug when he greeted her.

"Whoa," he said, "maybe you should go away more often. Teasing …. "

Gary took her hand in his and pulled her suitcase with the other.

On the way home, they stopped at their favorite pizzeria and shared a large thin-crust, white-cheese-and-artichoke and a couple of beers.

"So you've really gotten into this trunk thing?"

She nodded; her mouth full of pizza. "Yep," she said, once she cleared her throat. "This is really fascinating, Gary. Most of the stuff is very old, way before my parents would have bought the house, and yet it makes me feel closer to *them* somehow."

Gary listened attentively, his eyes holding hers just a moment too long.

"What?" she asked.

"No, nothing. I know you love history and a good mystery too, but it sounds like you're looking for something that may not be there, babe."

"What do you mean by *that?*" she said.

"Nothing, Karen I'm sorry. I just know it's been rough on you losing your mom this spring; that's all."

"I'm not trying to substitute her presence with this trunk, Gary, if that's what you mean."

"Jesus, Karen, I said I'm sorry. Forget I mentioned it. Should be fun for you to research."

The conversation died, and they were silent through the remainder of the meal. Gary turned up the radio on the drive home.

Karen settled into her old life for the next few days: phone calls with work colleagues, lunch with her best friend, Denise, and her normal daily routine.

"So tell me again how you found the trunk," Denise asked one day at lunch.

Karen took a sip of iced tea and placed her crostini back onto her plate. They were sitting in a European café, her favorite place in downtown Denver. "Wouldn't have found it if I hadn't gone back to the house to check the attic. Very strange little room inside the front dormer."

"So what's in it, anyway?" Denise said; then quickly added, "And how did all the stuff get into it in the first place, do you think?"

"Funny you should ask. I've been wondering the same thing. None of my mother's things are in it—not even her wedding gown or my baby clothes. It's possible she never knew it existed, I suppose; and yet, she was surely up there in the years we lived there."

"Might have just been a dusty old attic back then; maybe she wasn't," Denise said.

She nodded. "Although, when I was there, I had a strange feeling that I had played up there in that little room. I don't know—I was only four when we moved. How much does a four-year-old remember, huh?"

Denise nodded. "So when does it arrive?"

"Any day. Seems to be stuff from nearly every decade, from the late 1800's through the mid '80's. There are four or five journals I think, though I haven't rummaged through it all. But the photographs are fascinating, and the war medal; the baby things and clothing are really in good shape."

"I would really like to see them," Denise said.

"Absolutely, stop by sometime this week."

"Need to hit the ladies' room," Denise said.

Karen watched her best friend wind her way between tables. She envied Denise's body. It was obvious she worked out every day. At 5'5" Denise was slim but muscled and looked thirty instead of forty-two. Her perky new short haircut brought out her blue eyes. Karen suddenly felt old or worn out perhaps.

On the day the trunk was to be delivered, she scurried around the house trying to decide where to put it. She wanted easy access, but she needed room to sort and organize. She'd prefer the office, but she shared that room with Gary, and he'd just be in the way. Karen paced for an hour after the phone call notifying her they were en route. When the shipping company finally arrived, she led the husky young men to the back sunroom where they uncrated the trunk and placed it dead-center. Now that it was summer, it would be warm enough to spend daytime hours back there and not have Gary underfoot. As the men left, she tipped them a few bucks and grabbed the phone.

"It came!" she said when she reached Gary at his office. "Hope you don't mind losing me for a few weeks." She laughed.

Gary responded with a half-laugh of his own. "Would I notice?"

"Are you ever home long enough *to* notice, Gary?" She heard the anger in her voice and regretted it immediately. Why couldn't she just let it lie? She was tired of arguing; that's all they seemed to do lately. "Forget I said that," she said, before he had a chance to react.

After a brief silence, she continued. "I've also decided it's time to go through mom and dad's place. I wanted to get it on the market at the same time as the one in Oklahoma anyway, so this will push me to get it done."

"Sounds like a plan …" Gary sounded totally distracted.

"Too much enthusiasm, Gare; can't handle it. See you at dinner. We're eating in."

That evening, she heard the garage door roll to a sharp stop, and a moment later Gary called from the kitchen.

"Back here," she yelled.

He followed her voice. "Holy crap! That's a lot of stuff, babe. Hope we hadn't planned to use the sunroom this summer." He gave a slight chuckle.

"Don't start," she said.

"You got a system?" he asked, leaning against the wicker sofa.

Karen sat in the middle of the room with the trunk beside her. She was trying to arrange each item and photo by date, as best she could. She was quickly becoming encircled in history.

"Yep, always. I'm sorting by age, or at least I'm guessing. There are some pictures from clear back to the land run, and this teaching certificate is dated about that far back. See?"

Gary sat on the floor and she handed him things as she talked. "Interesting," he said, "what's this?" He pointed to the Purple Heart.

"Well, I'm guessing by the year this picture is dated, that the medal belongs to this fellow. She held up a photo of a WWII soldier. "But I really don't know. I'll have to look up some military websites."

Gary picked up a rather dog-eared black and white. He held it so she could see. The woman's curly bob and belted shirt-dress suggested the 1940's. The husband appeared to be the same man as the soldier she had identified with the Purple Heart.

"Big family—three kids and a new baby." His voice softened and sounded somewhat distant. "Lucky couple," he said.

She glanced up at him, but he had already returned to the present.

"So your game plan is …?" He handed the photo back to her and she placed it on the 1940's pile.

"Gonna go through it chronologically and research as I go, starting with this photo of the Edmond coaling station and the man and his family standing beside it. Hazel, the woman I told you about at the historical museum? She said to call or e mail her any time."

Gary nodded and reached for her hand. "You know I support you in everything you do?"

She looked down at the floor. "I know; I know you do."

After Gary went upstairs to change, she sat in the sunroom awhile longer. As tears slid down her cheeks, she wondered where things had taken that turn—that turn where they couldn't go back and change it. When did that fork in the road happen for them? She couldn't remember. It had happened so gradually; she hadn't even noticed. One minute they were young and in love, and the next, fifteen years had passed, and she didn't know *what* they were.

Gary *had* been there for her, though; he was right. He'd been there when her father had a stroke in the middle of the night. Twenty-nine years old, and she'd had to face the death of her fifty-eight year old father. He'd sat with her during the two year death-watch as her mother died slowly of lymphoma. Such a God-awful, horrible disease.

Shit, she thought, *I need to get a handle on myself. Whatever has been going wrong, I need to face it and fix it.*

Going through her mother's two-story would take months. Karen sighed deeply as she dragged dozens of empty boxes up to her parents' bedroom. They'd lived in the house for thirty-four years, her home since age five. So many memories to pack up, along with the "stuff." It was all hers to do, with no siblings to share the burden. And as soon as that thought formed, Karen froze. Just as she had in Edmond, she once again considered the possibility of her biological father having married. And if he had, who was to say that she didn't have brothers or sisters?

For the next few weeks, she split her time between the piles in the sunroom and the piles in her mother's house five miles down the road. She wasn't making much of a dent in either.

One evening she walked into the kitchen with a pile of papers in a file folder and dropped them on the counter as Gary opened a bag of take-out Chinese.

"What's this?" he asked.

Karen scooped a spoonful of sweet and sour chicken onto her plate. She licked her fingers where the sauce had run. "Ummm," she said. "Wanted you to look at those with me."

Gary opened the folder, ate with his right hand, and thumbed through the papers with his left. "Is this your birth certificate?" he asked.

"It is," she said. "And their wills and insurance papers and all that stuff. I thought I might find a copy of my adoption papers, but it wasn't there."

"So only your adopted parents are listed here?"

"Yeah, birth records were sealed when adoptions took place and I still can't request one."

"Are you wanting to dig further, Karen? You've never questioned this before."

"I don't know," she said. "It's just that since mother died, I can't stop wondering about my biological parents. I have no names even if I wanted to search."

She sat quietly as Gary flipped through the remaining papers.

"So what you're looking for is the order of adoption?"

"Yes, but I can't find it and I can't figure out why it isn't here?"

"Did your parents have a box at the bank?"

"A safe deposit box? I don't know. I never knew of one," she said, "But it has to be somewhere, right?"

"Just go to their bank and ask. You have the death certificate—that's all you need." She saw the question in Gary's eyes. "Ok, I hate to ask, but does this trunk you found have anything to do with this sudden interest in your parents?"

"I don't know," she said. "Maybe. I just have this gnawing feeling that I was intended to discover this trunk. Like it has answers for me."

Gary hesitated. "Looking into the history of the house is one thing, Karen. I understand your interest. But I think you're making this too personal," he said. "There's nothing that belonged to *your parents* in the trunk, right?"

She bristled. "Where's all that support you keep saying you give me, Gary? I don't know … I haven't gotten through everything yet."

Gary pushed suddenly from his bar stool and started closing the containers on the counter. He avoided her gaze.

"Were you going to ask if I was finished?"

"Karen, I don't want to do this. Your mother just died. You're on summer break which always makes you nutso, and you're involved in two huge projects. Why do you do that to yourself? You always do this—take on too much at one time."

She was halfway through the room before he could finish.

The next morning, on the phone with Denise, she reflected on last night's scene. "I should have let him have it."

"I understand," Denise said.

"I don't take on too much at a time, do I?" The phone was silent just long enough to ask again, "Well, do I?"

"You love your job and you love your projects. Who cares if you take on too much sometimes?"

"Well, apparently Gary."

The silence stretched for several seconds. Karen sighed deeply. "Thing is, I constantly complain about Gary never being home—his busy schedule. Maybe I do the same thing."

After she hung up, she sat at the kitchen counter drinking a second cup of coffee before heading to her parents' for the day. She and Gary hadn't talked this morning. He had slipped out early for the breakfast meeting downtown he'd mentioned last evening.

Maybe Gary's right, she thought. *Maybe I am staying overly busy to keep from missing mom.* She decided to surprise him with a home-cooked meal. She could even bake some fresh bread and make an ice cream cake. She started a grocery list and added wine at the bottom.

At 7:30 that evening the steak was still sitting in the refrigerator marinating, the salad had wilted, and the warm bread was no longer warm. She picked up the phone and tried Gary's cell one more time. At eight she sat at the counter and sliced the steak she'd just taken off the grill. *I'm the one who stays too busy, Gary?* she thought. *Really?*

Around midnight Karen lay on the sunroom sofa and watched him in the dark: hands in pockets, shirt un-tucked, blue blazer draped over his right arm. He stood at the bottom of the stairwell staring into space. Was he considering retracing his steps and leaving again? Wondering what he'd say if she were awake? She cleared her throat to let him know she was there. When he turned, she slipped from the sofa and walked to the kitchen for a glass of water.

When she came back, he was gone. She could hear the faucet running in the upstairs bath. She slowly climbed the stairs, placed the water glass on the night stand and pulled the sheets over her just before he entered the room. The mattress sagged as he lay down beside her on the king sized bed. The 18 inches between them felt like 18 miles. She closed her eyes.

The next morning, she squinted at the clock on her bedside table. She'd slept late. The tempting smell of coffee wafted from downstairs, but she stared at the ceiling a few minutes longer before dragging herself from bed. A few moments later she shrugged into a robe and slowly took the stairs, wondering whether she should simply let things be until they had time to sit and talk. Gary would be racing to a meeting downtown at his office. It would be foolish to start something they couldn't finish.

She hadn't needed to worry. The pot was on Warm and half full. A brief handwritten note sat beside it on the counter. "I'll be home early tonight. I'll bring dinner."

Taking her coffee cup to the kitchen table, she sat and let the steam rise to her face. It melded with the streaming tears and dampened her cheeks. She would shower and call Denise. *If only mother were here*, she thought. The tears seemed endless as they dropped from her chin line onto the wood surface.

Denise was waiting in the coffee shop across from her favorite park when she arrived. The Colorado spring was almost over. June was the prettiest month in the city. The air smelled of Golden Raintree, and their blossoms drifted onto the wrought iron table where they sat and talked for the next two hours.

She chose to agree with Denise that there was, most likely, a simple explanation for Gary's late night; though she refused to let go of the fact he hadn't bothered to call or that her lovely dinner had gone to waste. Businessmen wined and dined; they listened and cajoled and sucked up. Why even suspect anything else? She had no reason to doubt Gary.

"I find myself doubting everything and everyone these days, though," she confided. "I'm at loose ends, Denise. I feel ungrounded, unsure of my whole life."

"That's normal isn't it, hon?" Denise said. "Your mom—I mean it's only been a few months."

Karen nodded but she tipped her head in a question mark. "I *guess*," she said.

"But?"

"But … I don't know. I feel like I'm being pulled apart. Like—I want to go somewhere new and exciting—leave the boring life I've fallen into. At the same time, I want to hide in my nest and never come out."

She looked up to meet Denise's eyes. What a terrible thing to say to your best friend. She shook her head. "I'm so sorry. Just ignore me. This stress of cleaning out two houses and working with realtors and these dumb histories—I need to just slow down and breathe."

Denise smiled and reached for her hand across the table. "I didn't take that personally, Karen. It's ok. We all feel like that at some point. I get it. But it sounds like it's more than that."

"There's nothing keeping me here, D," she said. "I'm no one's daughter any longer; no one's mom, no one's sister, not even a wife most days. It feels like Gary has left, just like my dad."

"You mean your biological father?"

"Yes. I have dreams of seeing him on the street. I know I've never met him, never even seen a photo, but I recognize him. I know his eyes. But a few seconds later, he's disappeared into the crowd, and I can't find him."

"Is this new?" Denise said. "I mean, since you mom …?"

"Yes … really since I went to the house—those journals—all that history. It's brought it all back—questions I never asked—never really ever wanted or needed to ask. But being there. Knowing that was the last place I was ever with him—it's a deep hole—deeper than I expected. I wonder, you know, is he still there? Right around the corner? Did he die in Vietnam? I have nothing but questions now and two dead parents with no answers for me—if they ever had any."

"What *did* your parents tell you?"

"College kids—students—too young to care for a baby. I don't even know for sure if they were married before … you know…before she died giving birth to me. It was war-time—Vietnam, Cambodia—war protests. That's about it. I wonder if they did know where he went."

"Is there a way to open the adoption to find out?"

"The process is daunting at this point. I don't know if I really even want to. Maybe that's the issue, huh? Part of this bigger dilemma. I want to know and I don't."

Denise sighed. "You'll do it when you're ready. But for now maybe you need to start with your marriage. Gary is here—right now—and you two need to talk and figure things out. Do you want the marriage, Karen?"

She stared into her empty cup as if it might hold the answer. "Gary is safe, comfortable, familiar—always has been. He's that nest I want to hide in at the same time I want to cast off and fly away." She sighed openly. "I know … you can't do both."

"You'll figure it out, my friend; you always do. My advice? Tonight … just let him talk. Be quiet and listen."

Karen straightened her back and let her shoulders fall and relax.

"Thanks," she said. "I'll try."

"Sometimes love has nothing to do with marriage, and sometimes marriage has nothing to do with love."

"Amen," Karen said.

Karen avoided the sunroom that day. She talked to herself all afternoon and was going to play it as Denise had suggested. True, he had said he'd be home early. True, she'd spent an entire afternoon cooking. And true, he hadn't called to say he'd be late. But she hadn't exactly told him her plans; hadn't even apologized for walking out on him the night before.

She was in the kitchen when Gary opened the back door earlier than usual; his hands full of white paper bags of take-out. She noticed the logo of an Indian restaurant they frequented. Gary knew she loved their food and it didn't take a second to realize he was trying to apologize. She shook her head and felt a smile form. And though she tried to return to her anger; it just wouldn't come.

"Oh, my gosh, Gary. Did you buy enough for an army?"

He chuckled. She hadn't heard him laugh in ages. It felt nice. She took a couple of bags from him and placed them on the counter. "Pour us a glass of wine and I'll set the table," she said.

For the next half hour they tiptoed around the details of last night. A new client. A meeting that ran late. A dead cell phone. "I'm really sorry," he said. "I saw the mess in the kitchen this morning. I'm sorry you went to so much trouble. I had no idea."

Karen put down her fork and waited for him to finish. Once he made eye contact, she spoke. "I'm sorry I walked out the other evening. That's no way to figure things out, I know."

"I didn't mean to be condescending that night, Karen. I'm just worried I guess. I don't want you to keep questioning what all these old things have to do with your own life, you know?"

"I know," she said. Then she smiled. "Sounds like we have a draw, huh?"

*

Two weeks later, Karen phoned to tell Hazel the abstract had been correct. "I just finished reading Lily's diary. I'm sure her son, Davis, built the house." She asked if Hazel could do some further research to confirm it.

"I'll keep looking, dear," Hazel said, "but it does sound like the dates match up. He'd have been a young man at the time."

After she hung up, Karen looked again at the old newspaper article she'd been holding. The photo had been taken July 11, 1888—the day the Edmond coaling station opened. The woman, Lily, appeared to be pregnant; she gazed with pride at her husband who smiled broadly toward the camera. She held the hand of a small boy. Karen closed Lily's journal and thought about the woman's life.

What a lot of guts that must have taken. Oklahoma in the 1880's. Barren red dirt, harsh conditions. Her mind churned. How much must you love a man to follow him into Indian Territory and the unknown? And how strong Lily had been, to not only face the hardships, but to be strengthened by them. She decided to frame Lily's teaching certificate and hang it in the office with her own.

Three days later, Hazel phoned from Oklahoma. "Well, appears you were right, my dear. Davis Lee was born in Albuquerque, New Mexico in 1885 to Lillian and Charles Lee. The land records confirm that he built, but never lived in, your house on Fourth Street."

Karen hung up with Hazel and returned to the sunroom. The trunk was half empty now. On hands and knees, she bent down and pulled out several more items. She placed them on piles already marked: pioneer days, WWII, Vietnam. Some heavier items had shifted to the bottom, so Karen carefully wove her hand through a few layers until she felt a firm rectangular object. What she pulled out was a thin brown leather book; the size of a ledger. The loose yellowing vellum pages were held together precariously by leather tie strings. She opened it gingerly to the first page. The broad strokes of handwriting suggested they'd been written by a man. The first date made her anxious to continue.

January 1, 1920. I'm not much of a writer so my annual notes to posterity will be brief again this year. I am happier in Kansas City then I have ever been and have no regrets about leaving Edmond behind. I miss Willard and Elizabeth and mother, of course, but I will never (hopefully) find myself in my father's debt again. The women are abundant, the booze flows (despite prohibition) and good times are to be had for young men like me in K.C. Life couldn't be better. DL

D.L. Karen considered the initials. Had to be. She turned a few more pages and felt more certain as she read the next few notations.

∗

By the last week in June, her parents' closets had been emptied; the clothing taken to Goodwill; her mother's jewelry placed in her own safe deposit box and the furniture cleaned and ready to mark for auction. She was making progress. Karen walked to her mother's kitchen and groaned. She opened cabinet after cabinet filled with nearly forty years' worth of storing and saving and purchasing. When she got to the china hutch, she sat down on a dining room chair and sobbed.

Maybe she should take Gary up on his offer to help her and quit being so stubborn.

For the past month, she'd practically lived at her parents' house and Gary had taken on two large projects. An Asian investor had purchased several pieces of land in downtown Denver. Gary's firm had been chosen to design the high rise condos while trying to maintain the feel of the historic neighborhood surrounding them. Between his late nights and her busy days they'd had virtually no time together.

On a sunny afternoon mid-week, Denise phoned.

"Can I drag you away from boxes for awhile?"

"Please do," she begged.

Denise laughed her signature loud cackle, which made Karen laugh as well.

"I'll pick you up in fifteen," Denise said.

"I'm a mess but I'll at least wash my face before you get her," she said.

When the doorbell rang, Karen grabbed her purse and welcomed Denise with a hug.

"Wow," Denise said. "I should have been over here helping. You are so stubborn."

"Now you sound like Gary. It's summer break, for heavens sake. One of us needs to enjoy the time off," she said.

"There must be over a hundred boxes," Denise said as she glanced around the living areas. "I'm glad you decided to have an auction instead of doing that part yourself."

As Denise drove, Karen caught her up on the progress she'd made. When the car turned south out of the city limits, she turned her head to see where they were headed.

"What . . . are we doing?"

"My news," she said and grinned.

"No . . ."

"Yep, talked Ralphie into moving. We made an offer this morning and I wanted you to be the first to see it. Don't worry, it's not far."

"Oh, D, I'm so happy for you," Karen nearly squealed. "Well, drive faster, will you?"

Karen was truly pleased. Denise and Ralph seemed to have it so together. It wasn't like she and Gary had been fighting since that last blow-up, but she knew the only reason was their lack of time together. In six weeks she'd be back teaching and her nights would fill as well, and they'd see even less of one another. And perhaps they'd just keep plodding along until one of them grew too tired to try.

Chapter 4
April, 1922

Davis Lee found himself in a perfect situation at the poker table where he'd been losing for hours. It was late, well past midnight, on a crisp spring Saturday night. The dangling ceiling fixture in the back of the speakeasy gave little light. Not that it mattered. Liquor had dimmed the men's vision hours ago.

Davis hung with a group of young dandies in Kansas City, Missouri. His family wasn't well-to-do like the others', but his parents were highly regarded in Oklahoma. Davis had quickly learned to dress and act the part of the privileged shortly after his arrival ten years earlier. The other men seemed to enjoy his company, and he had slipped easily into their somewhat questionable lifestyle. They were playboys by night and fast talkers by day. They enjoyed the lively atmosphere that Kansas City provided during prohibition.

Included in this group was Boston Maddux, the man tapping his cards on the table, directly across from Davis. Boston had been named for his hometown, and his family was well known in the social circles back east. This night, after hours of poker, and full of gin, he boasted. "Boys," he said with a slur, "I have made so much money in oil this month, let's make this interesting." On top of the pile of cash already on the table, Boston added a wad of certificates worth well over a hundred thousand dollars.

Play immediately stopped, and whether or not he was bluffing his hand, no one was about to put that kind of fortune on the line in order to find out. The dealt hands folded silently around the table, and eyes shifted between the two remaining men.

Davis stared across at Boston, who sat there like a Cheshire cat, grinning from ear to ear, his cigar dropping ashes onto the saloon table. Davis recognized it for what it was – *you intimidating braggart.* "I'll take that off your hands, Boston," he said.

"Well, ante up then, Davis. Ain't showing my hand without cold cash."

Davis leaned forward. "Your paper doesn't look like cold cash, Boston. Who's to say it's worth anything near what you claim?"

"Anyone who watches the stock market knows what oil is worth these days, Lee. What the hell's the matter with you? Fold your hand and shove your money this way."

"Tell you what, let's make this interesting? Leave it all on the table. If my hand loses, you can throw me in jail until I make good on the bet. Plenty of other reasons for you to call the authorities with a tip or two anyway, after some of our recent 'business' dealings."

Boston sat back in his chair, not a bead of sweat on his thin upper lip. "Well, that might be more entertaining than winning your money, actually, Davis. But if I were you, I'd think twice."

Davis knew his own hand: a royal flush, ace high, couldn't possibly be beat. Boston was going to pay dearly for this bluff.

The men surrounding the table urged them on. There wasn't one in the group that wouldn't like to see Boston Maddux lose. Catcalls and whistles rang in the room.

"Lay 'em down, Boston; a week in jail for your fake money." Davis laughed heartily.

"Flush—king high," Boston said, fanning his cards out on the table. He started to gather the pile of money toward him, but Davis pushed his hands away and slowly laid down his winning cards, one by one.

Silence fell around the table, and Boston stood. "Come on, Davis, you know I was joking. I'd never give up a hundred thousand on a game."

"Really, Boston? Well, it seems the joke is on you, huh?" Davis rose from his chair and scooped the heap of bills and certificates into both hands. He folded it into a large wad and tucked it into the breast pocket of his coat.

"Davis, come on; I mean it," Boston yelled. "Take the cash but you can't possibly believe I'm going to let you have those damned oil stocks." His liver-colored face tightened with threat; sweat beaded on his brow.

Davis stood quietly for a moment. He and Boston were friends, after all. And he knew Boston had been simply showing off when he made the stupid bet. Still …. this could be the answer he'd been waiting for.

"Tell you what, Boston; we'll make it a loan. How does that set with you?"

"What the hell does that mean, a loan?" Boston hit the table with his hand and rose from his seat.

"Just what I said — a loan. I'll give it back to you in a few weeks; I promise." Davis was the Cheshire cat now. He had an idea that had been percolating for some time, and Boston's oil stocks just might make it feasible.

Davis watched Boston closely; keeping his eyes focused on the man's fists.

"You can't renege on a bet, Boston," someone in the room called out. "But if Davis is willing to give you back the stock, I'd think about listening to his offer."

"God damn," Boston raged. "Lee, you'd better get that damned stock back to me within two weeks, or I swear you really will be in jail. Better yet, I'll talk to the Pendergast family and make you disappear. Got that?" He threw his coat over his arm, slammed his gray fedora onto his head and marched from the room as a round of whoops and hollers broke out behind him.

*

The following week, Davis Lee sat in the dining car sipping a mid-morning Irish coffee as the train swayed gently along the rails toward Oklahoma. He held the hot cup to his lips allowing the moisture to steam up his wire-rimmed glasses. When the giggles behind him grew louder, Davis turned in his large leather club chair, let the condensation dissipate and took in the image of the starkly beautiful woman sitting two tables behind.

Her long auburn hair was pulled into a fashionable top-knot, and her hazel eyes caught the light from the small chandelier above her. Her laughter filled the car. Had she not been sitting with the portly old gentleman across from her, he'd have stopped at her table on the way back to his private compartment. Instead, he tipped his hat slightly and smiled as he passed by.

The train was an hour out of Edmond, traveling south from Kansas City. It would stop in his hometown just long enough for him to hop off before it continued to Oklahoma City and on to Gainesville. Davis lay down on the lower berth to rest his eyes. He was well aware that his appearance would be under much scrutiny by his mother when his parents met him at the station. She took every opportunity to find ways to bring him back home. It had been two years since Davis had last seen his parents, and he was here for what he hoped to be a short but productive visit.

The whoosh of the train's brakes and the clanging of the engineer's bell woke him from a deep sleep. He rinsed his face with cold water from the small sink; then wiped his wet hands along his head, catching any stray hairs that might have loosed themselves during his nap. Pulling his black felt fedora from the brass wall hook, he tilted his head into it, straightened his tie and grabbed his leather briefcase before exiting the compartment. As the door swung outward, it met with resistance, and behind it, the woman from the dining car pushed against him and peeked around its edge.

"I'm so sorry," he said. "Did I hit you?"

"Not at all," she replied, and she stepped back slightly to allow him to exit.

Davis' eyes moved past the woman, watching for her earlier escort. He hesitated just long enough to determine that she was traveling alone, or at least departing the train alone, and either way, he was left a clear opening.

"Here, allow me to help you with that," he said. He reached for the large round hat box, slipping it from her grasp as he slid through the door. "Please." He indicated for her to move in front of him, and as she passed, he allowed his hand to just graze her hip, the touch so slight she would not notice.

He wished he were at the bottom of the metal stairway so he could watch her long legs as her skirt rose and fell with each step. Instead he took advantage of the rear view, which he had to admit, was particularly impressive.

Davis knew he looked older than his thirty-six years; his hard-working, hard-playing lifestyle had etched some early wrinkles, but he also knew that his dark wavy hair held no gray, and his taut stomach and slender frame were an attraction to most of the women he met.

The woman stepped onto the platform and turned quickly. "I can take it from here," she said. "Thank you."

Davis held the satin strings of the hat-box tightly in his grasp a few seconds longer, holding it toward her but not releasing it. He grinned broadly. "Only if you tell me your name and where you're staying," he said.

Her crimson smile turned up at the corners and her gray-green eyes twinkled. Shaking her head slightly side to side, she laughed at his audacity. As she reached to take the case from him, her voice was clear and firm. "Belinda Price," she said. "I'm staying at the De Hoss Hotel downtown for a few days while visiting my great-aunt."

"May I call on you?" he asked carefully, putting aside his earlier cockiness.

She hesitated only slightly before answering. "That would be nice, Mr. . . . ."

"Lee ... Davis Lee," he said.

"Well, Mr. Lee, it was nice to make your acquaintance. Thank you again." She turned from him, hips swaying gently and heels clicking along the wooden platform of the train station.

He stood momentarily mesmerized and deaf to his mother shrieking from down the way, "Davis! Davis! Down here."

He waved a hand at his parents, retrieved his larger bag from the porter and tipped him generously. When Davis reached his mother, he lifted her face for a kiss and hugged her tenderly. "Mother, how wonderful you look," he said.

"I cannot believe how long it has been," she said. She dusted the shoulders of his wool coat though Davis knew there was nothing to be dusted.

"Son," his father said as he gave a nod. He extended his hand, and Davis shook it with a firm grip.

"Dad."

"Well, come on," Lily admonished. "Charles, grab those bags, will you?" She took Davis' arm and steered him down the wooden walkway of the rail station.

When they reached the car, his mother said, "Here, Davis, you sit up front with your father. It's much more comfortable than the rear seat."

"Lily, he's a grown man, for heaven's sake."

Davis shook his head. His parents would never change. They'd been playing these same roles since they migrated to Oklahoma. His father—gruff and demanding; his mother always smoothing and cajoling and getting her way.

Davis listened with half an ear as Lily chattered in the back seat. He watched the streets of Edmond roll past and noted the many changes since his last visit. There were new lamp posts on Broad and Main with three light globes each, and as his father turned the corner, he proudly pointed out the newly opened campground that provided shade and amenities for travelers coming through the city.

"Pretty classy," Davis said. He glanced at his father, and then turned to face his mother who sat stoically in the rear seat. "No wonder you all took first place in the Better Cities contest last summer."

His father pulled the shiny new Ford into the narrow drive along the west side of their two-story Victorian home at First and Broad and parked beneath the shade of a tall oak, several yards shy of the garage. Before Davis could object, his father pulled his bags from the rear of the automobile and clapped his large hand onto Davis' left shoulder without saying a word.

Davis noted a slight limp as his father led them toward the house. Charles had turned fifty-five last month; his mother would be fifty-three. They still lived in the family home they'd built in the early 1900's, one of the first lots sold from the old Clegern land holdings. Its white clapboard frame had been recently painted, and the red brick cove still stood in good repair.

"Here, dad, let me take that," Davis said, and lifted the suitcase from his father's grip. He crossed the porch and stepped into the floral wallpapered living room, tipped his hat into his right hand and threw it on the closest velvet settee.

His mother shrugged out of her jacket and reached for him with both arms. "Davis, Davis," she said, giving him an embrace. "You're too thin; you're going to blow away."

"Good grief, Lily," Charles said, "Let the boy be."

Davis chuckled. "Fine, mother, fatten me up this trip then."

"I'll go make some coffee. You settle in. You're up in your old room, of course." She pointed toward the steep stairwell.

Davis nodded and excused himself. He took the narrow steps two at a time to accommodate his long stride, threw his briefcase onto the bed and walked to the front window. His room overlooked the street and the large oak trees that lined the sidewalk.

In high school, he had often climbed from his window onto the front porch roof just above their parents' bedroom. He was forever getting caught sneaking back in at one or two in the morning, noticing at the very last moment his father's silent figure sitting in the hard, straight desk chair in the corner of his room.

Davis was relentlessly blamed for all of Elizabeth's and Willard's wrong-doings and often reminded, that as the eldest child, he was an improper role-model to his younger siblings. Elizabeth, two years younger than Davis, had learned early on from his mistakes. She rarely got caught in her parents' traps and assumed the guise of the innocent girl she pretended to be. They had often laughed, as adults, at Davis' reputation in Edmond as the town bad boy, a celebrity that followed him to this day.

His father still accused Lily of spoiling the children. Davis didn't remember it that way. What *he* recalled was the absence of a father all those years. He remembered being constantly under his mother's petticoats as she struggled with frontier life and thought fondly of their visits to the Kickapoo Reservation. She had taught him to read and write at an early age, had sent all three children to the public school under her constant tutelage, and arranged her college teaching schedule to be home in the afternoons.

As for his father, Davis had walked past the rail station each day on his way home from school and saw a hunch-backed man, much older than his years, sitting behind a large desk looking out his office window. He remembered the constant smell of liquor each time his father walked into the room. And he remembered the distance between his parents. His siblings had been smart enough to leave home for college as quickly as they could. He had hung around in the hopes of winning his father's affection.

"Davis," his mother called up the stairs. "Come help me with this heavy tray." Davis knew she had brought out the heavy silver serving tray, laden with sugar bowl, creamer, coffee urn and the *good* china cups and saucers from his Grandmother Rose.

"Be right down," he answered her.

On his way to join his parents in the parlor—he passed Charles' cherry-wood paneled office, and memories floated to the surface. His father had spent years behind the heavy mahogany desk, stern and serious, as he led the way for the changes the railroad would bring to the Indian Territory. Old photographs lined the walls. He glanced at the sepia of Edmond in 1887. A few wooden buildings, some tents, and the new brick rail station that stood alongside the coal and watering chutes. The station: his father's contribution to the Atchison, Topeka and Santa Fe Rail, and a lasting tribute to the "company man."

A large print of the land run hung in its place of honor on the wall behind his father's rolling desk chair. Davis had been barely five years old, and he wasn't sure if his memories were from experience or the constant telling of the story.

Davis took the heavy tray from his mother's arms and placed it on the coffee table. He sat down on the settee next to her.

"So, Davis," his father said, leaning forward in his chair. "What brings you to town?"

He thanked his mother as she handed him a steaming cup of coffee. He blew onto it gently and observed a slight frown on her forehead, aimed directly at his father. It eased as quickly as it came.

"Wait, Charles," she said," I want to hear about the young lady at the rail station first."

Davis grinned. "Now mother," he said, "you know nothing will come of that, and quit hoping to marry me off."

"You're thirty-six, Davis," she said. "You can't remain a playboy the rest of your life. You need to settle down, for heaven's sakes."

"Which is why I'm trying to gather information about his visit," Charles said impatiently. "You've avoided us for the past two years; guess I'm just curious as to what brings you back."

Davis had hoped to avoid this particular conversation until after dinner, but he knew his father all too well. Once he latched onto something, he didn't let go.

"When is Elizabeth coming down from Guthrie?" Davis asked his mother.

"Davis, don't change the subject." Irritation tinted Charles' words. "I want to know why you wrote that you needed to visit. So, out with it."

Lily's right eyebrow arched for a quick second. She looked at Charles and then turned to face her son. "Yes, Davis, dear, we are very anxious to know how you are."

Davis grinned. His mother was an expert at playing his father; he had watched it since childhood—her ability to soften any situation and turn it into her own. The day he left Oklahoma he had still been the twenty-six-year-old child of Charles Lee. Ten years later, it seemed his role had not changed. His parents' scolding did not sit well.

He took a sip of his coffee, placed it into the saucer on the table in front of him and leaned forward. "I have a proposition," he said.

"I'm listening," Charles replied, his eyes holding Davis' for a long moment.

Davis broke the gaze first, his fingers strumming his bent knees. The settee was suddenly uncomfortable. He stood and walked toward the heavily draped front bay-window and turned to his parents.

"I've pulled together a group of investors; we hope to buy land and build some homes, and I told them Edmond was the right place at the right time." He let his words sink in for a few seconds before continuing. "I'd stay a short while, of course, if the deal comes to fruition and over-see the project; be the front man so to speak since I know the area." His jaw clinched with tension, and he couldn't seem to stop the string of words. "I'd need a place to stay temporarily, but not for long." His voice trailed off into silence. It seemed to fill the room.

Charles remained quiet and contemplative. His furrowed

brow revealed his skepticism. Davis stood stiffly, waiting—for what, he wasn't sure. He didn't expect anything other than his father's silence.

"How about we save this for later," Lily said. She stood quickly and began gathering the coffee service together. "I'll have the beef roast ready before Elizabeth arrives. Davis, go take a short nap. You look just totally tuckered out." Smiling at both men, she left the room, and Davis took advantage of the opportunity and made a quick exit up the stairs.

Elizabeth's arrival from Guthrie cushioned the tension over dinner. A few inches shorter than Davis, she fit comfortably in his warm embrace. "My God, Davis, it's been way too long," she said. Dinner conversation settled safely around Elizabeth's stories of dealing with four teen-age children and her husband Daniel's new position as vice president of Guthrie Bank and Trust. When Davis asked about their younger brother, Willard, both women shook their heads in unison.

"Davis Lee," his mother said, "You really should stay in touch with your family. How can you not know about Willard's move to Texas? For heaven's sake, he's been there a year now."

Davis mocked them by hanging his head low to his chest, feigning guilt. He didn't acknowledge his father's head-shake from his position at the head of the table. Intended or not, he always felt his father's judgment. He had left Oklahoma with one purpose – to leave his family and all it represented behind him, and he had done just that.

Davis had never understood his father's anger; it simply seemed a part of him. He had been ten when the family moved into this house—the house his mother had longed for and saved for since arriving in Oklahoma. He had much preferred the simple life in the little pump house by the station. He sometimes longed for the days spent with his mother on the Kickapoo Reservation and the evenings when the five of them huddled for warmth in their tiny two-room house. But even then, his father had seemed distant and focused solely on the Santa Fe Rail, not on hearth and home.

After Elizabeth and Willard left for college, Davis had stayed on, taking his role as eldest son seriously. He worked and went to law school, contributed to the family coffers, but he never could break through his father's stone wall. Then one day he'd had enough and headed to Kansas City for a breath of fresh air and big-city life-style.

He had found plenty of that. Kansas City was full of young men like Davis: handsome, well educated, with good family backgrounds and wealth. It was true he'd fallen in with a rowdy bunch, but they were men in their twenties when he arrived in 1911 and they were enjoying life.

Prohibition had come last year, but it didn't affect Kansas City, Missouri. The Pendergasts made sure of that, and saloons and taverns flourished. It was in that environment that Davis found young men with similar likes, wants and needs: women, parties, booze and easy money.

After dinner, Charles offered cognac in his study, and the women excused themselves to clear the dining table and clean the kitchen. Davis took one of the upholstered wing-backs as his father pulled the bottle from the back of a cabinet, poured the whiskey and sat down beside him.

"So you want to be a developer now, do you, Davis?" he asked. "What made you come up with this scheme?"

"It's not a sch …"

Charles interrupted his son. "Davis, I know you too well. What's this really about?"

Looking his father directly in the eye, Davis said, "I hear old man Clegern is opening up the land just south of here. You used to be friends; figure he might sell me some of it. I've made a lot of money; want to invest it in something good."

"Not the rumor that has filtered down here in recent years, son," he said.

'Don't know what rumors you're talking about, but I can assure you I have the money to back this."

Charles nodded slowly. "Well, maybe so; truth is I don't believe it's your own money though, Davis. Who you conning this time?"

Davis had had enough of his father's barbs; he gulped down his whiskey and stood.

"I'll be staying overnight and moving to a hotel tomorrow," he said. "I'm going to do this with your help or without, father."

He walked into the large foyer between the office and stairway and grabbed his light-weight over-coat and his fedora from the umbrella stand. "Think I'll take a walk. Tell Elizabeth I will phone her tomorrow." He shut the heavy wood door firmly behind him and stepped into the cool damp April night.

Davis sighed deeply as he pulled on his leather gloves and looked up at the clear night sky. He suspected the rumors his father had mentioned included some of his business dealings that were on the fringe of shady, as well as his party life in Kansas City. People loved to talk. It was true; he'd worked some deals the past few years with some of his cohorts. Nothing illegal … at least so far, though close enough to be wary of Boston's threats to call the authorities. But Charles' last statement worried him. His father had been too close to the truth for his comfort. Davis didn't, in fact, have the money for this venture. He was subsidized by Boston's oil stocks. Oil stocks he would claim as his own to cut the deal.

Davis walked several blocks west on Fourth Street. As he passed the Hotel De Hoss, he glanced through the leaded glass windows into the hotel lobby in the hopes of spotting the lovely Belinda. Two doors down was the old Piccadilly Saloon, an establishment he had frequented all too often. Prohibition had shuttered the windows, but he knew the back door would still be ajar.

He was greeted with back slaps and offers of drinks from the younger men at the bar, but he took his Pimm's and approached a table of older gentlemen at the rear of the room. His father's colleagues nodded an acknowledgment, but no one offered him a seat.

He had hoped Clegern might be among them. Davis was about to turn around when one of the men spoke. "Evening, Davis. What brings you down south, son?"

"Your daddy know you're around?" The question came from the rear of the room and sarcasm dripped from the man's words.

Davis wasn't up for sparring with the old men, so he nodded a cursory hello and turned around. He climbed onto the only vacant stool, stuck between the end of the bar and a town drunk. He sipped his drink silently and nodded occasionally to the faces across from him.

Hours later, Davis opened the front door gingerly and tip-toed into the foyer. To his left, in the faint lamp light, sat his mother, hands folded in her lap and close to nodding off.

She opened her eyes at the sound of his footsteps. "Join me for a moment, won't you dear?"

Davis threw his coat aside and sat across from her.

"I spoke with your father," she said. "He wants you to stay and so do I. I've missed you, Davis."

Davis knew full well that this was not his father's decision.

"Mother, don't try to con a con." Davis grinned.

Her voice sounded tight in her throat. "Davis, please don't be so hard on your father. He loves you, you know?"

"He has a funny way of showing it, then." Davis straightened to rise from the settee.

"Davis, wait," she said. "I know you've had your differences, but it's time you two settle them, for all our sakes."

For the next half hour, Davis listened half-heartedly to his mother's excuses. He knew nothing had changed, nor would it. His father was not a man who could be pleased, and yet, here he was trying to do just that. He didn't know what sleight of hand his mother had used this time, but he agreed to stay with them a few more days until he could meet with Clegern.

Davis was unable to sleep. Aside from the conversation with his mother, something else was keeping him awake. He kept remembering the crisp sweet tone of Belinda's laughter in the dining car and the slight hint of gardenia that rose from her long porcelain neck. Oh, that neck that plunged to a hidden curve of décolletage. His morning plan was to walk in the direction of the Hotel De Hoss in the hopes of seeing her.

It would take two more days and several notes left with the desk clerk before she agreed to meet him for lunch in the hotel restaurant. He listened intently to the lilt of her voice as she told him of her concern for her elderly Aunt Mary, her sadness at being orphaned at twenty-five, both parents dying of pneumonia within weeks of each other, and of living in Chicago this past year pondering her future alone with no siblings. When her Aunt Mary had written with an invitation to visit, she had quickly accepted and found herself on a train to Oklahoma, although she had insisted on her own accommodations so as not to impose on her Aunt's good graces.

"She's more like a great Aunt," she explained to Davis. "My father's much older half-sister." Mary was a spinster and lived in a small frame house close to the university where she'd spent the past twenty years as a teacher at the Normal School. "We'd never met before," Belinda said, "but we're getting along famously, and I think I'll stay a week or so."

Davis was amazed at himself. For the first time in a long time, he hadn't monopolized the conversation, hadn't talked about himself at all, except to mention that he too was here for a rather short stay unless a business venture were to arise. When she wanted to know more, he dismissed it as boring work-talk and asked if he could see her again. A faint blush on her cheeks confirmed her willingness to do so.

Davis had kept up with the news of Edmond's growth over

the past few years. His parents had known H.W. Clegern for years. He had immigrated from Scotland in the mid-1880's and obtained a great deal of land during the run. He'd sold Charles and Lillian a small piece to build their home in 1903 and worked with Lily to get the Normal School built. Clegern's latest enterprise was an electric rail line connecting Guthrie and Edmond to Oklahoma City. He was an entrepreneur, always looking for the next deal.

Davis was more interested in his current land development. Clegern was building a house of his own on Fifth Street at the eastern edge of the family orchard and was going to divide the remainder of the property into housing lots. He'd named the area Capital View. It was this land that Davis hoped to divide with H.W.; land that would bring him a nice income and the respect of his father.

Davis had sensed Clegern's unspoken questions over the phone when he asked the older man for a lunch meeting at the Boulevard Café. As he entered the restaurant, he saw him sitting at the back of the restaurant reading The Edmond Sun. Clegern was a large, stout man whose hair had turned white since Davis had last seen him. Unlike his father, Clegern seemed to be in robust health. His posture was like a rod stuck down his charcoal gray suit-jacket. He seemed to fill not only the wide leather seat, but the café as well.

Davis waved and nodded; then took a seat across from him in the booth. "Mr. Clegern, good to see you again." He firmly shook the older man's hand.

"You too Davis; what's it been? Ten years since you left town?"

"Yes, sir, although I come to visit now and again, of course."

"And what brings you home this trip?" He looked directly into Davis' eyes, assessing the younger man's veracity.

For the next half hour, Davis discussed his plan to return to Edmond, buy into a land deal with Clegern and build homes from Fourth Street to Ninth.

"What's in it for me, Davis?" Clegern asked. "I own the land; I can sell it off myself. I don't need a partner."

"Well, sir, I'm sure that's true, but I also know you have to put a lot of money into preparing the land, having it assessed, and putting in the utilities before you can even begin to sell off individual lots."

The man's eyes told Davis he was listening.

"Plus, sir, I can give you cash up front, take some of the land off your hands, and you're in a better position financially to sell off the rest or build homes yourself to sell for a profit. I can buy you out of the land from Fourth to Ninth and from Rankin to Boulevard, and the rest is yours to do with as you like."

"And where are you getting the money to do this, Davis? I'm not giving it away, son."

"I've done quite well in Kansas City, sir, invested my money in oil, and I can sign over my oil stock in exchange for the land. It's a cash deal for you." The lie stung his tongue.

Davis knew Clegern would take the deal. Why wait for individual lots to sell when he could get rid of a large portion and have his money immediately? Sure enough, by Friday the deal was cut. They met at the bank, and Davis handed over the oil stock in the amount of $100,000.00. Davis made the bet that Clegern wouldn't try to cash the stock for some time. It would make the old man much more money than the land he proposed to develop. He would hang onto it, and Davis would begin selling off lots to cover his debts. He had no intention of actually committing fraud, or at least that's what he told himself. He'd sell a few lots for more than he'd paid, put the money aside, and in time pay off Clegern with his earnings, get back the stocks, and pocket the profits. It was a win-win proposition. In a way, Davis thought, Clegern was simply making him a short-term loan. As had Boston Maddux with his oil stock.

After their first lunch, Davis and Belinda met daily for tea in the hotel dining room. At four pm on Friday, shortly after his meeting with Clegern, Davis sat in what had become his favorite corner of the room. He enjoyed arriving early and watching her enter through the double glass doors. Davis had known many women in the past ten years; too many to count, but Belinda had a hold on him that he both hated and craved.

"How is your aunt doing?" he asked as soon as she was seated. Her Aunt Mary had fallen earlier in the week, and Belinda had been at her side each day since.

"I'm afraid not well, but thank you for asking," she said. "In fact, I'm moving into her house later today and will set myself up for when she returns home from the hospital next week. Her hip will never be the same, and she's going to need care."

"So returning to Chicago is not in your plans now?" he asked. His face lit up and he smiled broadly.

"Davis Lee," she said, "shame on you for being happy about an old lady's poor health."

"May I help you move your things this afternoon, then?" he asked, hoping she'd say yes.

A few hours later, Davis walked into the living room of his parents' house and called for his mother. Lily was on the second floor landing when he spotted her.

"Mother, may I borrow the car?" he asked.

"Well, of course, my dear; I'm sure your father won't mind. But if you're going into Oklahoma City, I have an errand for you."

"No, mother, but you'll be pleased as to my need. Belinda is staying in Edmond with her Aunt for an extended time, and I'm helping her move her things over to the house on University."

Lily's cheeks flushed with excitement. "You must invite her for dinner, Davis. I know it's only been a couple of weeks; I know; I know. I won't make a fuss, but it would be lovely to meet her."

Davis promised to arrange an evening soon. He had to laugh.

If his mother had her way, she'd have him married tomorrow.

A week later, after he had driven Belinda to purchase groceries, she offered Davis a simple supper.

"I have to cook something for Mary anyway," Belinda said. "Can you live on scrambled eggs for one night?"

In the kitchen Davis made himself useful by stirring the eggs, while Belinda scurried around the kitchen locating dishes, silverware, and glasses.

"Still trying to get my bearings," she explained.

Davis watched her slender figure, her tiny waist that accentuated a buxom bosom. He wanted to touch her, to know what lay under her long full skirt and her high-necked lace bodice. She had allowed him to take her hand on an evening walk earlier in the week. He wondered if she wanted more, as he did.

Belinda took a tray up to her aunt's bedroom, and then she and Davis ate at the long mahogany table. After he helped clear dishes, he turned to her. "Walk with me," he said, and she willingly followed him through the front door and into the dusk.

At the corner, Davis turned to Belinda and stared into her eyes. Taking her slender heart-shaped face into his hands, he bent to kiss her, but Belinda turned away.

"Mr. Lee, I hope I've not given you a wrong impression." Her formal tone startled Davis; he'd never been denied by a woman. In answer to his questioning eyes, she explained. "Davis, do you really think I could be in this small town very long and not learn about your past?"

His anger sparked for a moment, but he shut it down. "I don't know what you've heard, Belinda, but that was a long time ago."

"Really, Davis?" she said. "Why don't you tell me about a Miss Tennyson in Kansas City?"

Davis flushed and momentarily refused to meet her gaze. Then he watched her look of surprise when he began to chuckle.

"You have certainly done some research," he said. "I guess I'll be off then, but Belinda," he added, "I'm not going away, and I have plenty of time to explain anything you wish to know." He left her quickly, but on the drive home he wondered who had shared his past with her and just how much she'd been told. It didn't matter. He was enamored and had no intention of letting her go so easily. Her reticence only made her more desirable.

For the next month, Davis was frantically busy, courting Belinda each evening, spending his days with land assessors, city officials, utility companies, and architects, and avoiding Boston's efforts to reach him. He had received several phone calls from friends in Kansas City warning him Boston was on a rampage and trying to find him. Davis had promised to return the stock in two weeks, and at this point he could definitely be accused of theft. And theft of thousands of dollars would most likely be jail time. He begged the men to not disclose his where-abouts and they had promised. Luckily for Davis, Boston was not well liked.

Clegern was moving forward as planned, had sold a dozen lots between Second and Fourth, and the development was taking shape. He convinced Davis to put aside a small piece of land at the end of one block for a small park area, just large enough for a couple of oak trees, flowerbeds and a bench or two. He agreed with anything Clegern proposed and kept his fingers crossed that the oil certificates would remain in the bank's safe deposit box. Boston hadn't yet located him, and he hoped like hell the land sales would happen quickly. He hadn't really planned to steal the stock from a friend; he was simply borrowing it for a short time. But he knew he had to move fast.

Each Saturday, Davis took a break from work and walked the eight blocks to Aunt Mary's. His attentions had not been rebuffed, and Belinda seemed to be willing to give him a chance to prove himself. He even got her to leave Aunt Mary a few times for dinner, at the hotel restaurant and a time or two with his parents, at his mother's request. Davis was moving slowly to give her time, but the more they were together, the more deeply entangled he became. No other woman had ever held his attentions this long.

One morning when he arrived, Belinda met him at the front door in tears. According to the doctors, Mary's hip was healing nicely, but she was becoming quite cantankerous.

"Belle," Davis said, reaching for her hands which were clasped tightly in front of her. He pulled her arms apart, leaned into her face and made a goofy grin. "Let me see that beautiful smile of yours," he teased.

Belinda pulled her left hand away and swiped at his shoulder. "Davis, don't," she said. "Do you always have to be so light-hearted? You don't know what it's like taking care of an old woman day and night."

Davis pulled her onto the front porch and shut the door behind them. "I'm sorry," he said. He pulled the wicker rocker away from the wall and motioned for her to sit. "Tell me what's going on, Belle."

Belinda spent the next half hour regaling Davis with the specifics of housekeeping, shopping, cooking, and walking up and down the flight of stairs a dozen times a day. A few tears fell, and Davis handed her a clean cotton handkerchief embroidered with the letters "D.L."

Davis leaned forward and listened, not once interrupting. When Belinda took a long, deep breath and seemed to relax, he spoke.

"It won't be forever, Belle. Doc Smith says her hip is mending; she'll be on her feet in no time; you'll see."

Belinda huffed, "Well, I certainly hope so, Davis. It's not like we were ever close relatives; I just met her last month. I'm just so tired." She gave a long sigh.

"It's a beautiful day in May," Davis said, and he smiled. "I'm taking you on a picnic. Go on, go slip on some comfortable shoes. I'll take care of Aunt Mary."

As Belinda headed to her bedroom, Davis took the stairs two at a time. Aunt Mary's room was the second down the hall facing the street. He had visited before when Belinda served her meals and he liked the old woman.

She was sitting in a needlepoint-embroidered high-back looking through the thick foliage of the elm trees in the front yard. She turned as he approached.

"Davis," she said. "That you?"

"Yes, ma'am," he said as he entered the room. "Came upstairs to give you a hug. I'll bet you need one today." He leaned down and put his arms around the elderly woman, straightening her shawl as he released her.

"You're a good man, Davis Lee," she said. She looked directly into his eyes. "I knew your mother at the college, you know?"

Davis sat opposite her on the edge of the unmade feather bed. "Yes, Mother taught there for years; she said she knew you. She was on the committee that got the college built in fact."

Aunt Mary nodded. "Yes, your mother's efforts were well known when I began teaching there. I believe I met you once when you were about ten years old, in fact."

Davis smiled. "Can I get you anything, Miss Price, before I take Belinda for a picnic? We don't want you getting up while we're gone."

She shooed him off with her hand.

Downstairs, he scurried around the kitchen, and when Belinda popped in, he stood waiting, picnic basket in hand.

Before they left, Davis brought up a tray of tea and cookies; he pulled a single rose from the dining room centerpiece and placed it in a jelly jar at the last moment. He needed Aunt Mary in his corner if he was going to persuade Belinda that he was a good guy, possibly even good enough to marry.

They walked a few blocks to the park, and Davis unfolded a blanket he'd found in the hallway and opened a basket of things he'd pulled from the refrigerator.

"Davis," Belinda exclaimed. "How did you do all that in such a short time?"

They laughed as he pulled out jar after jar taken from Aunt Mary's pantry: pickled herring, peanut butter and jelly, pickles, and peach preserves. "Luckily, I grabbed a loaf of bread," he said. "We can spread the preserves on that for dessert."

"It's the best picnic I've ever seen," Belinda said as she settled onto the blanket.

Davis felt her relax, and he smiled inside.

They spent the rest of the afternoon sharing family stories, her dreams of getting a teaching degree, and his plans of completing the housing development as quickly as possible. Davis suddenly knew what he wanted, and it wasn't his father's approval or financial wealth and status.

A few hours later, Davis found himself humming and then whistling as he walked back to his parents'.

At family dinners, the tension relaxed somewhat between father and son. Davis was aware that Charles watched him closely, but he also knew that word on the street was that he had come home a changed young man who was doing well in the real estate business. It made Davis smile to prove his father's initial doubts unfounded.

If he had been a difficult child, Davis thought, his father had only himself to blame. He was a company man, nothing Davis wished to be. Companies owned you. His mother had raised the three of them in extremely difficult conditions while Charles focused on his career with the railroad. In fact if it hadn't been for Lily, they would not have accumulated the financial wealth or the status they now held.

Without a strong male role model, Davis had become an independent, strong-willed young man. Charles had waited too long to be effective in curtailing his son's need for adventure and acceptance.

Davis loved the energy of Kansas City. It had been a good fit. He knew that rumors floated back to his family about his womanizing, gambling and partying. But Davis couldn't have cared less. He had broken out of the small town pressures to be perfect, to be chaste, to be successful. And yes, he had stretched the limits; he was well aware of that. Yes, he had scammed a friend out of the oil stock in order to return to Oklahoma and prove himself the strong man his father had always wanted. But he had every intention of replacing it soon. And for the first time in a long time, Davis wondered about moving back home.

*

By June, Davis had sold three lots to farmers from Guthrie and was moving forward with his plans. The money he'd made, thus far, was safe in the Edmond Bank and Trust; the sale of one more lot would give him enough to pay Clegern and buy back Boston's stock with a sizeable profit in his pocket. He walked the property daily and stopped to check the progress of each of the three homes at the east end of his holdings.

One Saturday in late June, the entire family gathered in the Lees' backyard. Willard and his family had driven from Dallas and Elizabeth from Guthrie with her husband and four kids. It was a beautiful Oklahoma evening, with the sunset painting the backyard with tints of pinks and purples. The constant Oklahoma wind had even stopped for the evening. Lily showed Belinda where to set the potato salad and buns on the long fabric-covered picnic table. The children played hide and seek while the adults conversed and waited for the new Henry Ford charcoal grill to heat up.

Davis watched as Charles added more whiskey to his glass, walked toward his two sons, and topped off their drinks. "I hate to admit it when I'm wrong," he began. "But I have to say how proud I am of my three adult children. Davis, I'm glad things are going well and though I'm a bit surprised, so far things have gone off without a hitch."

"To Davis," Willard said, as he raised a toast.

Lily put her arm around Belinda for just a moment, giving her a quick hug. She walked to her husband as he stood in the center of the back yard. "Dinner is served," she announced, "that is, if your father can stop talking long enough to get that meat cooked."

Willard shook Davis' hand again and said, "I didn't think you'd ever wander back this way, big brother. I thought things were too good in K.C." He looked directly into Davis' eyes. "I have to ask you, though, what's the story with you and Boston Maddux?"

The mention of Boston made Davis nervous. Rumors certainly spread quickly, he thought. He wondered just how much Willard really knew. Davis took a moment to assess his brother's demeanor before answering. "I have no idea what you mean, Willard. Probably a female issue, though I don't recall." He gave Willard a wink to ease the tension. The rest of the evening passed in comfortable conversation, and family stories were shared with spouses and Belinda.

The next Saturday evening, Davis wandered into the Broadway Saloon before meeting Belinda for dinner. As he slid onto a stool at the far end of the bar, he heard someone call his name. When Davis looked behind him, his stomach turned once, and his breath caught between his ribs.

"Boston," he said as he stood to shake hands with the six foot man in a black Stetson and tweed jacket. Davis shook his hand vigorously and pointed to the seat next to him. "I'm sure surprised to see *you*," he said.

"Really, Lee? I sort of figured you'd be expecting me by now."

"How's that?" Davis asked.

"You damned well know, Davis. Don't act like you don't."

Davis had avoided a few phone calls and even a telegram, but he had no idea Boston would show up in Oklahoma. *Shit*.

"Thought you might do the right thing here, Davis. After all we're here in your hometown, right? Hate to see word get out about your lack of ethics. That would be a real shame," he said.

Davis stood and dropped a few coins onto the riddled wood bar as he turned to leave.

"Davis," Boston said sharply. "I want those shares returned by tomorrow, or I may just have to let the Pendergasts find you. I'll beat the shit out of you and ruin your tiny home town reputation to boot."

Davis bent over Boston until their eyes locked. "They are safe and in the bank and you will have them by noon."

Boston rose to his full height, towering over Davis, "Look, scum, you were to return those certificates a month ago. Don't lie to me again."

"Never," Davis said. "I told you—I just needed to borrow them for a few weeks, Boston. That business is completed; meet me here at eleven tomorrow morning."

Davis placed his hat on his head, waved his hand for Boston to pass first and spoke again. "I have another deal for you, Boston. The loan will have been well worth it, you'll see."

"You have till noon tomorrow, Davis, or I have an appointment with the elder Mr. Lee and then the Pendergasts."

Davis stood outside in the alley and cursed. Damn. It would be impossible to retrieve the oil certificates; Clegern had had them for weeks. Plus he didn't have the cash to even buy them back. He only needed to sell one more lot and he'd be out of the woods. Now Boston was here, and Davis had run out of time.

When she opened the door and saw his pinched pale face, Belinda asked Davis what was wrong. They sat in the darkened front parlor while Davis spun his tale.

"I shouldn't have borrowed from the man; I knew he wouldn't hold to our agreement," he told her, stretching the truth. "Now he wants the stocks back that I've already paid to Clegern for the land."

"Can't you borrow them back from Clegern and repay Maddux?" she asked.

"It's a business deal, Belle. Until I sell this last lot, I'm stuck; I can't ask Clegern to return the stocks now." Davis hadn't really intended to ask Belinda, but when she offered to speak to her aunt about a loan, he couldn't have been happier.

By eleven the following morning he had a cashier's check for ten grand from Aunt Mary plus the $90,000 in his savings account from the recent land sales. It was enough to pay off old man Clegern. Davis would get back Boston's stock certificates in return. He crossed his fingers for luck and walked into their meeting.

Clegern patiently heard him out before responding. "Davis, what the hell? I thought you paid me for the land with the oil certificates. That deal is done, son."

"Well, yes, sir, that's true." Sweat was pouring down the back of his starched white shirt. He was glad he had put on a jacket, even though it was too warm for one.

Davis thought for a moment. How was he going to persuade H.W. to return the damned stock?

It had worked yesterday with Belinda; maybe it would work again.

"Mr. Clegern, sir," he said. "I think I can explain." Davis kept his story straight. A friend had loaned him the certificates to help him out. He had intended all along to buy them back when he could. The friend really needed the actual stock.

Clegern hesitated. Davis felt the man's eyes boring through him. All he could do was wait.

"I don't know, Davis," Clegern said. "Seems to me I got the better deal here. Oil has gone up in price over the past few weeks, and I just see it continuing. Why should I give it back to you?"

"Well, sir, you aren't giving it back; I'm buying it back. Right?" Davis continued to sweat; the palms of his hands could have oiled the wheels on his old man's automobile.

Clegern shook his head in disgust and slammed his fist on the large cherry-wood desk he sat behind. "God damn," he cursed under his breath.

Davis waited.

"It could easily go down in this market, sir." Davis knew he sounded like a whimpering child now.

"Tell you what, Davis. Here's the deal. I like your old man; we're friends, so I'll do this for you."

Davis felt the tension in his body easing.

"You can buy it back, but I want what it's currently worth. Figure that's about $115,000.00 by now."

Davis felt the rug pull out from under him. "But sir, I have the hundred thousand here right now."

"Sorry, Davis, that stock is worth more than when you bought the land. I want its value, and I'm doing this only because I don't want your father to be embarrassed by you again."

Davis thought quickly. "Tell you what, Mr. Clegern; I have one last lot, and it should sell any day. They're moving quickly now that the subdivision is shaping up. When that deal closes, you get the additional fifteen."

Clegern thought for a moment; then walked over to the safe in his office.

An hour later, Davis walked toward the Second Street Saloon holding a large white envelope.

Boston looked pleased when he saw what Davis was handing him. "Well, I'll be damned. I didn't think you'd do it," he said.

"I have another deal for you, Boston. I have one more lot to sell in this land deal, and I'll cut you into the profits if you loan me back a portion." He gripped Boston's right shoulder for a moment.

"How much of a profit?" Boston asked.

"A couple thou'."

"How much do you need to borrow for that amount?"

Boston asked apprehensively.

Davis couldn't believe Boston would trust him again, but he watched the change in the man's demeanor. Two grand in a short amount of time was a damned good return, and apparently Maddux thought so too.

Davis hummed a tune as he returned to the bank to deposit Boston's fifteen thousand. Maddux was on the next train back to K.C. probably licking his chops. Tomorrow he'd write a check for that same amount to Clegern and be done.

*

On the 4th of July, the town of Edmond geared up for their annual celebration. Horse drawn carriages with local dignitaries made their way down Broadway followed by the local school band, the college football team, and small children waving American flags and throwing confetti at the crowd. Belinda stood next to Davis and he had his hand around her tiny waist.

Last week, she had admitted to him that Aunt Mary had cautioned her to take her time; reminded her Davis was a lovable scoundrel who had only recently returned to his roots. Belinda had listened and nodded her head in agreement, but, she admitted that his presence made butterflies rattle around in her chest. Davis had laughed at the thought many times this past week. He liked creating butterflies inside her, and he wanted more.

As a group of small children threw candy into the air, Davis bent his mouth to her ear for a moment, and they walked away from the crowd.

"I want you to see something," he whispered. "Are you up for a short walk?"

"Davis Lee, what do you have up your sleeve?" she asked.

Davis and Belinda walked a few blocks east; then turned south toward his land. As they rounded the corner onto Fourth Street, they admired the houses under construction, commenting on the details of each. At the empty lot next to the latest build-out, Davis stopped. He reached for her hand and turned her toward him.

"Belinda Price," he said, "I want to build you a house on this land. I want to prove to you that my last three marriage proposals were serious. I'm ready to settle down."

"Oh, Davis," she said, "Are you sure?"

"So sure I'm going to let you design every inch of it."

Belinda threw her arms around his neck. "You may be sorry about that part," she said. "I have very expensive taste."

The next month was filled with meetings, builders and the city zoning office. As promised, Davis turned Belinda loose with the architect, and the drawings were soon completed.

The building began in early August. Belinda insisted they didn't need much room for the two of them. She wanted a small, one-story bungalow; nothing like Davis' parents. It would still allow them room to start a family, and that was enough.

Davis was taking a gamble financially, but his heart told him he couldn't let Belinda go. He had needed to build and sell this next house to cover his debts. Now he had fallen in love, owed Aunt Mary ten thousand, and Boston an additional fifteen. Every day he woke with a small knot in his gut. If he and Belinda moved into the house, he had to rethink the plan. On top of everything else, his old man was pleased with him for the first time in his life; he didn't want to ruin that.

Belinda designed a simple one story Craftsman set back from the street to allow a narrow easement at the front. In her mind, she had already positioned two oak trees there for both privacy and shade. Once the house was plotted and staked, Davis knew he had to have more room to the east to accommodate a driveway and garage. Even though he didn't yet own an automobile, it was part of their future plans, and few people were building homes without one.

He met with the building and zoning commissioner. Although the lot to the east was sold, the owner had held off on a build-out; he'd never know if the plot was a few feet narrower than initially promised. With the help of the assessor, they re-drew the zoning map, extending Davis' lot line east by seven feet, giving him plenty of room to place the house and the garage comfortably on the lot.

The room lay-outs were simple: entry into a wide room that would serve as both living room and parlor. Dining room just behind with two doors into the kitchen giving easy access for serving guests. Just beyond the kitchen was a miniscule bath and a small, but efficient, in-door area for the wringer washer. An exterior door led down the steps to the front of the garage.

August turned hot and muggy, but one afternoon Belinda walked Davis through the house which was now fully framed.

She led him into what would be their bedroom. A large bank of windows faced the street and two smaller ones to the east would provide sunshine and views of the gardens she had planned. The back bedroom would hopefully become a nursery in time.

"Davis," Belinda said as they walked back through the house, "let's put in a telephone niche in the dining room."

Davis smiled and nodded. "Anything you want, my love."

"We can't enclose the dining room, Belle," he said. "It will make the house seem smaller than it is."

"All taken care of." She grinned. The architect had recommended they enclose four feet on one end and three on the other, with two eye-level red brick pillars at the entry. This design formed an arch between the two areas and left both rooms feeling open and spacious.

"Your parents want to purchase a small chandelier for the dining room when they are in Europe," Belinda said. "Are you ok with whatever they pick?"

"Mother has good taste. She'd never choose anything she thought you might object to, Belle. She is quite taken by you, in case you hadn't noticed."

Belinda laughed and took his hand. "Let me show you something." She led him just past the dining room into a connecting hallway and pointed. "I've asked for a door and a stairwell up to the attic."

"What in heaven's sake for, my dear?" Davis said. "There will be nothing but rafters up there, and it will make the house cold in the winter."

"They'll put in a wood floor, of course, and windows on the front and back under the gables."

"I thought we just approved a back room addition off the mudroom, Belle? How much space do we need for heaven's sake?"

"Oh, Davis." She tilted her head and smiled.

"Don't you do that, Belinda Price. You know I can't resist you when you flirt."

"We need the back room, Davis. Now that you're a builder, you'll want an office so you can work from home."

"It needn't be so big, Belle. Look at this drawing. It's as big as the living room."

"Darling, how you exaggerate. And best of all—I can see you from the kitchen whenever I need to spy on you." Her face crinkled with laughter.

"Well, as long as you keep tempting smells coming from the kitchen all day long."

Belinda put her arms around his waist and hugged him tightly. He lifted her mouth to his.

"When do we get to inaugurate the house?" he whispered.

"I think we at least need the walls up, dear, and a few rugs." They laughed. "And yes, most certainly, a marriage certificate, Mr. Lee. I am not a loose woman, you know, even though I am building a house with you."

Davis had never been happier. After the wedding, he'd find a way to repay Aunt Mary and Boston; he'd figure it out. For the first time in his life, he simply wanted a home and a wife and a family. He wasn't getting any younger, and he knew Belinda wanted children as soon as possible. He found himself whistling through the neighborhood each day on his rounds and counted the days to the wedding, which was planned for December.

A week later, the couple sat at dinner with Charles and Lily at the Boulevard Cafe. "We leave for France next Tuesday, Davis," his mother reminded him.

Davis nodded.

"I've told Belinda, but I wanted to be the one to tell you. I've requested your builder put in a lovely wall of bookcases around your white stucco fireplace. I hope you will like them. They are quite simple; nothing like your father's office; just white wood with glass doors to go with the style of the house. Don't say no."

Davis smiled at Belinda. "So you and mother are in cahoots against me before we're even married, huh? I think that I don't stand a chance against the two of you."

Belinda scrunched her nose. "And, she didn't tell you the best. They're bringing back Persian rugs for the living and dining rooms, Davis—real Persian rugs."

Davis turned to his mother and shook his head. "Now mother ..."

"Your father bought me the biggest steamer trunk he could find for the trip." She grinned from ear to ear. "And I intend to fill it to the top before we return. Who knows when we'll be in Europe again at our age?"

With dessert, Davis ordered a fine bottle of champagne and toasted his parents. "Bon Voyage." He winked and added, "And to father returning with a little bit of money."

Everyone laughed and enjoyed the remainder of the evening.

As they left the restaurant, Davis shook hands with his father and wished him a safe trip. Charles tightened his grasp and looked him directly in the eye. "You've made me proud these last months, Davis," he said. "I hate to admit it, but I never believed you when you first told me about this sche—plan, but it seems to have worked for you. And now you've won the heart of the nicest woman you've ever brought home."

Davis looked at his feet and listened.

"I guess I'm trying to say I'm proud of you, son." As Davis looked up, his father opened his arms and held him for a short moment.

"Thanks dad. Have a great trip." Davis felt a lump in his throat. If his dad knew the truth; he wouldn't be so proud.

*

By November, the house was looking solid and complete. The wood floors and the bathroom fixtures were scheduled for the end of the week. Things had gone smoothly with the building, and each day Belinda and Davis walked through the still forming house, watching it grow as one would a baby. Lily made good on her promise and the chandelier arrived by freight shortly after their return from Europe. The oriental rugs were rolled against the wall in the dining room which was awaiting finishing touches. Lily's steamer trunk was delivered to their house full of lace edged tablecloths and beautiful hand blown glass figurines from Venice, French antiquities from Paris, silk bed linens, and small framed oil paintings from Rome and Tuscany.

Davis watched as Belinda oohed and ahhed over each and every item; then pulled the heavy trunk up to the attic, huffing loudly just to make her laugh. "For our own trip in a few years, mother said."

He watched Belinda clap her hands like a small child, and he grinned with pride. God, how he loved to make her smile.

The wedding was planned for December eighth, and hopefully the completion of the house would correspond with their return from a honeymoon in New Orleans. Aunt Mary had been asked to give the bride away. She had laughed at the idea of an old lady with a cane walking her lovely niece down the aisle, but Davis had used his charms to persuade her.

"We'll decorate it with ribbons and roses, and you'll be right in style," he said.

Even with all the final building details and choosing furnishings and draperies, Belinda and Lily managed to plan a small family wedding to be held in the Methodist Church just a block from Davis' childhood home. Every day Davis walked through the house and saw Belinda in each detail. He had given in to every request, no matter the cost. This would be their home now.

Davis had put aside any thoughts of returning to Kansas City, and Belinda had no ties in Chicago. They would settle in close to family and raise one of their own. He couldn't wait to watch her walk down the aisle toward him.

Lily hosted an engagement party for the couple in early November. Belinda arrived early with Aunt Mary to help with last minute preparations, but she was quickly shooed out of the way by Elizabeth and Lily. She wandered back from the kitchen to the parlor where Davis, Willard and Charles stood sipping brandy in front of the fireplace which had been stoked to take the chill off the front rooms.

"There she is." Davis walked quickly to her side and pulled her into his arms. "My beautiful fiancée," he turned her toward the men, and she threw back her head in laughter and curtsied.

Aunt Mary followed Lily into the room and rested her hand on Charles' elbow. She whispered, "Could I have a moment?"

Willard took the old woman's arm and escorted her to a seat by the fire, and Belinda took the settee next to her. She patted Belinda's hand and motioned for Davis to come nearer.

"Davis," she said, "As you know, I had my reservations at first, but I've grown to love you as one of my own."

Davis took her hand. "I promise to take good care of her, Aunt Mary. I do."

"I believe that now, my boy," she said. "So I'd like you to keep the money I loaned you as a wedding gift. Can't start off a marriage in debt, you know?"

Davis stood speechless for possibly the first time in his life. It seemed that things were working out. They had to. He would do anything to prevent being caught in this scam—his father had been anticipating ever since he returned. All he could do was wait.

*

Thanksgiving Day started off cold and dreary. By ten o'clock the rain started, and within a half hour the temperature dropped and ice grew thick on the roads. Davis helped Lily in the kitchen while his father spent the morning holed up in his office. His mother had spent the past day and a half in the kitchen, preparing and baking. Elizabeth would bring several items. Willard's wife would most likely bring pies even though Davis had heard Lily specifically tell him not to worry with food. "Just drive carefully," she had admonished.

Soon the house was filled with the smells of Thanksgiving. The turkey roasted slowly; Lily asked Davis to chop onions and celery for the dressing. At eleven, Charles peeked into the kitchen and offered to assist. He heeded Lily's nonstop directions about wine and water and silverware. "Better get a move on if we're going to eat at two," Davis joked with his father.

"Be glad I'm even helping." Charles gave a grim nod. "Your brother will be late anyway—no rush."

Just before noon, the door bell rang.

"My heavens, I hope that isn't Willard and his gang already," Lily said. "I'll never get this meal finished."

Davis went to the front door and swung it open, half expecting to be pummeled by Willard's twin five-year-olds.

He was surprised to find Aunt Mary on the porch. She was accompanied by an older man he didn't recognize.

"Aunt Mary?" Davis said. His look was quizzical but welcoming. "Come on in."

Davis noticed Mary's colorless face. As she folded in on

herself, he and the other gentleman grabbed her just before she crumpled. They helped her into the living room and onto the nearest seat.

"Mary, are you ok?" he asked. "Mother, come quickly," he called loudly.

Lily and Charles reached the parlor together and raced to Davis' side.

Tears streamed down Mary's face now, and Davis reached into his breast pocket for a linen handkerchief. He looked up into his mother's questioning eyes.

"May I get you some water, Mary?" Lily asked.

Mary's tears turned to sobs and Davis knew something was very wrong. "Where is Belinda?" he asked carefully. "Isn't she with you?"

As the words began to flow from the old woman's lips, Davis faded into another space. He couldn't take in the news. It had no base of reality for him.

Belinda—dead—were the only two words he heard leaving Mary's lips. The rest of the story would filter into his consciousness in small bits over the next few days.

Around 10:30 Thanksgiving morning, Belinda had called to her aunt from the lower step. "Aunt Mary … the pumpkin pies are done, but I forgot to buy cream yesterday. I have to finish them before we head over to the Lees."

Mary called from the landing above. "Oh, darling," she said. "No one will care. Please don't go out in this ice storm."

"You can't have pumpkin pie without whipped cream, Aunt Mary. It's just to the corner and back." She grabbed her scarf and an umbrella. The blustery rain was icing quickly. She scurried up the street, her boots crunching the slush.

As she left Thompson's grocery, she tucked her head into her chest and began to walk quickly toward the house. She had one small package in one arm and her umbrella in the other. The sidewalk had turned to a sheet of ice; the two-lane street remained slush. She decided to take the lesser of two evils.

As Belinda stepped from the curb, she lost her footing. Things began to move in slow motion. She threw the paper bag with the cream onto the street and tried to stop her fall with that hand. At the very last minute, Belinda saw the driver's face, white with terror. The brakes only caused the car to go into a spin that the driver could not stop in time.

She was dead on impact. And as Mary finished the story Davis died as well.

On Christmas Day, Davis stood inside the living room of their home. The brass numbers 311 had been recently attached to the side of the front door just below the coach light. He had left the front door wide open and a cold wind came blowing through the rooms as he walked first through the bedroom, then back through the dining room. He closed the glass paneled door to the kitchen behind him, opened the folding doors to the back office she had planned for him; then retraced his steps. He admired the lovely blue and gold Persian rugs his mother had chosen for them as their wedding gift, the small, simple brass and glass chandelier she'd had shipped all the way from Paris. His heart had stopped beating weeks before. He wasn't sure it would beat again.

A For Sale sign stood in the median between the small but flourishing oaks. His new car stood in the split drive-way near the sidewalk. The white wood swing he had bought as a wedding present for Belinda hung on the end of the large front porch.

He had pulled off the scam remarkably well though he wished he'd been found out. Sitting out the rest of his life in jail might be preferable to this. He had nothing to live for. His children would not be birthed and rocked in the back bedroom. A daughter would not play in the attic playroom closet. A son would never climb out onto the slanted roof and jump to the grass below.

Someone else's dreams would fill the house. Someone else's

books would line the lovely bookshelves. Another couple would sit before the warmth of the fireplace and look out the perfectly placed windows onto the front flowerbeds. He would return to Kansas City as soon as the house sold with Boston's loan money in hand. His debts would be paid.

*

The house on Fourth Street sold in January to a young couple from Stillwater. They moved in with their two-year-old son and gave birth to a little girl in the front bedroom in April. The sun shone brightly each morning through the east windows overlooking the crepe myrtle and fell gently each night through the windows of the living room to the west. The house was warm and comforting and held wonderful smells from the kitchen oven. And the young wife spoke gently to her husband who sat in the back room office, and the third baby arrived the next year.

*

When Charles died three years later at the age of sixty, Davis made excuses to his mother; then asked Willard to take Lily to Dallas to care for her. Elizabeth sold the family home on First Street and all of its furnishings and divided the proceeds evenly. It was 1926, and Edmond was once again flourishing. Clegern had sold all his land. The University was doing well. Davis would never return to Edmond.

Chapter 5
Another Trip to Oklahoma

On July 1ˢᵗ, Karen answered the phone and heard Vickey Smith's voice on the other end. She had a full price offer. How quickly could Karen close?

She read over the documents, signed the contract and faxed them back the same day.

"Can you come for the closing?" Vickey said. "We can do it by fax and email, but it would be easier if you were here; I'll be honest."

She agreed to come as soon as Vickey had the closing date.

On the 29th, Karen landed at Will Rogers International Airport and picked up a rental car for the drive north to Edmond. The closing went smoothly, keys were handed off, and Vickey asked if she'd like to see the house one last time. She was surprised to find herself saying "yes" to the offer.

Vickey waited in the car while she let herself into the bungalow. As she walked from room to room, she felt the ghosts of the families she'd recently come to know. She could almost visualize Davis and Belinda bent over blue prints planning each stage of their new house—this house. She'd finished Davis' sad story just last week. Such a scoundrel, and yet Davis had loved his fiancée so much. It made her sad to think about him never getting to live in the home he'd built with the woman he loved.

In the rear bedroom, she stared out the window onto the backyard. She remembered a swing set where the wood deck now stood, just left of the concrete stoop and two stairs. It had been painted fire engine red; she was certain. Goose bumps rose on her arms and she trembled. It wasn't a vague sensation now; it was a memory. She had lived in this room with her parents, Angela and Richard, university professors, loving parents. Had they truly wanted her? Had her mother really wanted a child or was this forced upon her? Why had they agreed to take her? All the questions she'd had time to ask now had no chance of being answered.

As she did so often these days, she considered her own marriage. She had known before she married Gary that she did not want kids. Was it because of her adoption? She hadn't thought so at the time. But she had to admit, she was beginning to question a lot of things. She had known Gary wanted a family; had almost canceled the wedding over the issue. She shook her head. Too late for those doubts. As she locked the front door she said good-bye to the house on 4th Street one last time. She'd go home and put the trunk in the attic where it belonged. It was too late for answers now.

After Vickey dropped her at her motel room, she ordered room service and pulled Davis' diary from her overnight bag. She propped herself on pillows against the headboard of the bed and turned once again to the final pages.

In bold block lettering she read:

I don't know how to live without Belinda. How dare you, God? How dare you do this? Today should have found me on my honeymoon with the most kind and loving woman on earth. Instead, I placed a for sale sign in the front yard. I will return to Kansas City within the month.

She sighed. The intensity of his love was almost tangible. Had she and Gary ever had that kind of love—that passion?

Tomorrow, she would stop by the museum. She had found nothing but property records for the two families who owned the house between 1922 and 1936, the year Maxine and Robert Watson had purchased it.

She had stayed out of the sunroom for nearly a week; but a

few days ago, the trunk had called to her from across the room. When she lifted the heavy lid, something sparkled beneath some baby items. What caught her eye was the metal locking clasp of a once-white leatherette diary. The leather was creased and broken, and the journal was unlocked. Inside, she found missing pages right away, but the contents belonged to a woman named Maxine—a woman with a secret.

The first entry was dated 1945. Karen couldn't put the book down for hours. She had phoned the historical museum that afternoon to ask about the woman's identity, and just yesterday, Hazel had called to say she'd found a few letters that might shed some light.

When Karen opened the door to the historical society the next morning, Hazel was waiting in her office just down the hall. She rose quickly and gave Karen a hug. "Miss your visits," she said. "You've been working very hard on this research, haven't you, dear?"

"I can't seem to get it out of my mind, even when I try. I'm busy going through my parents' house, and yet I continually find myself spending more and more time in the past."

"I don't have to tell you that I understand. You know where *I* work." Hazel chuckled.

"So what's in these letters you say you've found?" Karen said.

"Some pretty interesting stuff. I think you'll agree. But take them home and take your time, dear."

Karen gave Hazel a warm hug as she said good-bye. "Please stay in touch." Her voice quivered.

"I will, my dear. Keep me up to date on what you're finding, ok?"

Karen nodded. She hated that this might be their last visit in person. On the way to the car she stumbled over a broken piece of curbing and hit her big toe hard on the edge of the cement. It made her cry, but not from the pain of the toe. *We'll stay in touch*, she told herself.

She phoned Gary a few hours later to tell him she'd be back by nightfall

"Figured I'd hear you were staying awhile," he said. "When you get back, Karen, we need to talk."

She wanted to ask *what about?* But she knew the answer; so instead, she repeated her flight information and hung up.

As she drove home from the Denver airport later that evening, she considered turning around. She was tired. Tired from living in the past; tired of missing her mother; tired of learning about people she'd never known. She was suddenly unsure why she was spending so much time on things that didn't pertain to her. *Gary is right,* she thought, *I do busy myself to avoid.* Maybe this whole project had just been a way to fill her mother's absence.

She loved history—taught history—but the obsession she was experiencing with the items in the trunk was not normal; even she had to admit that. It was as if she couldn't stop; as if she knew something more was coming; yet she'd found nothing of her mother's in the trunk to suggest that.

She was also surprised at this sudden desire to know her past. It had never seemed important before. Why would she now, at age thirty-nine, even care? The idea of not having a parent had hit her hard. She wanted to know about her biological mother, and she wished she'd asked Angela while she was still alive.

As for her real father, it was obvious he hadn't cared to ever find her; why would she want to begin searching for him? And who said she even wanted to search for him? She pulled into the drive and put her head on the steering wheel, trying to clear her thoughts. She had no idea where this spiral was taking her. She was suddenly exhausted.

She walked stiffly from the garage into the back hallway and followed the lit lamps toward the rear of the house.

Gary was waiting in the living room, sitting rigid in a chair he never sat in. She put down her bag and settled herself onto the floral sofa. He wasted no time.

"I'm moving out, Karen." His voice was flat and matter of fact.

She found herself standing before he could say another word.

"No ... no, I won't hear this." She ran from the room, and Gary followed.

"Karen, look at me. You aren't happy; you haven't been happy in years. Neither of us has."

"I know that, Gary, but why now? Is there someone else?" She couldn't stop the words from flying from her mouth.

"There's no one else, Karen. Let's be rational."

"I don't want to be rational right now," she said. "I'm tired. I need some rest. I can't do this with you right now." She headed toward the stairs. A few moments later, in front of the bathroom mirror, Karen faced herself head-on.

"You've wanted this yourself, so why are you acting like you don't?" she whispered. As much as she hated to admit it, she'd wanted to be the one to confront the situation—to be the one to blame and shame his long hours at work, his inattentiveness to their marriage, his weekend golf outings. She wanted to be the one to say all that and see him squirm. He'd beaten her to the punch, and she didn't like it, not one bit.

"Are we going to talk about this?" Gary was standing just behind her. She wasn't sure how long he'd been there.

"I have every reason to want out, Gary," she said. "But how the hell do you have the balls to stand there and ask for this?" She watched his face mirrored beside hers.

"*You* have every reason? What do you mean, Karen? I work hard to give us the best money can buy. I understand when you're at school three and four nights a week with activities. I put up with your nose stuck in a book nine months out of the year. I even tolerate your moodiness in the summers when you don't have the distraction of work."

He threw up his hands and bounded through the bedroom.

She could hear his heaviness on each step and heard the back door slam behind him.

She sat on the end of the bed and stared out the window, wishing for darkness. Summer dusk hung for hours before the sun set at ten.

He's the one who's never home, she told herself. He's at that firm ten hours a day. How could we have had kids with his busy career, his need to be at constant meetings, to be at the club rubbing elbows to keep the firm going. Deep down, she knew that wasn't the whole story; might not even be true. She was furious that he'd brought this up right now. She was trying to sell two houses, grieve her mother's death, and the trunk ....

The stupid trunk. Why had she ever brought it into this house? It was just one more thing interfering with her time, and it felt like the final wedge between them. Well, fine, he could have a divorce, but it was going to cost him dearly.

She went downstairs and sat in the darkening sunroom. She picked up file folders, photographs, and books; then threw them into the trunk and slammed the lid. Kicking it would feel good, but instead she stood in the center of the room and let go.

"Mother, where are you when I need you?" she cried out. "Why didn't you clean out the damned house before you went?" A rage had taken over her body, and tears and snot soaked the front of her shirt. *Why didn't you try harder to live?*

She was still there when she woke the next morning. Her body was crumpled into the corner of the sofa, her head tilted sideways onto an arm of the couch. Her neck would be cricked for days. She picked up the wads of Kleenex from the floor and walked toward the stairway, stretching her back and neck and feeling a sudden need for food and a hot shower.

Twenty minutes later, she wrapped herself in a towel and pulled her wet hair into a pony tail. As soon as she entered the bedroom, she realized something was amiss. She walked through the open door of the walk-in closet and found empty hangers on the floor and their largest suitcase missing from the far corner.

Karen felt as empty as Gary's clothes rod.

An hour later, she was pacing the floor; her cell phone tucked between her shoulder and chin. She gathered the final few items strewn along the floor and placed them into the trunk. She was done with the damned thing.

"I have to admit; the empty closet surprised me, Denise. In the past he's taken an overnight bag at most. This feels different."

"Are you all right? Do you need me to come over?" Denise said.

"No, I guess I was more prepared for this than I thought. I suppose it's been coming for some time." She hesitated before finding the courage to say it out loud. "I think I'm mostly pissed that he upstaged me. I wanted to be the one to walk out, you know?"

"I know," Denise said, "ego and all that. We're never really ready for loss though, no matter how much warning we have. You call if you need anything, ok?"

Karen agreed, and they set a time and place for lunch later in the week.

She busied herself for the remainder of the day. Late that afternoon, she once again found herself with Maxine's diary open in her lap. Beside her were the letters Hazel had located—letters written between Maxine and her husband, Robert, a World War II pilot. She slid the rubber band from the bundle of letters. As a history teacher she was anxious to read his accounts of the war. She would follow Maxine's dated journal entries at the same time. As she thumbed through the pages, a crumpled piece of stationary fell onto the sofa—a letter dated November, 1944. "Dear Maxine, good news ..."

Just then the phone in the kitchen startled her back to the present. Gary was calling to tell her where he was staying. They were cordial and civil on the phone. They just needed some time apart, she told herself. He'd be back soon.

As she settled back onto the couch, she thought about Lily and Belinda and Maxine. Women like me, she thought. Searching, surviving, and finding themselves.

Chapter 6
November 1, 1944

Earlier this morning, and just weeks after his twenty-fifth mission, Bob Watson was issued the required discharge papers; they read February 1, 1945—three months from today. He had been sent to Polebrooks, England as part of the 95th Bombardment group in June of '41, five months following America's entrance into World War II. By the following February, he was a member of the 8th Air Force in France. Now, nearly three years later, Bob stood in the barracks and re-read the brief lines of the typed document. A mixture of anticipation and hesitancy filled him. Bob reached for the small silver frame he kept in his locker. He touched the face of each of his three children as they smiled up at him.

His last furlough had been in the winter of 1942, two years ago this Christmas. Tommy, at age five, had been old enough to remember him and to once again miss him when he left. Jeffrey, not quite three, barely knew his dad outside the picture frame on the fireplace mantel. Amy had been conceived shortly before he returned to England. He knew her only through pictures.

The boys were now seven and five, and the photos his wife Maxine sent every few months confirmed their physical changes and their new talents. A recent one showed the boys all decked out in their homemade Halloween costumes, Tommy a black cat and Jeffrey, a ghost. Tommy stood beside his big boy bike, training wheels now removed. Jeff's new bike with trainers appeared shiny red even in the black and white photograph.

Tears welled in his eyes, and he blinked them away.

Bob turned back to the letter he was writing to Maxine. He would be home for good just before their tenth wedding anniversary, and he planned to surprise her with a trip to Dallas where they had honeymooned.

"Dear Maxine," it read, "Good news. I'm being discharged on February 1st. Should arrive in OK City on the 3rd. Can your parents watch the kids that next weekend? I'm taking you away for our anniversary. It isn't Hawaii, honey but I think you'll like it. Hug Amy and the boys and read them a story for me. I look old and haggard, nothing like the guy in the photo on the mantel. I'm afraid the kids won't know who I am. One of my buddies has offered to take a picture soon, and I'll try to send it in a few weeks. Film is hard to come by, but Lewis has a camera so we'll try. I love you. I know how hard the past three years have been for you. All my love, Bob."

Bob licked the three-cent stamp and pressed it on the sealed envelope. In his mind he added another note. *And it's been rough on me too. I will never be able to tell you what I've seen over here. I just pray that the nightmares stop when I get back to you and to our bed. Maybe the warmth of your body will take them from me.*

The nightmares had worsened the past few months, though they'd started from the moment he reached France. Each bombing, every loss of a friend, and every midnight raid absorbed into muscle. The memories came to life late at night, not long after taps and he hadn't slept well in weeks. Each time he closed his eyes, the movie reel whirred and the images played on the screen of his mind.

The 8th AF was activated in January of 1942, and a month later Bob and his B17 with the name Betty Lou inscribed on its side began flying missions into France. Everything he and the other pilots knew by then had been learned by experience and experiment, every mission a learning exercise.

Each of the four squadrons was made up of eight to twelve

bombers. Each bomber held a ten-man crew, and Bob realized quickly that he was now in charge of ten boys, young men in their early 20's with little experience. Most of them had never set foot in a plane.

Frostbite, trauma and terror were what awaited them. The thin, freezing air from the altitudes they were flying was something Bob had never experienced. The cold killed, and the air was un-breathable.

There was intermittent activity followed by weeks of stressful boredom. The men released their tension with card games, drinking, fighting and an occasional leave where they sought out the local English women for warmth, decent food and comfort. Bob waited for night missions that didn't come.

Finally, on October 9, the call came. The four engine heavies, the heart of the 8ᵗʰ's bomber force, headed out for the first time and at high altitude. The town of Lille served as the French steel and rail center that fed Hitler's war machine. After months of training they were filled with the desire for combat, but the gunners were not prepared for what they met in the skies. It was the 8ᵗʰ's first real brawl.

At 3:30 Bob's crew lifted off. Cloud cover helped them along and they successfully rained down bombs that put the center below them out of commission. But on the return, all hell broke loose.

Bob first felt—then saw—the horrendous fiery explosion just ahead of him. He watched in horror as he saw the escape hatch of the lead plane open and a young man begin his jump. Suddenly the right shoulder strap of the young soldier's parachute caught on the handle, and he hung outside the bomber with the inboard propeller inches from his head.

Focus, Bob yelled to himself. *You aren't hit; focus on your own men.* But he could not take his eyes off the movie playing out before him. There was nothing but twenty thousand feet of air between the soldier and the ground. "Jesus," Bob yelled, out loud this time. He pulled his own plane steady, pushed the engine hard; he had to get his men out of there—now.

Then the unimaginable happened. He watched as another soldier pulled the young man's strap free, and the two parachuted out together, followed by the rest of the crew. Bob watched as the pilot, his best friend in the squadron, wasted precious seconds as he struggled to keep his bomber in the air.

"Put it on auto pilot," he whispered. "Get the hell out, Lewis." The seconds stretched as he watched and waited. Nothing. He prayed silently. *Jump,* he was screaming inside.

The bomb bay door had been left open. Where the hell was he? Why was he trying to be a God-damned hero? The plane was nearly out of sight, falling quickly, when Bob spotted him. With seconds remaining before he would be too low to jump, Lewis stepped into the doorway, pulled his cord and released his parachute. With any luck, ground troops would find them quickly. That's all he could hope for now. Bob radioed the remaining two planes. "Veer right and head to base."

Bob gave a sigh of relief and radioed his instructions to the bomb bay. "Veering from formation," Bob announced. "Bombardier—drop your load; I need lift."

The British spit fires hovered around him and the remaining bombers, drawing fire from the German Messerschmitts and returning tremendous blows to the enemy. Bob pulled to the right, easing out of formation. The planes ahead of him and to his left were taking a beating. Just as he eased away from the group, one shell after another shook his B17. Bob felt the strikes six inches below his feet on the length of the bomb bay door. "God damn," he said. He turned to his co-pilot. "Let's get the hell out of here."

Later he would count the thirty punctuation marks along the side of the plane. He limped back to base that day without casualties but with a metallic taste of fear in his mouth. A taste that, even after twenty-five missions, would not go away.

During each mission, Bob held the lives of his crew in his hands. He flew the Betty Lou with precision as they approached each target area. From their bases in England, the bombers of the 97ᵗʰ hit railroad marshalling yards near Rouen in Northwest France and oil targets in Leipzig and Brux.

And soon he would be heading home to try to forget it all.

*

November 24, 1944

Maxine Watson pulled the heavy velvet drape to the side of the window and drew a heart in the light glaze of frost; then wiped it away with a long sweep of her hand. Outside, the oak trees appeared black against the gray November sky and the patches of dirty brown snow.

"Mama, Mama," a small voice called from the back bedroom. Maxine pulled herself from the worn brown corduroy rocker and strode across the living room, through the dining room and down the short hall. As she entered the back bedroom, she glanced out the rear window at the bare pecan trees that hung over their garage from the neighbors' yard. Yesterday, she had promised herself to pick up the pecans from the ground and shell them for Thanksgiving pies.

"Hey, munchkin," she said as she lifted fifteen-month-old Amy from the crib. "You're starting to outgrow this crib, aren't you?" she cooed. She had told Bob in her last letter that she had to have a bit of money to purchase a bed for Amy, but his return letter was either lost in the mail or delayed. Who knew what happened between his army base in Europe and their home at 311 E. Fourth Street, Edmond, Oklahoma. She would often get no word for weeks and suddenly receive five letters in a day. Maxine hated those long stretches of silence. During the night she saw body bags and planes falling from the sky, and during the day she'd suddenly feel tears streaming down her cheeks and realize she was waiting for that dreaded uniformed stranger to knock at the door with news she couldn't bear to hear.

She didn't know where she'd put a bed anyway. The two boys slept together in a full size bed at the back of the room. The crib was squeezed along the inside wall to protect the toddler from the cold draft that always seeped through the east windows, especially when the wind howled as it did today.

"Let's get you changed and find those brothers of yours," she said.

A few minutes later Maxine set Amy on the floor in the kitchen and handed her a large metal mixing bowl and a set of measuring spoons to keep her occupied. Tommy and Jeffrey scampered around in the large room just behind the kitchen, off the narrow laundry area. The previous owners had used it as an office, but it had now become an all-purpose room for three small children under the age of six. Just after Christmas, she had told the boys they could move their toys from their cramped bedroom to the back, so that Amy could nap without their constant noise. It was cold back there; there were windows on all three walls, and the heat from the old furnace in the basement just couldn't stretch that far.

"That's mine," Tommy screeched, and Maxine heard Jeffrey, the six year old, thump to the floor, followed by a howl and then sobbing. She knew Tommy had once again plowed poor Jeffrey to the ground. Tommy was only fifteen months older than his brother but two sizes larger already. They were so close in age; he couldn't understand that he actually hurt Jeffrey when they fought.

She hadn't reached the doorway before both boys were wrapped around each leg, tears streaming and denying that either had caused the row. "I guess you'll both get to spend time alone for awhile," Maxine said. "Tommy, you go to my bedroom and Jeffrey to your own. Fifteen minutes," she added.

"It's not *your* room," Tommy said in defiance. He had

inherited his father's temperament, and having lived with Bob for ten years, she knew that Tommy was going to try to win every battle. "It's *dad's* room," he said, his face flushed red with anger.

"Fine," Maxine said as she bent down to his face, "then go to your dad's room *now*."

Once the boys were settled and quietly looking at their favorite picture books, Maxine placed her grandmother's wedding-pattern quilt on the living room floor, and Amy crawled onto it, stuck her thumb in her mouth and nodded off.

Maxine slumped into the rocker and watched her sleeping blond-haired toddler. Amy looked so much like Robert, more than either of the boys. It made her smile and she walked over to the wall-length mantel above the glass faced bookshelves that she loved so much. She traced each framed photograph with her index finger. There they were on their wedding day. Robert towered over her by a foot. His 6'2" body was surprisingly thin in his army uniform. She barely remembered the depth of those aquamarine eyes as he smiled down at his new bride. Had she really felt that happy, that proud? Her pale ivory wedding suit set off her dark hair and eyes. Maxine sighed deeply. *How young we looked*, she thought as her mind wandered into memories.

*

She had met Bob, a Lieutenant in the Army Air Corp, in Oklahoma City in the winter of 1934. Their nights were filled with dancing and drinking at the Tinker AF Officer's Club. The world was fine, and life was just beginning. They were twenty-three; as handsome and as beautiful as either would ever be.

One night after they'd danced the jitterbug until dawn, Bob said, "Let's go, babe."

"Go where?" she asked.

"Let's get married."

Maxine had feigned innocence and said, "Mr. Watson, I am

way too young for marriage, thank you." But he pulled her into his arms and lifted her high, then slid her slowly down until their lips met.

They'd known each other just five months, and Maxine at first thought he was teasing, maybe hoping she'd sleep with him. She went home that night assuming the five whiskeys had loosened his tongue, and she didn't say a word to any of the girls before undressing for bed.

Maxine bunked with three other young women in a postage stamp apartment in town, across from the library and down the street from the IGA where she worked day shifts making thirty-five cents an hour.

"You dead on your feet?" asked Wanda when Maxine tip-toed in. Wanda was the only roommate Maxine had warmed up to. They had met at the YWCA where both had taken rooms until they could locate a place of their own. Maxine hadn't wanted to invite the others, but Wanda had reminded her that their grocery store paychecks wouldn't stretch far. So the four women had moved into Mrs. Bridge's large, brown brick two-story. The Depression had forced the older woman to turn it into a two-bedroom apartment plus the suite that remained her own.

The next day Bob had shown up with a tiny white box, and in front of Wanda, Beth and Lois, he got down on one knee and opened it, slipping a gold band with a small diamond chip onto her finger before she could do anything but accept.

*

Maxine folded Bob's letter and placed it on the desk in the living room. It had slid through the metal mail slot onto the wood floor around one o'clock, but she had left it sealed on the desktop as a gift to be opened later. She had waited until all three children were napping and the house was quiet.

Looking out the front window, she watched the squirrels scamper along the bare oak branches and race down the large trunks where they sat cracking open the nuts they had stored in the fall. She loved the two oak trees in the easement out front. They had been there at least twenty years already, and she hoped the boys would be climbing them for the next ten. Tommy could already shinny up the trunk to the lowest branch. Jeffrey frowned and his lower lip quivered as he watched his brother climbing higher than he could go. He cried the day Maxine removed the training wheels from Tommy's bike. He watched his brother fly down the sidewalk toward Boulevard Street as he fell further and further behind, pumping as hard as he could, doing his best to keep up. That's the way it will be, she thought, for the rest of their lives …Tommy moving on, trying things first, reaching life milestones before his brother. Amy had come along three years later, too young to ever compete.

Our tenth anniversary. I wonder if that will even happen once he hears. She absentmindedly rubbed her belly. She was barely five weeks pregnant and would be three months along when Bob returned.

The baby, she thought: the baby Bob knew nothing about. Now he was coming home, and the secret would be revealed— revealed and explained and prayed over and hopefully reconciled between them … if that was even possible. How do you tell your husband you became pregnant with his best friend's child while he was off protecting his country? Do you wait until he walks off the train? Do you write him the news so he's prepared? She knew she had to tell him in person. What was another ten weeks? She would soon know how strong their marriage was and if he loved her enough to stay.

Tears stained her face as she wondered what her future held. Her child; Jim's child. Would Bob allow it to be his child as well? She hadn't had contact with Jim since early November. Their last argument had been over her refusal to divorce Bob and marry him. Maxine picked up the phone, waited for the dial tone, and slowly rotated the finger wheel to A - D - 2 . . . she hesitated as the disk swung back to center, then quickly dialed the 7. Her heart lurched when Jim picked up on the third ring.

"Jim," she said, so softly she wasn't certain he heard her. "I have to talk to you."

Jim's deep voice responded immediately. "Is something wrong? Is it the baby?"

"No, no, everything's fine. Bob's coming home for good. He'll be discharged in February."

The silence stretched to breaking. Maxine started to cry and considered hanging up.

"I see," he said finally. "And your plan is to … do what?" His tone shifted to anger and frustration. "Shit, Maxine, do you not realize I'm half of this … this … problem?" He drew a deep breath before he continued. "So you haven't told him?"

"No, it didn't seem right to do it in a letter."

"Maxine," Jim said. "It's like a bandage. Just grab the edge and rip it quickly. He'll be less hurt; if there is a less."

Maxine cringed. "I have to tell him, you know?" Maxine said before hanging up the phone, "about *us*."

"I know. I'll deal with it. I've lost a best friend, but I lost him a year ago when I fell in love with you," Jim said. "Do what you have to do."

That night she lay in the darkness listening to the trains rumbling through the city. Maxine couldn't shut down her thoughts. Jim's voice had been so cold; it chilled her to think that he might hate her. She could no longer accept the very love that she wanted so badly not to lose. Yet, she wanted him to want her, wanted him to plead with her again to leave her marriage and make the farm her home. The boys might have loved the old ranch that had been in Jim's family for three generations. The farm sat on the northern edge of town and produced wheat and cattle, both badly needed commodities during war. It had also provided Jim with a II-C exemption when every other able-bodied male had been 'scripted.

Though neither man would admit it, she knew Jim's deferment had come between the two men, even before Bob shipped out in '42. Jim had felt equally betrayed when Bob failed to correspond during the next three years. Their high school bond of football and later, partying and girls, simply ended. Their only remaining connection had been Maxine. Just before he left for England, Bob asked Jim to take care of Maxine and the boys, especially if he didn't make it back home. Jim kept his promise, making weekly Sunday check-in visits.

In the darkness, she smiled for the first time in weeks. This past March an unusually late ice storm had hit quickly on a Saturday afternoon. Power lines, as well as phone, hung limply to the ground under the weight of the ice. Maxine had made a large pallet on the kitchen floor in front of the gas range. The boys were ecstatic about sleeping in jammies, coats and mittens inside their sleeping bags. To them it was a camp-out. Oh, to be a child again, she thought.

She was in the kitchen the following morning when the doorbell rang, followed by a dampened knock. As she walked through the living room, she spotted Jim peeking around the corner into one of the large front windows.

He could have been her brother; they were so similar in height and coloring. His dark eyes glittered in the frosty daylight as he waved at her through the glass, a broad grin spreading across his handsome face.

"Get in here," Maxine said when she opened the door. "Not that you'll be any warmer than you are out there."

Jim laughed and held up a brown grocery bag filled to overflowing. "Treats," he said. "I'd take off my coat, but it must be 40 degrees in here. I just heard in the store that power should be back on by this afternoon though."

They spent the next few hours gathered around the warmth of the open oven door. Jim rigged coat hangers into prongs for marshmallows. They wouldn't brown, but they were hot enough to melt the chocolate squares onto the graham crackers he'd brought them.

"Chocolate," the boys exclaimed.

"Jim, where did you find chocolate and how much did you have to pay?" Maxine asked. The government had rationed anything not deemed a necessity for several years. The boys hugged him enthusiastically, pulling her into Jim's arms as well, with a loud round of 'thank you's.'

After she encouraged the boys to bundle up and go to the back playroom, Maxine held Amy on her lap and sat on the floor next to Jim as he leaned back against the lower cupboards. Amy fell asleep a short time later, and the conversation progressed from weather to farm news to deeper issues. He rarely talked about his decision to accept a II-C status; had never shared what it felt like to be one of the few men under sixty in the small town.

"When I walk into Johnson's feed store each Saturday, I feel the eyes on me and the question marks behind them. I don't have a limp or an eye patch so of course I look like an able-bodied man who should be fighting for his country."

"I had no idea what a stigma that was for you," she said.

"Well, taking care of you and the kids has sort of made up for it," Jim said. "Gives me a purpose, besides growing beef for the troops." He grinned sheepishly.

"It must have been a hard decision to accept the deferment," she said.

He nodded. "I won't lie. There have been days when I wanted to walk into the recruiting office and sign the papers. And just as many when I've been glad to be here instead."

"What would you have done if your father had still been living?"

"I'd be in that damned foxhole, Maxine." He looked away from her and she thought she saw a glimmer of wetness in his eyes.

After a moment, she took his hand in hers. "Well, I, for one, am glad you're here. What you provide is important, Jim. Beef and grain for the troops are as important as standing beside them in battle."

He shook his head to the negative. "Thanks," he said, "but not sure that's true."

At three o'clock, every light in the house popped on at once, and the boys yelped with delight.

Maxine laughed. "Well, obviously we had the house well lit when the storm rolled in. Stay for dinner," she added. "You never do; please stay this time."

Jim accepted quickly and pulled a few more items from his grocery bag. Together they created a meal of hot dogs in buns, pickles, canned green beans and pears. Maxine poured out the now lukewarm milk and opened a can of apple juice. She laughed. "Guess the fridge needed cleaning anyway."

Jim and Maxine side-stepped in the small kitchen; bumping into each other from time to time. The ice storm created a warmth between them, a comfort and ease with each other they hadn't recognized before. Jim read a book to the boys while Maxine dressed Amy for bed.

"Thanks, Uncle Jim," Jeffrey said, looking up from his pillow. He and Tommy could have been twins; they also could have been Jim's with their muddy brown eyes and dark skin. Once the kids were asleep, he and Maxine settled into the living room, close to the wood floor vents where the hot air from the furnace rose to warm them. Jim turned the knob of the upright wood radio a few times until he found a local station clear enough to hear a Frank Sinatra tune crooning at them.

He sat on the sofa beside Maxine, pulled a small bottle of Jim Beam from his back pocket, and poured a healthy amount into the two cups of coffee she had brewed for them. Jim raised his cup in the air and clicked the rim to hers. "To heat," he said.

She nodded. "To heat!"

And to heat it had quickly grown. Maxine hadn't been held by a man for two years. When Jim put his arm around her and pulled her to him, her response was immediate and intense. The urgency she felt between her legs made it impossible to stop something she knew they would both regret. She wanted it too much. Not just the physical act itself, but the warmth, the intimacy, the comfort.

The next morning just before dawn, Jim turned over in bed to kiss her good-bye. "Don't get up," he said. "I can see my way out before the kids wake up."

Maxine wanted to talk; to make sure they both agreed this could not happen again, but he was gone too quickly, and by the end of the week, Jim had stopped by daily.

Maxine thought about that night as she lay in her now cold, empty bed; that night and all the others that had come after. In those weeks everything she loved about Jim had surfaced. His strength, his dependability, his wise way of looking at the world. She loved it all and found it amazing that it had taken so long for her to see the very qualities Bob had obviously seen in his friend of so many years. Another unsettling question surfaced as well. Had she ever loved Bob this way?

By the end of summer, Maxine had thought about ending the affair; had grown weary of making excuses to the children, family and friends, even to herself. The initial excitement had turned to guilt, and each time Jim left, Maxine swore she would not continue. The pregnancy had surprised them both. Her periods had always been irregular, but somehow the one she missed in mid-October was too obvious to ignore.

Maxine called her best friend, Lorraine, one morning in early November. She answered on the first ring.

"Can I come over?" Maxine asked.

Later that week Lorraine drove her north to Guthrie to a physician recommended by a friend. Maxine's hands shook as she walked part-way into an alley and entered the rear door of the doctor's office. Illegal or not, she would discuss her options with him. The physician refused to advise her though he would perform the procedure in a safe, medical environment if she chose to do so. Yes, it was feasible to terminate; costly but feasible. But it had to be soon.

When they got back into the car, Lorraine turned toward Maxine, and her eyes asked the question she couldn't utter.

"No," Maxine said, though she wasn't completely certain for another week. Not until the phone call to her mother on Thanksgiving.

Her mother's shock was obvious by her long silence, but she listened to Maxine for quite some time. "What does your heart tell you, darling?" her mother asked quietly after hearing the news. "God will tell you what to do if you listen."

"God wasn't taking care of me very well, then," Maxine said.

"Bob is a good man. Jim is a good man. I'm just sorry you had to fall in love with both of them, if you did."

"Bob *is* a good man, mother," Maxine said, "though I don't think I've ever loved a man until now." Tears ran, and through a snotty snort, Maxine began laughing at the incongruence.

"If you keep the baby," her mother said, "you simply have to be ready for the consequences, and you have a hard decision to make."

The decision wasn't very hard, Maxine thought as she untwisted her nightgown and brought herself out of her reverie. Ten years of marriage to a good man and three children; who leaves that for the unknown?

*

On January 31, 1945, Maxine picked up the newspaper from the front lawn and pulled her heavy cotton chenille robe tighter against the cold. "Brr," she said as she took the three wide concrete steps in two strides and headed for the front door. The grass was brown and prickly, and the plantings around the front of the house bent their stiff necks to the ground. *Three days*, she said to herself. *I have three days to figure this out.*

February third came all too slowly for Bob, all too quickly for Maxine. She stood in their bedroom with the light streaming through the windows behind her and looked at her image in the full-length mirror behind the closet door. Turning side-ways she checked the seams of her silk hosiery. Her tall, slender figure helped hide her condition. Her eyes moved to her midriff and she thought she saw the faint outline of a small bulge. Lorraine had come earlier for the kids. The drive from Edmond to the Oklahoma City train station would only take a half hour. She had tentatively decided to tell Bob about the pregnancy as soon as they got home, or even before that, in the car … if she could stay calm, and if she didn't back down.

When Maxine arrived at the station, there was a good-sized crowd milling about. Many residents came with flags in hand to welcome the troops each time a group returned. Their arrivals were always posted in the local paper. The country had given its all to win this war with the purchase of war bonds, acceptance of the lack of provisions, even all the resources from oil to steel that had been supplied to the war effort. Not to mention, of course, their sons and daughters, many of whom were coming home wounded both physically and mentally, if they came home at all.

Bob's parents were sitting on the farthest wooden bench inside the cavernous brick waiting room of the rail depot. Their eyes were glued to the long expanse of windows and the tracks just beyond. They rose when she entered, and Bob's mother gave her a cursory hug; his father nodded. She could feel the distance that had grown between them over the past year.

"You didn't bring the children to meet their father?" her mother-in-law accused, "Maxine!"

"I need to see him alone for awhile, Barbara," Maxine said sharply. "They will be at the house."

"And I suppose we will not be invited," Barbara added.

"Barbara, please …" she pleaded. "Please let me have Bob

home for a couple of hours. We'll meet you for dinner at five; I'll bring the children. Please do this for me."

The train pulled in at exactly 1:05, and the families watched as fourteen soldiers leaped from the passenger car two steps at a time and raced toward the station.

Maxine's tear-stained face must have softened her mother-in-law.

"I will not tell you that I understand this, Maxine, but I will respect your wishes."

Maxine exhaled deeply. "Thank you," she managed, as Bob walked through the waiting room door and into the arms of his wife and parents.

They made arrangements to meet later at the Holiday Inn on May Avenue. It was her father-in-law's favorite buffet and she hoped it would appease them just a little. Bob took her hand and they walked through the dirty mounds of ice that still lined the parking lot. Maxine looked up at his thin, ashen face. "You look exhausted," she said. She couldn't take her eyes off him. "I can't believe you're really here."

Bob bent to kiss her softly on the lips. "You have no idea," he said quietly.

Maxine handed him the keys to the car, and Bob opened the passenger door for her. As he slid behind the steering wheel, she knew for certain; it would not be today. A thick solid silence enveloped the space between them for a short while.

"I see what you mean about the hard winter," he said, nodding to the split branches in the trees along the highway.

"Don't worry about the kids not recognizing you," Maxine said a few moments later. "They've looked at the new picture you sent them every single day. That was such a good idea. In fact," she added, "you have been sitting at the end of the dining table for weeks." They both chuckled; relieved to break the ice for a moment.

Small talk was all either could manage for the next half hour.

It had been so long since Bob had last been home. As he made the turn into Edmond, Bob exhaled deeply. "What about Amy? What do I do?"

"Just be yourself. She'll warm up to you. She's a really outgoing kid, probably because she has two older brothers who encourage her. She'll know her daddy." Bob nodded but his worried look remained through the rest of the drive.

A deep breath whistled through Bob's teeth as he pulled into the split driveway and pulled to the back of the Craftsman, parking in front of the one-car garage. Maxine put a hand on his shoulder and squeezed. A gentle "Wow ... home," escaped his lips, and he sat for a moment as Maxine opened her door and walked toward the house. She glanced back as she climbed the wooden steps up to the back door and unlocked it. Bob finally grabbed his duffel bag from the backseat. She watched him survey the entirety of the house. She knew what he was thinking. He had made it home. He reached toward the bare branches of the neighboring pecan tree that hung over the side fence. "I'll take care of that," he said. Opening the back screen door, he dropped his bag in the laundry room and followed her into the kitchen.

"I'll make a pot of coffee," Maxine said, "Are you chilled? I can turn up the heat."

Bob walked on through the kitchen, through the dining room and down the short hall to their bedroom. He lay down atop the thick feather coverlet and looked out the open Venetian blinds onto the front yard. The gray sky, the brown grass, the black barren tree trunks and the thin sharp stalks in the flower beds stared back at him in their dreary dark colors of death. Bob closed his eyes to them.

The doorbell rang ten minutes later. Bob opened the front door, and Lorraine scooped the boys into the living room toward their dad as she held Amy for a moment longer. He lifted both boys at once, one in each arm as they squealed and shrieked.

"Daddy, Daddy," they said over and over again.

He held them to his chest, and two sets of small arms wrapped around his neck. He turned as Maxine walked through the archway of the dining room toward them. Taking Amy from Lorraine's arms, she walked toward Bob. She gulped back the sobs that stuck in her throat. She could swear she felt the baby in her belly turn. Sliding the boys to the floor, Bob gazed with amazement at the tiny mirror image of his wife, and took the toddler from her. "Thank you God," she heard him whisper so softly no one else heard.

For the next few days a fog lowered itself over the Fourth Street house. She watched as Bob spent most of each day playing with the boys in the backyard and reading stories to Amy in the antique rocking chair they'd bought when Tommy was born. As he'd suspected, Tommy had seemed to adjust to his return quickly, but Jeffrey squirmed from his arms each time he reached for him. Maxine assured him this would be temporary. "Just give him time to get reacquainted," she said.

He avoided neighbors and friends who wanted to visit and refused to take the phone when his mother called each day. One afternoon he wandered into the kitchen and put his arms around Maxine from behind. He felt warm and solid. He didn't seem to notice when she moved his hands from her belly.

That week Bob slept fitfully on the couch in the living room, assuring Maxine that it was temporary. He had to readjust to civilian life; had to stop hearing the shriek of nightly air raid sirens; had to re-learn how to sleep in quiet, on something other than a cot. Hands flailing at Maxine, he grabbed her hard as she woke him from nightmare after nightmare. "Where were you?" she asked several times.

Sweat beading on his forehead, body shaking, unable to breathe, Bob would lie back against the sofa pillows and gaze up at the fear she knew was in her eyes. "It's ok," he would say, "It's over. I'm ok."

After three nights of being woken with night terrors, Maxine asked Bob to sleep in their room. "Maybe it will help," she said, "being close to someone."

He hung his head for a moment. She recognized in his face the feelings swirling through him—guilt, fear, passion, longing for touch. The very feelings she was experiencing at that same moment. "I'll try," was all he said.

Bob took his time in the bathroom while Maxine waited, lying on her back, considering the cobwebs on the ceiling fixture above her. She vowed to clean them the next day. She thought of a dozen other things except Bob's presence. When he finally climbed into his side of the bed, Bob pulled the covers over him. Maxine slid a bit closer, placing one leg over his. He responded by placing his right arm under her and pulling her head onto his chest. She curled into him snugly. Within minutes, he began to snore.

On Saturday morning Maxine's parents arrived from Nebraska and took over the house in a flurry of presents and hugs. Amy's third birthday would be celebrated upon their return. On the drive to Dallas, the car was stuffed with silence, and the old 1937 Buick cruised along, radio softly purring with Perry Como and Dina Shore on WKY. The Hotel Adolphus looked much like it had in 1934 as Bob drove up the circular drive and parked under the covered entrance.

"Oh, Bob," Maxine said as she choked back tears. The night before he had agreed to tell her where they were headed so she could pack, but he had made no mention of this part of the surprise.

As they settled into their room, Maxine unpacked a few things taking note of the one double bed. She would not reach for him tonight although her body ached to be held. He needed time, she knew. The wives had been warned in their monthly meetings at the base that their husbands were coming back as different men. He had never written her, nor would he now talk about, what he had experienced the past five years, and she could only guess at what horrors had lodged themselves in his memory. *How can I add to that?* she asked herself. But she had to tell him and soon.

She sat stiffly at dinner and watched Bob down one whiskey sour after another while she sipped a white wine spritzer. Asking about the war seemed unseemly; talking about the children brought thoughts of the baby that would arrive in July. So she sat quietly as Bob occasionally asked a question about safe topics like holidays, birthdays, friends he hadn't seen in years. When he moved toward the bar, she suggested walking off their large dinner, a suggestion that went unacknowledged. It was nearly midnight when they returned to their hotel room. Leaning against Maxine, Bob wobbled into the elevator and up to their seventh floor room before collapsing onto the bed fully clothed. Maxine slipped his shoes from his feet and loosened his tie. Placing a blanket over him, she kissed his forehead, crawled in beside him and fell into a troubled sleep.

"Stop," he screamed, "Down … Go … the bombardier's hit … pull up, damn it!"

Maxine startled awake, glancing at the clock. Two in the morning. Bob was writhing about, hands in fists, yelling loudly, but sound asleep. She had to shake him numerous times before he woke just enough to turn on his side and quiet down. Her heart was pounding and she realized she was holding her breath. It would take hours for her to return to sleep.

When Maxine asked about his nightmare the following morning, Bob shook his head no. She watched as he ordered room service and climbed back into bed. Seconds later, she felt his hands under her black lace gown as they followed the curve of her body.

"I've missed you," he whispered as he pressed his body to hers. "I've missed you so much, Maxine."

Beneath his weight, Maxine let the tears fall and prayed he'd think it was cries of passion. Oh, my God, she thought, I can't do this; but as Bob plunged inside her and quickly gave a shuddering gasp, she knew it had to be now.

When Bob released her and fell onto his back, Maxine rolled onto her side, raised herself up on her left elbow, and faced him. Every sentence Maxine had practiced flew from her mind. Jim would be proud. He had told Maxine to rip the bandage quickly, and she had. Two words. "I'm pregnant." The room filled with unspoken words while she waited.

Bob had adjusted to the sounds of bombs dropping from the sky onto the targets below his B17. He had gotten used to listening for proof that he'd hit the target, a shipyard near Rotterdam, a submarine base along the French coast. Nothing had prepared him for the sounds of his wife's words.

Maxine sat up and looked at her hands crossed on her belly as if they could bring her solace. Bob's face melted and she waited for words that didn't come. He rose from the bed and slipped on his flannel robe, walked to the chair in front of the window and sat down, then stared blankly at the floor for a few moments.

"Whose? . . . Whose child is it?" he whispered. When Maxine didn't answer, the anger roared. "Whose baby is it, Maxine!" he yelled. "I want to know now, damn it! Whose?"

"Jim's," Maxine answered. "It's Jim's."

He hadn't threatened to kill anyone. He hadn't said more than two words as he paid the hotel bill and had the concierge bring the car around. Maxine would have preferred anger over the silence.

They found a feeble excuse for her parents when they returned early from the trip. Bob had come down with a cold, and they shouldn't stay longer in case of infection. He set up a roll-away in the back room, and when the boys asked where he was putting their toys, he attempted a small measure of humor. "Over in the corner; dads like to play with toys too you know."

By Tuesday of the following week Maxine thought she would suffocate in the thick quiet. She had tried twice to call Jim since their return from Dallas. Each time she had gotten a busy signal. She didn't think Bob had spoken with him either. The telephone sat in the carved wooden niche in the dining room, and Maxine would have heard any conversation. After lunch, she zippered the boys in their jackets and sent them out to play, put Amy down for her afternoon nap, and found Bob out on the front porch swing. She stood in front of him and cleared her throat. "Bob," she said, "we have to talk. We can't continue like this."

"You're right, Maxine," he offered. "We can't."

Thinking she had finally gotten through to him, she sat down on the other end of the swing.

"That's why I'm seeing Jim this afternoon," he added.

"What? Why?"

"Because, as you said, we have to figure this out. And man to man, we will."

*

He had considered calling Jim, but he wanted the element of surprise. The bastard, Bob raged, the gall. He hadn't wanted to hear Maxine's insistent explanations; didn't want to hear about it from anyone but his best friend. Best friend, shit. He turned onto the gravel road to Jim's place and a few moments later, slammed the gearshift into Park, spit on the ground beside the car, and walked in full uniform to the front door of Jim's farmhouse. As if he were on reconnaissance, he tentatively turned the knob and entered the house, hoping to find Jim cowered in a corner.

As he cautiously crept into the small living area, Jim appeared from the kitchen. The smell of bacon wafted into the room with him. "I thought I heard a car coming up the road," Jim said as he walked toward Bob. He put out his right hand; then let it drop gradually to his side when Bob refused it. Jim gave a deep sigh, stood his ground, and motioned for Bob to take a seat on the couch. Jim took the large overstuffed chair to his right.

"I think I'll just stand, if you don't mind," Bob responded. "I don't have much to say, and it won't take long."

"Bob …" Jim stammered, shaking his head, eyes closing for a brief moment.

Bob interrupted, "Shit, don't say anything, Jim. What is there to say? You're sorry? You didn't mean for it to happen? What? My best friend, Jim?" he asked.

Jim rose from his chair, and both men stood silently in the center of the room, facing each other with eyes cast downward at the fraying gold rug between them. Then, without thinking, Bob rushed at Jim, pushing him several times in the chest with both hands until he had him against the back wall.

"Go ahead," Jim said calmly. "You deserve to hurt me. Hell, I'd hurt me too if I knew how."

Taking one last shove, he heard Jim's head knock against the wall but he knew he hadn't hit him hard enough to wound him. Shaking it off, he backed away in anger. "You don't deserve to be hurt, you bastard. You deserve to rot in hell."

Bob crossed the room, slammed open the screen door, and strode quickly to the drive. As he backed up, then threw the car into first gear, he glanced over to see Jim watching him. He cursed under his breath, as he saw his best friend raise an open palm. Stretching the middle finger of his left hand high into the air, Bob shifted and the car surged forward, leaving deep ruts in the gravel.

*

Maxine was on the phone with Lorraine when she heard the car pull into the drive. "Gotta go," she said, "Bob just drove up."

"Remember what I just said," Lorraine insisted. "Do not talk about this tonight. Whatever happened, happened. Let it go. Don't escalate it. Give him time."

"Yes, I got it," Maxine said. "I'll see you soon."

Except for the boys' constant chatter and Amy spilling her milk, which had become a nightly occurrence, the table that night remained unnervingly silent. As Maxine removed the dinner plate from in front of Bob, he grabbed her wrist; then quickly let it go. When she returned from the kitchen with two cups of coffee, he had left the room.

Later that evening, after the nightly rituals of Bob's story time with the boys and rocking Amy to sleep, Maxine once again offered coffee, and this time he accepted. They sat like statues on opposite sides of the dining table for several moments, and just when the silence became unbearable, Maxine startled with surprise as Bob began talking. He was calm and quiet, his deep voice barely audible. "Do you want to know?" he asked. "About what I saw, I mean?"

Maxine silently nodded.

He rocked onto the back two legs of his chair, rubbed his chin for a moment, and began.

"A piece of me died as I watched other guys coming in dead or wounded. Every mission, I made it back with my crew and plane intact. God was with me, I guess. Oh, we took flak many times. The plane was always riddled with bullet holes along the sides of the bombardier, but they'd fix her up and we'd head back out on the next run."

He took a sip of coffee and Maxine reached over to fill it, but he motioned for her to sit.

"But the worst … the worst was seeing them haul off guys with severed limbs, watching guys holding the hands of butchered friends. We didn't even have time to react. Within an hour, their personal belongings were stuffed into bags, their bunks stripped and there was no sign they had ever existed. Just gone."

Tears streamed down Bob's face, landing on the damask tablecloth, but Maxine could sense he wasn't done. "And I kept wondering why. Why not me? And then I began to think, because I have a family waiting back home who needs me and God damn it, I will get back." He grew quiet.

"Do I, Maxine, do I have a family?" he whispered.

Nearly overturning her chair, Maxine raced to his side and took his face in her hands and lowered her eyes to his. "Yes, Bob," she insisted, "You do have a family. We're right here."

She kissed his eyelids and tear-stained cheeks, and lifting himself from his chair, he took her in his arms and led her to the bedroom. It was the first time they'd had sex since the morning in Dallas, only this time it was slow and gentle and reeked of love.

The next morning Bob slept late while Maxine took care of the kids and household chores. At 1:00 when she put Amy down for her nap and shooed the boys outside to enjoy the unusual sunny February day, she slipped into the bedroom and gently touched his shoulder. One minute she was leaning slightly over him and the next she was laying on her back on the floor with Bob's right hand in a fist around her neck. "Bob," she screamed, "Bob, it's me, don't…"

His eyes finally focused on her face, and his body went limp. He sat back on his heels with his left hand on his forehead, begging for her forgiveness. Maxine sat up as well and put her right hand on his knee. "It's ok, honey. We'll get through this." But she wondered how.

The following morning as she sipped coffee at Lorraine's house, Maxine said, "I'm afraid to leave him with the kids. I just don't know if I'm strong enough to help him, you know?"

"And don't forget you're in your fourth month, Maxine. Or do you want to lose this child?" she asked pointedly.

"No, Lorraine, I do not want to lose this baby. I know it would make life a lot easier for everyone else, but not for me."

"Have you talked to Jim since Bob went over?"

"No, but I'm going to call him from a payphone before I go back to the house. They were best friends, Lorraine. If anyone can help Bob, it's Jim."

Lorraine shook her head and released an incredulous laugh. "Maxine ... honestly." And she left it at that.

A short while later, Maxine pulled into the parking lot of the Red Owl supermarket and found a pay phone on the side of the building. "Jim, it's Maxine. Can we meet somewhere? I don't have long, in fifteen minutes, at Fink Park, please?" she begged.

He was waiting by his battered Ford pick-up when she arrived. Maxine raised her hand, then pulled further into the parking lot behind a stand of trees before approaching him. He nodded but neither reached for the other. Jim led them into a clearing behind a stand of cedars. Arms crossed over his chest, eyes constantly glancing from the ground to Maxine and back, Jim listened for a few moments.

"So let me get this straight," Jim said. "You want me to try to talk to a guy who was facing death overseas for five years while I sat here with a II-C exemption, screwing his wife?"

Jim turned from her and faced the small man-made lake. Lowering his voice, he added, "Shit, Maxine. What I want to say to him is 'I love your wife; she's having my child; she's leaving you to marry me'."

Placing a hand on his right shoulder, she turned him gently toward her. "Jim," she said, "I loved you. I still love you. I would never have let this happen if I hadn't. But can't you see? We can't do this to Bob. It's not me and it's not you .... *We* cannot do that to Bob."

"No, Maxine, there's where you're wrong. I could."

The warm sunny day turned chill, and Maxine let out a long sigh before walking toward her car.

"Maxine," Jim called after her. "Give me some time. Let me think."

She didn't look back but she nodded her head in agreement; then drove a few blocks south and west to her beloved Fourth Street house. Driving up the tree-lined street, Maxine took time to soak it in as she approached the driveway. The oaks would bud out soon and the grass would grow again. And surely life would return to some kind of normal.

They had bought the 1922 Craftsman with the few pennies they had scraped together during the five years before Bob had been commissioned overseas. She had walked through the front door, had seen the original wood floors, the white brick fireplace and glassed-in bookcases, and had fallen in love.

Bob had argued that Edmond was too far away. Even though he spent much of his time in the Armory up the street, his training base was ninety miles north. When begging hadn't worked, Maxine had resorted to her last line of defense. "It has a wonderful attic for a playroom," she had said flirtatiously. "And we could have a lot of fun trying." He could never resist, she remembered. But now, if he left her; he would never let her keep the house. If he legally accused her of infidelity, she might not even keep the kids; except for the unborn baby, she thought.

How had this happened? she asked herself. *And how many times have I asked myself that question?* she added. Bob had been gone so long; so very long. She had stayed faithful all those years. Amy had been conceived on his last visit, two years ago. Two years. What damned military didn't allow their soldiers furlough? It was no excuse, she knew. But how long can you live without touch, without feelings, without love? She had been honest with Jim; she had truly loved him, even if he didn't agree. As common and predictable as it sounded, she thought, it had just happened. *No excuse, Maxine,* she thought. *Now make this right.*

A month passed, and Maxine's belly became more pronounced each week. Bob hadn't reached for her since the night he had shared his demons. She knew that each time he saw her naked body, he thought about Jim. They hadn't discussed past, present or future. It was like they were living on a movie set, saying their lines on cue and acting for the audience. By mid-March, Bob had made no attempt to find work. The psychiatrist he was required to see every other week at the V.A. hospital insisted he must give it time. Maxine questioned that, but she agreed not to push. The military paycheck came in monthly, but that wouldn't last much longer. She hated to ask her parents and would definitely not approach his. All she could do now was wait and pray.

On April first, Maxine watched Bob dress and head for the garage without stopping in the playroom to tousle the boys' hair as he always did. His look of determination took her off guard. Through the kitchen window she could barely see him as he lifted the garage door. She raced to the kids' bedroom where she could get a clear view. His back was to her for a moment but as he turned, she took in a gasp that nearly took her to the floor.

"Oh, no; oh, my God, no," she said as she flew through the house and out the side door. "Bob, what are you doing?" she screamed as she watched him walk toward the car, rifle in hand. "Bob." She forced herself to quiet her voice. "What are you doing? Talk to me."

He opened the trunk and placed the rifle carefully inside it; then turned toward Maxine.

"One of my buddies had his head shot off, do you know that?" His eyes were distant and unfocused. "Clean off." He hesitated. "The first round severed him at the neck. I threw it into autopilot and stood on the catwalk of the bomb bay shouting for the rest of the crew to jump. Abandon ship was for your brothers, not yourself. Somehow the plane made it to the base. I never expected to make it back."

He turned to Maxine and his eyes had cleared. "I'll see ya, Max," he whispered, "for dinner."

Maxine raced into the house, heart pounding. She hesitated momentarily, weighing her options. She didn't know what would happen if she called the police. She didn't want Bob to be arrested; she simply wanted him safe. She dialed the familiar number. When Jim answered, she simply yelled, "Bob has a gun. He went west on Fourth Street. I don't know what to do."

*

Bob drove slowly five miles west of town to a reservoir where he and Jim had shared target practice hundreds of times. It was an old shooting range on the other side of a small lake. He had spotted dust behind him a few times but he wasn't worried. As Bob rounded the curve of the lake, he looked behind him and saw Jim's truck churning up a wall of red. Bob pulled into the dirt lot and was opening the trunk when Jim turned the corner, threw his truck into park and approached him.

"Well, of course," Bob shouted. "The II-C is going to save the day, right? Maxine couldn't let well enough alone, huh?"

Jim climbed from the car but stood silently watching Bob's erratic moves. "Ain't worth it, Bob, ain't worth your life," he finally said.

"And how would you know that, Jim, my best friend, Jim? Huh? How much combat did you see the past five years? Too busy fucking my wife, I guess."

"That's not how it was, Bob, and you know Maxine better than that. I may be an asshole and I may have betrayed you, but you know Maxine better than that."

"Why don't you enlighten me then, Jim?"

"Put down the gun first," Jim said.

Bob looked down at the M1 Carbine in his hands. "Maybe I'll just shoot you instead of myself." His voice was agitated, his hands shook and he pointed the rifle at Jim.

"Put down the gun and we'll talk. Then you can shoot me, ok?" Jim asked.

"Well, this could be an interesting story," said Bob. "I'll just hold the gun while I listen."

Jim walked over to an old railroad tie and sat down, leaving room for Bob at the other end.

"It was my fault," Jim said. "Don't blame Maxine. It just happened, over time, you know? You were gone; you asked me to keep an eye on her and the kids. I went over every Sunday to make sure she was ok, roughhouse with the boys, fix a few things when she needed them."

He stopped just long enough to assess Bob's demeanor, then went on. "She invited me to stay for dinner and Sunday evenings are hard, but I always refused. I knew I was falling in love with her; I tried to stop going over, but if I didn't, she'd call and ask. And one night after that big ice storm last spring, the kids were asleep, we were sitting there on the couch listening to the radio, and it just happened." He looked directly into his friend's eyes. "You love her, Bob; you know why I love her. It ain't really any different except; except it was just wrong."

He had Bob's full attention. Bob laid the rifle on the ground slowly, putting both elbows on his knees and leaning his face into his hands. Neither man said a word for some time.

"Don't ask me to forgive you," Bob finally answered. "Because I can't; I can't ever."

"That's not important. Can you forgive Maxine?" Jim asked.

Bob lifted his head from his open palms and turned to look Jim square on. "Maybe," he said.

"Then don't do anything you'd regret," Jim said, nodding his head at the rifle.

"And what about this baby?" Bob asked. "What the hell do we do about that?"

"I don't know," Jim answered. "I've given that a lot of thought. It's my kid but mostly it's Maxine's. She chose to keep it; she wants to raise him – or her; it was her choice. I wanted to marry her, you know. I wanted to take her clean away from you. Hell, I didn't even know if you were coming back, you son of a bitch; you never even wrote me all those years. Wouldn't see me on your last visit."

Bob shook his head; his shoulders slumped forward. Without another word, he picked up the rifle, walked to the car and drove off leaving only a cloud of dust that filtered over Jim's hunched body.

*

At 6:30 Maxine paced the house from playroom to living room, down the hall, into their bedroom and back to check on the kids. Over and over she circled the house. She had called Lorraine and talked briefly. She had dialed Jim's number numerous times over the course of the last two hours. No word from him or Bob, either one. She kept envisioning one man, then the other, laying bloody somewhere on a dirt road. Maybe Bob had intercepted Jim before he could even leave the house.

She turned on the radio and sat all three children in front of it. Bobby punched Jeffrey to get the best spot. Amy picked up her baby doll and pressed a plastic bottle to its mouth, cooing softly. Maxine watched the tender family scene unfold, and she begged God to bring them both back home; both men whom she loved so dearly. How many times had she prayed for Bob's safety over the last five years? How many times had she longed for Jim's warm body next to hers each Sunday night? What in the hell had they done to each other?

At 7:00 o'clock she knew she had to do something. She had tucked the boys in early and watched their long eye lashes close as they nodded off to sleep. Amy had required rocking, but she too was warm under her soft pink hand-knit afghan.

Lorraine picked up on the first ring. "Can you come stay with the kids and let me borrow your car? I have to go out and look for them." Just then Maxine heard the car pull slowly into the driveway. She stretched the phone cord into the hall and watched through the window in the kids' bedroom as the headlights lit the door of the old garage. She could see Bob clearly through the back window, and as he approached the house, he looked up and locked her eyes briefly.

She met him halfway as he walked through the kitchen. She threw her arms around his neck and waited uncertainly. In response, he pulled her to him carefully and gently.

"You're safe," she said as she tilted her head under his chin. "And Jim?" she asked.

"Not sure any of us are safe in this world," Bob said slowly. "Are we ever really safe?

*

The next morning Bob woke to a quiet house. A note with his name scrawled on top sat on the kitchen counter. Maxine had taken the three children for an early walk to the park a few blocks away. He poured a cup of coffee from the pot Maxine had left plugged in and walked down the rear steps into the backyard. Walking the perimeter of their property, he checked the wood fencing and from a distance looked at the roof which had weathered another Oklahoma winter fairly well.

A few shingles needed to be readjusted and tacked back down, but otherwise the house looked just as it had two years ago. Jim had obviously helped Maxine repair the back screen windows; he could see the patching when the sun hit them just right, and he had probably kept the ivy from overtaking the garage and shed, taming its invasive growth before it could creep beneath the eaves and cause damage to both roofs. Bob couldn't help but wonder how yesterday's resolve could have dissipated so quickly. At the time, Jim's question of forgiveness had seemed possible, but this morning brought doubts and the festering anger that lay beneath.

He wasn't certain now what he had intended to do when he drove off half-cocked with his rifle in the trunk, but he had promised Maxine late last night that he would call his shrink. She had insisted on locking his army issue Carbine in the basement along with his hunting rifles and gear. Jim's explanation now solidified the betrayal Bob had felt for months; it reconfirmed for him the fact that Jim had taken advantage of Maxine's loneliness and frailty. Jim's question kept echoing through his mind; the thought bouncing from one conclusion to the opposite. Could he forgive Maxine? Could he accept this baby as his own? Jim had actually said he could give up the child; he could walk away. What were his words? It was more Maxine's baby anyway; she had been the one to insist on keeping the child.

Picking up a handful of loose pecans, he crushed them easily in his right palm, then threw the shells hard against the side of the house. He hadn't been in hand-to-hand combat, but he knew he had the strength and will to kill a man. Hell, he had probably killed scores from the air.

*

A half hour later, the boys raced Maxine up the front sidewalk to the porch, and she let them win, pretending to be winded and tired as she balanced Amy on her left hip. "Go on in," she called to them as they swung open the front door. "I'm going to check the flower beds."

Placing Amy on the ground, she bent down on one knee and swept away the layer of leaves and mulch, looking for the signs of the tulip bulbs she had planted in the fall. It had been warm and sunny for a couple of weeks, and she had hoped to have them in full bloom by mid-April. As she raised herself from the damp ground, she felt a hard kick on the right side of her distended belly. She pushed against the tiny foot, hoping to move the baby into a different position. Her fingers did a quick count for the millionth time; thirteen weeks remaining. As much as she tried, she could not stop thinking about the events of yesterday. What if Bob had succeeded in killing either himself or Jim? It was too much to consider. Taking Amy by the hand, she started up the front steps just as Bob walked from the house onto the porch.

Without thinking, she raced up the short steps and wrapped her arms around his waist, burrowing her head beneath his chin, forcing him to take her in his arms. When she pulled back slightly, his look of confusion and uncertainty made her wince. "Oh, Bob," she murmured, "do you hate me so much?"

His mouth twisted into a forced smile. "I don't hate you, Maxine. If anything I hate myself. If I hadn't left you; if I had loved you better, maybe things would have been different. Maybe you would have been stronger."

"Can we sit for a moment?" she asked carefully. When he nodded ok, she opened the door and called for Tommy to take his little sister to the playroom with Jeffrey.

Bob took a place on the right side of the swing. Maxine slid next to him, closer than she thought he might want. "You were in combat, Robert."

He turned sharply at the sound of his full name and faced her.

"I know it's easier to hate Jim; to blame him for everything; but the truth is I made a choice and you have to understand that I am as much to blame as Jim." She hesitated briefly, questioning herself before she even said the words. "We haven't been close in years, Bob; maybe we never were." Tears were now trickling from the corners of her eyes. "When did that happen? When did we stop loving each other?"

"I've always loved you Maxine," he answered harshly. "Maybe you didn't love me, but I love you, and I always have. Every day I woke up and prayed that I'd get back home to protect you and take care of you. It wasn't my own life I was worried about; it was you and the kids. That's all that mattered. Do you not understand that, Maxine?"

He stood quickly, setting the swing into a jerky sideways motion, and Maxine had to grab at the armrest to right herself.

She watched his back as he headed across the lawn and turned toward the garage out of her line of vision. Maxine's mind tried to react to Bob's words, but a flood of feelings crashed through her, drowning out all thoughts. The truth stuck in her throat, and she choked out a low guttural moan, a sound released at the news of a sudden death.

Maxine checked on the children and placed a crock of leftovers into the oven to warm. She walked to the living room and sat in the rocking chair in front of the window, barely aware of the full greenness that had descended on the yard the past few days. It had warmed enough for the buds to burst forth on the oak trees and the crepe myrtle. The lawn was alive again and the spring bulbs showed sprigs of leaf tearing from the garden soil. She didn't know how much time had passed, but she was startled awake by the sound of Bob's duffel bag hitting the wood floor as he shifted an armload of clothing for balance. Her mind yelled stop but the words wouldn't form before he turned from her and walked toward the back of the house, stopping only long enough to kiss the top of each small head before walking to the car.

Lorraine and Maxine took advantage of the warm sun later in the week as the boys climbed the jungle gym and Amy poured sand through an old flour sifter Maxine had salvaged from the trash.

She released a long sigh. "Bob called again last night from his parents," she said. "At least he's checking on us each day."

Lorraine took a sip of her tea and placed the cup back onto the saucer that she cradled in her lap. Maxine felt her friend's watchful eye as she placed her own cup on the tabletop her baby now provided. She saw the quick shift of Lorraine's gaze as her eyes moved from Maxine's belly to the ground in front of her. "Go ahead," she said as she shifted in the uncomfortable kitchen chair they had dragged to the backyard. "It's ok. I'm sure every one in town is looking at my belly. I can lie about my due date but I can see the fingers counting as I walk away."

Lorraine's focus turned to the three children who played in innocence and safety, calmly unaware that the ground on which they were playing was a shifting fault-line. "You look too thin, Maxine," she said. "You need to put on some weight to nourish the baby."

Maxine nodded her head as Lorraine's words slowly made their way to her consciousness.

"I wish I knew," she said.

"Wish you knew what, honey?"

"If I ever loved him."

Lorraine's body shifted closer to her best friend but she kept her hands locked on her teacup.

"If you ever loved Bob? Or Jim?" Lorraine asked.

One tear streaked its way down her left cheek and she looked directly into Lorraine's eyes.

"That day; the day Bob showed up with the engagement ring." She hesitated. "I should have had the courage to say 'no' but I didn't. Everyone was standing around, bursting with excitement. I wanted to feel it too, the excitement. I tried so hard to feel it. I wanted to be married to Bob. I knew he was a good man and would be a great father. I just didn't love him, not really."

She felt Lorraine's hand reach for hers, and she clasped it tightly. In Lorraine's eyes, Maxine saw her own reflection mirrored; a pale, thin pregnant woman, and in the background, three small children who needed her.

"Let me take the kids for the evening," Lorraine suggested. "You need the break and I love having them."

Maxine considered the offer and called to the kids. "Want to go home with Aunt Lorraine?"

The boys yelled with excitement. "Can we stay over? Please?"

Maxine laughed. "No, no sleep-over, but dinner and you can stay up till 10:00 o'clock."

Soon after Lorraine left with the children, Maxine made a phone call.

At seven, Jim arrived as she had requested, right on time as usual. They had the house to themselves, and the quiet was stifling. Jim took the chair farthest from the sofa where Maxine sat gently rubbing her left temple. She saw Jim shift uncomfortably, but she took her time, forming her words carefully before she released them.

"You look good," she said, opening the tunnel between them.

"And you look very … well, pregnant," he said as his mouth widened slowly to a faint grin. "I haven't seen you for awhile; the baby must have doubled in size by the looks of it." His smile faded quickly. "Look, Maxine," he began, but she interrupted him immediately.

"We have to talk, Jim. I have to talk," she corrected herself. "Bob moved out …"

"I heard," he said. "At church last week."

"What are people saying?"

"I think they just know how hard it's been for Bob. Coming home after all he went through over there. Not about the pregnancy, Maxine."

"This baby," she began again. "This baby has to save us; somehow it has to save all of us."

"I don't understand."

"Jim, you are the father of this child. Bob is the father of my three children. Somehow, this baby has to help us come together, not tear us apart."

Jim moved forward to stand, but Maxine pleaded, "No, please hear me out."

"Maxine," he said, "I can't do this. You have to know something. I love you; I've begged you to leave Bob and let me take care of all of you. You don't love him, Maxine. I know that. You aren't the kind of woman who throws caution aside to have an affair. We love each other and we need to be together. That's what this baby needs to do, Maxine; bring *us* together."

When he moved toward the door, Maxine reached it first. She stood facing him, shaking with sobs she wouldn't release. When he reached past her for the doorknob, she knew he felt her pregnancy, his baby, push against him. She heard him groan with desire as he pulled her into his arms and pressed her face against his chest. She felt his hands along her hair; then he cupped her chin and looked down at her with longing. Maxine wanted to push away, but she wanted much more to respond, and she did. Kissing him hard on the mouth, every feeling she had been tightly clutching exploded into a physical ball of desire that carried her toward his lust. As they moved toward the bedroom door, Jim continued to kiss her mouth and caress her body until they felt themselves backing onto the bed, and at that point nothing could have come between them.

An hour later, they sat over coffee at the dining room table.

"You won't leave him, will you?" he said softly.

"Bob is my husband; we have three children together – a family; he's just home from being gone for five years, Jim. We don't even know each other anymore."

"Then why bother to try now, Maxine?" His anger grew louder.

"For the same reason you know you're going to walk out that door tonight and let me go. Because you are his friend. Because you are a good man and I am a good wife."

Their eyes met briefly before he turned to the bedroom to dress, his steps, creaking on the hardwood floors, the only sound.

It would take six weeks of phone conversations and weekend visits before Bob agreed to move back home. On the 4ᵗʰ of July, he turned the crank of the wooden ice-cream bucket as Maxine brought out sugar cookies iced with sprinkles of red, white and blue. They watched the children play with sparklers as the night lengthened, and then lay on a blanket looking up at a midnight blue Oklahoma night filled with fireworks from the near-by park and the stars that appeared intermittently between booms. Maxine lay by Bob. Amy tucked herself between her two brothers, and the three lay with their heads at their parents' feet. He spread his fingers wide along Maxine's engorged middle; then turned to face her. "Maxine," he whispered. She turned to meet his gaze. "Why did you choose me over Jim?"

His question surprised her but her response came more quickly than she'd imagined. "Because I have always loved you; I was too immature to realize it, and then the kids came so quickly."

"And you love me enough now to let me father this child?" he asked.

"Oh, Bob," she said as tears streamed down her cheeks, "I want that more than anything. But only if you're sure, if you're really sure."

"This baby is your child, Maxine—ours. You have carried it for almost nine months; you chose to keep it when you could have made a different decision. Who fathered him or her doesn't matter. It's yours and yours alone."

Maxine leaned into Bob's chest and wept. "She will be very lucky to call you dad."

A week later, Maxine answered the doorbell in an old housecoat and an apron white with flour. When she saw Jim, her hands went to her mouth, leaving a trail of powder.

"Is Bob home?" he asked before she had a chance to speak.

She couldn't think of anything to say except "yes." She pointed toward the garage, and Jim turned without hesitation and walked to the rear of the drive.

*

Bob had his head under the hood of the Chevy, wiping oil from the dipstick when he heard a familiar male voice call his name. He looked up briefly and returned to the task of carefully inserting the stick into its tube. Resentment rose like bile.

"Gotta minute?" Jim asked, as he walked cautiously up to the rear of the car.

Bob couldn't believe it. He shook his head in disgust and wiped the remaining oiliness onto his over-alls. After putting the hood of the car back down and checking to see it had latched, he looked at Jim directly. "I suppose," he finally said.

He indicated the back steps though both men barely fit on the width of the cement landing. It was fine with Bob; he didn't care to look at the other man's face.

"Remember that sophomore dance we went to that spring—with the twins?" Jim gave a slight chuckle.

Bob had no clue how to respond, so he remained silent.

Jim cleared his throat. "We both thought we'd get lucky that night, huh?"

A deathly silence filled the little space between them.

"Oh, shit, Bob, I don't know what the hell I'm saying or why I'm here." He pulled his fingers through his hair and combed it backward, letting it flop back into place.

This time, Bob stood and looked down and directly into Jim's eyes.

"If this is an attempt at an apology, I don't accept."

Jim stood to meet Bob's height. "I just think it's time, for Maxine's sake, for the kids' sake, and hell, the baby's due soon. Shit, Bob, I just think it's time we put this aside if we can."

Bob squared his jaw and his chin moved forward. He bit his upper lip before he replied. 'Let me get a couple of beers." He opened the creaky screen door, and Jim waited on the bottom step. When he returned the two men moved onto lawn chairs in the grass of the backyard.

Bob was surprised that Jim made no attempt to apologize; just took the same stance as he had at the shooting range. And once again Jim took full responsibility and offered to bow out of the picture as far as the baby was concerned.

"So what does that mean, exactly, Jim?" Bob asked.

"I'll sign adoption papers. Whatever it takes for you and Maxine to be a family again."

Bob showed almost no emotion, and felt even less. He looked at Jim and nodded an "ok."

Suddenly Jim leaned forward in his lawn chair to within inches of Bob's face. "Tell me what happened over there. You never wrote me once, you son of a bitch; friends don't do that."

His question angered Bob for a moment, but as he looked into the face of his friend of twenty years, he saw true concern and interest. Something inside him slipped back in time and he began to talk. Over the next hour, Bob answered each question Jim asked of him. By five o'clock the two men had had enough honesty for one day. Neither quite understood what the afternoon had meant or whether they'd ever see each other again, but for now it seemed best to leave things as a truce.

*

On July 28, 1945, Elizabeth James Watson came into the world to change the lives of her mother, two brothers, older sister Amy and her two dads. The children waited outside the hospital lined up according to height as they held hands with each other and with Lorraine. Maxine stood at her hospital window and held the pink-blanketed baby high enough for them to see her from the sidewalk below. She blew them each a kiss and turned back to the brightly lit utilitarian hospital room. Bob took a new bouquet of flowers from the nurse and placed them on Maxine's bed table. He pulled the card from the tiny envelope, glanced at it, and handed it to her. It was signed simply, "Jim".

Maxine saw in her husband's face the muddled mixture of grief, and sorrow and pain she had added to his traumatized soul, and yet overlying those deep feelings was a recent layer of peace, and God willing, a new layer of happiness was growing just below.

The house on Fourth Street would be waiting for her return to its warm yellow kitchen, the back bedroom newly painted pink for both girls, and the love that cloaked each and every room of their home. With any luck, Maxine thought, this child would bring them all together in the future. She would never give up hope of that happening. For the moment, she was content to hand the tiny bundle to Bob as she drifted quickly off to sleep.

Chapter 7
Looking Back

Their longest separation had been early in the relationship. Karen had met Gary in her fall semester Biology lab, freshman year of college. She'd explained that math and science were not *her thing*. Her nose was usually stuck in a novel or history book—usually history, she'd told him.

Gary had laughed. "Stick with me, kid," he teased. "Nothing but A's on this transcript. And math and science *are* my thing."

He seemed a bit cocky but not in an abrasive way, and within a month, she was tutoring him in American History and was even beginning to understand his after-class reviews of mitosis and meiosis.

Karen received a B in Biology at semester's end, and Gary proudly displayed his C+ history grade.

"Guess I'm the better tutor," he said.

"Or you didn't study as hard as I did," she replied, pressing a teasing finger into his chest.

That spring they saw little of each other. On occasion, she would spot him in the Student Union, never with the same girl twice. He'd always approach her to ask how classes were going, but he never called. There were only two women's dorms; he could find her if he wanted. She continued to stick her nose into history books and English Lit and put him out of her mind.

It was spring of senior year in Statistics 101 before they had a conversation beyond a "good to see you." Gary had waited outside the door at the end of the first lecture.

"Good to see you," he said.

Karen nodded agreement.

"Be glad to study together."

"I'm sure you aren't in any class that consists of dates and places," she teased.

"Nah, never ... leave that to the likes of you."

"What does that mean?" she said, feeling just a little offended.

"Teasing," he laughed. "So how about it? Library at 6:00?"

Two months later, he'd still not asked her out, and she accepted that he had no interest in her aside from tutoring. She was headed on to grad school in the fall anyway; she convinced herself she didn't really care.

Then in mid-April, as the Colorado spring came earlier than expected and tulip bulbs peeked their heads through the soil in the campus gardens, she was called to the hallway phone and heard his voice on the other end.

"Want to go for a drive or get a bite of lunch?" he asked. Just like that—out of the blue.

He met her downstairs in the foyer and walked her to his red Corvette convertible parked a few spaces down the block. She would later insist it was the car and not the man who had first appealed to her, although they both knew differently.

By the end of the summer, they'd become lovers, and Karen spent most of her time at the apartment he shared with two other guys. One morning in July, she had woken to find him staring out his bedroom window looking forlorn.

"What's wrong?" she asked groggily. "Something happen?"

Gary sat down on the edge of the bed and held her face and kissed her deeply.

"Well, that was nice, but it didn't answer my question." She felt a sudden concern as she observed the wan look on his face.

It was a long moment before he spoke. "Karen, I've been accepted to the School of Architecture in Chicago. Won't you please consider getting your teaching degree there?"

She was stunned. "You never mentioned this, Gary. All these months. You never said."

"I didn't want to say anything because I didn't think I'd get accepted, and I didn't want to upset things figuring I'd be staying in-state."

"And so you just didn't mention …"

She was too furious to continue. She pushed past him, hit the shower, and didn't speak to him for the next week, and when she did, she assumed it would be the last time.

She had been the one to call, kept it simple and asked if he'd meet her for coffee on Saturday. They met at a local pancake place, gave each other a cursory nod and said nothing more until they were seated in a cracked orange vinyl booth at the rear of the restaurant.

Gary sat and blew gently on his coffee. He picked up sugar packets and laid them back down. He tapped his fingers in the silence. He looked like he was waiting for the proverbial ax to fall, she thought. She almost felt sorry for him.

She broke the silence. "It's only two years," she said, twirling her knife through the paper cup of softened butter beside her plate.

"Go on …" he said. His eyes squinted in anticipation.

She finally looked up with wet eyes and reached for his hand across the table. "It's only two years," she repeated. "We can do this long-distance thing, right?"

Gary's eyebrows lifted with unspoken questions.

"Well, can't we?" she asked again.

He slowly placed his napkin on the table and turned in his seat, putting his feet into the aisle and lifting himself from the booth.

Karen steeled herself and waited for him to walk out. Instead, he slid into the booth beside her and took her in his arms.

"I'm going to kiss you," he said. "Just warning in case you're embarrassed the whole place is watching."

She had no time to object although it never crossed her mind to do so.

For the next two years, they both immersed themselves in their graduate degrees. Architecture demanded every waking moment of Gary's days, but he called every other night without fail.

Karen was the one who periodically questioned how wise they had been to make this commitment; this promise she might not be able to fulfill. She knew Gary would never cheat; once he made up his mind about something, he was in it all the way. That's one thing she'd learned about Gary Reynolds. Whatever he did, he gave it his all.

Her resolve was the one in question. She was lonely and very much alone. Roommates and friends had gone their separate ways at graduation; to grad school, or to husbands and babies or directly to careers. And that first winter, Denver was cursed with well above average snow falls, keeping her huddled in the warmth of her apartment except for classes.

She signed up for summer school to speed up her degree, registered for an extra heavy course load the following fall and managed just a few weeks with Gary in Chicago between sessions. If she was going to be faithful, she had to stay busy, she thought.

"The truth is," she told her mother during a weekend visit at home, "I'm not sure I want this."

"Karen," her mother said, "what in the world? You were so certain."

She felt reprimanded. "Were you so certain, Mother? With daddy?"

"I never doubted from the moment I met him," her mother answered, "but if you do—if you do doubt—you need to end this before Gary gets hurt."

She gave a slight nod. The thing was—Gary wanted children. He wanted a wife and family and a home. She wasn't sure that was what she wanted. "He never mentions my desire to teach. He doesn't seem to understand that what I want is my career."

Her mother reached for her hand and held it. The intensity in her eyes surprised her. "I understand more than you'll ever know. I fought those same demons before we were blessed with you. Your father and our parents wanted a grandchild from the time we married. I put career first—right or wrong; but it was different back then. Times have changed, honey. You can have it all if you want."

"But what if I don't know what I want? What if I don't want kids?"

"Then you'd better be making that very clear, my darling daughter." She reached for the check, ending the conversation.

The next day, she followed her mother's firm advice.

They argued for days over the phone. "I've been expecting this," Gary said, "but I never said I didn't want you to have a career, Karen. My God, you're getting your masters degree so you can teach. Do you really think I don't understand that? But this is about something else, and you need to figure out what it is."

She didn't have time to figure it out. *Or maybe I hadn't wanted to.*

June slipped past. She knew Gary was half expecting her to end the relationship at any time. She knew he felt her uncertainty, but it was still exactly that—uncertainty.

She watched the National Democratic Convention on television that summer. It was July of 1993, and women gathered in force outside the convention to push their agenda to candidate Clinton. Things had improved, but not enough. There seemed to be a backlash and a full-scale attack on what were seen as radical feminists.

She didn't consider herself a radical feminist, but she supported the women standing outside Madison Square Garden. Abortion, equal pay, equal jobs, health care, day care, and discrimination were still concerns to most women, and to her. Though there was a trend toward two-working-parent-families, there was also a great fear that women couldn't, in fact, have it all. She took this as proof that her decision to have a career instead of motherhood was the only reasonable one.

She got her master's degree in December that year and had no trouble finding a high school teaching job in the Denver area. The day she got the offer, she invited Gary for Christmas with her parents, and during his visit they planned a spring wedding.

By the time they married, Karen was convinced career and children did not mix well. She insisted that waiting a few years would be best for both of them professionally. He wanted to start a family immediately; the arguments became heated. When she was being honest with herself, which occurred primarily after each fight, she became aware of something deeper. Under the guise of politics and women's rights lay a fear, and she couldn't put a name to it. The fear sat silently year after year; sometimes Karen forgot it was there; other times it threatened to choke her. She tried a few times to explain her feelings to Gary, but she was too uncertain herself. She couldn't blame her mother for dying in childbirth. But her father had simply left without looking back.

Gary had apprenticed in a Denver firm that later turned into a full-tine paid position. He worked his way up the ranks until starting his own firm three years ago. They avoided the conversation about kids and raced into their careers with all the gusto they had. That had been sixteen years ago. Now he was forty; she was thirty-nine. And here they were, in the same place they'd been when they married. Nothing had changed.

*

And today, standing before the mirror putting on her make-up and brushing out her long hair, she was startled by the realization that she still felt that same fear and still hadn't identified it.

Though they talked almost daily about practical matters, Gary did not mention moving back. It made her sad to think they would give up this easily, without even a fight. She'd been so convinced he'd come right back home. After a week, she found herself ruminating on that last night. He hadn't said the word—divorce—but were they headed there? Perhaps there was another woman—someone younger, someone who wanted children. Maybe it was just a mid-life crisis. When was the last time they'd made love? She couldn't even remember that. Her mother's death, the funeral, the trips to Oklahoma—all of that had taken her far from her marriage.

The house grew emptier with each passing day. She kept herself busy with her parents' house and the trunk. She wandered into school one afternoon and checked on her classroom, not that there was anything to check on. She had lunch with Denise and met a few other coworkers on Saturday. And each day she woke up wanting Gary back just a little bit more.

The trunk filled her days again. Not just the diaries, but the research she was doing on nearly every object it contained. She hadn't had time to do the other million things she usually did to stay busy in the summers. Instead she woke early, threw on grungy old jeans or shorts, a comfortable, stretched-out-at-the-neck, over-washed t-shirt and raced to the sunroom. She stopped to make a fresh pot of coffee or grab a snack, and she almost resented the interruptions from Denise to go to the mall or have lunch out.

"Karen," Denise said during one early morning phone call, "I'm starting to feel neglected here. After all, we only have a few more weeks of summer break. God knows, these school years get shorter every year."

"I know, I know—I'm sorry. Ok, tomorrow I swear. I'm almost through reading Maxine's diary. Should finish today."

"Well, ok ... Monte's at noon?"

"I promise."

"Tell you what ... I'll pick you up."

She smiled at her friends' lack of trust. "I'll be ready," she said. She clicked the end call button and opened to the fragile linen page she'd just read. Just then a thought crossed her mind, and she grabbed a lined, white note card from her stock and jotted three things:

Pick up laundry

Get toothpaste and milk

Call dept. chair re: 1st day team meeting

In the past her lists would have been three pages long. Lists that she crossed off; the remainder diligently transferred to a new card. Her book club was coming up, and she hadn't started the novel. Her needle craft bag had sat neglected in the den since her return. And she'd volunteered to bring food to the Teacher First Day brunch. She had time for that. She'd told her tennis foursome she'd hurt an ankle on her trip to Edmond—tripped on a step and twisted something.

The trunk had become her Pandora's box.

The next day, after sorting through some of her stacks, she called Hazel. "Would the Historical Society want some of these items?"

Hazel sounded thrilled. "Absolutely. Anything you want to pass along, dear."

"A few clothing items are in pretty bad shape, but most everything else was protected in the trunk all those years."

"Particularly interested in 1800's and early 1900's," Hazel said. "Seems like anything from WWII is pretty common, but we'd love women's clothing or any war memorabilia like medals and ribbons."

"I have some of both," she said.

"Well, dear, take your time. You want to see if any of these are actual relatives of yours; you never know."

"My family—well, my biological grandparents—apparently came from Kansas. My parents bought the house in 1968—doubt if there are any connections."

After she hung up, her last words hung in the air. If that was true, then—what was she looking for? She shook her head. The question stayed with her through the day, and even Maxine's diary couldn't hold her attention

The next morning she woke with a start. Lily, Davis, Maxine and Bob. Were there more pieces to the puzzle?

Two weeks later, on a Sunday morning, Karen answered the phone and was surprised to hear Gary's voice. "Want to go to IHOP?" he asked.

She grinned from ear to ear. "You remembered that?" she said.

They sat in the rear of the restaurant in a cracked orange vinyl booth.

Karen was the first to speak once they'd ordered. "We can make this work, right?" she said.

Gary grinned, rose from his seat and slid in beside her. "I'm going to kiss you," he said, "in case … well, you know…"

A few days later, they had dinner at the house to discuss their future.

She rambled about nothing in particular as she scurried around the kitchen while Gary sat stiffly on a barstool watching her. She was nervous they might be making the wrong decision, yet she also knew she didn't want a divorce right now. Her life was in too much turmoil.

Gary pulled the chair out for her to be seated at their formal dining room table. She had pulled out all the stops; white linen and candles and his favorite chicken cordon bleu. After polite conversation about each other's wellbeing, he spoke.

"We are not twenty-four years old any more, Karen. And we're almost too old to begin a family. So putting aside all that mumbo jumbo we've always fought about, why don't we try focusing on the present?"

She nodded. "So what is it that we're fighting about?"

He put his napkin on the table and pushed back his chair. He sat quietly for a moment. "I'm not really certain, Karen. It seems like the old issues dissipated, but we kept fighting their ghosts. We've gotten stuck in a blame game; the way I see it."

"I agree, Gary, but it's become an indelible pattern, and I'm not sure how we fix it. I don't want to play a blame game, not really. You're never here; I'm never here; you're too busy for me; I'm too busy for you. We each have our careers, our own friends; it just feels like we live separate lives. When was the last time we had something in common?"

"Well, I liked the chicken cordon bleu." His eyes lit with humor.

"You know what I mean," she said.

"Well, maybe we need to find something in common. You hate golf; I hate tennis. Even with your summers off, I can seldom find time to travel. Any ideas?"

She shook her head. "Not really. But I wish I did. Where do we go from here?" Her voice was somber, and she was close to tears. Maybe this really couldn't be fixed.

"Well, why don't I move my stuff back in, and we continue to talk until we figure it out?" he said. His eyes were warm with concern and understanding.

Had she stopped noticing that love? She wondered. "We need to put a timeframe on it, I think," she said. "Don't you think?"

He nodded. "I suppose. Otherwise we continue doing this to each other, and we find no solutions. I'm willing to keep talking if you are. What do you think? Three months?"

She agreed. "Three months—October—Halloween?"

"An appropriate make-or-break night, I'd say." She smiled at his attempt at levity.

The next evening he pulled into the garage and parked, and she stopped what she was doing and welcomed him with a hug.

"Wanna go to a movie later?" he asked.

She wanted to ask why, since they never agreed on movies. She liked romantic comedy; he preferred Iron Man. But she'd agreed to give it her best shot, so she helped him with his duffel bag and then went to change. Whatever he wanted to see would be fine. She could always nap through it. God knew she was tired enough to do that.

*

In August, Karen watched the red and white For Sale sign go up in her parents' front yard. She'd taken all of the items her own house could handle, held an estate sale for the rest, and the old house sat empty except for ghost memories that called to her from every room.

Just days before, Gary had grunted with exertion as he pulled the heavy corded rope that lowered her parents' folding attic stairs. He gave her a hand as she carefully climbed them.

"Just throw down any boxes you find up there," he said. He waited just below the square opening in the hallway ceiling.

"Looks like the Christmas decorations," she called down. "Here you go."

They were light, and she had no difficulty tossing them to Gary's waiting hands.

"Just a few more … looks like some of my old childhood stuff. Don't drop the teddy bear," she chuckled. "I'm sure it's quite valuable."

She looked around to see if she'd missed anything, then carefully handed the last of the boxes through the opening. She climbed down, brushed her hands of dust, and sighed. Thirty-odd years of memories in five small packages.

The wilted Christmas decorations went directly to the outdoor dumpster. She brought home the two boxes full of her childhood and placed them in the sunroom next to the trunk. She'd only recently finished piecing together the story of Maxine and Bob, at least as clearly as she could. They had lived in the house another twenty-five years. She'd never know what became of them.

But in the spring of 1968 her parents had purchased the

house on Fourth Street. Karen knew most of that story—how her grandparents had surprised the young couple with the down payment when they graduated with doctorates and moved to Oklahoma. She knew they'd been professors at the college for two years before they adopted her in July of 1970 and that they had remained at Central State for another five years before getting jobs at the University of Colorado. Her mother had died in childbirth; her parents had taken her as their own. But there was a missing piece. She still hadn't found the adoption papers that would provide her with the name of her birth father. There had to be a record somewhere.

Once again she wondered what she was looking for. She was close to forty. How old would he be now? What would be gained even if he was alive? Would he even want to know her? Her thoughts swirled. Why hadn't she asked? Would her mother have told her who he was? Perhaps. If she had asked. But she hadn't.

The next morning she sat on the floor in the sun and opened one of the cardboard boxes from her parents' house. She picked through wrist corsages, yearbooks, and tattered birthday cards—nothing of value. She turned to the next. As she slid a knife along the packing tape of the second box and watched it fall open, she gasped.

Inside were a dozen diaries in her mother's handwriting. She had a vague memory of a few of them—a hardbound cream and pink with gold-edged pages; a fabric-covered booklet with hearts and angels embossed on the cover. Her heart raced to read them immediately, but her mind was not ready for the secrets they might unveil. She folded the sides into themselves and pushed it away.

The boxes sat there staring at her for days before she found the courage to open a journal and begin to read. Its broken spine and worn appearance suggested its age. The first entry was dated shortly after her parents' wedding. She sprawled out on the couch with the warmth streaming through the glass walls.

So happy. We have interviews in Oklahoma next week. It would be wonderful to find positions at the same school. It's a small college, but a very pretty town—hilly and green and not far from family. Keeping my fingers crossed.

Classes at her high school would begin the following week. Karen should be making lesson plans, getting her room ready for the first day of school, but she couldn't force herself away from the sunroom except to grab more coffee and an occasional snack.

Chapter 8
November 1, 1969

Angela Johnston glanced at the Currier & Ives wall-calendar in her kitchen and shook her head. She could see her husband, Richard, in the next room, crumpled in a straight-back kitchen chair in front of his makeshift desk. He had constructed it a year and a half ago out of an old wood door he had found in the garage the day they moved into their new home. The open three-panel folding door that enclosed the back room was a sign that he was available, at least for the moment.

"Honey," she said, "do you know it's November First already? Your mother's birthday is next week, and we've planned nothing." As she waited for his response, she pushed aside the blue-checked curtains above the kitchen sink and looked out to the side yard, now accumulating a fine covering of snow from the freakish early storm that had moved through central Oklahoma overnight.

"She's not expecting anything much," he said. He sounded distracted. "Why don't we just have dinner here?"

"I suppose." She rolled her eyes and sighed; he couldn't see with his back toward her. Angela knew that would mean a weekend, or at least an overnight, visit from her in-laws since they'd be driving down from Kansas. As much as she loved Richard's parents, she dreaded his mothers' constant badgering about starting a family. It was the last thing she wanted to deal with right now.

Angela and Richard were second-year professors at the local state college; Angela in the English department, and Richard in

the newly formed Computer Science Program. Their joint
income barely covered their student loans, gas in the VW Beetle,
and the mortgage payment. Their parents had surprised them
with the down payment on a small 1920's Craftsman in the
historic area just south of the campus. Although it did allow
them to walk or bike to work, Angela knew that the underlying
motive and the unspoken expectation was for the couple to
establish roots, make a commitment to the university and
hopefully fill the three-bedroom home with grandchildren. She
had no intention of doing that any time soon.

Angela walked the few steps into the rear office and stood
behind her husband. "Whatcha looking at?" she said, as she held
out a fresh cup of coffee.

He was frowning at the pile of papers he was grading. "These
test scores are horrible. I'm questioning if it's just freshmen in
general, my teaching skills, or their lack of focus." He stretched
his back and took the mug from her. "Thanks."

Angela nodded and sat down across from him on an old
daybed they'd dragged in from the curb not long ago.

"I'm facing the same thing ... only I add to the list: pot,
alcohol and LSD." Although she and Richard had graduated less
than two years ago, the world had changed quickly. She
overheard student conversations daily as they arrived and left the
classroom; half the time they were discussing last night's party or
how they could score some Mary Jane.

"Well, I don't know, but it's sure frustrating. Hell, I worry
that my department head may look at these scores and question
my teaching ability, you know?"

Angela stood to leave and as she passed, she rubbed his
shoulders. "When are you going to buy a decent chair? You're
killing your back."

A half hour later, she watched as Richard wrapped a gray
wool scarf around his neck and tugged on his knitted ski cap. She
kissed him good-bye as he opened the door, letting in a blast of

cold air. "Brrr," she said, "You may get to campus in five minutes this morning." She straightened his scarf. "I'll be right behind you," she said. Her first class was at eleven today.

As her students shuffled into the classroom, Angela stood at the chalkboard in front of the room finishing an outline of today's lesson. Jennifer Anderson, a 4.0 sophomore who sat in the front row, walked in with Mark Roberts, who sat next to her.

"I don't care what you do," Angela heard Jennifer whisper. "I'm not going. It's illegal, Mark."

"It's a rally, Jen, nothing more."

"Yeah, well, my parents will kill me if I lose my scholarship. I can't risk it, Mark, sorry."

Noticing Angela a few feet away, Mark shook his head to stop the conversation.

After class, Angela surreptitiously watched as the two continued their earlier argument, stuffed notebooks into backpacks, and were the last to leave the classroom. She wondered what rally Mark had been referring to. She'd check in the faculty lounge before her next class.

At two o'clock Angela locked up her office and walked across campus to meet Richard. The early morning snow had melted with the mid-afternoon sun. They walked hand in hand up the slightly steep incline of Boulevard Street; heavy book bags full of student work hung on their opposite shoulders.

Rumors about the anti-war rally were flying in the hallways of the English building, and Angela was torn. She was not much older than these students, and while she didn't want to be friends with them, it was important to her to be someone they could turn to. In the past month, she'd helped a girl with a positive pregnancy test, referred a young man suffering from nerves to Student Services, and counseled several others with relationship problems.

She knew how difficult college transitions were. As a freshman, she had returned from Christmas break to learn that her roommate had died of an overdose. And there had been many times in graduate school when the workload had been so stressful she had considered dropping out. She gave the credit to her academic advisor and her favorite professor, Laura Jenkins. Without her, she might have never completed her doctoral thesis.

"Richard, I don't know what to do with this information. If I report it to my Department Chair, he'll go immediately to the Dean, and then I lose all credibility with my students. I've worked hard all semester gaining the trust of these kids."

"What exactly did *you* hear today? Because in my ten o'clock class, I overheard something about a rally tonight."

"Rally, protest—not sure. I also overheard that student protests are planned on the Norman and Stillwater campuses next week. I guess it had to hit the central plains at some point but it frightens me. Look what happened in D.C. last month and in Boston."

"And Chicago," Richard added. "Now it's this damned lottery bill. Every guy on campus will be facing the draft. Hell, that puts us up to 400,000 troops over there if Nixon gets this passed. Why the hell did we stick our noses into another country's business anyway?"

"Do you have a lot of grading or prepping to do tonight?" Angela asked.

Richard looked down at the intensity in her eyes and shook his head. "I know where you're going with this, you know?" His mouth twisted sideways in good humor. "Ok, just this once; we'll check it out, but we're not getting involved."

At seven that evening, Angela reminded Richard of the time, and they drove the few blocks from Fourth Street to the college and parked in the faculty lot just north of the main campus. The sounds of angry voices, megaphones, and music led them to the football stadium. *Not a huge crowd*, Angela observed; *may be nothing significant.*

As they entered the stadium ticket-entrance however, the noise level grew. Fifty or so students milled around, looking uncertain. Angela and Richard worked their way through the small crowd, and he led them toward the far side. "The last thing we need is for Dean Hayes to walk in and see us here. Being non-tenured, we could easily be dismissed," Richard said.

"This is our personal time; we're not at work. How could they do that?"

"Fraternizing with students is in the professional handbook, Ang. It's a no-no."

Angela frowned and glanced around to see if she could spot any of her students. No one tenured wanted to teach the freshmen or sophomores. Upper level classes were taught specifically to English majors. Shakespeare, Faulkner, Steinbeck. Angela couldn't wait to get her hands on those syllabi, but she had to pay her dues for a few more years to get there.

She knew Richard was right about their presence. It could definitely be misconstrued. She pulled the fur-lined hood of her red nylon jacket over her head and let her eyes glide over the crowd and to the outskirts of the stadium, watching for security or administration. Just then a tall young man in an army fatigue jacket jumped onto the second row of bleachers with a megaphone in his hand. He had scruffy stubble that hadn't quite formed a beard and long brown hair pulled into a shoulder length pony tail.

Richard took her hand and they moved a few yards closer.

"Thanks for coming out tonight," he boomed. "We have a lot of work ahead of us and a lot to talk about. But we need numbers," he stressed. "A week from tonight, rally number two; bring at least one friend. Our numbers will double instantly."

He pleaded with them. "We cannot sit idly by and do nothing while Nixon doubles the troops. If this lottery passes, we're pawns of the government. Let the Viet Cong take over; what business is it of ours? It's just another goddamn way for

America to make money off of war and try to control the rest of the world."

Angela watched as the crowd grew agitated. A buzz of murmurs began to spread, then grew louder. He had them now, she thought.

The young man pushed on. "Let's fight this, people! We have to fight! What do you say?" he yelled at the crowd.

The students chanted. "Draft beer, not boys!"

The chanting grew louder. Their self-proclaimed leader raised a fist into the air and yelled into the megaphone, "Not one more dead!"

The crowd responded, "1-2-3-4, we don't want your fucking war!"

As their voices gained volume, the hair on Angela's arms bristled. Off to her left, she spotted several of her students: Brenda Caudell, Jesse Matthews, Jennifer Anderson. Angela felt the first stirrings of fear for her students, for herself, and for the country. The anger and rage that spewed from the crowd put them all in danger. If they didn't stand up and fight, they faced dying for a cause they didn't believe in. But by doing so, who knew what these young people would suffer instead? She could feel the tide turning.

Throughout the week, Angela and Richard talked of little else. Neither had chosen to discuss the rally with their students, taking the stance that the less said, the better. Angela knew the administration had to be aware of the student gathering by now. She and Richard were afraid of feeding the fire of discontent by addressing anything outside of the normal curriculum. If they even opened it up for discussion, they created an environment of debate that could grow volatile. And the flames of that fire could easily roll back on their careers.

The following Thursday, the day of the second rally, a blanket of tension covered the campus. Each faculty member received a perfunctory note in their staff mailbox from Dean Hayes. *The college will not condone unauthorized student gatherings. College facilities and public areas cannot be used for political meetings.* He urged the faculty to report to their Department Chair or directly to him upon hearing any rumors or discussions about such meetings.

That evening, just after dinner, Angela insisted they walk to campus for the second rally.

"I really don't think that's wise," Richard said. "I let you talk me into going last week. We just can't risk this, Angela."

"We won't stay," she insisted. "Let's just check it out and make sure things don't get out of hand." She glimpsed a slight weakening in his demeanor. "Richard, please."

A short time later they stood in the faculty parking lot with a dozen other professors concerned for their students' safety. They talked quietly among themselves about the recent shifting tensions and the dean's directive. Security stood at the entrance to the stadium, which remained empty. As dusk turned to night, everyone shook their heads and headed back home. Angela sensed that something wasn't right.

And sure enough the next morning, she stopped in her tracks as she glanced at the college newspaper stand. An overnight edition had appeared with large, bold headlines: Protest Rally Successful. And just below: "Decision to join Students for a Democratic Society. Plans made to combine efforts with Norman and Stillwater for future demonstrations in OKC." The young man she'd seen last week was quoted, "Come next week, bring one friend, our numbers will double again."

Angela had to give them credit for persistence, but she wondered where they had managed to meet. *Off campus, no doubt.* She headed into the English building to prepare for her nine o'clock class. As she walked toward her office, she saw the crowd of students gathered outside her closed door, every eye watching her arrival. She hesitated for a brief moment; then approached them.

Jennifer Anderson stood up quickly. "May we speak with you,

Dr. Johnston?" She appeared to be the group spokesperson.

"Sure, Jennifer—just let me get my coat off, and we'll move some things around so you can squeeze in." Angela unlocked the door and pushed her two conference chairs aside.

She nodded at each student as they found a space on the floor or stood along the wall. She prayed her officemate would be late today. Angela took note of the changes she'd been seeing this fall. Students who had always come to class clean-shaven, well-dressed and well-behaved, were gradually taking on new personas. Bell bottoms were frayed; some sported peace symbols and fringed leather vests. A few bandanas held back lengthening hair. And yet beneath the newly donned façade of activism the same bright eyed, intelligent and searching students gazed at her.

Angela chose to stand behind her desk, her hands knotted tensely together. "What's up, guys?"

Jennifer spoke. "Dr. Johnston, we came to you because you're always cool. We need your help. We can't meet in the dorms; we'd be kicked out, and we have nowhere safe. Can we please meet at your place?"

"Oh, guys ..." Angela began, but Jennifer cut her off.

"We're not asking for much, honest. We understand you're faculty and all, but we need a place to meet, to make signs and banners for the upcoming protest. No one will ever know. If you let us use your house, we will never mention your name. It's off campus and you'll be safe, we promise."

Angela hesitated and looked intently at their faces. She knew they were right. Central was mostly a commuter school, and except for a few sororities and fraternities, the majority of students lived in the dorms.

"Oh, guys .... I understand what you're doing. I even support your right to meet and to voice your feelings. But being part of this would put my job in jeopardy, and my husband's. Several of you have him for classes, too. Do you want him to get fired?"

"Please just think about it, ok? Talk to Dr. Johnston."

Jennifer hesitated before playing her final card. "After all, you know, if this draft lottery goes through, he won't be exempt either. It won't matter if you're married or if you're in college, this affects all of us from here on out."

Angela cringed at the thought of Richard's number, encased in a blue plastic capsule, being pulled from a hopper.

"Let me talk to him." Angela's voice was soft and careful. "But don't plan on it. By the way, where did you all meet last night?"

Several students attempted to get Jennifer's attention, shaking their heads "no." Jennifer acknowledged them but answered anyway. "The downstairs cafeteria in Wantland Hall."

Right on campus, Angela thought. *Right under the administration's nose.*

A cloud of tension covered the campus the rest of the week. Administration was furious they had been undermined, but they also knew that the students wanted and needed adult support in some manner. The Provost called an emergency meeting to discuss how to allow for freedom of speech but maintain control and student safety at the same time. It was a delicate thin line they were all balancing.

"Are you crazy, Angela?" Richard said when she shared the students' request. "You know how damned lucky we were to get teaching positions at the same school. You want us to jeopardize that? Absolutely not."

Angela pushed on. "We can always say we're tutoring if anyone sees them at the house," she said, "because Richard, really, how can we deny them?"

"Angela, no, I can't let you risk our jobs."

"And what will happen when you get your draft notice once this bill is approved?" she asked. "Where will our jobs be then?"

He shook his head and gave a long sigh. "You're right about one thing. It could be us as easily as them. I'm no more protected than they are."

The next morning Angela tried again. "Richard, I'd like to give Jennifer an answer today. I don't want to go against your wishes, but how can we turn our backs on them when we feel the same as they do? This isn't just their battle, Richard; it's ours and our country's. We have to protest this before it's simply a done deal."

Richard shook his head. "Damn it, Angela, you just make things so hard."

"I make them hard or you make them hard?" she said.

"SDS under our roof. I cannot believe this is happening." He shook his head and walked away. Halfway out the door he turned and looked at her. "This will come back to haunt us; you just watch."

When Jennifer walked into the classroom that morning, Angela called her to the front and they set the time and date for the first publicity committee meeting of the SDS. At the last moment, Angela said, "Jennifer, I know you know this, but you must be careful. You absolutely have to keep this secret."

"I promise," Jennifer said. "Only the SDS kids."

The following Tuesday evening, a dozen students arranged themselves in unobtrusive groups of two and three, left plenty of time and space between each, and walked nonchalantly toward the Johnston's front porch.

Mark Roberts rang the doorbell at seven thirty with Jennifer by his side, and Angela opened the door and welcomed them into their home. Every few moments the doorbell rang again until everyone had gathered in the small living room.

"Oh, wow, look at this." "Man!"

Angela could hear the hushed comments as the students looked around her house, and she beamed. She was proud of the warm wood floors she tended with such care, the antique crystal chandelier hanging above their garage-sale dining set, and the glass-fronted bookcases spilling over with her literary library. She loved the glow of the kitchen visible just beyond.

"Gosh," Jennifer said, "Dr. Johnston, your house is totally cool."

Richard said hello to the group and showed them the front bedroom where they threw their coats and jackets onto the bed. Angela had worried about her husband's resistance most of the afternoon, but he seemed to be making the best of things.

Mark and another young man pushed the worn corduroy sofa and maple coffee table to the side. Then they carefully rolled up the rug from Richard's grandmother and placed a black plastic tarp in its place. The girls produced poster board and bags of markers, scissors, and paint.

Angela returned from the kitchen a few moments later with plastic bowls of chips and popcorn. Richard helped her carry in a dozen bottles of soda pop and ice. The students worked on hands and knees as Jennifer handed out supplies and made suggestions for slogans. Angela couldn't help but notice how the young woman had become Mark's second in command.

Richard had told her he'd be staying in the back office, leaving the students to their work, but Angela noticed him nervously pacing from one window to the next, peeking at the front walk and the neighboring street. After his third round, his shoulders seemed to relax and he joined her in the kitchen.

Someone asked to put a Beatles album on the record player, and Angela followed Richard back into the living room as he placed the record onto the turntable. The sounds of "Let it Be" floated over the room, and before they realized it, Angela and Richard were caught up in the excitement and enthusiasm of the evening. Jennifer smiled at Angela and handed her a poster board and markers. The normally quiet house suddenly felt warmly chaotic.

Angela smiled at Jennifer's rapt attention to every word Mark spoke that night and watched the girl laugh at each of his attempts at humor. She stayed to help Angela clean up, while Mark helped Richard with the furniture. As they left, Mark held the door for Jennifer and they stopped for a moment on the covered porch. Angela noticed Mark take Jennifer's hand as they walked down the cement steps and onto the walk.

As she shut the door, Richard reached for her from behind. She nestled backwards into his arms. Then he turned her to him and bent to kiss her, but before his mouth reached hers, she whispered, "Thank you."

Over the next few weeks the students turned the bungalow into a publicity headquarters for the newly formed chapter of Students for a Democratic Society. During the day, the girls in their mini-skirts and go-go boots and the guys in their bell bottom pants would come and go as quietly as possible. One evening a week, Mark led the SDS meetings in the secrecy of the old 1922 Craftsman house.

Richard's initial concerns seemed to lessen as the weeks went by. They were just far enough from campus that students could walk through the residential neighborhood without raising attention. There had been no suspicions so far.

In mid-December the first draft lottery since the 1940's was signed into law. Although large protests erupted around the country, the students at Central State marched quietly around campus, protest signs waving in the cold Oklahoma winter wind. The situation remained peaceful, and college officials watched and waited anxiously for winter break to begin.

Two days before the month-long Christmas holiday, Angela's phone rang and Richard shared his afternoon. "I was hiding in my classroom grading final exams when the door opened, and Mark Roberts asked to speak to me."

Richard described the events as they had played out, and Angela listened without interrupting. "I thought he simply wanted to thank us for helping them this fall, but when I told him we knew what we were getting into, he interrupted me. Come to find out, he and Jennifer have been dating and she's pregnant."

Angela gasped. "Oh my gosh, no."

"I wanted to laugh when he said that somehow Jennifer had gotten pregnant. But I didn't say that to him. I felt really sorry for the kid. The sexual revolution may be in full swing, but a pregnancy on campus is another matter."

"You're right about that," Angela said. "This won't be easy for them. So why did he come to you?"

"Well, he says they can't talk to their parents and he's upset that Jennifer is making this her decision and not including him. She says it's her body; it's her decision."

Angela straightened in her chair and held the phone tighter. "It is her decision, Richard."

"Well, Mark feels it's his decision too; he wants the baby, and he wants to marry her."

Angela hesitated. "So what does he want us to do, Richard? He obviously came to you for something."

"He wants us to meet with him and Jennifer and persuade her to listen to him."

Angela nodded. "What did you tell him?"

"Well, shit, Angela, I didn't really know what to say, but I looked at the kid, who looks all of fifteen, shoulder-length hair, frayed jeans and a peace symbol around his neck. He's not exactly a father figure."

Angela couldn't help but chuckle at Richard's description.

"So have you made a decision? What are you thinking?" She was more than aware of his reluctance to getting involved in the kids' lives. But she also knew that Jennifer had become one of his favorite students. Just as she did in Angela's honors courses, the girl learned quickly and was one of the few students who truly understood the concepts of programming. She had formed a study group for the other female students in the class at Richard's request. Not only was Jennifer gifted academically, she had quickly taken on a leadership role in the anti-war group. The once reticent girl had poured herself into the work of the SDS this past month and managed to keep her straight A's while spending long nights in their living room making signs, banners, and buttons to fight the draft vote.

"I asked how we could possibly initiate that conversation with her," Richard continued. "Mark says he can get Jennifer to stay and clean up after their last SDS meeting tomorrow night, and hopefully she'll agree to let us talk to her." Richard didn't sound convinced. "I really don't know how we can keep getting involved in these kids' lives," he said.

"Well, if I recall, you agreed to let them use our home."

"Yeah, at your insistence. You were the one who wanted to go to the first rally," he countered.

"Richard, we're involved. How can we turn our back on Mark and Jennifer now?" But as Angela hung up the phone, she found herself wondering if this was wise. She supported Jennifer to a certain degree. As a woman, granted a young woman, but still . . . it was Jennifer's body; her college education; her career. A pregnancy always affected the woman more, and she didn't feel comfortable supporting Mark in this attempt to convince Jennifer to carry the baby to term.

The next evening Jennifer arrived at the house first. Richard welcomed her and told her that Angela was in back preparing a snack. She walked through the living and dining room to the back kitchen. "I love that little telephone niche in the dining room," Jennifer said as she joined Angela. "I hope Mark and I can have a house just like this some day."

Angela turned toward her in surprise. "That's the first time I've heard serious commitment from you or Mark," she said. "Are you guys talking about marriage?"

Jennifer smiled sheepishly.

Angela hated knowing about the pregnancy, but she and Richard had promised Mark they'd talk to the two of them together, and it wasn't her place to say more.

The meeting was short, a summary of the semester's

successes and a budget report. At eight, after hugs and happy holidays had been exchanged, Mark asked Jennifer to stay, and Angela and Richard offered seats at the dining room table. Jennifer's eyes narrowed and her mouth pursed in anger.

"I've told the Johnston's about the pregnancy, Jennifer. They've agreed to talk with us."

As soon as they were seated, Jennifer went on the attack. "I appreciate everything you are trying to do for us, Dr. Johnston, I really do, but honestly this is my decision, and Mark had no right involving you."

"We just care for both of you, Jennifer, and we simply agreed to be here while you talked; that's all," Richard assured her.

Angela nodded in agreement, and Mark pressed his hands together and leaned forward.

"Jennifer, this is my baby too; whether you agree with that or not. I won't sit by and let you make a decision without me. That's just not fair. Abortions are illegal and dangerous; if you're even thinking about that, you need to tell me."

"I don't have to tell you my plans, Mark. I may choose to, but I don't have to."

"I'm the father of this baby, Jennifer. You can't just cut me out of the decision."

"And you aren't listening to me, Mark. I love you but right now I just wish I hadn't even told you. I really do."

"Don't say that," Mark said. "Let's just talk this through."

"Honestly, I'm tired of talking, Mark. We've done that for a week. I have options; I'm simply going to consider all of them."

"There are NO options," Mark said.

After a short while, Jennifer sat back in her chair with a look that said she was finished with the discussion. She sat with her arms across her chest.

Richard spoke up in an attempt to ease the tension. "Jennifer, you know Mark wants to marry you, right?"

She nodded. "I want to marry Mark but ..."

Richard cut her off. "But you aren't sure you want the baby. We all understand that. Completing your degree, going for your post-grad, your career. It's a difficult decision. But I have to agree with Mark that it needs to be a joint decision." He looked to Angela for support.

Angela had one arm around the back of Jennifer's chair; she squeezed the girl's shoulders. She had remained silent, letting the two of them debate, but now she sat forward and looked directly at Jennifer, then at Mark. "Jennifer, you're a young woman, you do have options if you act quickly, but this does need serious thought. I want to support you whatever you decide. But I also understand what Mark is saying. He just wants to be part of the decision. I suggest you guys keep talking and include your parents if you can."

Angela watched as Jennifer bristled in response to her remarks.

Glancing at Richard, Angela's heart beat quickened. She hadn't thought about the possibility of a baby for a very long time. She felt like a hypocrite. Did she ever listen to Richard when the subject of babies came up?

"I wish Mark hadn't brought you into this," Jennifer said. "I don't think there's anything left to say, do you, Mark?"

"Only that I hope you'll let me be part of the decision, Jen."

Angela leaned forward to give the young woman a hug, but Jennifer pulled away.

"We'd best be going," she said directly to Mark. He stood and followed her to the door.

After the young couple left for campus, Angela straightened the living room and put the dishes in soapy water to soak. She looked for Richard in the back room office. His chair was vacant. She walked the house; then turned on the porch light to see if he was outside on the swing. His jacket still hung on the old umbrella stand just inside the front door along with his scarf and boots. Just as she felt the first twinge of concern, she heard the hallway door to the attic stairway creak loudly, and she turned to see Richard as he closed the door. His face was flushed.

"Babe," she said, "why were you in the attic? It's cold up there." He gave a slight smile and shrugged without answering. "We'd better get some sleep," he said. "We both have early classes."

As she brushed her teeth and prepared for bed, Angela glanced at her birth control pills. She slid her fingers over the round plastic dispenser and hesitated. Then she filled the glass with water and swallowed the white tablet.

Tuesday rolled into Friday, and when Jennifer walked into Angela's eleven o'clock class, it took all Angela had to refrain from asking the girl to stay after. Jennifer had turned in her Honors work packet and told Angela she thought it was A quality work. Angela had no doubt of that.

The Christmas holiday meant that students left campus for a full four weeks. Angela and Richard welcomed the reprieve from the war protests, the weekly SDS meetings and even Jennifer and Mark's issues. First thing Saturday morning, Richard dragged the Christmas tree they had purchased the evening before into the corner of the living room where it would shine through the large front window. That afternoon Angela dragged their few boxes of decorations from the attic.

Following her directions, Richard tacked greenery along the arch that separated the dining room from the living area and around the red brick dividers. When they were finished, Richard handed Angela a package from her mother-in-law that said Open Me Now.

"Oh, dear," Angela said when she opened the box. Her shocked expression turned to peals of laughter as she held it up for Richard to see.

"What in God's name is that?" he asked as he grabbed for the plastic Santa head. It had a red velvet cap with a furry white tassel and a gold metallic string, that when pulled, played Jingle

Bells.

Angela insisted he get a hammer and nail so she could hang it immediately, even though he loudly objected. "My mother," he said, shaking his head in amazement.

That evening, they trimmed the tree, sipped cider and began their second Christmas holiday together in Oklahoma. The old Craftsman house fit the Currier and Ives vision of what Christmas should look like. Once Angela finished placing the last of the silver tinsel on the tree and Richard plugged in the lights, they sat on the floor together in the dark and admired their handiwork. A Christmas album played softly in the background, and the peace felt good after the hectic fall semester.

After a few moments, Angela smiled up at Richard and asked, "What were you doing in the attic the other night?"

He hadn't anticipated the question. Having no time to think of a lie, he looked into Angela's warm brown eyes. "When we first bought the house, I thought how perfect it would be as a playroom," he admitted. "Remember when we first saw the large closet under the front eve?"

Angela nodded. "Like a dollhouse, we thought. I remember. You said you'd finish the walls and ceilings and once they got older, the kids would have a hide-out right inside the house. What made you think of that, Richard? The talk about the baby?"

"Yeah, I guess," he said. "I wonder if you will ever want that, Ang."

She quietly rose and turned down the volume on the record player.

Angela and Richard promised not to open a book or syllabus for the first two weeks of the holiday break. Even the trip to Kansas on ice-packed roads was a welcome change of pace. Niggling thoughts about Jennifer kept surfacing in Angela's mind, but she kept pushing them down. Her parents kept the conversation focused on their jobs, the college, and the war that refused to end.

But at Richard's house Christmas Eve, his mother broached the baby question head-on.

"So, Angela," her mother-in-law said. "Are we going to have baby toys under the tree by next Christmas?"

Angela paled in silence while Richard stepped in.

"Mom," he said, "Please. We'll let you know when we're ready for babies. Angela is focused on getting tenured right now, and it's only our second year on staff."

"Well, I understand, but you aren't getting any younger. Why, I had both of you boys before I was twenty, and here you are nearly twenty-five. Angela, really darling, we love you so much, but you can't put your job before family, can you?"

Angela bit her tongue; she would not cause a fight on Christmas Eve. Inside she was seething. Richard reached over and put his arm around her. "Things have changed, mom," he said.

"You mean Women's Lib?" his mother asked. She stood. "I'll get the brandy snifter."

On the drive back to Edmond Christmas night, Angela put her hand on Richard's as he gripped the steering wheel. He seemed tense and out of sorts. "Are you upset about your parents asking?" she said gently.

Glancing over at her, Richard said, "No, are you?"

She shook her head, and the subject was dropped, but she knew he was as disappointed with her as his parents were. The baby discussion had taken place a few months after their wedding, shortly after they received their PhDs and again last summer. Women's Liberation said she could have it all. Angela wasn't willing to take that risk. Yes, she wanted children, but she had worked hard for her doctorate and for this position and no, she did not believe you could have it all. It just sounded too easy.

*

January 16, 1970 found both students and professors bleary eyed, barely managing to make it through the morning class periods. Afternoon students were somewhat more engaged. At four o'clock Angela took Richard's excited phone call and ran the short distance to the Engineering and Computer Science building, forgetting to grab her coat. Shivering, she let herself into Richard's office where she found Mark and Jennifer talking with Richard about Christmas gifts and holiday parties. The office held three chairs comfortably. She walked around the desk and stood behind Richard, putting her hands on his shoulders.

"Didn't want to leave you out of this," Richard explained. He nodded at the kids.

Mark spoke first. "We spent the month talking with our parents and to each other," he said. "Do *you* want to finish?" he asked Jennifer.

"We wanted you guys to be the first to know," she began. "We've—*We've* decided to continue with the pregnancy. But we're giving the baby up for adoption."

Angela let out a small gasp.

Richard said, "That's wonderful, kids. You made the decision together. Good," he repeated.

"Congratulations," Angela added, "I'm glad it was mutual."

Angela was pleased they'd made the decision jointly, but she wasn't sure they had made the right one. Abortion was a difficult choice as was marriage and children; but adoption? Did they have any idea how hard it would be to give up this baby?

January and February literally blew through Oklahoma. The heavy wool rugs kept the wood floors a bit warmer although Angela wore socks round the clock. Classes were going well, and the SDS group had gone underground for awhile; the students concentrated on early semester course work.

Since Christmas, Angela had found herself walking the hallway from their front bedroom to the one at the rear. One morning in late February, she left Richard to his newspaper and coffee and found herself there again. It was a wonderful room with one small window looking over the backyard and the neighbors' pecan trees. The two larger windows on the east lit the room with early morning sunshine.

She opened the tiny closet to the left of the doorway and peeked inside; then walked to the center of the room looking past the boxes they had stored there and the over-stuffed and ugly brown pull-out sofa that no one could sleep on. She visualized the room painted yellow with white lace curtains and a white wicker bassinet and a small wicker chest of drawers. A changing table over by the windows. An animal carousel over the crib that waited for the newborn to grow out of the bassinet. Humming to herself, she let the thoughts settle into her consciousness.

*

The Oklahoma wind blew in a warm April and an early spring. The Dogwood trees bloomed earlier than ever, and even the Crepe Myrtel outside her bedroom window had budded out. It would be a late Easter this year and Angela was looking forward to another short break from classes. The past few weeks she'd noticed Jennifer looking tired and pale and one afternoon she stopped her as she was racing from class.

"I'm fine," Jennifer said when Angela asked about her health. "Just tired all the time."

"To be expected, I guess," Angela replied.

"It's been hard, you know. Mark has been there for me constantly. But I had to have a meeting with Dean Mumford last week regarding my pregnancy."

"I wondered if Administration was going to step in," Angela said.

"She was very nice. Told me I could be brought before the Women's Counsel but she wasn't going to recommend that. I think she feels being pregnant and unmarried is probably punishment enough." Her smile looked forced.

"It's got to be hard. I'm sorry. Your friends?" she said.

"Some have stayed friends; others dumped me right away.

Once in awhile in the cafeteria, I feel like a pariah but I refuse to drop out of classes. I'm not due till July so I have plenty of time to complete this semester."

"If you need anything, call me, ok?" Angela said. "I know Richard and I have stepped back but we were really forced to after being reprimanded. That doesn't mean we don't care."

"I know," Jennifer said. "We understood. Honestly."

"Well, just know we're here for you and for Mark, ok?"

She gave Jennifer a warm hug before the girl headed to her next class. All afternoon, it bothered her, though. What a hard thing for a nineteen year old to deal with. But Jennifer had a strength she wasn't sure she'd ever had at that age. She was a determined young lady for sure.

"She's holding her head high and doing what she needs to do," she told Richard that evening. "You've got to give her a lot of credit."

"And making straight A's in my class as always," Richard said. "I'm glad Administration backed off on considering expulsion. I guess the times really are changing."

"Well, I wouldn't go that far," Angela said. But inside she did agree with him. Times were definitely changing.

Just after Easter, a letter arrived from the Selective Service and Angela cringed when she saw the envelope she cringed. "Richard," she called as she walked to his office. When she handed it to him, they both held their breaths.

But the letter inside was simply a reminder to make certain he had registered for the draft. "I didn't think it could be," he said. "The numbers they called last month didn't include my birth date, but next month I suppose it could."

"Don't even say that," she said. "Don't even think it."

Their arguments had ceased for now; too busy with classes to do much of that these days anyway.

*

On May 6, Angela and Richard's students had had enough. They took to the streets, two hundred strong, and along with several hundred from Oklahoma University in Norman, they gathered to call for a general strike. The students clashed with two busloads of police and thirty-five Highway Patrol Officers, and someone pulled out a Viet Cong Flag. Before it was over, several protestors were injured and three arrested.

The next day over two thousand gathered in a peaceful march to protest the arrest of the flag-bearing student. At Phillips University in Enid, thirty students and faculty began a three-day hunger strike. And in Stillwater, at Oklahoma State, a smaller group marched peacefully through the streets of the small town.

At noon, Angela was on campus, holed up in her office. The worry lines had deepened over the past nine months, and she found herself unable to concentrate on academics. Her eight o'clock class had been half-full; at ten, the room was nearly empty. Angela knew that Mark and Jennifer would be leading their classmates in today's march. Mark had phoned the night before to tell her about the young man who had been arrested for waving the V.C. flag. The students were outraged and crying *Freedom of Speech*. They were gathering today to protest his arrest and to call for a general strike of all classes.

At one o'clock, Richard stood in the doorway of Angela's office.

"What? What is it?" she asked. She stood and moved quickly toward the door, meeting him just inside.

"I just got a call from Jennifer. She didn't have your office number. Mark has been arrested and they need bond money."

"But what ..."

"I didn't ask questions, Angela. There wasn't time. She hung up pretty quickly."

"Well, let's go," Angela said.

"No." Richard's face was stern.

"What do you mean, no?"

"I mean—we've done enough, Angela. There is too much at stake here."

"Well, I'm going. You can stay here and be safe. Those kids need us right now, and we have the money to help. How much is it, anyway?" said Angela.

"$75.00 that we don't have," he yelled as she grabbed her purse and left the room.

Angela found Jennifer hunched in a straight-back metal chair in the waiting room of the Oklahoma City jail, its torn orange plastic seat poking into the backs of her legs. Her six month belly was pretty much hidden by the navy blue and white plaid mod maternity jumper she wore. It was not unlike the hundreds of other plaid jumpers on campus.

She looked frightened and exhausted. *And oh, so very young,* Angela thought. After giving her a quick hug, Angela approached the desk sergeant behind the window. Within a few moments the supervisor accepted her check and made a call for Mark to be released, and a half hour later, they walked into the sunlight and to Angela's car. Angela watched as Jennifer walked quickly to the vehicle and climbed into the rear seat of the VW without saying a word to either of them.

"I can't thank you enough, Dr. Johnston," Mark said. "How can we repay you?"

By now Richard's anger had worn off on Angela, and her tone was sharp when she spoke. "You can repay me by not doing anything foolish like this again, Mark."

She shifted the VW into gear and backed from the parking spot.

Mark sat beside her in the passenger seat, and Jennifer was wedged tightly behind him.

As Angela glanced into her rear-view mirror, she saw Jennifer sitting rigid with rage.

"We agreed to march, Mark, we didn't agree to get arrested. What were you thinking? Do you know how lucky we are that

Angela is helping us? And you wanted to be a father?" Tears welled in her eyes.

Angela watched Mark's face redden in response to Jennifer's harsh remarks. Then she spoke quietly, "Guys, I love you both, you know that. I've stood with you for months now. But Richard is right about one thing. This can't happen again, Mark. Getting arrested is not ok."

"I know," Mark said. "But you weren't there; you don't understand. You have to stand up for what's right."

"What is right, Mark, is *you* taking care of Jennifer and putting this baby first. Even if you are adopting out, she is your number one concern, got that? You can repay us $5.00 a week for awhile. Now let's get you both back to campus."

Richard was waiting at the house when Angela opened the front door. He stood red-faced and rigid in the center of the room, glaring with anger. She had never gone against his wishes before. She knew things were escalating between them and she wasn't sure she was prepared for what might come next.

Angela shrugged out of her jacket and threw it on the nearest chair, then turned to face him.

"Richard Johnston, don't say a word to me."

"I cannot believe you did this when I made it very clear we were not giving them the money. Hell, Angela, we don't have it to spare. You seem to have forgotten we are a couple and we make decisions together. I don't know you anymore."

"And I don't know *you*. We agreed to get involved in the lives of these kids, Richard. You and I—we made that decision together. When did *you* stop acting like we were a couple?"

"You've become a bleeding heart, Angela. I hate this war as much as the rest of you, but there are proper ways to channel that energy, and protesting and burning flags isn't one of them!"

"Go ahead, Richard, say the rest."

Richard ran his fingers through his hair, brushing it back from his forehead and took a deep breath. "You don't want me to do that, Angela. Trust me."

"Say it, Richard. This is about your job, not mine. This is about you wanting me to start a family and give up my career. This is all about you." She turned quickly and walked into the bedroom, rattling the door as it slammed shut.

Angela and Richard retreated into a cold war. They ate together, slept together and went to their respective classrooms and offices each day. Neither wanted to address the blow-up; afraid that talking about it might somehow push them further toward the abyss. Whatever thoughts Angela had considered about getting pregnant were put aside; she would not give in to demands or threats. But she also did not want to lose her marriage and going silent and sitting still seemed to be the safest decision for now.

Two weeks later, Angela's phone rang. Dean Hayes was on the other end asking her to come over to his office in Old North. All winter Angela had dreaded this call. She and Richard had two years under their belts, making them eligible for tenure in five more. Her hands were shaking as she sat in the small waiting area. Richard walked in two minutes later looking just as pale as she felt. He took her hand and tried to smile.

"It will be ok," he whispered. He refused to take the easy road of blame.

Dean Hayes stood as they took the seats directly across from his imposing desk.

"You've seen the photo, I assume," he began. He held up a black and white glossy. It was the same photo that had appeared in the Oklahoma City paper last week.

Mark stood defiant in front of two police officers; it had been taken just moments before they had arrested him and hours before she had bailed him out of jail. She knew what this meant; Dean Hayes knew of her involvement.

Angela nodded silently.

"Dr. Johnston," he said addressing Angela. "I believe I've

made my position about staff fraternizing with students very clear since you arrived. Particularly in lieu of what's been happening on campus this year. I've been told you participated in SDS meetings, is that true?"

"Sir," Richard interjected.

"I believe I'm addressing your wife, Richard." He turned to Angela and waited.

"Dean Hayes, I cannot deny that the students held meetings in our home but in my defense, I felt it was better they be safe and have adult supervision. I didn't encourage it but I did allow it."

"This photo was released last week by the FBI and sent to every campus administrator. I believe you know the student involved."

Angela glanced at the photo again and nodded.

"And did you or did you not post bail to have Mr. Roberts released?"

"I did. His parents live out of state. Yes, I did." She left it at that.

Turning to Richard, he asked, "You were aware of these meetings in your home?"

Angela interrupted, "Dean Hayes, my husband warned me not to get involved. He had nothing to do with the decision. I'm the one to blame, and I'm the one who should be disciplined."

"You're both good instructors," Dean Hayes continued, "it makes me sad to do this, but your actions were completely against school policy and my direct instructions."

Angela felt her stomach clinch and her heart lurch.

"However, we'll take this as a first offense. You will both receive a formal reprimand in your personnel file, and any further actions of this type will be cause for dismissal."

As they walked from the Dean's office, the relief Angela felt brought her to tears. But the angry words between her and Richard over the past month still hung in the air.

*

Following Mark's release, Angela had dropped him and Jennifer at their respective dorms and had gently told them that she and Richard would have to end the use of their home for future SDS meetings. Since then, Jennifer had been cautiously polite in class and had avoided any personal contact with either of her instructors. The sudden change had been difficult for Angela. She didn't like losing her connection with her students. Richard, on the other hand, seemed greatly relieved which angered Angela even further. They hadn't spoken of it since the meeting with the Dean.

It was true. He had warned her that she was putting their careers in jeopardy; had told her not to get involved. But she wasn't like him. Richard could speak out about his opposition to the war, but he didn't put actions behind his words. She had been willing to do both and she wasn't ashamed of that.

Classes wound down in mid-May and final exams were scheduled in two weeks. Angela and Richard were counting the days to summer break. Some of the tension had lifted since their meeting with the Dean. Perhaps his leniency had rubbed off on Richard, she wondered. She stopped going to the 'baby's room' and made the decision, alone as always, to put any thoughts of motherhood off for another year or two. Luckily she had said nothing to Richard in the past few months about her maternal yearnings. *It was probably just hormonal,* she thought, *or empathy for Jennifer.*

She admired the young woman for being able to hold her head high and continue attending classes despite her obvious pregnancy. An Honors student, campus leader; it couldn't be easy. Angela saw the young couple walking campus arm in arm nearly every day. Mark appeared to have taken Angela's advice and was constantly at Jennifer's side. She hadn't asked about the adoption or if they'd found a family for the baby. Heeding Dean

Hayes' advice, Angela kept personal matters out of her classroom for now.

But she thought often of the heart-breaking decision Jennifer had been forced to make. It couldn't be easy giving up your first-born child for adoption. *Maybe one day it won't be so difficult for women*, she thought, but at the moment it was.

Angela was at home grading exams one afternoon in late May when the phone rang, and she heard Jennifer's voice.

"Dr. Johnston, Angela—may I come to the house to talk to you?"

Angela frowned with curiosity. "Of course, is two thirty okay?" She set the meeting for mid-afternoon, knowing that Richard would be in class. She made iced tea while she waited for Jennifer to arrive. At two thirty on the dot, Angela welcomed Jennifer, and the two women sat in the living room.

Jennifer pushed herself back in the overstuffed recliner and put her feet up as Angela set a tray of glasses, sugar and lemon and a small plate of gingersnap cookies onto the coffee table between them. "Sugar?" Angela asked.

Jennifer shook her head, "Just a slice of lemon, please."

"Are you comfortable? Can I get you anything?"

"Truth is I'm never comfortable these days. I'm as big as a house. My mom keeps wondering about twins, but the doctor said absolutely not, only one heart-beat."

"Well, it won't be too much longer. When is your due date?"

"August 12, they think. Ten weeks. Hard to believe."

"Any luck with adoptive parents?" said Angela

Jennifer took a cookie and laid it on the napkin. "Well, that's sort of why I'm here. Dr. Johnston ... Angela," she corrected herself. "Have you and Mr. Johnston ever wanted to have a baby? I mean, have you ever tried or anything?"

Angela shifted forward onto the edge of the worn sofa and looked closely at Jennifer's serious face, questions forming around the edges of her mind.

"Well, I've felt a lot like you the past few years. Although Richard and I married a year before we finished our doctorates, I wanted to wait on starting a family until I was ready to put a child before my career. I felt like it was my decision to make, even though Richard and our parents would have liked for it to happen sooner. I just wasn't ready."

Jennifer nodded.

"You know," Angela continued, "I've worked so hard for my education, years of time spent preparing for this, and it will be a long time before we are tenured and making good money. A baby, right now, just doesn't fit the plan."

Jennifer's face fell a little, and she pursed her lips. "Well, Mark and I were wondering—how you might feel about adopting our baby? I could continue with classes this fall and babysit for you all the time so you could keep teaching. And you wouldn't have a long pregnancy to go through or morning sickness or any of that. We just thought maybe ..." Her voice drifted off.

Angela felt the blood rush from her head as she tried to sort out what Jennifer was asking. There was no way this could work. And yet—why had she been walking the extra bedroom placing baby furniture in her mind if she wasn't ready? Why had she found herself in the baby department at Kmart? She had to admit that until her recent fight with Richard over her involvement, over-involvement Richard accused, with her students, she had given serious thought to becoming pregnant.

Something inside her stirred. She grinned broadly at the girl.

"You're serious?" she asked. "You'd trust Richard and me with your baby? You'd be able to give up the child to people you know?"

"It makes perfect sense, Angela. Mark and I wouldn't have made it through this year without you and your husband. Letting us use your house, supporting the pregnancy, getting Mark out of jail, not to mention understanding when I couldn't make it to class." She looked intently into Angela's eyes. "Plus you're great together. Who better?" she asked.

"Oh, Jennifer," she whispered. Tears welled in her eyes. "What a gift."

They parted a short time later with an agreement that perhaps they could make it work.

Angela couldn't wait for Richard to walk through the door. After Jennifer left, she had called him and told him to cut short his office hours and come home. She'd refused to tell him why. She knew just how she was going to approach him.

At five thirty, Richard pulled into the drive and jumped from the car. He bounded up the steps, onto the porch and quickly threw open the front door. "Angela," he called out when he didn't see her. He walked through the dining room into the kitchen, peeked into the laundry room and into his back office. "Angela," he called again.

"Back here," she replied, "in the other bedroom."

She heard him walk back through the dining room and into the hall outside the bedroom door. Richard stood in the doorway, his mouth open and slack. He shook his head twice.

Angela stood in the middle of the room. She had pushed the boxes and the old sofa back against the wall. On the floor were large pieces of left-over sheets of poster board from the SDS meetings, cut into patterns. Bassinet to the rear, a rocking chair in the corner, crib in front of the windows, and changing table against the front wall. She had marked each piece so he wouldn't be confused.

"You're pregnant?" His eyes widened, and a grin began to spread.

"Well, sort of," she said. "Come, sit." She sat on the sofa and patted the cushion beside her.

Over the next half hour she told him about Jennifer's visit. "What do you think?" she asked somewhat hesitantly. She watched the hesitation on his face turn into a smile.

"I think it's a hellava idea," he added, reaching for her and pulling her into his arms. "Wow."

Angela leaned against his chest, and they sat quietly for awhile. Richard bent and kissed her neck; then in the silence he grinned and shook his head. "A baby."

Though neither mentioned the added blessing this child brought to them, Angela knew it was a godsend. If Richard got his draft notice this summer, they would be protected. He could avoid the damned war that seemed to never end.

Chapter 9
The Search Begins

Halfway through the first diary, Karen realized she'd never fully appreciated the challenges her mother had faced as a woman in the seventies. Between the lines of handwriting, she felt Angela's torment over the possibility of losing everything if she tried to have it all.

She turned the yellowed pages and read another entry:

Tonight we let the kids use our house for their first SDS meeting. After everyone left, Jennifer Anderson stayed to talk to me for a few minutes. She's in my Honors English class. I figured out why she stayed when I saw Mark take Jennifer's hand as they walked down the steps of the front porch. They make a cute couple.

Her hand flew to her mouth as she read the last line. Jennifer—Mark—she wondered. She began flipping through pages, checking dates and a few events here and there. It was in here; she knew it.

She grabbed the next journal.

March, 1970—April—May. She stopped.

The entry read:

Jennifer came to see me today. She'd hoped to find a good stable couple to adopt the baby but nothing has worked out for the poor girl. She said she'd like Richard and me to adopt her unborn child. Maybe because I want a baby so badly, I said yes. And I hope we don't regret this decision. This will take Richard out of the draft, at least for now. What an amazing day. We'll have a baby by mid-

summer. I've decided on a pale mint green for the walls since we won't know the sex till the birth. Mark has agreed and will sign the adoption paperwork.

Karen threw the journal aside. It was all there; she had the name—the name of her father.

"Gary," she cried out, "Oh, my God, Gary."

She was shaking and sobbing when Gary reached her. He held her until she calmed to a quiet gasping breath.

"Karen, what is it?" he finally asked. "Talk to me."

Her parents had never lied about her adoption, but what angered Karen was the fact that her mother and father had known her biological parents so well. The adoption had been planned months before her mother had died in childbirth. Why had Angela never told her? The excitement of finding the identity of her biological parents was now tempered by her parents' lies of omission.

Jennifer Anderson. Angela and Richard Johnston. Three of her parents were dead. Karen wondered about Mark Roberts. Was he still alive? Was it time to complete the puzzle? Or should she leave the past unearthed?

Once she got past the initial shock, Karen gave herself a week to slowly re-read and process the information in her mother's diaries. Angela had written a lot about that spring of 1970; the months leading up to the adoption. There were a few clues about Jennifer's insistence that she and Mark give the child up though he had fought the decision. It was obvious how much the young couple loved each other, and the devastation he had felt the day she died—her birthday—the day she'd always celebrated with parties and childhood glee. But each added piece of information begged for another and the puzzle she was piecing together had gaping holes and jagged edges everywhere.

She spent hours on the computer plugging in every search word she could think of. She found a half dozen Mark Roberts but none close to his age or place of birth. His name was not listed on the Vietnam Vets Memorial Wall site. As hard as it was to believe, there was nothing on *her* Mark Roberts. It was like he had vanished.

She sometimes stood at the windows overlooking the lush green of their Colorado backyard for an hour or more before realizing how much time she'd lost in the past. Denise stopped by on Wednesday to check on her and to remind her of their first day luncheon obligations. School started in six days.

On Friday evening, she approached Gary in their home office. She stood in the doorway; hand on hip, a determined scowl on her face.

"We're going to Oklahoma, Gary. I have to find him."

Gary looked up with little visible emotion, as if he'd been waiting for this announcement. "I don't disagree, but are you sure you're ready? I mean, it's been thirty-nine years. You've never met the man. I just don't want you to get hurt."

"I know," she said, "but to answer your question—yes. I'm ready no matter how it turns out. I need to meet him, if only once."

And so, on Monday, they boarded a Southwest non-stop flight into Oklahoma City, grabbed a rental car and drove downtown to the county court house. The clerk on duty retrieved the microfiche films from 1970.

The record of marriage listed birth dates in Kansas for both Jennifer and Mark. The ceremony was witnessed by Angela and Richard Johnston. Karen's birth record was there. And just below was the adoption paper, signed by her adoptive parents. But no name or signature of her biological father.

Her next step was military records. They took the elevator to the third floor and asked for assistance at the desk. Within minutes, the woman had located the information.

The name of Lt. Mark Roberts had been pulled in the June lottery of 1970. He received orders to report for duty, but apparently had joined the Air Force before that induction occurred. His boot camp start-date was three weeks after her birth. That realization gave her chills. How could he watch his wife die, give his baby to another couple, and report for duty three weeks later, knowing he was headed to Vietnam? Gary held her as she wept tears of grief for this man she'd never met.

Gary read over her shoulder as her finger traced from left to right along the next lines of print. Injured in Operation Homecoming, Cambodia, April 12, 1973. Released from duty August 1973 following medical treatment, San Antonio, Texas, USA.

1973—she would have been three years old. It would seem likely he had returned to the central plains. Kansas was his birth state; only miles from Oklahoma. So, why …? She didn't want to finish the question. But, why had he not?

As she closed the military computer site, she turned to the clerk who had helped her retrieve his records. "Where do I go from here?" she asked.

"Census. IRS. His home town. Those are all options," she said. "Start with death records though, if you want to be certain he's still living."

Still living. He couldn't be more than fifty-eight years old. Deep down, she felt a knowingness that he was still alive.

It was nearly six in the evening when they walked down the courthouse steps. Both she and Gary needed rest. They drove toward Guthrie and pulled off I35 at a Holiday Inn Express and Suites. At least they had room service, sparse as it was. Gary ordered burgers and fries and they settled into the room for the remainder of the evening.

Neither felt much like talking. *What was there to say?* They would go to Kansas the next morning and continue the search. For now, she just needed sleep.

The next morning she ordered coffee to their room. She hadn't slept all night, but she didn't want to wake Gary too early.

Within an hour they dressed and were driving north on KS-2 to Kiowa, Kansas, the small town where her father had been born. Another helpful government clerk welcomed them to the records office at the county court house and began yet another computer search. Birth records showed Mark Roberts, born to Margaret and Gene Roberts. No listed siblings. Death record—none. Karen sucked in a deep breath. Gary squeezed her hand. But they hit a wall at that point. No Kansas tax records for anyone with that name. No property purchases either. And no marriage certificate recorded, at least not in the county.

"Let's grab a bite and come back," Mark said. "I have a thought."

By 1:30 they had found a lead by tracing back to Mark's parents, Margaret and Gene Roberts. Margaret's one sister had died in 2000. Gene had two siblings: a brother who had died in Korea and a sister, Helen, still living in Kiowa.

Karen called information and received a phone number; the automated voice put the call through. She waited through three rings without breathing, and then a woman's voice came on the line.

"I'm sorry to bother you," she said, "But I'm trying to locate Mark Roberts and it appears that you may have a nephew with that name?" Her voice held the question mark.

There was a moment of silence on the other end before the woman responded. "I did have a nephew; my brother's son, but I haven't heard from him in many years."

"I believe he was my biological father," she explained. "And I'm here in Kansas trying to locate him. Would it be possible for us to visit with you?"

The woman agreed to meet and gave Karen driving directions.

She shook her head as they headed for the car. Was this the link?

Helen Taylor, maiden name Roberts, answered the door of a

small house in the countryside just south of town. She greeted them warmly and invited them to sit at the kitchen table where she offered iced tea and some packaged cookies on a plate.

Karen accepted the icy glass but passed on the Fig Newton's. Helen sat across from her and they spent a few moments with introductions and explanations. Karen described the past few months and the journals she'd discovered.

"I found my adopted mother's journals as we were emptying out my parent's Denver house and I've pretty well proved that my biological father was Mark Roberts. Anything you can tell us would be appreciated."

"It's odd you should show up right now. I was just thinking of Mark the other day," Helen began. "The last time I saw him was during a visit after he got back from Vietnam. Marge and Gene stopped in around the holidays that year with Mark in tow. He was ... what? Probably about twenty-five or so. He'd been wounded and walked with a bit of a limp; not bad though. A year or so after that, I heard from Gene that Mark had returned to classes and was headed to Oklahoma State in Stillwater for an Engineering degree."

She stopped and took a sip of tea and bit into a cookie, her eyes looking far into the past. "You know he didn't say two words that whole day, and I remember wondering if he was going to be ok. You know what I mean?"

Karen nodded and Mark spoke up. "Do you know where he went after that?"

"I wish I did, for your sake, Karen, but I really don't. Gene died a year later of cancer and I'm ashamed I sort of lost track of Marge not long after that."

Karen knew Gary's deflated expression mirrored her own.

"Mark just seemed to vanish. I tried looking him up once or twice. Was going to reach out after Gene died. Family you know. But if he ever got any of my cards, I never heard. I finally gave up many years ago."

Karen felt like crying, but Helen looked about as sad as she felt. "Well, it was worth a shot and I thank you so much for your time." She stood to leave but Helen stopped her in her tracks with her next statement.

"You know, Karen, I did communicate with him during the war though. Now, where did I put those letters?" she said.

Karen held her breath. *Please have them.*

"I'll be right back. I'm sure they're in a box somewhere; help yourself to more tea, dear."

Karen turned to Gary and whispered. "Oh, my gosh, Gary, do you think?" She was interrupted by Helen's voice calling from the front of the house. She arrived a moment later with a battered old shirt box and placed it on the table in front of them.

"Maybe these will help, dear. I'm sorry I can't do more, but I just have no idea where Mark went when he left Oklahoma."

Karen thanked the woman and picked up the box. She couldn't wait to get some place quiet to go through the correspondence.

Helen walked them to the door. "Please stay in touch, and please tell Mark to phone me if you locate him."

"I will," Karen said, "and thanks again."

Gary reached for her hand as they walked to the car. "You alright?"

She nodded. "Let's stay the night so I can go through these, Gary."

"I'm sorry we didn't get further." he said. "But I wasn't too surprised. That happened with a lot of guys when they got back from 'Nam. They didn't re-integrate well and a lot of them did the same thing. Disappeared."

Karen read as many letters as she could that night in the motel. Gary went into Kiowa for pizza and beer and sat across from her at the table as she read aloud at times. By 9:00 p.m. she was exhausted and closed the box. She was numb inside from the horror of her father's experiences in Cambodia, but it only made her desire to find him in person that much stronger.

"So, what do we do tomorrow, babe?" Gary said.

"I have no idea," she said. She wiped tears from her cheeks. "Where do we go from here?" she asked. "I don't know what to do next, but I'm not giving up now."

Chapter 10
September, 1973

Mark Roberts grimaced as he bent to retrieve his Air Force-issue duffel bag.

"Thanks," he said. He shook hands with the kid who had pushed his mandatory wheel chair through the double glass doors of the VA Hospital in Oklahoma City. He could see his mother's car parked along the curb of the circular drive. She had driven down from Wichita that morning. He waved when he spotted her, and she pulled forward to the curb.

It was an unseasonably hot day, and Mark was already sweating through his uniform. He felt a little wobbly but he took it slow. His mother was halfway out the driver's door when he waved her off. "I can do this, mom," he muttered under his breath.

His six foot frame needed another thirty pounds before he'd rid himself of the skeletal image he saw in the bathroom mirror each morning. As he stepped forward, his body listed to the right, reacting to the tightness on his other side. Everything along there felt shorter to Mark – his left leg, arm, even his shoulder and neck. The muscles seemed locked in a taut vice, holding together the underlying tissue and once-broken bones.

Rehab had been hell for the past four months, but at least he was back in Oklahoma and out of San Antonio. It was in Texas that he'd survived a half-dozen surgeries as the military doctors pieced him back together with sutures and staples, and inserted metal plates, pins and screws. He had so much steel inside him, it was a wonder he didn't clank as he walked toward the car and opened the passenger door.

His mother attempted an awkward hug across the steering wheel, gave up and pecked his left cheek with a light kiss. "Ready?" she asked.

Mark ignored the question. "Dad couldn't face me?"

"Oh, Mark, he'll be here tomorrow; he will. It's so hard for …" Her voice trailed off.

His mother and father had visited several times, both in San Antonio during his surgeries and in Oklahoma City during his long and difficult rehab. He knew his physical wounds had affected his dad the most. He glanced over at his mother's profile and realized how much she had aged while he was gone. He knew it tore her apart to realize that a mother's love was just not enough to heal his wounds, to erase the scars, no matter how much she desired to do so. He was healing physically; he wasn't sure about the rest.

"Not a big deal," he said.

The fact that he could now maneuver without a cane had been last week's miracle, though he kept one near-by should he have to manage more than a few stairs. He wondered if he'd ever reach a point where he even wanted to leave his room to use it.

He noticed his mother glancing at him whenever freeway traffic eased enough for her to do so. The drive to Edmond, this time of day, would take twenty minutes. He could find nothing to fill the silence, so he let his mother ramble on about the weather, his father, and her bridge group, as he nodded and responded with an occasional "oh" or "good".

Once off the Broadway curve, they entered the outskirts of Edmond, a sleepy college town north of Oklahoma City. As they drove along the tree-lined streets by the university, Mark steeled himself for the moment they would turn into the drive of his red brick duplex. He had considered going on to Kansas with his parents for a few more weeks, but he knew he couldn't avoid the past forever. Might as well face it now and get it over with.

He spotted the house a half block away and closed his eyes against the sight. Three years ago this week he had exchanged his war protest signs for a rifle – his number pulled easily from a lottery jar he'd heatedly fought against. He had buried Jennifer, his wife of two months, handed their newborn baby girl to her adoptive parents and turned into someone who, to this day, he did not recognize. His mother parked the car in the driveway and quickly rushed to the passenger door, one hand out, in case he needed to steady himself.

"I'm fine, Mother," he said tersely. "Thanks," he said more gently.

He retrieved his bag from the back seat and walked along the short sidewalk and up the two steps to the front porch. His mother followed close behind, her arms now full of grocery bags and her purse.

The key turned the tumblers, and he let his mother walk through the door ahead of him. Mark watched as she clicked on light switches and walked to the thermostat in the hall to turn on some cool air.

"I'll just put these groceries away," she said as she headed back to the kitchen.

Mark turned to his right and walked directly to the bedroom he had shared with Jennifer for those few short weeks. He knew his mother would have removed any personal reminders, but she couldn't wash away the memories that hung in the air like a heavy fog. His heart fluttered with fear for just a beat.

Mark teetered from the doorway to the edge of the bed, glanced at the old armoire against the wall, and looked out the front window at the untended yard of dead grass. He could hear his mother busying herself in the kitchen; the refrigerator door swishing open and shut, the squeak of the oven door, items sliding onto cabinet shelves. As he listened and stared, his vision blurred— like looking through the empty bottom of a glass as you down the last drop of liquid.

He lowered himself onto the bed; his head fell into his open palms, and in a moment he was in another hospital—one he never wanted to see again.

*

After just five weeks of marriage, and two weeks before he was to report for duty, her contractions started. At the hospital, no one seemed overly concerned; Jennifer was near enough to full-term, the baby's vitals were strong, and even if premature, the consensus was that she or he would be healthy after a short stay in the preemie ward. Angela and Richard raced to the hospital as soon as Mark called. Both his parents and Jennifer's lived in Kansas and were headed south when things went to hell quickly.

In the delivery room, Mark stood beside Jennifer, letting her grip his hand as tightly as she needed. He was white with fear, nineteen years old and totally unprepared for what he was watching. Three nurses moved in and out of his peripheral vision; he had given up trying to tell them apart. The doctor had been called the moment they arrived, and he walked into her room wearing green scrubs and a wide smile shortly after Jennifer's water broke.

Mark felt totally inept and extraneous, but Jennifer would not release his hand. Even if he'd wanted to slip aside, he couldn't. He watched her face contort with each contraction. The doctor pressed his hand against her belly, checked to see if the baby was head first, and reassured them that things were on track, even though a bit early.

Mark heard him tell one of the nurses to prepare the nursery for a preemie, and she rushed from the room. Another nurse wiped Jennifer's forehead and murmured encouraging phrases. "Good job, Jennifer." "Breathe." "Don't push." "Push."

He wanted to be saying those words, but his wife's distorted face, heavy panting and cries of pain frightened him, and he couldn't think. Mark finally bent to kiss her forehead and mimicked the nurse. "You're doing great, Jennifer. It will be over soon."

That remark had gotten him a furious look and another wrenching scream. He knew she wanted to curse at him, but her energy was focused on her writhing belly.

The first nurse now stood behind Mark. "You ok, dad?" she asked. "Don't need another patient lying on the floor." She smiled, and Mark relaxed his body slightly.

The physician let Jennifer take a break from pushing, and she laid her head back onto the hospital bed, exhausted. Mark heard caution in the doctor's voice when he asked, "The adoptive parents on their way?"

Mark nodded yes. "And Jennifer's mom and dad, and mine."

Jennifer's belly rose as if carried upward on a high tidal wave. Mark gasped at the force of it. Jennifer cried out and grabbed his hand again, clasping harder and harder until Mark's fingers turned white.

Jennifer responded to each order to keep pushing; take a deep breath and push harder. Mark looked at her pale, sweat-covered face, still lovely to his eyes.

"The baby's into the canal," the doctor reported, "and crowning. I can see a black head of hair, Jennifer. Give me the biggest push you have, ok?"

Mark was growing giddy. Even though they were adopting to people they loved, it would always be his child—his child and Jennifer's. They had created a beautiful tiny being.

The next thing Mark knew, he was being pushed to the back of the delivery room where he stood like a stone. The two nurses on each side of Jennifer began CPR. An oxygen mask appeared on Jennifer's face, another IV entered her arm and time slammed into slow motion. A third nurse ran into the room, and the obstetrician yelled orders. "Call for an OR; grab the IV; we're going in."

Mark kept yelling, "What's happening?" One nurse took a moment to touch his arm. "We're going to the OR for a cesarean."

"But ..." Mark couldn't say it. *Is she alive?* Her once pale skin was now white, and he could see she wasn't breathing on her own.

"You can follow us to the doors," the doctor yelled as he raced from the room. The three nurses briskly wheeled the hospital bed through the door and were practically running as they reached the end of the hall and turned left.

As the doors to the operating room opened, the physician motioned for Mark to step into the room, and a nurse had Mark in a mask and gown before he took three steps.

"We have to save your baby. Do you want to watch the delivery?"

Mark felt the shell of his body and an emptiness within. He couldn't answer, but he couldn't leave Jennifer, especially now. He nodded "yes."

The nurse led him behind a glass partition in the scrub room. As fast as they had raced just moments before, it now felt to Mark like hours were passing, as the team prepped her for the procedure and the doctor made the incision.

The whiteness of the room made him dizzy. He suddenly lost vision, but the voices around him were loud and clear. "BP?" "Oxygen levels?" "Heart rate?"

He leaned forward onto the cold glass which seemed to clear his head.

Another physician, paddles in hand, stepped quickly to Jennifer's side, suddenly blocking Mark's view. His heart pumped faster; what the hell was going on?

"Clear."

He walked the length of the window; he could barely see Jennifer's body covered from the waist down in blood-spattered white sheeting. He wanted to claw his way through the glass.

"She's failing!"

"Step back!" Another round of paddles to her heart. Another deeper incision.

The digital monitors to Mark's left flat-lined, and he heard someone in the distance.

"She's not responding, Doctor."

Moments later, the doctor lifted the tiny pink infant and announced, "A girl."

The baby was handed off to a nurse and whisked away.

The words that followed stopped Mark's heart. Turning to the attending, the physician announced, "Time of death …."

Mark's hearing shut down as his body fell into a chasm of shock and disbelief.

Pulling off his surgical gloves, the physician walked swiftly through the swinging doors, reached Mark and put a hand on his shoulder. "I'm so sorry, son. So sorry. We just couldn't save them both. I'll have answers for you in awhile."

And then it seemed that everyone dissipated into thin air. The once full OR was suddenly empty except for the attending physician who sutured Jennifer's abdomen and one nurse who stood silently by Mark's side. "Do you want some time alone with her?" she asked. Mark's head nodded without conscious effort, and she led him into the OR.

"Take all the time you need."

Mark lost track of the next few hours after he fell into his mother's arms in the waiting room. Angela and Richard, Jennifer's parents and his dad, stood by in helpless shock. The hospital staff offered an adjoining room, and the seven of them sat together and wept in the oppressive silence.

A few hours later the doctors concluded that Jennifer had suffered an amniotic embolism, a rare complication where the amniotic fluid enters the blood stream of the mother. The infant was pronounced a viable baby girl and placed in an incubator in the pediatric special care unit where she would be monitored carefully over the next forty-eight hours. They walked as a group to the nursery and stood in front of the glass partition, gazing longingly at the tiny beings that formed a quilt of pink and blue blankets and knitted caps.

Mark was allowed into the room with the adoptive parents after all the legal details had been completed. Mark held the pink bundle only once, and his earlier good-bye to his wife was followed with a tearful good-bye to their daughter. He kissed the top of her tiny head, reluctantly handed her to Angela and rushed from the room, clutching his throat to keep the screams inside.

Fourteen days later he was inducted. Barely a week after his wife's funeral. His daughter was at home with the Johnston's. In his starched and pressed Air Force uniform, Mark climbed aboard a transport plane headed to basic training in North Carolina. Three months later he'd be in Cambodia.

The unnamed baby girl would later be given her biological mother's middle name and her adoptive great-grandmother's first—Karen. Karen Ann Johnston, 4 lbs. 1 oz., born 7/19/1970.

*

"Will you be all right tonight, son?" his mother said as she walked into the room and gently touched his arm.

He turned and looked blankly toward her. A moment later her arms encircled him, and he cried deep wet sobs down the front of her dress. They sat on the bed for some time before Mark could gather his grief back inside him. He physically shook off the despair.

"I'll be fine, mom," he said, though he knew differently. "Honest. I'll even eat that chicken pot pie I know darned well is in the oven." His attempt to lighten the mood helped them both.

She blushed slightly. "How did you know that?" she said, slapping at his shoulder.

Mark walked her out to the living room and hugged her

tightly before opening the front door. He saw the hesitation on her face, and he forced a slight smile.

"Call me if you need anything," she said as she turned to leave. "I'm staying at the Holiday Inn up the road; I knew you'd need some time alone." She hesitated. "And dad will drive down from Kansas tomorrow, I'm sure."

That first evening, as the sun moved to the west and the light in the living room grew dim, Mark sat rocking in the recliner he'd nearly forgotten they owned. His parents had continued to pay the rent on the duplex each year, certain he'd return. Instead he'd re-enlisted for additional tours until now ... Two blocks away, in a historic yellow house, lived his child, his birth child. What would she look like at three years old? Was she a tiny Jennifer or a blend of them both? Did he want to know? Not now. Not yet, he thought. As he fell asleep, he saw the small face that had begun to haunt his dreams—the face of a young girl who slid in and out of his nightmares.

It was nearly a week before Mark ventured into the garage and shifted his Jeep Renegade into reverse. His mother had visited every day, and it was apparent to Mark that she watched for signs he knew she didn't want to find. His father was suddenly busy with work; too busy to make the two hour trip.

The previous night at dinner, she had pushed Mark to call the Johnston's, but he'd stood, red-faced and hurled his plate across the kitchen. His mother had blanched with shock.

"When I'm fucking ready," he had yelled. "When *I* am fucking ready, not you!"

As the plate shattered against the wall, he ran in shock to her, fear in his eyes. "Mom, are you hurt?" he asked. He checked her legs and ankles as she assured him she was ok, but her face told a different story. He had hurt her deeply, and he crumpled into his chair and hung his head in shame.

A moment later, he felt her tender touch on his shoulder; then she held his head against her apron and stroked his hair as she had when he was a child.

He felt a chair scraping against the floor and looked up to see her sitting beside him at the table. "You'll do things when you are ready, Mark; I know that. Do you need me to stay the night?" "I just want to be alone." He couldn't deal with the remorse he was feeling with her right there. "I'll clean up, mom."

So she'd left the dishes soaking in the sink, reluctantly hugged him good-bye and said she'd be returning to Wichita to check on his father the following day. Mark could barely look at her as he walked her to the front door.

Early this morning she'd stopped by on her way back home. "I'm sorry about last night, Mom," Mark said. "I don't know what's wrong with me. Please bring dad down for a visit soon."

She nodded and touched his chest one last time. "Call me; I'll worry."

Shortly after she left, Mark pulled on his stiff left leg, forcing it into the Jeep. He felt the sharp stab of pain, but he knew he had to fight the demons and get on with his life. Mark backed down the drive, and at the corner he considered options. If he took a right and drove two blocks, he'd be faced with the truth. Instead he turned left and headed to the interstate.

In the past few days, Ryan and Jeff, his college buddies, had left numerous messages on the new answering machine. An underlying concern was transparent in their "where the hell are you?" They shared a dorm room at O.S.U. where they were completing PhDs in Engineering. Mark remembered clearly the day that dream had been ripped from him as he opened the white rectangular envelope from the Department of Defense. He turned onto the overpass and headed north toward their apartment in Stillwater.

"We're in here," Jeff yelled when he heard the knock. "Come on i ... oh, my God—Mark!"

Ryan raced from the kitchen; shoulder slaps ensued, then handshakes, until all three men gave in to an embrace.

For the next few hours, conversation revolved around parents, girlfriends, classes and jobs.

"Are you thinking about coming back to school?" Jeff asked.

"We missed you at graduation, you asshole," Ryan, said.

"Really? I don't remember getting any mail over there in my foxhole. Must not have missed me too much."

"Hey, I'm sorry about that, Mark, seriously. But you know, junior and senior years were unbelievably tough, and grad school? Forget that. No excuse, I know."

Mark forced a look of understanding and waited for one of them to ask about Nam. About his wounds that nearly killed him. About the rainy monsoon season. About the time his M16 jammed. You'd think he'd been away at summer camp or something.

"Wait till you see this girl Jeff is dating." Ryan mimicked large breasts and laughed.

"Hey, you shouldn't be looking anyway." Jeff sat up proudly and grinned broadly.

The afternoon tone had been set. Light banter, casual catching up conversation, and in a way it felt like old times. Except—for Mark—the old times seemed a lifetime ago. Recent times made it impossible to feel a part of any of it.

He gazed at the piles of math and engineering books covering the kitchen table, the mounds of clean and dirty clothes strewn around, the remains of a previous meal still in pots on the stove. Mark managed a constant smile and nodded and listened.

"Shit, yes, you're staying over," Ryan insisted a few hours later. They headed for the bars shortly after.

At eight o'clock that evening, they ordered another pitcher of 3.2 beer at the Mason Jar. Jeff poured the last of the brew into his glass and raised it in another toast.

"To getting the hell out of that hellhole," he yelled loud enough for the room to hear. "Am I right?" He was joined in unison by nearly every college kid in the bar.

"Not another American life!" they cried.

Mark stared Ryan down. He didn't want the attention, and the noise of the bar was starting to make him nervous. "Stop, man," Mark said.

Ryan's look was one of bewilderment. "Why the hell not celebrate? You made it back alive, and you killed a lot of the bad guys."

"It wasn't like that, Ryan," he insisted. It was hard to make himself heard above the din.

Ryan persisted. "Well, the ceasefire agreement was nine months ago; why the hell are people still losing their lives? You aren't defending that fucking war, are you?"

"You forget that I was part of that 'fucking' war, Ryan. That was me over there getting shot at."

Mark was practically in Ryan's face when Ryan backed a bit and said in a calmer voice, "I know that, buddy. I'm just saying what more will it take for us to get the fuck out for good?"

Mark looked up just in time to tilt his head away from the spittle flying through the air directly at him. "Baby killer," the guy hissed as he walked on past and out the door.

He looked at Jeff and Ryan. "And that's why I'm not celebrating. Let's get the hell out of here."

The next morning Mark's head throbbed as he opened his eyes and wondered where he was—a feeling that had grown way too familiar the past three years. He held his shaking right hand with his left, rolled to his side and spotted Ryan sprawled on the couch. He assumed Jeff had been the only one to make it to the bedroom before passing out. "Shit." The word stretched through clinched teeth. He rose from the living room floor and stumbled to the bathroom.

A half hour later, the three men were sitting in a pancake house downing as much protein, sugar and caffeine as they could manage.

"Man," Ryan said, "when did we stop drinking?"

Jeff laughed. "Question might be, 'when did we start?'"

Mark downed three aspirin with his orange juice and waved for the waitress to top off his coffee. She walked toward them in her pink and white striped apron, mousy brown hair twisted at the back of her neck. "You boys look a little under the weather," she said. She smiled as she filled each of the cheap white ceramic mugs on the table. Her rough, weathered hands gave away her age.

Jeff took her courtesy as interest and began to talk. "My good man here," he said pointing directly at Mark, "just got back from Nam. If that isn't something to celebrate, I don't know what is."

Reading her name-tag, Jeff continued. "Betty," he said, "this guy was my college roommate, and he came back alive. Do you believe it? My best friend, and damn it, he came back fucking alive."

Betty looked carefully into Mark's eyes. "Welcome home, son," she said. Her eyes saddened. "Two of my nephews were killed outside Phnom Penh, three days apart. Glad you're home safe."

She turned to go, then over her shoulder called, "On the house, boys." And she walked through the swinging door to the kitchen.

Mark knew he should get back to Edmond. He knew he should let his parents know his whereabouts; his mother would be worried if she'd tried to reach him. But he couldn't face the empty house. "Mind if I call my folks from the apartment?" Mark said; then asked if he could stay another night.

Both Jeff and Ryan had to hit the library to study. They gave Mark the door key and agreed to meet back at the apartment for dinner. As he stepped through the doorway, a sudden blackness seized him.

This should be his apartment, his life. He hadn't asked to go to Nam; hadn't asked to give up his education and his career, and nearly his life. His stupid lottery number had sealed his fate. He had fought that lottery hard; had formed the SDS on campus and marched for months, even ending up in jail just two months before Nixon's damned lottery pulled his birth date.

Jeff and Ryan, and most of his friends had managed to escape, and it pissed him off. He even wondered if Jennifer would be alive today if he hadn't gotten drafted when he did. He was convinced his enlistment had created enough stress to cause the baby to come early. None of it made sense. Mark headed for a hot shower and a shave, but not before he grabbed a bottle of Coors from the refrigerator.

*

Cambodia

Betty's mention of Phnom Phen had rattled in his chest. Her nephews had been only two of the nearly two hundred guys killed in that bloodbath. His division was three days behind, in time to clean up the mess and send the body bags back home. What he remembered most was the solid silence just before the reverberating rounds of ammo. That wasn't quite accurate, Mark thought. There was no complete silence in the jungle. There was always an underlying cacophony of insect noises, and a ceaseless hum of mosquitoes encircling their bodies.

Mark's platoon had arrived during the eighth year of the war. American troops were heading home just as he arrived, but there was plenty of war left to be had.

Along the banks of the Mekong River, Mark discovered that basic training in Carolina bore no resemblance to how he would live or fight over here. After he clambered from the transport, stood in line to salute his newest platoon leader and sweated through his first set of khakis, he had been shown to a tent housing fourteen men with inches between makeshift beds. They were one notch above cots, with a few springs and a one-inch mattress thrown on top. He was given a set of sheets which by morning were soaked with sweat and would never dry in the moist air of the jungle. Within a week Mark wrote home, asking his mother to send as many pairs of white cotton socks as she could afford.

During basic training, he had gotten used to being jabbed and harassed in the mess hall, given no time to eat, and dropping pounds. Here, if you could stomach the food, you could eat as much as you wanted. You needed all the weight you could gain before the heat and the long marches sweated it off you. The new recruits stuck out: fresh uniforms, dry skin, feet with flesh. It would take less than a month for Mark to look like his seasoned peers.

*

After two nights in Stillwater with the guys, Mark declined their invitation to stay longer. He recognized their busy class schedules, but it was their total disinterest in the past three years of his life that made his decision. "Nah," he said, "I gotta get back and figure out my next move."

Next move. *What does that even mean?* He wondered as he drove the I-35 toward Edmond. A job, obviously; he had to pay the bills now. Beyond that, his vision faltered. He needed a bachelor's degree to continue in Engineering, but he wasn't sure he could stay in a town where memories hunkered around every corner. A bigger city would be best, but even Tulsa wasn't far enough from his grief. Wichita, where his parents lived, would be an option, but he wasn't sure he wanted them hovering.

He let out a long sigh and turned up the radio in the Jeep. Marvin Gaye belted out "What's Going On?" Pictures clouded his mind so he cranked it louder, then louder again. The Stones enveloped him. He didn't hear the sirens until the Highway Patrol car was parallel on his left, the officer behind the wheel waving his hand emphatically for Mark to pull onto the embankment.

"Shit," he said as he rolled down the window and waited for the officer to approach.

"Young man, I've been following you for the past three miles with my lights and siren on. Wanna tell me what in the world is going on?"

Mark couldn't meet the patrolman's eyes. "Get out of the truck slowly and put your hands up," the officer said.

"May I ask why you're stopping me?" Mark said.

"I'll ask the questions here, son, if you don't mind." He did a quick frisk, smelled Mark's breath and checked the movement of his pupils with his flashlight.

"You were speeding back there, but what I want to know is why you didn't respond to my directions to pull over?"

Mark refused to give excuses. Who the hell cared if his wife was dead and his daughter lost? Who the hell cared that he'd been inches from death several times in Nam? Who the hell cared, period? Mark shrugged his shoulders and remained silent.

"I asked you a question, young man," the officer barked.

When Mark refused to answer, the officer, now red-faced with anger, shoved the ticket into his hand. He shook his head. "The next time you see flashing red lights, you pull over. This will be in your record; next time will be a second offense."

The officer motioned for him to get back into the Jeep. "I oughta take you in for defiance," he said. "Turn down your radio, put your cruise-control on, and focus."

"Yes, sir," Mark answered. He thought about saluting. Sir, yes sir! He stepped up into the Jeep. There was a rage inside him that wanted to beat the shit out of that cop, but he pushed it under the surface and took off.

As he pulled into the drive alongside the darkened house, he recognized his parents' car parked at the curb. Damn it! They were sitting on the top step of the porch and both stood up, swiped at the back of their legs and waited for him to reach them. It was difficult to tell whose smile was the most forced.

"Hey, dad," Mark said, as he stood before the elderly man. His father reached out a hand for Mark to shake, wetness in his eyes clearly shining in the darkness. Mark bent slightly and reached out his arms. The two men embraced tightly a brief moment. His father seemed to have shrunk several inches, and was thin and pale. Mark looked at his mother for answers, but it was obvious that discussion was off bounds for the moment.

His dad cleared his throat of emotion. "Decided to stay a night or two, Mark, if that's ok with you," he said. He went on to explain business in Oklahoma City, too far to drive from Kansas several days in a row, the need to have a place to stay. Mark bought the story to keep them both from lying further.

"And I suppose that picnic basket has a full meal inside?" Mark smiled as he nodded toward the wicker container at his mother's feet.

His mother scrunched her nose and smiled. "Gene, get that cooler from the trunk too, will you please?"

"Come on in and make yourselves at home," Mark said as he unlocked the door.

A short while later as they ate at the kitchen table, Mark had to admit his mother's cooking had never tasted better. "Sure beats K-rations," he said as he reached for another piece of fried chicken. He watched as his father picked at his food. He'd eaten nothing on his plate.

"I'll have some more mashed potatoes as well," Mark said. "Biscuit, dad?"

The older man coughed. "Nah, had a late lunch," he offered. "But it is delicious, as always, Marge." He patted her hand.

As his mother cleared the table and insisted on washing the dishes, the men retired to the living room. The rental house had come furnished with a few sparse pieces of uncomfortable furniture. Mark pointed to the over-sized Mediterranean sofa covered in a print of olive green and gold velveteen.

"That's probably the most comfortable, I'm afraid, dad."

Mark grimaced slightly as he lowered himself into the recliner—his left side an on-going dull aching pain.

They slipped into a moment of silence and stared longingly at the floor; then both spoke at once.

"Mark …"

"Dad …"

Mark laughed. "Go ahead, you first,

"Mark, I know it's hard but I want you to know that I can listen … when you're ready that is, I can listen."

"Coffee?" his mother called from the kitchen.

Both men called out "sure" in unison.

After the nine o'clock news, Mark helped his parents put fresh sheets on the dilapidated mattress in the second bedroom and bid them a good night's sleep. He lay in bed for a half hour then quietly walked to the kitchen. The floor boards creaked as he tip-toed to the refrigerator and downed a beer. He opened a second. He needed to sleep.

Over breakfast the following morning, his mother approached the subject again. "Mark, don't you want to see her? It's been three years."

Mark's fork dinged the side of his plate as he placed it forcibly onto the table, but he breathed deeply and waited to speak.

"She has a life with her new family," he finally managed. "Mom, don't you get it? She's not mine; I have no right to even see her."

"That's not true, Mark Charles Roberts, and you know it. The Johnston's wanted you to be part of her life; that was the agreement early on; that they would parent, and you would still have visitation."

Mark bit his lip until he noticed the metallic taste of his own blood. His father sat stone-still and sipped his morning coffee with the newspaper creased awkwardly on his lap.

"Not going to talk, are we?" she said finally.

"Nothing to talk about, Mother."

"Mark, she's two blocks away. She's growing up. She has a right to know her real father; she has a right to know you, whether *you* want to know *her* or not."

Her next words sliced through his silence like a sword. "I've seen her, you know."

Mark's dad looked up, apprehensively.

And this time Mark could no longer hold it in. He pronounced each word slowly. "You—did—what?"

"I've seen her—many times, Mark. Angela and Richard wanted it."

"I cannot believe you would ... you never told me this."

"You were thousands of miles away trying to stay alive, Mark. And you'd written the Johnston's you wanted no more contact. Did you really want me to write in a letter how beautiful your daughter is?"

Mark stood quickly. The chair behind him tipped enough that his father grabbed for it. Mark threw his hands in the air, dropped them over his head, then down his face. Why couldn't people just allow him to forget?

Anger trapped his ability to speak for a long moment. Then he sat back down hard in the kitchen chair and faced her.

"I asked the Johnston's not to send any more photos because I was dead and dying, Mom, don't you understand that? I cannot believe you went against my wishes."

"I had to go against your wishes, son. I didn't agree with your decision, and I wasn't about to never know my own granddaughter. And she is beautiful, Mark. She looks so much ..."

"No, stop!" Mark screamed before she could say the words. "I mean it, Mother, stop. I don't want to hear another word."

Mark's dad reached for his forearm, but Mark pulled away.

"Son," his father said, "Your mother ..." He had no chance to continue.

Mark leaped away from the table and out the front door,
letting it slam behind him. He could imagine the scene he'd just
left, as it continued to play out. As the roar of blood in his veins
slowed, he felt the shame again. It seemed like all he felt any
more was rage and remorse. He'd make it up to her later, he told
himself, and to his old man.

The next day, the late September sky suggested autumn. As
he stood on the back stoop with his coffee, his mother's feet
padded across the kitchen linoleum. Mark walked back into the
house to confront her.

"What's wrong with dad? He's thin as a rail, and he barely
eats anything."

She finished pouring the coffee, stirred milk and sugar into
the cup, and finally met his eyes. They were full of sadness. "Sit
down."

Last night's argument still hung between them. He had come
in late, after his parents had gone to bed. He'd been piss drunk,
and he was feeling the effects.

"I guess I'll just say it, Mark. Your father has cancer—liver.
He found out last month."

"And you kept it from me?" He took a deep breath. "Seems
like I'm surrounded by secrets; just like in Nam."

She reached across the table and took his hand. "Mark,
you've been badly wounded. Why would we add that stress to
your recovery? We intended to tell you."

Mark's throat closed in a gulp, and his gut contracted.
"What's the treatment?" he asked.

"He starts radiation next week. That's why he insisted we
come down to see you now. In case he can't make the trip later."

Mark stood and walked to his mother; he lifted her out of her
chair and into his arms. He couldn't find words; he simply held
her for a very long, silent moment. When she finally pulled away,
she kissed him on the cheek; her own tears joining his. "Just pray
for him, Mark. That's all we can do."

He heard his father turn on the bathroom shower. "What are his chances?"

"No one knows that, son. But he's a fighter as you know."

Mark nodded. "Both of you are, mom."

"I've watched you recover for months now, Mark. *You* are the fighter."

Mark didn't feel like a fighter; when he did feel anything, he felt like a failure. He'd let his wife die, given away his child, killed Cambodians he never saw, and then there was the worst: the thin he would never speak of.

Just as basic hadn't prepared Mark for war; war hadn't prepared him for a job in civilian life. There were few positions that involved flying a fighter plane over the Oklahoma wheat fields. He was also unprepared for the reactions his presence often evoked. One afternoon, he sat in the waiting room of a small business as the receptionist announced his arrival to a prospective employer.

"Mr. Clements will be right out," she said. She gave him a smile; then looked to her right at the partitioned work stations just beyond. Mark followed her gaze and was suddenly aware of a dozen sets of eyes on him. Though they all seemed to be roughly his age, he noticed that none wore his signature clipped haircut. Even without his uniform, it was easy to spot the military. And as Mark had come to realize—the military was not popular.

Following a brief interview, Mr. Clements walked him to the reception area and shook his hand. "Thanks for coming in," he said. His voice didn't sound very thankful, Mark thought. Heads turned as he walked out, and Mark was suddenly aware of an underlying current of hostility that ran through the office. He knew he wouldn't hear from Clements.

The next Saturday evening, Jeff and Ryan picked him up on their way to Oklahoma City for a night of bar-hopping.

"What's with the hair, man?" Jeff asked.

Ryan ran his hand along Mark's scraggly spiked brown hair and laughed.

"The sooner I grow this out the better," Mark insisted.

"What the...?"

"You know what I mean, Jeff. Lots of people don't want to be reminded of what a buzz cut symbolizes these days. May grow it shoulder length again, know what I mean?"

"Don't ever be ashamed that you went, Mark," Ryan said. "Sure, some people think you should have crossed the border into Canada, but who the hell are they to judge?"

"Yeah, well, I'm just trying to get a fuckin' job," Mark said. "And I don't need people staring at my head."

A few hours later, the three men downed a second beer. They'd been in the bar less than a half hour when Mark was approached by three tall thin men, each in ripped blue jeans, with pony tails and silver studs in their left ears.

"Hey," Jeff barked as he watched the three position themselves directly in front of Mark. "What the hell do you guys want?" He leaned forward and waited.

"Where are your medals, asshole?" one of the men said as he poked a finger into Mark's chest.

"Yeh, how many gooks did you kill over there?" said another. "Or innocent people?"

"Wouldn't find me over there playing war for the President," the third man yelled.

"Why don't you three leave him the fuck alone?" Ryan yelled, throwing his chin forward, daring them to step one foot closer.

"Ryan, let it go," Mark said, and he turned to the three. "We were just leaving—but not because of you."

The tallest of the three raised his fists and came at Mark full force. Mark put his combat techniques to use, tucked and ducked and came up just under the guy's chin, blood splattering the man's anti-war t shirt.

As his attacker fell backward, Mark returned to Nam. He

grabbed the guy by the front of his shirt and pulled him back up; hit him again; pounded his body; and caught him on the left eye. The guy crumpled.

Jeff and Ryan were on top of him when he came back to the present. "Mark, stop!" Jeff yelled as he and Ryan lifted Mark to his feet. "Shit, the cops will be here any minute."

Mark shook his right hand as it began to swell. Good thing his injuries were on his left side, he thought. He nodded at Jeff and Ryan. "Let's get the hell out of here. I don't need jail time."

As they rushed the door, Mark turned one last time. "Get up, you pussy coward."

By mid-November Mark's initial relief of leaving the war and the military behind dwindled into a deepening depression. The anti-war movement was still raging and had spread its hatred to veterans, as well. Mark had been one of them three years ago— long hair, peace symbols, protest signs—now *he* had become the enemy.

Though the war was officially over, hundreds of American civilians and combat troops were still in Nam. His thoughts circled and spiraled for hours. Would he do it differently if he had to do it again? He questioned if Jennifer might be alive if he hadn't been recruited. If he'd fought it; if he'd taken her and run, would she be with him now?

Yet somewhere between Jennifer's death and his arrival in Cambodia a short few months later, something in Mark had shifted. He had quickly bought into a sense of duty, and it had actually been a comfort to follow directions without thinking. Now—he no longer had that easy escape and suddenly, thinking was all he could do.

The empty Scotch bottles clinked against each other as he emptied them into the trash each Monday morning. He prided himself that at least he wasn't turning to acid or even pot, like many returning vets had done. During the day he hit the pavement looking for work; at night he drowned in the pain.

One afternoon as he turned the corner toward home, he saw a green Buick creeping slowly down the street, the man behind the wheel straining his neck to peer at the house. Mark pulled the Jeep into the drive instead of following. Two days later, as he watched through the front window, Mark spotted the same car as it slowed once again. He stepped toward the front door and onto the porch just as the Buick sped up.

"Mom," Mark said into the phone the following day. "Have you talked to the Johnston's recently?"

"No, Mark, you made your wishes pretty well known a few months ago," she said. "Why?"

"Just wondered," he lied. Why would Richard Johnston be watching the house if he didn't know Mark had returned? He questioned his mother's honesty, but he let it go.

Mark welcomed his parents' offer and drove to Kansas the day before Thanksgiving. He was tired of fighting his way through interviews, only to be told he didn't have the right skills. It was becoming obvious that two years of college and several tours of duty in the military were not enough. It didn't seem to matter that he'd fought for his country for three damned years. In fact, he knew it worked against him. His hair had grown longer; he'd tossed the uniforms and bought civilian clothes, but somehow it still showed, and he knew it.

It was one of those occasional warm Novembers in Oklahoma. The oaks had managed to hang on to their leaves although most of their color had seeped to gold. The winter wheat was coming in green; a few fields of corn stalks remained unscythed. Mark drove with the windows down, and his left arm hugged the side panel of the Jeep. The lined two-lane highway was empty except for a Chevy truck that had passed him ten miles back. Mark turned the radio to a country station, and for the first time in nearly four years, he felt the taut springs inside him begin to unwind. As the mile markers along old highway 66 ticked off larger numbers, Mark's thoughts took him back to Cambodia.

*

Cambodia

As a pilot in the Air Force, his first tour was marked by several *operations*, a fancy word for the mostly bungled war efforts in Vietnam. In November, Op Ivory Coast was his first failed mission. Sent to remove U.S. troops from the Son Tay prison, the Special Forces he dropped found it empty … the American prisoners moved to another site. Faulty intel was prevalent and became the soldiers' worst nightmare—an enemy equal to the Viet Cong they were fighting.

Op Jefferson Glenn was a series of botched attempts to assist the South Vietnamese military. After one mission, Mark heard one of his colleagues voice his own opinion—"Oh, my God, why didn't they teach me anything in flight school?" Mark was finding the war just as he'd suspected—a major clusterfuck.

It was in Lam Son in February of '71 that he suffered his first injury: shrapnel in his right leg bad enough to land him in the infirmary for a few weeks. The mission was a month-long offensive to sever the Ho Chi Ming Trail supply line. Mark bombed U.S. aircraft and abandoned equipment to prevent them from falling into enemy hands. The Pentagon was confident that American firepower would guarantee victory. The truth looked much different: 215 dead; 1149 wounded; 38 missing, 108 helicopters lost and 7 fighter bombers downed. The operation was a fiasco and half the troops on the ground were captured. He often wondered if anyone was in charge.

That day, Mark had taken a hit along the right side of his bomber. He was one of the lucky ones. The bombardier in front of him wasn't so lucky. Mark lay in the camp hospital and hoped to be sent home, but every time he closed his eyes he saw Jennifer lying cold and dead in his arms. He knew he'd rather face his own death here in the jungle than to face the one back home.

Each afternoon his favorite nurse, Jacquie, delivered mail to the injured troops. She always announced the return address, and the guys responded with cheers. Mark received regular mail from his mother, but there were weeks in the field when unexpected letters showed up— letters that had grown unwelcome over time.

Today, Jacquie stood by Mark's bed and hesitated as she read the Edmond address. "Angela and Richard Johnston? Looks like a thick one, Mark."

He grabbed the letter from her and shoved it under the covers. Mark waited until she walked away and everyone else grew busy reading letters from girlfriends, fiancés, and wives. The manila envelope was unsealed. Mark pulled out a half-dozen black and white photos: his daughter kicking at a crib toy that hung above her, asleep in her pram in the front yard, Richard waiting with arms opened wide as she crept toward him. She was nearly seven months old. Mark glanced around and quickly tucked the pictures back inside without reading Angela's handwritten note. If nothing else, it confirmed his decision.

Mark re-enlisted for a second tour after a few weeks of R & R and was transferred to the 7th A.F. division. Operation Freedom Deal was into its second year at that point. The targets of his F-4 Phantom were base areas and border sanctuaries of the People's Army of Vietnam (PVAM) and Khmer Rouge. His boundaries were tight—a 30 mile deep area between the South Vietnamese border and the Mekong River. Nixon's orders were clear— "Bomb the living bejeezus out of them." Mark did his part by dropping a hundred tons of ordnance.

It was easy to call out orders to "drop" when you couldn't see the enemy below you. But there were days he'd like to forget. On occasion, as the smoke rose from the fields below, Mark glimpsed blurry images running into the surrounding jungle. He wanted to believe they were uniformed military, but in his heart he knew they were frail, small villagers running for their lives, leaving behind the bodies of wives and children in the bombed-out area he had created.

Within two months Mark's target territory was expanded west of the Mekong; though most of his sorties struck targets outside the authorized zone. Falsified reports kept them legal. He sustained three minor shrapnel injuries in the next year and a half that left scars on his right forearm and left thigh, and a line of ugly stitch marks down the center of his back.

Time moved quickly in a seemingly endless war. The day he received a package from Angela with news of Karen's upcoming second birthday, he responded with a one line letter. "Deep in jungle. Please do not send further correspondence."

*

Thanksgiving was bittersweet. For the past month, he'd called his father at least once a week, but he hadn't seen him since starting radiation treatments. When the thin frail man opened the door, it took all Mark's strength to not break down. "Dad," he said as he hugged him gingerly, "how the hell are you?"

His first holiday back in the states might possibly be the last with his father. When his mother brought out pumpkin pie and coffee, Mark turned to her. "Have any wine in the house? I think we could all use a drink."

On the drive back to Oklahoma, Mark felt his sadness build into anger. How dare this happen just as he got back home. Hell, he hadn't had time to grieve Jennifer or the war, and he hated God for this next test.

Every morning Mark woke with a hangover, showered and cleaned himself up and answered job ads. The liquor bottles doubled, and he continued to avoid seeing his daughter. Late one afternoon, following another round of interviews and rejections,

Mark drove past the neighborhood park on his way home. He slowed the Jeep and turned into the lot. He would walk off his fatigue and frustration.

As he passed the playground, he spotted Angela Johnston. She was lifting a small figure in a pale-blue snowsuit into a canvas swing. Mark froze as he saw the tiny face of a miniature Jennifer smiling up at her mother, swinging her legs and begging for a push.

Angela turned just as Mark stepped behind a tall cedar. He was not expecting the bowling ball that hit him in his gut, and he dropped to his knees on the dead brown grass. Mark gave a muffled cry, and tears stung his cheeks. "No," he said. "Please, God, no."

In mid-December the first snows hit the plains from Nebraska to southern Oklahoma and lasted a week. It was unusual, but after years in Nam, Mark was accustomed to unusual. Between his increasingly infrequent job interviews, he stayed drunk. It numbed his memories and smothered his feelings.

One evening, after a few beers, he wrapped his wool scarf inside his ski jacket, tugged on his knit cap and headed toward campus. He had avoided their old haunts, but tonight he braved both the cold and the past. Four streets west of his duplex, he walked into Pete's, a college hamburger joint that he and Jennifer had frequented. The food was cheap and the happy hour beer nearly free. The little bell on the door jingled as he shut it and walked to the bar. College kids filled the place at eight o'clock, and every table was loaded with glasses and pitchers and baskets of fries and onion rings.

"What'll it be?" the bartender called from the till.

"Jack Daniels, straight up," Mark answered. The kid looked all of fifteen, and Mark considered how war made you grow old.

As he downed the drink and ordered a second, Mark grew warm in the crowded room. His slipped off his jacket and threw it over his gloves and scarf on the stool next to him. The bartender swept the empty glass toward him and filled it with the amber liquid from the whiskey bottle. As he did, Mark sensed someone beside him. He turned.

"You military?" a short college kid with too many beers in him asked Mark.

"What's it to you?" Mark countered.

"What branch?"

"I said, "What's it to you, man? Air Force, why?"

Mark sensed the noise level lessening, and he stood from his stool. "Hey," he said, "I'm not looking for a fight, kid." Mark stood a good six inches taller, and his military muscles tensed in preparation. He almost laughed.

The kid turned away, and Mark thought it was over until he heard the next two words. "Baby killer."

The words were barely out of the college student's mouth before Mark had him on the ground—punching and punching and reaching for a pistol that wasn't there—and suddenly he realized he was not in Nam. By then he was covered with a dozen young men, and the police had been called. He spent the night in jail with no one to call to post bail. Mark felt a loneliness rise through the booze. The following day he walked out of the city jail with the familiar feeling of remorse flowing in his veins. At home he replaced it with the flow of booze. And almost nightly the face of a small girl flowed through his nightmares.

A few days later, the doorbell jarred him awake, and Mark groggily pulled a bathrobe from the piles of clothes on the floor. He slipped it on over his sweat-soaked t-shirt and boxers and dragged himself to the front door.

"Dad?"

His father stood there wrapped from head to toe in black. Long overcoat, leather gloves and boots, and his favorite wool driving cap. He could be mistaken for Death himself.

He handed Mark the newspaper wrapped in plastic from the

front porch. Without a word, he walked into the living room, droplets from the melting snow hitting the wood floor. He stood hands on hips amidst the disarray, and Mark watched him assess the situation.

He stripped off one glove and then the other, clambered out of his wet boots and stood in his coat and stockinged feet.

"What is it, dad?" Mark said.

"You're not really asking *me* what is it, are you, son? I mean, my God, look at you."

Mark's jaw set tightly, but he had no escape. He stood in his near nakedness smelling of liquor and sweat and something he couldn't name—something he hadn't felt since his last days in Nam. Those days flashed in Mark's eyes before he could stop them; they included the vision of the small girl.

*

Cambodia

Shortly after Nixon signed the Paris Peace Accord in January, Mark received orders for an expanded bombing campaign. Peace was far from any one's mind it seemed. His platoon began dropping bombs daily. As the Communists drew a tighter ring around Phnom Phen, he jumped into the cockpit of his B52, completed a hundred sorties and dropped tons of ordnance. He had learned to act; not think. Thinking got you nowhere when there was nothing you could understand. It fit him well. Nothing in his life, thus far, had made sense.

Finally, his release date was just weeks away. He took R & R in Hawaii for three of those, and upon his return, Commander Thompson called him into a private meeting.

"One last sortie. Come on Mark, you've given us three tours, go out with a bang." Little did he know how loud that bang would reverberate.

*

He was suddenly aware of his dad's presence. "I don't know what the hell you mean, dad."

"Mark, your mother and I are worried about your drinking. Look at this place," he said, waving his arm around the ramshackle room. He pointed at the unread newspapers piled high in the corner, crusty plates and dirty glasses on every surface, and beer-stained carpets and rugs. There were glass rings on the wood coffee table, and the kitchen sink was full of dirty dishes and food debris.

"So I have a few drinks here and there; it's not like I get drunk every night of the week, dad. After nearly dying, don't you think I deserve a little relief?"

He knew his dad was having none of it, but he wasn't about to back down. He'd told no one about last week's night in jail, and he wasn't about to go into more rehab of any kind – physical or mental.

"Let's go get some breakfast, dad. Did you drive clear from Wichita this morning?" Mark was quickly picking up food cartons and beer bottles from the living room floor, and he scurried them into the kitchen. He called down the hall. "Let me get on some pants and let's go out."

When Mark returned to the living area, he saw his dad sitting on the sofa flipping his gloves from one hand to the other, over and over again. He felt like shit. Not just from last night's binge but because he was adding to his dad's pain, as if liver cancer and radiation weren't enough. His father had removed his cap in the heat of the room, and Mark shivered with fear and regret when he saw the bare bald head.

"Please don't do this right now, Dad. Ok? Let's talk over breakfast."

He watched as the older man sighed, rose from the sofa and struggled with his balance. During one brief moment, Mark glimpsed in his father's eyes a look of disgust tinged with despair.

He walked out of the house, leaving the old man no choice but to follow. Mark sat in the Jeep and waited for his dad to climb reluctantly into the passenger seat.

At the IHOP on the other side of town, Mark broke the silence that enveloped the space between them. "I'll quit, dad. I don't want you worried about me, ok?"

He made a promise he didn't intend to keep, but he had to give his dad some relief. "I'll call the VA tomorrow."

"I hope you will, son. Your mother needs you."

Neither mentioned the next round of treatments or the likelihood of his father living till summer. Mark wanted to simplify the man's life, but he seemed to always complicate his relationships. He saw the opening of that draft notice back in 1970 as the end of life as he'd known it. The losses that spilled from that white envelope were too many to count.

They had known it was coming. Once the lottery system passed in Congress, college no longer kept any physically able male out of the melee. But Mark's birth date hadn't been drawn and he had hoped it would take at least another year for them to find him.

The day he was handed his orders felt like a punishment from God himself. The government post mark made it unnecessary to even open the envelope: except he wanted to know how long he had with Jennifer before they took him.

Canada was an option; hundreds of men had made that decision, and Mark gave it careful consideration. But leaving behind a pregnant fiancé who faced giving up her first born child, seemed unduly cruel. He immediately filed for deferment to slow down the process, met with an Air Force Recruiter to avoid the Army, and moved the wedding to June.

Despite an eight-month belly protruding from her wedding suit, Jennifer had glowed with happiness and pregnancy as Mark placed a simple gold band on her finger and pledged his love. Mark's joy was tinged with fear. It was tinged with self-doubt.

How could he be marching against a war one day and submitting to active duty the next?

That night as he sat with a bottle of Jim Beam that seemed to empty itself, Mark fell into a rage. How dare they think he was a drunk! He was a vet. He had seen death; he had escaped death. He had a right to an occasional drink. Ryan and Jeff had their nice apartment and their degrees and what the hell did he have? He threw the bottle across the room and watched it shatter against the wall. As he passed out, he saw his father's face at the door, although he knew the old man had driven back to Kansas hours ago.

He woke up during the night needing to pee, and as he walked to the bathroom, his right foot hit the slivers of glass from the broken bottle. The sharp pain and the gush of red made him sick. He laid in his own urine and blood and wept for the first time in three years. The following morning he called the mental health facility for an appointment.

A week later, in the cold white waiting room of the VA Hospital in Oklahoma City, the receptionist called his name. He followed her to a modest office down the hall.

"Dr. Smith will be right with you," the petite woman said as she pointed to a worn blue-tweed chair no more comfortable than the ones in the lobby.

Mark felt an unexpected warmth in the utilitarian office space. Family photos covered the metal desk, crayon drawings were taped to the walls, and Lucy and Charlie Brown gazed down at him. "Psychiatric Help – 5 cents . . . The Doctor Is In." Mark's mood lightened a degree, and he managed a smile when Ralph Smith walked in and shook his hand.

Mark liked the fact that the psychologist listened instead of talking. "I don't think I really need help, doc, but I promised my parents I'd come in to check it out."

Dr. Smith nodded. "Go on," he said.

Once he opened up, he knew he couldn't stop. Before he realized it, Mark found himself vomiting out the words as fast as they would come—the pregnancy, Jennifer's death and the paralyzing guilt of simply handing over his child and walking away. He had never wanted that; Jennifer had pushed him into that decision.

As he talked briefly about his last flight, his wounds and near death, and his return to a home and a country who found him invisible, Mark shed hot tears. What followed was inevitable—anger and more anger just below the bubble of grief.

"What we did was wrong, and a waste, and I don't try to justify it like a lot of vets. Some of them have to believe it was right, so they don't have to face the fact that there was nothing in Nam worth being paralyzed for the rest of your life. Nothing was worth killing people. I won't justify what the fuck we did over there."

An hour later, Dr. Smith looked at his watch and straightened his tie. "Well, Mark," he said, "I think it's fair to say that we have a lot of work to do."

Mark nodded in agreement. They scheduled a standing weekly appointment for the next month. When Dr. Smith opened the office door, Mark hesitated and pointed to the desk. "How many kids you got?" he said.

"Three," Dr. Smith answered. He pointed at the tiny framed school pictures, one by one. "Martha, ten. John, eight. Ralphie Jr., six. Just started school this year."

Mark felt himself tearing up, and Dr. Smith noticed.

"It will get easier, Mark," he said, "I promise. And one day you will know your daughter."

Mark gave in and responded to the therapist's good-bye hug. It might get easier, but he would never know his daughter; of that he was certain.

"See ya," he said as he walked toward to the lobby and a pay phone.

He told his father about the appointment, and when his mother came on the line, Mark insisted she not hide his father's prognosis. As he drove the Jeep back to Edmond, he knew what he needed to tell Ralph Smith at their next visit.

*

Cambodia

On April 12, Operation Homecoming dispatched C-141's to Hanoi, North Vietnam, and Saigon to pick up released prisoners of war. Mark's crew took off at 0200 for Hanoi, picked up forty released American soldiers, and continued down the runway for an immediate return to base. Mark heard, and then felt, the bullets penetrating metal.

The plane felt unresponsive in his grip for several seconds; then he pulled the C-141 upward, hitting a fence and then a vehicle before gaining lift. Once airborne, Mark realized his left side had taken the hit.

There was no way to know where the blood was coming from. It seemed to be everywhere from his neck down, and he suddenly had no feeling. As the blood dripped onto the cockpit floor, Mark gave an urgent command to his co-pilot. "Take the stick, Max, I'm hit."

*

His parents were good, kind people. They'd done so much for him, and he'd failed them miserably. He knew it, but he didn't know how to fix it. For months, possibly longer if he was truthful, he hadn't wanted to be alive. He'd hoped the liquor would either kill him or, if nothing else, destroy enough brain cells to erase the past four years.

A few days later, Jeff called from Stillwater. It had been over a month since they'd spoken. Mark felt he and Ryan were avoiding him, but he didn't know why. What the hell had he

done except return from an unpopular war that even he had
protested?

When Jeff asked if he'd gotten a job, he cringed. "Yeah," he
said, "just a crap one, but it'll pay the bills." He'd finally taken a
job at the dry cleaning shop up the street.

"Well, great," Jeff said. After a moment, Jeff spoke carefully.
"Have you considered completing your degree, Mark?"

It was nothing he expected to hear, and it took a moment
before Mark could respond. "An occasional thought," he said,
"but ...."

"It isn't any of my business, man, and I know I've been an
asshole since you got back, but you need to do this, Mark. Hell,
Ryan and I'll be rich before you can even compete if you don't
get started."

Mark felt an anger rising though he wasn't sure why. "You
know, Jeff, it isn't as easy as all that. Am I supposed to sit in
classrooms where Jennifer and I used to hang out together? Hell,
I can barely make myself get up and go to work every day."

"Mark, I may be wrong, but how else are you going to move
forward?"

"What if I don't want to?"

"Well, I can't answer that but let me ask you this. If you can't
go backward and you can't face the present, seems to me you
only have one direction to go. Maybe it's time. Hell, what do I
know, Mark? I've never been where you are. Just think about it."

"I will." He started to hang up the phone but grabbed it back
at the last minute. "Jeff! Are you still there?"

"Yeah, buddy, I'm still here. Why?"

"Thanks."

"Always here for you, man."

After he hung up, Mark sat in the darkened kitchen and let
Jeff's words settle. Maybe he needed to grab this life raft. He
needed one to survive the sea of booze he found himself
drowning in. He could ride it a short way for now; no

commitment; see where it took him.

A few days later, he walked from his duplex on Second Street toward campus. He'd avoided this area of town for months. Mark followed the route he and Jennifer had taken a hundred times from the SDS headquarters at the Johnston's on Fourth Street to their dorms. He quickened his pace.

As he approached Pete's Patio once again, he smelled the grease, and the smoke made his eyes tear. He popped in for a moment, half-expecting to see her there with a dozen other familiar faces. But of course, they'd all graduated while he'd been battling the Viet Cong, and Jennifer had died.

"May I get you something, sir?" a young acne-faced kid asked him. Mark felt off-kilter, and he touched the back of a chair to balance himself.

"Huh?" he finally managed.

"May I get you a table, sir?"

Sir! Mark nearly laughed. "No, thanks." He turned quickly and headed up Boulevard Street. Every few steps he saw her braided brown pigtails up ahead; the olive green of her wool beret; the multi-colored crocheted scarf his mother had made for her that first and only Christmas.

He lowered his head and walked faster. But then he saw her brown and white saddle Oxfords coming toward him; her silly red rubber galoshes he'd teased her about that spring. He spun around and quickly walked toward home.

A block further, Mark stopped as if he'd hit a wall head-on. No. He turned back toward Old North Tower and the administration building.

A short while later, as Mark wiped the perspiration from his forehead with a tissue from the box of Kleenex on her desk, the student assistant in Registration handed him forms to re-enroll. "Do you have your transcripts, sir?" she asked.

This time Mark did laugh out loud. "I'm sure you'll find them right in that computer," he replied.

As he walked back home, Mark turned off an internal switch. "No more thinking," he said. He walked the first block, and then the second, before his heart started pounding in his throat. I can do this, he thought. I need to do this.

He passed his duplex on the corner of Second Street and continued to Fourth. One more block, a right turn, three houses further, and he would be in front of Richard and Angela's yellow Craftsman. He would walk up the steps he'd walked so many times, where he'd held Jennifer's hand and sat at their dining room table discussing the pregnancy. He smelled the acrid alcohol of colored markers as they made protest banners and signs each Friday night. He could see Jennifer's head swing back quickly in laughter at something inane he had said.

He made it past one house before his panic spun him around, and he sprinted to the corner and the two blocks home. He threw open the refrigerator door, took out his last two beers and downed them quickly; then reached for the bottle of Scotch on the top shelf of the cupboard.

He felt the bottle suck his spirit into its liquid haze, and he felt himself going under. What was it Dr. Smith had said? Sucking his soul dry.

One evening, just as he was closing down the store, Mark looked up to find deep blue eyes staring into his.

"Are you closed?" she asked.

"Nah, I'm in no hurry," he said. He reached for the pile of sweaters in her arms.

"Thanks," she said.

"Tomorrow afternoon, ok?"

"Yes, fine."

Mark saw her staring as she waited for the ticket, and when he handed it to her, she spoke. "I know you," she said. "Mark Roberts?"

He looked closely. Something about her did seem familiar.

"Freshman chem, years ago," she reminded him. "Patty —

Patty Nolan back then. I'm married now."

Mark nodded. "I remember you, yes. How are you?"

"Married, one kid already, working—you know the routine. How about you?"

"Nam for three years," he said. "Right after sophomore year. Just back actually."

"Well, good to see you," Patty said as she waved good-bye. Then she turned abruptly around. "Mark? Would you like to come for dinner soon? My husband, John, lost his brother over in Nam. Maybe you guys could talk a little?"

Mark considered for a moment before accepting. He'd had no company for months except bar hopping. No one to talk to.

"Good," she said. "Friday night this week ok with you? Seven?" She wrote her address on a dry cleaning slip from the counter and handed it to Mark.

"Sure, sounds good."

On Friday evening, Mark bought a bottle of wine at the liquor store on his way to Patty's.

After introductions, Mark and John sat in the living room as Patty finished up the last minute details of the meal.

"So you were in Nam?" John said.

Mark nodded, but he felt his body go rigid. Maybe this had been a bad idea. "Cambodia, actually. Last years of the war."

"Air Force—Patty mentioned," John said.

"Yeah, drafted spring of sophomore year, and I didn't want to go Army so I went ahead and enlisted. What branch was your brother in?"

For the next ten minutes, both men sat forward, leaning into each other, eyes intense but the conversation remained factual, unemotional—male.

"Would you enlist if you had it to do over?" John asked when Patty called them to dinner.

"Go back? God, no. I can't imagine anyone going back."

"You didn't feel a moral obligation?" John said.

Mark grimaced, "Hmmph, moral? There was nothing moral about that war. I can tell you first-hand. Nothing moral or sane or anything close to that. The television shows you the war, but it doesn't tell you a thing about it."

John's face closed, and he motioned for Mark to sit. The silence grew until Patty sat down across from Mark. Her next words made Mark cringe. "John's brother died in a battle with the V.C. in a little jungle village west of PhuBai. He enlisted because he believed in the war," she explained. "John didn't go, so he feels he didn't do his part."

"Your number never came up?" Mark asked.

John shook his head, no. "Should have gone though," he said softly.

Mark wanted to end the conversation badly, but he couldn't just let things hang.

"Hey, man, no disrespect to your brother, and I'm sure he believed in what he was doing. We all did. We all bought into the bullshit we were told. Hell, I was decorated just for being gunned down in my plane. Truth is none of us were heroes."

John stiffened again.

"Look, I'm sure your brother felt differently. I don't mean to tear him down."

Mark stood and stared down at John and Patty, placed his napkin carefully back onto the table. "I think I'd better go," he said. In spite of Patty's insistence to stay, Mark made his way out of the house and to the car.

He hadn't eaten a bite, but he was never hungry for anything but booze these days. Some of the guys in rehab had been given Thorazine to deaden them. Anyone got emotional, Thorazine was the military's answer. He wished he had some. He wouldn't mind being a zombie right now.

*

Christmas day was almost too much for Mark's senses. He'd been in Nam and Cambodia for the past three seasons. The smell of cedar from the Christmas tree rose to his upstairs childhood bedroom, along with the sweetness of nutmeg and clove from his mother's pumpkin pie cooling on the counter in the kitchen below. Mark lay in bed and stared at the ceiling. He knew his mother had been preparing for hours already. His last Christmas in this house had been the year he and Jennifer told their parents about their pregnancy. Mark thought about how young and naïve they had been.

He forced himself to the bathroom, brushed his teeth and threw on a pair of old high school football sweats. He cringed as he pulled a pant leg up; the cold made the wounds hurt. Moments later, he stood at the top of the stairs, his hand frozen to the banister. A sorrow wrapped his soul like a damp wool blanket. It took several minutes before he managed the first step down the stairwell to the living room. His bare feet padded down the carpeted steps, and just as he reached the bottom of the staircase, his rigid heart seemed to soften.

A few steps away, his parents' densely decorated tree twinkled red, blue and gold even in the mid-morning sunshine that made its way through the heavy brocade drapes. Elaborately decorated packages were piled on the white cotton batting of snow beneath the tree. Those that didn't fit under the low branches lined the back wall. His mother always over-did the holiday for her only child. Apparently this year would be no different. "Merry Christmas," he called into the kitchen.

His parents must have been standing close by; they popped into the living room together. "Merry Christmas, son," his mother said as she grabbed him for a hug. "Hungry?"

For the next hour he sat on the sofa alongside his father sipping coffee until it became too cold to drink and taking occasional bites of home-made streusel. His mother handed out packages and exclaimed over her own. After all the gifts were unwrapped, Mark spotted one more, clear to the back and close to the wall. He walked to the tree and bent to reach for it.

"Hey, is this one for me?" he teased. He pulled it along the tree skirt and into his arms, and as he did, something inside gave out a sound that he swore was a "moo". His forehead frowned into a question mark.

"Don't get mad," his mother said. "I just thought …"

Mark sat with the gift in his hands and sighed. He knew her intentions were good. He didn't feel angry; just very, very tired. "Mom, I know. Let me think about it, ok?"

His mother smiled and offered more pastry. After she left the room, Mark's dad gave a slight cough that made Mark turn toward the sofa. His father's face was ashen but his eyes burned into Mark's.

"Dad, what is it?" he asked as he pulled himself from the floor and onto the davenport beside him.

He only heard two of his father's words. *Two months.*

Mark closed his eyes against the rest of the sentence and reached for his father. The two men embraced; then pulled apart quickly.

"Doctors are always wrong," his dad insisted and made a half-hearted attempt at a smile. "Don't worry yourself, son." He patted Mark's hand. "This damned coffee is cold again, Marge," he called into the next room.

A few moments later, Mark entered the kitchen with tears in his eyes and put his arms around his mother's apron-covered waist. She turned to him and held him as she had when he was a boy. He had known since his dad's first visit, but he hadn't wanted the truth—could never face the truth. A part of him wished he had died on that last mission.

*

Cambodia

As Mark slipped into semi-consciousness and his body slid to the left, he heard his co-pilot, Max, yelling. "Shit, Mark!"

Max grabbed for the radio while simultaneously taking the controls, "Bobbi Jo to base. Bobbie Jo to base. We've taken a hit. Have medics waiting."

Mark closed his eyes; then opened them in slits. He had to stay awake if he was going to make it. He focused on Max. His co-pilot pulled back and lunged the plane into a wide arc as he radioed the rest of the crew they were headed back. The Bobbi Jo would evacuate no more Americans today.

He would later learn that the left side of his plane was riddled with fifty-nine holes. But for now all he was aware of was the air rushing through, and Max working to right the plane and lower his elevation enough to crawl back to DaNang. The blackness of the blood coagulating at his feet matched the darkness sucking him in.

Mark awakened later that night. White coats filled the medical tent. Several planes had taken hits that day. One of the white coats walked toward him when she noticed his open eyes.

"Hey, sailor, you look like shit." She had a kind smile. "Let me get a doc."

"Sending you back to the states ASAP," the physician reported. "We get you out of here tonight, you'll be in San Antone in less than 48 hours. I've done all I can do to stitch you up, but it'll take some surgeries to repair the nerves."

"Do I have anything left?" Mark said.

The physician sat down on a stool next to the gurney. "Mark, I'm not gonna kid you. You took a bad hit. But yes, you have everything left that it will take to put you back together the right way." The men shook hands, and Mark let himself drift into the drug-induced sleep that pulled him under.

In San Antonio, the heavy metal doors of the transport opened, and Mark and the other injured soldiers were welcomed by more smiling faces in white. They looked like angels, Mark thought. But after two months of surgeries, rehab, physical therapy, more surgeries, and a lot of pain, Mark was forced to revise that image. Maybe not angels.

He rarely talked during those months. He washed down his pain pills. He slept any time he could. He went inward. He'd left for Nam a broken man and come home in pieces so tiny he wasn't sure he even existed.

*

Mark left his parents the following morning and headed back to Edmond for New Year's Eve. His last words to his father were a promise he intended to keep. After he walked into the duplex, he made an immediate call to Jeff and Ryan. "Gonna pass on the partying this year, guys," he told them.

"Good thing," Jeff said. "I'd kick your ass if you even thought about it."

Ryan grabbed the phone. "Hey, Mark, get your ass up here in a few weeks. Maybe we can tutor you through your piddly bachelor's degree in Engineering."

Mark couldn't remember the last time he'd laughed out loud. It felt remarkable. It wouldn't take that long to catch up with Ryan and Jeff, he told himself. Maybe they'd move to Austin for jobs. The place was booming with IBM, university research labs and oil. He let himself plant that small kernel of hope.

At their next appointment, Dr. Smith watched as Mark tapped his right foot rapidly and rocked back and forth in his chair. The psychiatrist waited patiently for a good five minutes. When Mark finally registered the silence, he stood and paced across the threadbare gray carpet to the far side of the office and back.

And then it was like a flood surged up and over the treacherous rocks that Mark had been hanging onto for years. When he looked up, Dr. Smith was floating in the tears that filled his eyes, and then he crumpled into his chair and felt himself dying.

"I can't …" Mark sobbed. "I can't …" The words became a small rubber ball caught in his throat.

He felt Dr. Smith touch his hand just once, and Mark knew the doctor would wait as long as it took. But Mark wasn't certain he had the strength to dive that deep. He stepped to the edge, stared into the deep waters, and threw himself into the river of Jennifer's death.

Well below the surface, he saw her in the distance. She held a small pink blanket in one arm and waved for him to join her with the other. Mark was gliding toward her; he could feel her pull. He swam forward with all his strength, the weight of the water fighting every stroke and just as the current stilled, she faded to foam.

Mark pushed upward to the surface and crashed into the air his lungs were screaming for. It was the screaming that woke him, and he realized the cries were his own. Mark felt something break loose. His breath returned in long, jagged gasps. Dr. Smith rose and pulled Mark from his chair. Wrapped tightly in the man's bear hug, Mark realized for the first time how frighteningly similar the cries of grief were to those expunged in death.

*

Cambodia

Mark had bombed targets. He tried to see them as black painted X's—no people, no village huts, no innocent civilians. He was given his coordinates, flew over the area and ordered his gunner to release. Thousands of bombs, dropping one after another; as many as four hundred shells at a time. From high above the jungle, Mark watched the explosions as they hit the ground. You couldn't allow yourself to think, let alone feel, if you were going to do your job.

After the bombing raids came the search and rescue operations for American soldiers. You flew your transport into the area and landed quickly, then shut the door when you were at your load capacity. Mark wouldn't think of the men he left behind as he ordered lift-off. Once or twice, bodies dropped as the doors slammed shut. Part of the job.

And then came the day when Mark awoke from the propaganda and bullshit. He'd taken R & R in Saigon. Not a long leave; just a weekend for some booze and women, and he'd had both that night. He called to the other drunken airmen as he left the grass-roofed bar, joking he couldn't get it up one more time and was headed to the shitty place Saigan called a hotel.

He jerked the Jeep into reverse and spun the wheels with speed, laughing and hollering to his buddies. "Get your asses back before two o'clock," he yelled. "Transport arrives early." Suddenly his rear passenger tire rolled over something hard in the road. "Shit," he cursed, throwing it into Park. If he'd ruined a god-damned tire, he'd be called on the carpet. He was drunk enough to land in the brig.

Mark jumped from the open Jeep and walked around to see if the tire was too damaged to limp on back to his room. His mind cleared with an immediate sobriety.

"Oh my God," Mark whispered. He looked around. He was alone in the black night on a Saigon street, drunk and smelling of whore.

He fell to his knees and took the girl's hand, praying for a pulse. She appeared to be five or six, long dark hair covering a face he wouldn't allow himself to look at. Her dark navy dress had ridden up her body on impact, showing her grayed and dingy panties. He pulled the skirt down over her knees. She was barefoot, and in her hand was a small package folded in newspaper. Where had she been going at one in the morning? Why was she behind his Jeep and not on the sidewalk? He knew he was trying to rationalize this mindless death—this mindless death that put blood on his hands. For the first time he saw the enemy face to face, and she was six years old.

Mark doubled over and puked, wiped his mouth on his sleeve and returned to the Jeep. He turned the key, put the Jeep into drive and drove slowly to the hotel four blocks down the street. He had another beer in his room and passed out quickly. The next day, he told himself to forget.

*

In Dr. Smith's office, Mark saw the young girl as in a dream: warped and fluid. "I've never told a soul," he said. "I left her," Mark sobbed, "just like we left all the other bodies; left them for the living to find and bury." Mark shook his head. "But she was six years old; no one deserves to be left dead on a dirty street."

Dr. Smith sat back down behind his desk. He took a prescription pad and wrote for a moment. Then he looked deeply into Mark's eyes. "Not much older than your daughter, am I right?"

Mark wanted to die; to die and give her back her life. But God wasn't going to let it be that easy. He wept openly. "And I get a medal pinned to my chest for bravery under fire." He shook his head. "A God damned war hero. I wish I'd died the day we were nearly shot down."

Mark fully believed that he'd been saved so he could remember all the death he'd caused. Three years of bombing and killing, and he couldn't even die correctly. It was going to be a long road back to sanity, he thought. But now, perhaps, he could grieve.

*

Two days before the start of spring semester classes, Mark sat in his living room and stared at the carefully wrapped gift his mother had bought for her granddaughter. She'd told him it was a Fisher-Price Barn with all the animal sounds Karen would learn.

Last night he'd made good on his promise to his father, and the battered metal trash can lid now covered the bottles whose contents had gurgled down the drain. His texts were stacked on the dining table along with composition books and folders.

Mark threw on his parka and gloves. The Oklahoma wind was blowing hard as it always did in January. He picked up the package and walked through the front door and took a right turn at the corner On Fourth Street, Mark stopped and gazed. How many times had he and Jennifer walked these streets? How many nights had they held each other, encouraged each other, loved each other? He thought back on the dozens of anti-war marches they'd walked together, holding hands between them and holding peace signs with the other.

He saw her crying as they told her parents about the baby. He remembered her angry face as she refused to marry him and forced him to accept the adoption, and he saw her big blue eyes at their wedding. Sobs choked without warning, and Mark walked the rest of the block, eyes blind with tears. In front of the Johnston's house, he pulled himself straighter and prayed they wouldn't see him.

Mark stood on the uneven, cracked sidewalk under the tall oak trees and glanced around at the familiar surroundings. Richard and Angela had been much more than their college professors. He and Jennifer owed them so much. He would soon be in classes. Perhaps he'd see them on campus. But he knew he wouldn't visit this house again. He placed the package by the front door, turned and walked back down the steps and onto the sidewalk toward home.

Chapter 11
The Search Continues

The next morning Garry mapped out a possible plan. They would return to Edmond and try to find the people who had lived in the house after her parents moved to Colorado. It was a shot in the dark. The house had been rented numerous times in the past thirty years. But perhaps someone knew something. She was struck with a sudden idea. Vickey Smith might be able to help. She picked up her cell and punched in the realtor's number. Vickey agreed to meet them at the real estate office in two hours. Gary pulled into the parking lot around ten o'clock.

"You may have gotten lucky." Vickey had done her homework while Gary had pushed the rental car hard. She brought up the screen on her computer and motioned for them to take a seat. "Okay," she said, "1975—the house is rented to Sam and Marjorie Mills. They stay in the house for over ten years, which is amazing. So in 1985, Shirley and Sam White are the next renters."

Gary wrote down the information. He repeated. "Sam and Marjorie Mills ... in 1975?"

"Yes," Vickey said, and she glanced at Karen. "Right after you moved with your parents to Colorado."

"Ok, we try to locate Sam and Marjorie next I guess," Karen said with a sigh.

"That, and ..." Vickey hesitated. "On the northwest corner of Fourth Street; that house has never sold. Woman's name is Wanda Rose. She'd be about the same age as your parents. Also,

I thought about the possibility of checking student records at the university. Maybe he went back to school on the G.I. bill."

Karen shook Vickey's hand and thanked her profusely. Vickey reached out and hugged her. "Good luck," she said. "If I think of anything else, I'll call you."

Gary drove straight to Fourth Street and parked in front of the two-story home on the northwest corner, just across the street and two doors past her parents' house. They weren't wasting time with Sam and Marjorie. Karen slammed shut the rental car door and stood there for a moment. Gary waited by her side as she adjusted her skirt, pulled her hair behind her ears, picked at a nonexistent piece of lint.

"Karen," he said. "Think positive."

She gave him a smile of gratitude. How had she almost lost him the past few years? How had she ever thought this man was not all she needed him to be? She reached for his hand and let him lead her up the front steps.

"Mrs. Rose?" Gary said, as a white-haired stooped-shouldered woman opened the front door. She answered in the affirmative, and as Gary explained their desire to find a student who used to visit the Johnston's thirty years ago, Karen heard how ridiculous that sounded, but she smiled and nodded hello.

Mrs. Rose unlocked the screen door and motioned for them to come in. "Have a seat," she said. They complied with her instructions and sat stiffly on straight-back chairs that had to be from the 50's. They watched as she settled into a worn brown suede Lazy Boy recliner. She took her time adjusting to the seat that had permanently formed to her body years ago.

"I knew Richard and Angela Johnston quite well," she began. "Professors at the college, as was my late husband. We socialized a bit."

"Did you know their students, Mark, or Jennifer?" Gary asked.

Karen shifted to the front of her seat in anticipation.

"Knew of them, of course. After the girl died … early birth, you know? So sad. Anyway, Angela and Richard took that little baby home from the hospital a week later once she was out of the incubator, and I've never seen two people so much in love with a child."

Karen sat with her hands squeezed together and her mouth half open. *I was that baby*, she *thought. That was me.*

"And the young man?" Gary asked.

"Yes, well, thing is—Angela wanted the boy to be in the little girl's life. She used to tell me how she'd written him letters—over to Vietnam, you know—and how he'd written a few times, but then he wrote and asked her to stop sending pictures of the child. And so after a couple of years, Angela just gave up, I guess."

Karen felt like she was going to burst.

"So, here's the thing." Wanda Rose seemed to be enjoying her audience. "Angela and Richard waited until the young man came home from the war. He moved back here to Edmond and started back into school. They thought he'd want to get to know his daughter; thought he'd want to be part of her life, but he'd have none of it. And it made Angela so angry and so sad, she would cry. Oh, lordy, it would break your heart."

Wanda sat quietly, shaking her head and sighing.

Karen wasn't sure the woman was going to speak again. She looked at Gary, and he raised an eyebrow. "Mrs. Rose," she said, "I hate to rush you, but do you know where my father is?"

The old woman looked startled. "Oh, my … well, of course. *You're* Karen."

She rose quickly from her chair and stood in front of Karen, took her hands in her wrinkled aged ones, and kissed her on the forehead. "God moves in mysterious ways," she said.

In the next half hour, Wanda told them what she knew. Mark had returned to Edmond, finished his degree and went on to Stillwater for his doctorate in Engineering at Oklahoma State.

She lost track of him at that point. After Karen's parents moved to Colorado, Angela sent Wanda Christmas cards, family photos, and occasionally mentioned Mark. Angela had continued to hope that Mark might reach out to his daughter. He'd settled in Kansas City, Missouri, last she heard.

A short time later, they thanked Mrs. Rose and drove to a near-by Starbucks. Gary brought out his laptop. All it took this time was an online query of white pages, and they had an address and phone number. Now came the hard decision. She looked at Gary.

"Let's sleep on this," he said.

As much as she wanted to keep plowing forward, she knew he was right. She needed a plan. What if her father didn't want to meet her? She'd been thinking only of her own needs. But it had been thirty-nine years. *What if I ring the bell and he denies me? What if he tells me to go away?* Was she ready for that tremendous hurt?

Once again, they took a motel room east of Edmond. She tossed and turned all night. After two nights with no sleep, she felt wrung out and fuzzy brained the next morning. Gary looked exhausted as well.

Thursday morning, they took turns driving to Kansas City, a five-hour drive on the Interstate, stopping only for a fast food lunch. It helped settle her nerves to take the wheel every couple of hours. At four o'clock, Gary pulled into the city limits and followed GPS toward the address she had written on a yellow sticky note. It stared at them from the dashboard of the car.

A half hour further, she watched as they passed a commercial corner with the usual amenities—grocery, salon, hardware store—and turned right for a few blocks. Large stone pillars marked the entrance to an obviously upscale subdivision. Each home sat on an acre lot backed to dense woodland and probably a stream running below, she thought.

Gary took the winding streets to the left and parked along the curb, a distance from the house. A gentle rain began to pepper the windshield. The car was silent with their screaming inner dialogue. She took his hand in both of hers. "I love you," she said.

He put his right arm around her and pulled her as closely as the bucket seats allowed. He chuckled. "That's why I like those old '70's bench seats, you can kiss a girl."

She grinned, thankful that he hadn't left her.

"What do you want to do, babe?" he asked.

"If he doesn't want to see me; that's his problem," she said. "This is my need."

He nodded and pulled the car forward and onto a brick paver driveway. She sighed deeply and slowly opened the passenger door.

Gary stepped halfway out of the car but no further. She glanced over and shot a questioning glance his direction. "I'll just give you a minute before I come on up."

"Ok," she agreed. She walked to the two-story manse and rang the ornate bronze doorbell. She heard movement inside as she listened to her heart pounding in her chest.

A tall, slender, handsome man with salt-and-pepper gray hair answered the door.

She stepped forward. "Sorry to bother you, but are you … Mark?"

He interrupted immediately. His face was full of emotions, like a comedy and tragedy theater mask at Mardi Gras. "Oh my God. You are a clone of your mother."

She knew he meant her biological mother, Jennifer, but Karen wasn't sure she was ready to hear this. Her throat closed down, and her lungs forgot how to breathe. How could she look like someone she'd never even met? It was too much to take in.

She moved slightly toward the door and watched as her father's face broke into pieces of sadness, disbelief, and then, unexpectedly, anger.

"I'm sorry, Karen," he said gently, "I just can't."

As the door shut, Karen began to shake, as if the August warmth had suddenly turned to winter. It happened so quickly. One moment he was standing in front of her, and the next he was gone—again. Her eyes filled with tears as the chill grew inside her.

As she slid into the seat of the car, she met Gary's questioning look. "You ok, babe?" he asked. "Do you want me to go talk to him?"

Her face was frozen, and her lips refused to move. She shook her head determinedly.

Gary put the car in reverse and backtracked to the freeway. He took an on ramp toward the city, glancing at her every few seconds.

She began to sob. No words—just giant icicles melting on her cheeks.

Gary was silent, but he reached for her hand and squeezed. "I'll find us a hotel room for the night," he said in a quiet voice. "We can talk there."

Then suddenly, Karen banged her fist on the dashboard and screamed in rage. Gary turned quickly toward her, his face a mask of fear. He signaled a right turn and took the next exit ramp at top speed. At the first stop light, he turned into a residential neighborhood and parked. She could not stop smashing her fist onto the top of the glove compartment. Her hand was bright red with the effort, and her screams softened to an ugly howl. The physical pain felt good.

"How dare he?" she yelled. "How dare he do this to me?" She felt Gary reach for her hand, but she pulled away and continued to hit, harder and harder.

"Karen," Gary called out, "Stop it! Stop it right now. You're going to hurt yourself." He grabbed her hands and held them tightly, and her howls lessened and turned to simple sobbing sounds.

She finally let him take her into his arms as she cried deep, tearless sobs that wracked her body. As she began to calm, Gary pressed her head under his chin and held her protectively.

"It'll be all right, honey," he said. "It will be ok. Let's find us a room for the night."

As the rage dissipated, her body folded upon itself like a ragdoll, and she leaned her head against the window as Gary drove silently across town. Within a few minutes, she fell into a stupor that looked and felt a lot like sleep but wasn't.

Karen was inconsolable for the next hour. She'd pace the hotel room and cry; then bang something with her fist and rage. When she was finally spent, Gary ordered a light dinner to their room and walked her to the bed. Karen watched as he pulled back the spread, plumped a pillow, and sat her on the edge. He took off her shoes, massaged her feet and laid her down on the crisp white sheets like an invalid.

She was an invalid, she thought, and an orphan. With that fleeting thought, she felt Gary's soft kiss on her forehead, and she fell into a chasm of dark sleep.

Chapter 12
The Search Ends

She wasn't sure how long she'd slept, but when she opened her eyes, the room was dark except for a dim desk lamp. Karen saw her husband sitting on a chair just a few feet away, watching her closely, as if he hadn't taken his eyes off her the entire time. He was there. Gary was always there for her. How could she have ever questioned that love?

"I can heat up the soup," Gary said, and he sprang from the chair.

"No, Gary," she croaked, her voice tight and painful from her earlier rage. She patted the bed beside her, and he smiled gently.

She curled into his open arms once he was settled under the covers and didn't move for hours. When she woke again, the room was in total darkness, and she leaned into him carefully. She felt his arms and his arousal, and they made love in slow, careful movements that felt to Karen like both dying and coming alive.

They didn't talk that night, but early the next morning, she woke first and tiptoed out for coffee and cinnamon rolls from the hotel coffee shop. She let the door close loudly when she returned to the room, and she watched him sit up with swollen eyes and a night's growth of beard. His hair stuck up in a messy Mohawk.

Karen suddenly laughed. She wasn't sure if it was from fatigue, acceptance or relief that she was still alive.

As they ate, they discussed the next step.

"I think you've gotten your answer, babe," Gary said. "I just don't think you should even tempt another rejection." He hesitated when he saw her face fall. "Maybe Mark will change his mind and he will find us; he will find you, Karen. But for now …."

"I know you're probably right," she said as she licked icing from her fingers. "Yesterday was like reaching the depths of hell. But by God, I'm not letting him get away with this, Gary."

He looked surprised. "What do you mean?"

"As I said yesterday, this is for *me*, not him. I am due explanations, information—whatever. I am due this, and he can go to hell for all I care for refusing to even see his own daughter. How dare he turn his back on me again, after leaving me thirty-nine years ago?" Her anger grew with her words. "He left me. He left *me*."

"I don't think it's a good idea, Karen," Gary said again. "But I support whatever you decide."

An hour later, after making love one more time, showering and dressing in a navy skirt and white silk blouse, Karen climbed into the driver's seat and waved to Gary. "I'll see you in a few hours … hopefully," she called through the open window. She saw Gary shake his head and scratch his chin. She knew he would worry until she returned.

The hotel was thirty minutes by freeway to her father's mini-manse. The closer to Mark's home she got, the tighter the vice in her gut turned, until she was almost sick to her stomach. She pulled into his subdivision and found the street; then parked in the drive, just as they had less than twenty-four hours ago. She sat for a moment and went over the details of her plan. She wasn't going to let him shut the door against her again today; that was, if he even opened it. He probably had cameras along his property and was, even now, aware of her presence.

She sat and gazed at the two-story stone and stucco home that spread the length of half the property. It seemed to go on forever. She couldn't help but wonder how many bedrooms and baths her father had in this monstrous place. The home appeared to be less than ten years old, so if she did have siblings, they had probably been raised in another home in the area. This must be his retirement home, she thought. She placed her Coach bag over one shoulder and straightened her skirt. She wouldn't be denied again. This was her life and her history, and she was going to get answers today.

The bell chimed a melody inside, and a woman about ten years younger than her father would be opened the ornate door. Her gray hair was cropped short; she was petite and stylishly dressed. She smiled at Karen and opened the door wide to allow her to enter the large Italian marble foyer.

"I'm Marlene," she said as she reached to shake Karen's hand. Her generous, warm smile helped unwind the knot in Karen's stomach. At least she'd gotten this far.

"Nice to meet you," Karen acknowledged. "I'm …"

"Yes, Mark has told me all about you," Marlene said. "Please come in."

Marlene led her into a living area filled with soft cushioned sofas, over-stuffed chairs and European décor. Velvet brocade draperies hung from ceiling to floor, where they puddled fashionably at the base of each window.

Karen settled into the softness of the over-sized arm chair. The two women sat and talked for nearly fifteen minutes before she wondered if this would be the conclusion of her visit. No mention had been made of her father. She kept glancing toward the entry, half expecting him to step into the room.

Karen told Marlene about her mother's recent death and her discovery of the trunk in the Edmond house which had forced her to look for her biological father after so many years. Marlene listened, nodding occasionally as Karen opened her heart to this stranger. There was something about this woman that reminded her of her mother, Angela; something gentle and warm and genuine. Karen found that she liked this woman, and she felt the humming of tension leave her body.

"Mark talked of you often over the years, Karen," she said. "We never had children of our own, so I think Mark always felt a deep affinity for you."

Her words pleased Karen, but she was surprised. "But he never wanted to meet me," she replied. "My parents wanted him to be part of my life, but he refused."

"I can't answer that, I'm afraid," Marlene said.

They sat in silence for a moment or two. When Marlene offered iced tea, Karen accepted and watched as the woman walked toward the rear of the home. Marlene had barely left the room when Karen's father walked in and lowered himself into the chair his wife had been occupying. She saw the left foot drag and a slight shadow of pain on his face. *War wounds?* She considered.

She assumed he had been close by and probably heard the women's entire conversation. *Fine*, she thought, *I don't have to repeat my life story.*

She wriggled in her seat slightly as she and Mark gazed at each other in silence. Seconds later Mark leaned forward, placed his head into his palms and stared at the floor. Karen was uncomfortable. Should she speak first? Was he going to be able to even stay in the room with her? After yesterday's cold reception, she was at a total loss.

When Mark lifted his head and sat back into the large armchair, he sighed deeply and began to speak. "I'm sorry for how I treated you yesterday, Karen. I ... It was just such a shock to see your mother staring back at me. I just went numb."

She simply nodded and let him continue. Marlene returned and set a tray of glasses and a pitcher of iced tea on the ottoman between them, excused herself and walked from the room, leaving the two of them alone.

"Why did you come, Karen?" he finally asked.

"I think you know the answer to that question," she said.

"Why didn't you ever look for *me*?"

He shook his salt and pepper head, acknowledging the question. Karen watched him as he took his time answering. He was a handsome man; graying primarily at the temples, with warm brown eyes, and he was taller than she'd expected. *He must be over six foot*, she considered. And he had obviously taken care of himself over the years. Except for his slight limp, he seemed as fit as a man half his age. Karen was suddenly surprised at herself. She felt a sudden calm come over her as she waited for her father's answer. It was not what she had expected to feel after yesterday's fury and rage.

"This will take awhile," he finally said. Then Mark smiled warmly at her. "But it's time."

Karen told him what she needed most, which was to know about her real mother, their marriage and her birth. Where he had been for the past thirty-nine years could come later. She listened closely, sipped her iced tea occasionally and let the information soak into her like a sponge.

Mark described Jennifer as best he could after so many years, and Karen was unexpectedly pleased to hear how much she was like her mother. Jennifer had also been working toward a teaching degree, had been a straight 'A' honor student, and an active and vivacious young woman at twenty-one. They had been sophomores in college—just kids— Mark told her.

"But you loved her enough to marry her, pregnant or not?" she asked.

"I wanted to keep the baby." He hesitated. "I wanted to keep *you*; wanted to marry Jennifer and have a family. But I loved her enough to respect her wishes, and I finally agreed to the adoption." Mark lowered his gaze from hers before he continued.

She heard the shakiness in his voice and knew he was close to tears, but she had to move forward. "Tell me about my mother's death," she asked.

"Oh, Karen, that would take me awhile. It almost killed me," he said as he shook his head. "Can we do that part later?"

She watched the sadness in Mark's eyes, even after all these years.

Their short three months of marriage left Karen with little family history, except the knowledge of how deeply in love they had been. Mark reached into the pocket of his starched white shirt and handed Karen a photograph taken at their wedding. Angela and Richard stood to the right of the smiling wedding couple—the couple who would give them a daughter in a few short weeks. At that moment none of them could guess the tragedy that would accompany that happy moment.

"You can keep that," he said quickly.

"Thanks," was all she could manage. She was suddenly unsure what she had hoped for from this meeting. He was right. It had been a very brief marriage during a difficult war, and thirty-nine years had passed. It was an extremely small piece of his life, she realized. What had she expected?

"Your mother was brilliant," he added, "and kind and understanding. When I got the draft notice, after a year of protesting the damned lottery, it hit her hard." He looked fully into Karen's eyes for the first time. "I was convinced for a very long time that that was what had killed her." Tears appeared in the corners of his eyes, and he squeezed them shut for a moment.

"Thing is, Karen," he added. "Your mother knew we were too young to raise you. The adoption had been planned from the moment we knew Jennifer was pregnant. We would never have been good parents to you."

It was the first time she'd thought of his absence in that way, and Karen found herself understanding, though she preferred the anger she'd felt earlier.

"Is that why you stayed away? Because you didn't want to be a parent to me?" she asked.

"I stayed away for a lot of reasons, Karen," he explained. "Yes, I knew Angela and Richard were good parents and you didn't need me, but also the things I experienced in Vietnam changed me into someone I didn't want you to know." "Tell me, please," she pleaded. "I really need to understand this." She met his eyes and added, "I think your absence somehow affected me deeply. I've never had children; I've fought the idea for so long and yet a part of me—deeply hidden—has wanted them all my life."

She watched as Mark fought internally with how much deeper to take this conversation. He seemed visibly agitated now. She didn't care. She needed this.

"I never got over the death of your mother," he said. "Karen, I'm sorry for that because it kept me from knowing you as well. But I could not face losing Jennifer, the one person I had loved more than life itself."

"Did you blame me for my mother's death?" she asked.

"Oh, no, never," Mark replied. "I blamed the war, the government, myself for going, but never you."

Karen began to weep, and Mark reached in his jeans pocket for a handkerchief and handed it to her. She looked at him and saw intense sorrow. She knew it was true; he had never gotten over the guilt of going to Vietnam after promising Jennifer he would never go. How very sad. She suddenly felt sorry for this man—Mark—a man who had produced her, but who, in every other way, had never been her father. She hated that she understood. It wasn't fair. She needed to despise his cowardice; needed to feel her own sense of rejection and righteous indignation. But somehow she couldn't.

So she expressed, as best she could, how good her life had been. How she had known of her adoption and how much she had loved her parents; how she had never felt unloved, not once. What wonderful parents Angela and Richard had been.

She spoke to him as one adult to another now; not the

grieving, lonely, angry child that she was suddenly aware she'd been for many years. "Mark," she addressed him as she would a stranger. "I came here because I needed to know why you never wanted to know me. It was that question that altered my decisions for so many years. It was buried so deep, I didn't know it existed until I read my mother's journal last month."

He nodded. "And the ugly monster finally showed itself?"

"Yes, something like that. Gary, my husband, has said for many years that there was something deeper; something I hadn't faced, but I didn't believe him. I didn't want to believe him."

Mark reached for her left hand and held it in his warm bear-like grasp. "Karen, I'm so sorry for being so weak. You aren't the only one with ghosts."

He told her about coming back from Nam as a worn and battered soldier and a widower; how he had considered visiting her as a toddler, and his decision to leave it lie.

"I honestly thought I would poison you, Karen. I was so toxic when I returned. And when I saw you with your real parents, especially with Angela, I knew you were loved and didn't need me mucking things up."

He stood and came toward the sofa where she was sitting. "May I?" he asked. She nodded permission. "I'd like to hold you for a moment," he said softly. And this time he let the tears flow openly.

Karen turned to her father, and he gently placed his arms around her as they both wept. They embraced for less than a moment, and then Mark moved back to his seat. "Would you stay for lunch?" he asked with hope in his eyes.

There were dozens of other questions; thirty-nine years of questions and just as many life experiences for her to share with him but she knew it would take time. "I can't today. Classes start next week and I need to get back to Gary and return to Denver, but soon," she said as she stood to leave.

Several hours after she'd left the motel, Karen parked the car in front of their room, closed her eyes for a moment, and felt a smile form on her lips. When she looked up, Gary was standing in the door way; anxiety and fear on his face.

She grabbed her bag and the photo Mark had given her and raced into his arms.

"Tell me all about it," Gary said, "but first, let me tell you how much I love you."

Karen nudged him with her shoulder. "I already know, my dearest husband," she said. "I already know."

Not all of the answers came that day, but they would come over the next few years. A quiet unplanned reconciliation began that afternoon, not only with her father but with her husband of fifteen years.

Life was funny with its twists and turns. Theirs was a simple story really—a story as old as time—of losing one thing and finding another.

Her parents' house sold, and Karen returned to work and her life. She mailed a large package to Hazel for the historical museum. Then she carefully wrapped everything else from the trunk in tissue paper, and Gary hauled it to the attic. Perhaps Karen would add her own journals to the already full trunk some day, and she couldn't help but wonder who might find it in the future. A child of her own was doubtful, but you never knew. She wasn't yet forty and Gary was more than willing. Or maybe it would just simply be the next owners of their house. She would leave it behind as a legacy to whoever climbed the steep stairs to the attic, some day, years in the future.

The End

Dedication

To Mike and Michelle who support me through life every single day.

To my family and friends who encouraged me throughout this journey.

Thanks to my editor, Evelyn Duffy, for her keen eye, her attention to content and historical accuracy, and for making this a much better read.

And last but not least, to the professors and mentors who urged me forward with critiques, edits, and cracked whips.

Made in the USA
San Bernardino, CA
18 February 2017